C000062941

LOTTIE BEAUCHAMP'S WAR

*In a war, you'd want
Lottie Beauchamp on your side…*

By

PAULA NAPIER

Copyright © Paula Napier 2023
This book is sold subject to the condition that it shall not, by way of trade or
otherwise, be lent, resold, hired out, or otherwise circulated without the publisher's
prior consent in any form of binding or cover other than that in which it is
published and without a similar condition including this condition being imposed
on the subsequent publisher.
The moral right of Paula Napier has been asserted.

Most of the characters referred to in this book are fictitious. Any resemblance to actual persons, living or dead is purely coincidental. There are however certain references to some individuals, who were prominent at the time. Furthermore, some of the locations actually existed as well as certain events, which does not alter the fact, that it is a work of fiction.

For Mum & Dad.

There were many brave women who served during the Second World War. Some of their stories have been slow to come to light. I imagined what it would be like to have met them and from this, 'Lottie Beauchamp's War' evolved. The main character of this book, the story and the dialogue are fictitious. Although Lottie is my creation, she walks among many wonderful people who did exist in those times.

"Adversity alone has the unique power to inspire exceptional clarity…
and unleash your most potent forces."

Erik Weihenmayer

CONTENTS

PART 3

PART I

CHAPTER 1

5th October 1939, Cambridge

On this day, Hitler launches his "last" Peace Offensive to the West.
This is rejected by Prime Minister Neville Chamberlain.

Before it came into view, everyone could hear the roar of the engine. Her plane emerged through cloud into blue sky over Trinity College. She opened the throttle before turning upside down and falling to earth in a wide loop. There was a moment's silence from the ground and a collective holding of breath as the Tiger Moth levelled, before disappearing from sight, south-west of the River Cam.

*

The pilot hauled herself out of the cockpit and jumped to the ground where she peeled off her gloves, removed her goggles and leather flying hat and shook out her hair.

"Look after her, Hugh," she shouted to her co-pilot, above the noise of the engine.

"Of course! Do *try* not to get sent down!"

With that, she strode off in the direction of Newnham College, lighting a cigarette, barely aware of the small crowd that had formed on the bank of the river.

*

Heads turned as she strode down Newnham Walk, past the wrought-iron gates to the Porter's Lodge, where Lottie Beauchamp addressed the uniformed man with his greased hair, combed over to hide his thinning crown.

"Good morning. I was wondering if my luggage had arrived? I'm Miss Charlotte Beauchamp."

She seemed and looked, he thought, far more mature than her years and had the natural air of confidence of the upper classes. "Good morning, miss. Yes, it was taken to your room, yesterday evening. I'll get you your key and show you up." Mesmerised, he turned and took number eight from the highly polished board.

"Please don't trouble yourself, Mr…?"

"Long." In all his career, he'd not witnessed any student arriving by aircraft. Whatever next, he wondered, impressed but the sensation was tempered by a slight sense of disapproval at the audacity.

"Mr Long," she repeated, making his name sound almost exotic. "Just tell me where my room is. I'm very good at direction." There was a hint of irony that could have been mistaken for flirtation.

"Turn directly left and up the first flight of stairs to the second floor, miss." He was sucking a herbal tablet for his perpetual cough, a legacy of the Ypres trenches, and very nearly swallowed it whole.

"Thank you, Mr Long." She took the key and turned.

"Oh, Miss Beauchamp?" Distracted by the entirety of her, Harold had nearly forgotten the message. "Professor Garrod would like a word with you at two sharp, in her study."

"Sharp? I'll pop back in a while and I'm sure you will be kind enough to tell me where to report?"

"Of course." She was a spirited one and no mistake. He didn't detect any curiosity on her part as to why she'd been summoned so soon. Smiling, she turned and disappeared, it seemed, into the fabric of the building.

*

It felt, to Harold Long, career porter, a breath of life had entered the elegant college with its immaculate gardens and overwhelming sense of order and it would doubtless add a little colour to the place. Cambridge, as a whole was about, he was certain, to experience something of a bumpy ride but he wondered just how long she would last before the weight of rules and regulations slid down from on

2

high, engulfing her in its control and finally squeezing out any attempt at non-conformity. Taking out his handkerchief, he discreetly spat a gobbet of mustard-yellow phlegm, folded it neatly and returned it to his pocket. He found himself musing on the lovely Miss Beauchamp. If only, he thought, he'd been younger, more attractive and of a better class.

CHAPTER 2

5th October 1939

Newnham College, Cambridge

Also on this day, Poland is invaded for the final time.

Lottie opened the door to her room and surveyed it: To the far left, a single bed with a thick blanket and hot-water bottle, under the window a desk and chair, and a battered armchair. It rested on a rather threadbare rug that might have once been vibrant but had faded to almost nothing over many years. In the corner of the room was a washbasin. Her cases had been stacked neatly beside an impossibly small wardrobe. That was it. "Welcome home!" she muttered and made her way to the sash window that overlooked the gardens, where fellow students stood talking in the sunshine. It seemed a world away from the creeping conflict that was making its way across Europe like a toxic spillage. Events had turned so quickly from a summer of uncertainty to Hitler invading Poland and then, in an instant, war had been declared. With a sigh, she took off her flying jacket and threw it over the armchair, wondering what Professor Garrod wanted so soon. Perhaps it was a glass of sherry to welcome the new intake. Looking at her watch, she realised she had about half an hour to change and find the Professor. Sitting on the end of the bed, she bounced up and down a little. To her dismay she heard an irritating creak of aged bedsprings as she sank into the well of the lumpy mattress. Removing her boots and trousers, she replaced them with a tailored emerald dress and stockings and re-applied her lipstick. Regarding her appearance in the cracked mirror above the basin, she pulled a face and grinned.

*

Professor Garrod was sitting behind a large desk, covered with papers and artefacts.

"Come in, Miss Beauchamp," she said, looking her up and down through rimless glasses, as though examining something quite unusual. "Take a seat."

There were no other students in the room, so Lottie presumed she'd been wrong about the drinks. She'd been in awe of the Professor's work for quite a while and here she was, sitting opposite her.

"Thank you." Lottie looked at the chairs but both had items on them. "Is that... is that a human skull?" she said, eyeing one of the objects, wondering if it was that of a monkey.

Professor Garrod, Lottie noticed, had mousy hair, quite thin lips and a rather pointed nose, giving her rather a severe appearance.

"Yes, it won't bite you. Just move it to the other chair." She addressed her without looking up.

Lottie held it up with one hand, at a distance and addressed it. "Alas poor Yorick! I knew him Horatio."

"He was alive about two hundred years before Shakespeare," said the Professor. "And I know not whether he was 'a fellow of infinite jest' or 'of most excellent fancy'. I *do* however know his tragedy was a musket shot to the head." She didn't bat an eyelid but there was a hint of a smile on her colourless lips. "Sit."

Lottie balanced the skull carefully on a pile of books on the adjacent chair. While the older woman shuffled some papers on the desk, Lottie looked around the room. It was a complete treasure trove of antiquities re-buried among paper, books and dust. She'd have wandered around but it wouldn't do at this point.

Clearing her throat, the Professor pushed the papers to one side. "Right, how are you settling in?"

"Well, I've only just arrived..."

"So I gather! I heard your *arrival*, as did the Vice Chancellor and just about everyone else in Cambridge, I imagine."

"Right." Lottie realised with a sinking feeling, this wasn't a 'welcome chat' with a small glass of sherry, after all. The realisation that she'd made a terrible first impression jolted her.

The Professor removed her spectacles, put her hands together and rested her chin on her fingertips. "Miss Beauchamp, this is an academic establishment, not an airfield or indeed a flying circus."

"No, I..."

"Lord knows, women here have enough of a fight to be taken seriously, without the frivolous behaviour of new students setting us back decades. You are an ambassador for intelligent women and I don't need to remind you, I'm sure, that we are at war. Am I making myself clear?"

"Of course. I apologise for the disturbance... unreservedly," she added.

"I'm sure you're aware an airport has just opened down the road, so in future, if you eschew conventional modes of transport, I strongly suggest you use that."

"Of course."

Professor Garrod seemed to lose interest in her at that point and she picked up her glasses and pen and resumed reading.

"Will that be all, Professor?" Lottie wasn't quite sure what to do.

She nodded but when Lottie got to the door, she spoke again.

"Imagine yourself to be in an orchard of abundant talent, Miss Beauchamp. Do try to remain on the tree until you fully ripen and get picked for greater things. Don't become a windfall, to simply rot in the long grass of mediocrity."

"Yes, Professor."

*

Lottie shut the door behind her, feeling a little flattened by her first encounter with one of the greatest academics of her time but she acknowledged, she did have a point. It had been a bit of a stupid stunt and Hugh had warned her not to do anything "daft" but up until now, she'd flown almost every day and performing a loop was like sneezing. Next term, she vowed to take the train.

*

Making her way back to her room from her meeting with the Professor, a rather plain-looking girl with mousey hair, carelessly pinned up, bumped into Lottie.

"Hello," Lottie said, smiling. "Gosh, you're in a bit of a rush, aren't you?"

The girl, slightly breathless, apologised. "So sorry! I was just trying to locate one of my cases. It was sent ahead but seems to have gone missing on the train."

"Lord, I'm so sorry. Can I help in any way? I'm Lottie Beauchamp – Room 8."

"Phyllis Lowe, Room 9 – I don't think so but it's very kind of you to ask. It's just, well, a bit of an inconvenience." She looked a little flushed.

"Do you need anything?"

"Thank you, no. I've informed Mr Long, the Porter. He's going to send word to the station."

"I'm sure it will turn up." Lottie thought it was a rotten thing to happen on the girl's first day and she was, under the circumstances, being very calm.

"I do hope so. It has an awful lot of stuff in it. Books and clothes and so forth."

"Look, I was going to try and find somewhere to get a cup of tea. Why don't you join me and hopefully your case will have turned up by the time we get back?"

The girl looked a little embarrassed. "Well I didn't mean…" she began. "I mean I don't want to make a fuss."

"You're not. I spotted a rather nice-looking tea shop on King's Parade. They had some marvellous-looking scones in the window. Shall I meet you by the Porter's Lodge in say, ten minutes?"

"That would be lovely."

*

Phyllis Lowe was waiting for her when Lottie arrived. Her rather long pointed features and bright round eyes had become quite animated, reminding Lottie of her younger brother Archie's lurcher.

"I'm so relieved!" she said, beaming. "My case is on its way to the Lodge."

"That's very good news, Phyllis," Lottie said. "Let's go and celebrate. As we're to be neighbours, I want to hear all about you!"

"There's really not an awful lot to tell." She looked panicked and added quickly, "Well nothing of interest, that is."

"That can't be true. Where are you from?"

"Gloucester."

"You didn't choose Oxford, then?"

"No, always Cambridge for me. I'm a great admirer of Professor Hawcroft."

"Hawcroft?"

"Head of Classics. A great talent. What about you? What brought you to Cambridge? You seem very, well… glamorous." She chose her word carefully then blushed. "I mean you must have heaps of suitors!"

Lottie laughed. "What a dull thought! My family home is in Suffolk. I was all set for finishing school in Switzerland but luckily for me, The Brig, that's what we call my father, finally agreed I might be less of a financial liability here and, as my eldest brother graduated from Trinity, it seemed the obvious choice."

"You must know people here, then?"

"A few. What about you?"

"Nobody. We're very ordinary; my father's a doctor. We live in a very sleepy village. I managed to get a scholarship to my school."

"Clever girl!"

She blushed. "Not really. I'm just good at remembering things."

"No," said Lottie, putting her cup down and regarding Phyllis through half-closed eyes, "I have a sixth sense about genius."

Phyllis shook her head and they both laughed.

CHAPTER 3

February 14th 1940, Cambridge

On this day, a Nazi spokesperson announces that U Boats have the right to attack United States ships en route to Allied ports.

L iving in the college was a joy but draughty and in the mornings, Lottie could see her own breath as she discarded the tepid hot-water bottle and braved getting out of bed to venture across the room to make a hot drink. Not that she enjoyed her early morning tea much anymore, since sugar was on ration. She sighed and pressed her nose to the cold window pane. Last night, a hoar frost had crept in and settled, draining the world of colour and white-washing the gardens, making them glitter in the sunlight.

*

Later that morning, she sat at her desk in her room, legs covered with a blanket and with a two-bar electric fire positioned near her feet. She'd forgotten the coldness of her room for a while, absorbed in reading about Gertrude Caton-Thompson's excavation at Hamamieh. What impressed her most was the archaeologist's meticulousness in recording her finds. Since the end of 1937, Caton-Thompson had been excavating in Yemen. Lottie wondered if she would ever get to work with her. Rumour had it, she and her counterpart Freya Stark hadn't been seeing eye to eye. Once again, Lottie imagined herself in the heat of the African continent, scraping away the earth, inch by inch to reveal the past, while living among exotic dark-skinned people with strange voices and foreign smells rising up from the ancient, scorched earth. She was disturbed in her reverie by an envelope being slid under the door. She stretched and with a yawn, picked it up, intrigued by the flamboyant handwriting. Slipping out the single sheet of paper, it read:

Dear Miss Beauchamp,

Your brother Hugh told me you are studying in Cambridge. If you are not too busy, do come to tea on Friday at three.

Yours truly

Eleanor Goldman

Baroness von Haastein

The address on the embossed paper was House Cottage, Kettle's Yard. There was no telephone number. Who, she wondered, was Eleanor Goldman? It wasn't a name she'd heard her eldest brother, Hugh, speak about. If nothing else, out of curiosity and politeness, she would go and in any case, something about the handwriting was intriguing. Putting the note on the corner of her desk, she remembered she'd agreed to accompany George Melrose to a valentine jazz party that evening. He was nice, nothing more, nothing less; the sort of eligible boy young women longed to meet. Impeccable manners, good looking, great pedigree but he lacked any sense of adventure and she realised with a smile, when all was said and done, he really would find her quite unmanageable. He was, indeed, as many would have recognised, punching above his weight. Hearing a knock on the door, she got to her feet, reluctant to dispense with the blanket.

"Half the florist for you, Lottie," said Phyllis. "And *five* cards!"

"Goodness!" said Lottie. "Come in. Who can they be from?"

"I don't know, but they've made the rest of the corridor feel very jealous. None of us have so much as one," she grumbled. "Have you got lots of vases for days like these? I mean, surely this isn't the first avalanche of flowers?" She grinned.

"Well, no... I don't have emergency flower holders. That would feel presumptuous and no, this is very much a first!"

"Right," said Phyllis, purposefully. "You'll have to resort to jam jars. I'll go and get you some from the kitchen, while you open your cards."

"You don't have to do that, Phyllis," said Lottie, looking bewildered at the bouquets of flowers.

"I know," she said over her shoulder, "but it helps to be practical when trying to distract oneself from the realisation that it's Valentine's Day and yet again, the Post Office has forgotten the plainer old Bluestockings."

Embarrassed and curious, Lottie opened the envelopes and pulled out cards with hearts and anonymous messages of hope. It wasn't that she didn't like boys, they just didn't feature in her immediate plans and this outpouring of romantic love for someone who to them must be a stranger, felt a little desperate. Eager to get back to reading about Hamamieh, with Phyllis's help, she quickly arranged all the flowers and spread them round the room, before going to her wardrobe and pulling out a red dress, hanging it on the back of the door. That, she thought, would do and seeing it there, would serve as a necessary reminder to get ready and go to meet George.

CHAPTER 4

February 16th 1940, Cambridge

On this day, the Royal Navy seizes the German steamer Altmark in Norwegian waters and frees two hundred and ninety-nine prisoners of war.

It was snowing as Lottie made her way to House Cottage, Kettle's Yard. Her feet had chilblains from the constant cold and she pulled her collar up and the belt of her coat tightly round her, against the biting fen wind that whipped its tongue around passageways, in defiance of the buildings. Bicycles were rendered useless as the snow quickly confiscated them. Students remained indoors wherever possible, huddled in common areas smoking, reading or listening to the wireless, venturing out, only to attend the occasional lecture that hadn't been cancelled.

*

At the door, she rang the bell and waited, blowing icy breath into her cupped hands. The woman who opened it, was a surprise. Tall, handsome with olive skin and long, curly, dark hair that was streaked with white, untidily piled on her head and held in place with a couple of well-used artist's paintbrushes; the Baroness, Eleanor Goldman, smiled down at Lottie.

"Come in, my dear. You must be frozen. I quite forgot the time!"

"Thank you." Lottie stepped in and found to her joy, the house was warm. She removed her coat and beret and looked around in wonder at the paintings that seemed to cover every inch of available wall. "Oh my goodness, you're an artist!"

"I am." Eleanor smiled, opened a cigarette box and fixed one into a tortoiseshell holder. "Do you smoke?"

"Occasionally."

"Would you?" Eleanor offered her one.

Lottie took one.

"Come upstairs to the fire." She eyed her and suddenly laughed. "But maybe someone as pale and beautiful as you might just melt like a snow princess."

"I don't think I could ever get warm enough in Cambridge to melt," said Lottie, with a grin.

"Tea or would you like something a little stronger? My personal afternoon favourite on a winter's day, is brandy."

Lottie followed Eleanor as she swept majestically through into a long living room stuffed full of plants, pottery and canvasses of anonymous figures in various poses. It smelled of wood smoke and turpentine.

"Brandy would be heaven."

"Perfect. Make yourself at home. We're going to get along, I can tell. How is Hugh?"

"Very well, I think. He's waiting to be called up." Lottie wanted to ask Eleanor how she knew her brother but it might appear rude that she didn't already know.

"Terrible business! Hitler is a madman. I fear for my relatives in Europe."

"Where are they?"

"Germany... Hungary." She shrugged. "Who knows, now? To be a Jew is not safe anywhere, it seems."

"I'm sorry. It must be a frightful worry?" Lottie's face had quickly become flushed from the heat of the fire.

"Of course." Eleanor sighed. "But there are small things that bring light to this world of dark, like beauty. Do you see beauty in things, Lottie?"

Lottie thought for a moment and smiled. "Yes, I'm sure I do." It was a strange question with an obvious response but it made her question herself. Did she appreciate beauty or just wander through life, taking it for granted?

"Good! People who don't see and *feel*, aren't worth bothering with." Eleanor shut her eyes for a moment and inhaled, lost in thought.

Lottie found herself staring at her host and quickly, she averted her eyes. "When did you last hear from my brother?" she said, changing the subject.

Eleanor considered for a moment, before answering, "A while. He was never a writer. You know that he sat for me?" she said, matter-of-factly. "And we became friends. Very good friends."

"No, I didn't." Lottie struggled to imagine Hugh agreeing to be painted. He'd certainly never mentioned it or the Baroness. Were they lovers, she wondered? There was no denying that Eleanor was exotically beautiful but surely the age gap would have precluded it. Attempting to be discreet, her eyes scanned the walls.

"He's not in this room. Maybe later I'll show you. It's one of my personal favourites." She spoke softly, with an accent.

"I'd like that." Lottie wasn't sure she would really, given that most of the portraits in the room were wearing very little but she was curious. "I saw from your invitation, you're a Baroness," she said, taking another sip of brandy and enjoying the burning sensation as it travelled down her throat. "Is the Baron here?"

"No. He's dead."

"I'm so sorry…"

"Don't be." Eleanor waved her hand, dismissively. "He died many years ago. He was old and thank God he missed this Hell!"

Lottie nodded. The brandy and heat from the fire had made her feel a little lightheaded and she could feel her eyelids becoming heavy. She got to her feet and regarded the paintings, one by one. "They're very interesting," she said, having never seen anything quite like them before. She was very familiar with hunting scenes and still-lifes of dead pheasants placed next to iridescent bunches of grapes or ancestral portraits with eyes that followed one around the drawing room or up the stairs, in silent judgement. But these were different. More abstract. The faces of the figures were indistinct, yet tangible and the paintings changed, like magic, with the light. Eleanor joined her and regarded her expression, through her kohl-lined eyes that made Lottie think of Cleopatra on her way to meet Marc Anthony.

Raising her hand she put her fingertips under Lottie's chin, tilting her head upwards. Lottie could smell her warm, brandy-breath and for a moment, taken aback, she thought she might kiss her. Instead, she smiled and said, "I wonder if you will sit for me, sometime, Lottie Beauchamp…"

It wasn't, Lottie felt, a question, more prophesy.

CHAPTER 5

12th May 1940, Cambridge

On this day, Hitler orders the invasion of France.

Almost as soon as Lottie got into the daily swing of her Bluestocking life, Cambridge began to change. Senior male students studying arts and associated subjects were being 'called up' to fight or leaving to join the Civil Service. The under twenties and those studying subjects that might be useful in a state of war, like medicine and science, were however left to continue their studies. As bombs destroyed lives in London and major towns all over England, Cambridge, miraculously it seemed to its residents, remained relatively unscathed. Rationing's tentacles, however, reached out ever further and blackout put paid to what should have been a summer of parties on the river. Spring mornings continued as winter, as dawn was kept well at bay by the thick fabric that lined all the windows and the night streets were illuminated only by moonlight. The city, under cover of darkness, was unusually silent, save for the squeaking of the Air Raid Wardens' bicycle wheels as they diligently carried out their patrols, scouring the buildings for chinks of light that might betray the town to enemy aircraft.

As hardship grew against a backdrop of the news of Hitler invading the Low Countries, in his advance through Western Europe, Lottie studied and played as hard as she could within the confines of war, unwittingly breaking the hearts of young men who might never live to have them broken again. These were days of uncertain future, snapping on the heels of time and fuelling an urgency to live life at an accelerated pace. Boys craved physical love, leaving girls in a dilemma over convention and propriety. Marriage proposals were proffered like golden tickets to a sexual turnstile, in the expectation that one "might not return" and the boys' horror at the notion of dying "a virgin" or having no sweetheart waiting for them.

*

When she awoke on the twelfth of May, Lottie received a letter saying that her brother Hugh had joined the RAF to train as a pilot and her other brother, Archie, was highly likely to follow in some shape or form, as soon as he was old enough. Inevitable but news she dreaded. Boys playing at soldiers, she mused, recalling them playing with metal figures in bright uniforms and making the noise of gunfire as they knelt on the floor felling them with a careless flick of the finger, in mock battle. At the time, she had thought their games stupid and dull and had stomped off to ride her pony or climb a tree. A cliche, but it did seem like yesterday and, in the passage of time, it was. Folding her mother's letter that attempted but failed to sound cheerful, she buried it in her desk drawer to try to lock out the visions of real solders lying wounded on a battlefield and burning wreckage of aircraft spread across a town. What did they know of war, her beautiful, innocent brothers? They would be dressed as men but it was no more authentic than the costumes they donned as children for their make-believe plays. Her father, The Brig, had already returned to London to the War Office where Lottie knew he would do his best to support the new Prime Minister Churchill but he would no longer be able pick his own boys up and hold them to him, when they fell over, or comfort them when they had nightmares. Suddenly, they'd been fast-tracked, to adulthood. If she'd been allowed, she'd have joined them and every other brother or son, in solidarity. Instead, she'd be left impotent and under-utilised, waiting for news of them and opening the door to a grave-looking postman, clutching the dreaded telegram.

With a heavy heart, and feeling quite lonely, she turned off the lights and opened the heavy curtain a little and peeped down to the garden, searching for reassurance that the simple things hadn't changed. The oval moon cast its silvery light on the flowers and shrubs and for a few moments, all seemed comfortingly normal. What, she wondered, would become of all this and of them all? If France fell, it was only a very short hop across the Channel. What would happen to the farm? It had been in her family for generations and she couldn't bear the thought of the Nazis taking it over. It seemed pointless being in Cambridge, studying about digging up the past when all that really mattered at the present was not to be buried. It seemed ridiculous that she was sitting at university with a pilot's licence when she could be fighting alongside boys like Hugh. Picking up a piece of paper, she began to pen a letter to her father, imploring him to speak to Prime Minister Churchill and ask him to change the rules and allow women to serve alongside men, if they were willing and able to do so. If nothing else, the act of doing something pro-active made her feel a little better. The Brig, she was sure, would understand her frustration and would probably be sympathetic. Whether he would act upon her request was a different matter. When she'd finished, she addressed the envelope and blotted it decisively. It was gone eleven by the time she changed into her pyjamas and brushed her teeth.

CHAPTER 6

13th May 1940, Cambridge

On this day, Winston Churchill states – "I have nothing to offer but blood, toil, tears and sweat" in his first parliamentary speech as Prime Minister. German troops cross the Meuse at Sedan to trap Allies in the Low Countries.

"Lottie, it's me. Come down, I want to speak with you."

It was a little after midnight and she had just drifted off to sleep. Waking with a start, she recognised the voice as Robert Gilpatrick, a fresher from Trinity. He sounded very drunk.

Opening the window further and sticking her head out, she called down in a low voice, "Is that you, Robert? What on earth are you doing down there? There'll be Hell to pay if you get caught!"

"Come down, Lottie, won't you? I want to talk to you."

"You need to go!" she said in a loud whisper. "Now."

"I can't, I'm locked in. I must have fallen asleep in the flower bed." He began to giggle.

"You're drunk!"

"I'm drunk with love for you."

Lottie thought for a moment. She needed to get him out of the Newnham grounds before he woke anyone but she knew the college gates would be locked. Thinking fast, she told him to wait quietly whilst she let him in. Pulling a jumper and slacks over her pyjamas and grabbing her torch, she made her way out of her room and downstairs to the door to the courtyard. Unlocking it and staying close to the wall, using the light from the moon, she crept round the perimeter of the building. Coming up behind him and putting her hand over his mouth, she whispered in his ear that if he didn't do as she told him, they would both get sent down, and did he understand? He snorted with laughter, making her tighten her fingers until he stopped. Grabbing him by the sleeve, she dragged him round to the open door and pulled him inside, putting her finger to her lips. Something in her face must have registered with him as he nodded.

"Follow me and keep quiet. Understand?" She wasn't laughing.

"Yes. *Anything* you say, so long as you agree to marry me?"

Listening intently for any sound, she took him along the passage to the kitchen. She'd noticed some time ago where the key to the back door was kept. That, in turn, led to an external courtyard where the pig bins were stored. By the light of her torch, she found the small step ladder that was used for reaching the top shelf of the larder. Telling Robert not to move, she picked it up and let herself out of the door. The place was silent. She was well aware that some of the tutors' rooms faced the courtyard and if this was to succeed, they had to somehow manage it in complete silence. She placed the ladder against the wall that led onto a gully between two roofs and from there, out onto the street below. Robert seemed to have sobered a little under her command and she beckoned him to follow her, threatening to kill him if he made a noise. Compliantly, he weaved across the yard and, after two attempts, scrambled up the ladder. Motioning him to keep low, she joined him on the roof, pulling herself over the gutter and hauling the ladder up behind her, praying nobody would look out and see it. There was a bit of a drop on the other side that was too high for the small ladder but provided Robert eased himself over the edge, he should land on the pavement below without doing too much damage. He now seemed sober enough to find his way back to Trinity College but in any event, he would be out of the girls' college grounds.

Lying flat on her stomach, cautiously, she looked down into the street and listened. Generally the Air Raid Warden came by at around eleven p.m. before making his way east in the direction of Petersfield. She looked at her watch. It was eleven twenty. Hoping the siren didn't go off to signify a raid, she felt increasingly confident she would get away with this and nobody would be any the wiser. Putting her fingers to her lips and waving Robert forward, she told him in a low voice to relax and land softly. Given the amount of alcohol he'd consumed he shouldn't feel too much, she was sure. In any case, it was no higher than the hayloft at the farm and she and her brothers had spent years throwing themselves off it and had escaped any serious harm.

"I'm sorry," he said forlornly. "I suppose you won't even consider marrying me now?" With that, he disappeared over the edge and landed with a yelp on the pavement, below.

"For God's sake, be quiet!" hissed Lottie.

"I think I've broken my damned ankle!"

Lottie rolled her eyes. "Stand up!" she commanded, peering over the edge of the roof at him. "Stop fooling around."

"I can't," he whispered, hopping around. "I can't put any weight on it. I'm serious, Lottie!"

She hesitated for a moment before lowering herself down from the roof and landing next to him.

*

Half an hour later, under the cover of the shadows of doorways she managed to get him back, limping, to Trinity College, where she left him, throwing gravel up at the window of a fellow student.

*

On her way back to Newnham, she dodged a warden before scaling a rusty drainpipe that took the waste water from the roof, inching along a first-floor window ledge and hauling herself back into the gulley. Lying flat, she watched and listened for any sign of life, before lowering the step ladder back down, creeping across the courtyard and letting herself back into the kitchen. As she locked the door behind her and replaced the ladder and the key, she heard the creak of floorboards. Someone was coming down the corridor, towards the kitchen. Ducking down beneath the large oak table, she turned off her torch, held her breath and waited, praying they didn't shine a light around the kitchen and as luck would have it, they didn't. She couldn't tell who it was as they made their way to the refrigerator and felt inside. At most, Lottie was two yards from them and they yawned loudly. She heard the chink of glass before the door was shut and they moved off. Watching the beam of light until it had completely disappeared, she quickly undressed back down to her pyjamas and rolled up her jumper and slacks. If she was caught now, she knew she could bluff her way through it, saying she needed the bathroom but she got back to her room without further incident and once inside, she leaned against the closed door, feeling both relieved and exhilarated.

CHAPTER 7

Friday 17th May 1940, Cambridge

On this day, the German 6th Army captures Brussels.

Lottie sat in the university library, studying a document on excavation in Ostia, Italy, when she became aware of someone standing behind her. She turned to find a tall, clean-shaven man whom she judged to be in his mid-thirties. He was holding several books of what looked like poetry.

"Hello?" She smiled, a little distracted, wondering what he wanted.

He raised an eyebrow. "Archaeology?"

"Yes." The interruption felt a little intrusive.

"Hmm, a lifetime on one's knees, redistributing mud with a very small trowel, like chickens scratching for grains!" His expression was perplexed.

Lottie fixed her eyes on the books he was carrying and decided he was either a little mad or simply rude. "Poetry?"

"Indeed."

"A lifetime of scrabbling about in others' angst?"

"Touché!" He began to walk away, his elbows opening and closing like stunted wings while softly clucking like a chicken, before turning and giving her a broad wink.

Lottie watched his back for a second, before returning to her article. Shaking her head, she had no idea what to make of him. She wanted to laugh but more than that, she found she was very curious to know who he was. When she got up to leave, she casually asked one of the librarians, who she'd got to know a little, during her time at Cambridge.

The librarian frowned. "I think you mean Dr Lewis? He was in earlier, looking for books about Wilfred Owen. Bit of a dish, isn't he?"

Lottie shrugged. "Well, if you like that sort of thing, I suppose."

The librarian looked taken aback and slightly affronted. "He's very popular with the ladies."

"He just came over and spoke to me," she said quickly. "I just wondered who he was, that's all." With that, she smiled and turned on her heel.

*

At lunchtime, she found Phyllis and a few of their fellow students sitting on the lawn of Newnham gardens enjoying the sunshine, discussing Hitler's advance in Western Europe and the evacuation of Dunkirk. Things weren't going well, they concluded, wondering what life would be like under German rule. It looked more inevitable by the day and was really quite depressing. When Lottie joined them, a little breathless, she flopped down on the grass.

"The boys are threatening to cancel the cricket," she announced. "They're two men short, for the match against the Army, so I've been tasked with finding more players. Any ideas? We absolutely cannot let Hitler ruin one of the few pleasures we have left."

"At the rate things are going, we'll be playing the Hun," said Edith Jones, a rather short girl with round glasses who was studying physics. "What about Tom Bennett?"

"He's not a student. The rules won't allow it. You know how stuffy they are." Lottie lay on the grass and propped herself up on her elbow.

"What, even at this time?" Phyllis rolled her eyes.

"No. Stupid, stupid conventions. It's a shame. He's good but a groundsman is just that, sadly."

"Who's left the team?" Edith took off her spectacles to give them a clean on her dress.

"Wainwright and Simms. They've been called up. The way things are going, it might be the last game we get for the foreseeable future!" Lottie sighed.

"Well, I can't think of anyone," said Phyllis, retrieving a piece of grass from her brogue. "Anyhow, I really know nothing about cricket. It always seemed like an excuse for men to sit in deckchairs on the village green and waste the afternoon."

"There's loads to it, Phil! I used to play with my brothers and the local boys all the time," Lottie said, brushing a wasp off her dress and watching it fly off to the border and land on a pale pink gladioli.

"Oh, I know! What about that quiet chap, Jeremy Gordon?" Lorna Mayfield, biology undergraduate said, looking animated.

"Who?" said Phyllis.

Lottie frowned. "I know the one you mean. Scottish? Jesus College? Yes, he did play quite well in some of the inter-college matches. I'll send him a note, straight away." She got to her feet and headed off towards the Porter's Office.

*

When she returned some while later, she was clutching a letter.

"Still one short?" Edith scratched her head. "I really can't think of anyone else. I'm going to have to go in, in a minute and get my hat. This sun's really hot and I can't get a tan."

"Well, I'm determined the game will go ahead," said Lottie. "I'm going in to get some lemonade, while I have a think. Who wants some?"

There was a chorus of, "Yes, please."

*

The letter, she found out, was from the Baroness von Haastein, inviting her to a dinner party on the twenty-fifth of May. She said in her note that she had some interesting guests that she would love Lottie to meet and to RSVP to let her know.

CHAPTER 8

May 25th 1940, Fenners' Cricket Ground, Cambridge

On this day, the German 2nd Panzer Division captures the port of Boulogne-sur-Mer, ending the Battle of Boulogne, in Allied defeat.

Fenners' cricket pitch was shimmering in the late spring heat. Spectators sat in deckchairs or on the grass, drinking beer and lemonade. At two p.m., both teams emerged, the Army with eleven men and the University with nine. Gloomily the Varsity men tossed a coin and lost and the Army elected to bat first, taking up their positions. Just when play was about to commence a bespectacled, slim figure emerged, bearded, cap pulled down low, wearing Cambridge colours. The college supporters clapped as the team exchanged glances. None of them recognised the last-minute player but nonetheless, he was a welcome addition. Aubrey Williams, the team captain, pointed to the boundary and he nodded and moved into place. Two hours later, Cambridge, technically superior, were winning by seven wickets to four. When they broke for tea, the unknown player disappeared and only came back out to rejoin the team when play recommenced. By four o'clock, the Army had lost nine wickets and declared. The mystery player silently shook hands and left to the rear of the pavilion where cricket whites were hurriedly removed, rolled up and put inside a bag with the beard and glasses and replaced with a dress, brogues and self-satisfied smile.

*

"Who was he?" Aubrey said, leaning against the pavilion veranda and opening a bottle of beer. "Strange fellow!"

"I've no idea. According to the team sheet his name's I. B. Prince."

The team looked at each other, blankly.

"Which college?" said Richie Galbraith.

"King's, apparently." Geoffrey Saunders frowned.

"Damn fair fielder."

"Ask Peters." Saunders turned to where John Peters was standing. Peters, do you know a chap called I. B. Prince?"

Peters stared thoughtfully at his bat. "No, I don't think I do. What's he studying?"

"No idea. Curious." Williams raised an eyebrow.

"Does it matter? We won, even with a man down." Galbraith took his cap off and screwed up his eyes in the sunlight.

"I suppose it doesn't." Williams shrugged.

"Awfully odd he didn't come in for tea. Not on, really!" Saunders sniffed.

"No," Galbraith agreed.

"It would appear there's a letter at the post office for me," Williams said, changing the subject.

They all avoided looking at each other. Peters put the tip of his bat on the grass and did a few practice swings.

"Every time a letter arrives I think that's it, I'm being called up." Williams shook his head.

"We'll all be at some point. I can't see how we won't now Calais's surrendered and we lost so many in the evacuation." Galbraith chewed the inside of his mouth. "Ogilvy's brother was killed last week. That's why he's gone home, early."

"Yes, I heard, Grey's too. Both at Dunkirk." Saunders picked up his bag.

"I wonder who will be next." Galbraith trailed off.

"Who knows? Part of me is itching to get my hands on the bloody Hun!" Peters swung the bat fiercely, like a sword.

"Well, I'm off," said Williams. "After I've picked the letter up, I'm going to watch the girls play tennis at Girton."

"And we all know who will be playing!" Galbraith laughed, lighting a cigarette.

"Who?" Saunders looked innocently at both of them.

"Geraldine Simms!" He pretended to swoon.

Williams blushed. "Oh, quite possibly." He was non-committal. "I've been invited to drinks after."

"Lucky you! I bet Mavis Sefton will be there too. Can you get me in?" said Peters.

"Sorry, old boy. Strictly by invitation!" Williams swung his blazer over one shoulder and moved off with a wave.

"Oh well, back to my essay, then! I have a tutorial on Monday." Peters sighed. "Anyone going to the pub tonight?"

They shook their heads.

"If you want company, Sinclair will be there; he always is." Galbraith grinned and inhaled deeply.

"Nice to have the money," muttered Peters.

"I think the lab's just waiting for his liver," said Saunders, his voice drowned out by three Blenheim aircraft flying low overhead.

"If I go, I want to fly Spitfires," said Galbraith, spreading his arms, blowing his cheeks out and making a tuk-tuk noise.

"If I go, I just want it all over quickly," said Saunders, wiping his spectacles. "It's not a game, Galbraith!"

"Who said it was? I'm up for blasting the Luftwaffe out of the sky and saving good old Blighty."

"Good luck to you! Anyone walking into the City?"

"Yes," said Peters. "Something's just occurred to me," he said as they left the ground. "I. B. Prince from King's?"

CHAPTER 9

June 1ˢᵗ 1940, Cambridge

On this day, German bombers sink the French destroyer Foudroyant off Dunkirk.

It had been a bloody end to May. The Germans had won a massive tactical victory at Dunkirk despite the valiant evacuation of Allied troops and many thousands of young men had died. Still, families waited to hear from their loved ones and lived in daily dread of a knock on the door. Lottie walked through town, pondering on Churchill's speech. On Tuesday they had all crowded around the wireless at supper time, to listen to the new Prime Minister pledging Britain's "resolve to fight on for years and alone, if necessary." He predicted that since the battle for France was over, he expected the Battle of Britain would begin and if we failed, we would "sink into the abyss of a new dark age." Frightening words that had them staring at each other, in dismay. It didn't sound good and the following day, aircraft carrier HMS *Glorious* and two destroyers had been sunk by German battleships, off the coast of Norway. Everyone seemed to know someone who had perished at Dunkirk and to make matters worse, Lottie's brother Archie had received his call-up papers from the Army.

*

At the Post Office, Lottie bought stamps and posted her letters. Wandering back towards Newnham College in a sombre mood, a red MG car overtook her and stopped abruptly before reversing, level with her. She recognised the driver as Dr Gareth Lewis, the man who had spoken to her in the library. What on earth did he want now, she wondered, at the same time acknowledging he was very attractive with his light blue eyes and chiselled features.

"Ah, Chicken Lady!" he said, grinning.

Lottie really wasn't in the mood for banter. "What can I do for you?" she said a little coldly, not wanting to use his name as then he would know she'd asked about him.

"How do you fancy a trip out to Ely Cathedral? Don't say 'no', I absolutely insist!" He grinned and leaned over to open the passenger door. "Look, I'm really harmless and, to be honest, I could do with some company."

"Of a trainee archaeologist?"

"Yes. You can tell me about digging things up. I'm sure it's fascinating."

"What makes you think I want to spend time with you?" she said, trying not to laugh.

He looked a little wounded. "Well you might, if you try it? Look, if I give you my word not to recite poetry on the way and if you hate me by the time we reach Ely, I shall bring you straight back. I promise!"

"I might hate you already," she said, meeting his eyes.

"That would be a record and very sad. Come on, what have you got to lose?"

"Time. By all accounts it might be short."

People were beginning to stare.

"Have you been to the cathedral?" he said a little more seriously, resting his arm across the back of the passenger seat.

He had, Lottie noticed, strong and rather elegant hands. "No."

"Well, if you *are* a history student, you should. You could call it a field trip, if you like!"

A car behind tooted and he raised an eyebrow. "Well? I can't possibly move until you say yes and prolonging it will just annoy everyone."

With a shake of her head, Lottie slid reluctantly in beside him. "How come you have petrol to go on trips?"

"I've saved my coupons. A car needs to be driven once in a while, else it will seize up. I'm Gareth Lewis," he said, taking his right hand off the wheel and offering it to Lottie.

"Lottie…"

"Yes I know, Lottie Beauchamp," he said above the roar of the engine.

"How do you know my name?" she said, frowning.

"I asked," he said, matter-of-factly, pulling away rather fast and waving an apology to the driver behind.

"Why?"

"You ask an awful lot of questions for a chicken lady!"

"Haven't you got a wife or something to pester?"

He shrugged. "Somewhere. When last I heard, she was in Scotland."

"So, you just drive around picking up random students?"

"Not random! Carefully selected."

"Calculating!" She couldn't help laughing.

"I decided after our encounter in the library, we would get along."

"Encounter? I would say, more like ambush."

"I thought being an archaeologist you might dig deep and cure me of my literary melancholy." He took his hands off the wheel held his chest in mock pain. The car veered to the left and he grinned and grabbed the wheel.

"Highly unlikely, I would have thought."

As the car sped through the countryside, she wondered how she'd ended up in a car with this man, heading for an afternoon in Ely. Still, she thought, it was a bit of an adventure on an otherwise quite gloomy Saturday and although she didn't want to admit it, she did find him amusing.

CHAPTER 10

8th June 1940, Cambridge

On this day, the 5th Panzer Division Captures Rouen. Completion of the Allied evacuation from Norway.

The other dinner guests at Eleanor, Baroness von Haastein's house, were a mix of artists, writers and a politician. Lottie wasn't quite sure where or how she fitted in but she was grateful to be invited. "This is Lottie Beauchamp," Eleanor announced, on her arrival. "Don't you think she's just exquisite?"

She blushed as the rotund politician's eyes unashamedly undressed her. The others, who were mainly lounging on the battered sofas and velvet upholstered armchairs that, like everything in the room, bore the marks of crusted, splattered paint, smiled appreciatively.

"Come and sit next to me, Lottie," drawled an American woman, who was introduced as Doris Mulholland. "Keep away from Anthony Carlton! He's a rake." She was referring to the politician, who chortled with laughter at the insult. His stomach, the size of a full-term pregnancy, jiggled up and down.

A bearded, red-haired man, called Robert, was standing on the far side of the room, busy scrutinising some of Eleanor's new paintings and was so engrossed, he barely looked up. Eleanor kissed his shoulder lightly as she passed to fetch more wine and he looked round and smiled. "I really love this one," he said, pointing at a nude. "You just get better and better, Eleanor." He had a soft, Irish accent and he drew her into him and kissed her full on the lips. Whispering something in her ear, they parted and laughed, leaving Lottie under no illusion that they were lovers.

"Have some champagne, Lottie. Don't mind us, everyone's harmless!" The thin man with a rather large nose and ears smiled at her. "I'm Leonard Woolf and this is my wife, Virginia."

Virginia glanced across at her from where she was sitting, away from the other guests, in the corner of the room. She had an aura of melancholy and her dark eyes seemed to stare into the distance, as though absorbed with other, non-worldly matters. Eleanor looked at Virginia then back to Leonard and something unspoken went between them. Lottie opened her mouth to gush about how much she loved her novels but shut it again. Something told her it would be wholly inappropriate. She'd heard gossip of a passionate love affair between her and Vita Sackville-West and that Virginia was susceptible to spells of depression. It must, she thought, be awfully difficult for the devoted Leonard, who drew the conversation away from his wife like salt soaking up a spill.

"Tell me all about yourself," said Doris, taking her arm and leading her to a chair. "Eleanor tells us you're studying archaeology and that you fly planes? How interesting!" She was, Lottie estimated, in her early forties. Unconventionally dressed in baggy trousers and a cravat, she puffed away on a small cigar.

Lottie laughed. "Yes and it is absorbing but mainly only to other archaeologists. I'd hoped to get a spell studying in Egypt but what with the war, it seems unlikely."

"I hear they've found some quite interesting things in Suffolk," said Leonard.

"You mean, Sutton Hoo?" said Lottie.

"Yes, that's the place. Lots of seventh-century treasure?"

"Two hundred and sixty-three pieces, can you believe?" Lottie began, animatedly. "A local archaeologist, Basil Brown, began investigations in 1938 but because of their importance, Mr Philips, a Fellow of Selwyn College, took over." She stopped abruptly, conscious of not wanting to bore her fellow guests and aware that all attention in the room, bar one, had turned, once more, to her.

Robert was standing opposite, hand resting on the overmantel to the fire. "You really must paint her," he said to Eleanor, staring at Lottie. "She's quite flawless. She could be your muse!"

"I fully intend to, when the time is right." Eleanor fitted another cigarette in her holder and lit it, blowing a cloud of smoke into the air, adding to the opaque blanket that hung above their heads, drifting down among the clutter of pots, plants and spills of paint.

"For God's sake open a window!" said Doris. "Else in this fog, we'll all lose sight of each other and I want to know where Anthony is, at all times!"

Everyone laughed, except Virginia who jumped, startled by the sudden noise and looked pained as if her nerves had been jangled.

"You mean you'd miss me, Doris?"

"No, I want to know where your damn hands are!"

"The wrong kind of hands for you, methinks, Duckie?" He raised an eyebrow and made a circular motion in her direction with his pipe.

"What would you know about anything?" she said, pointedly. "You're a politician!"

"What's the latest from Westminster, Carlton?" said Leonard, sitting on the arm of the chair beside his wife.

"Well," he stared into the distance, thoughtfully, "everyone's running around Churchill like he's the Oracle, since Neville resigned. We have to face facts, France is hopeless and now the Italians have turned, he's our only hope but for all his bluster about fighting on, I honestly don't see how we can win this." Anthony refilled his pipe and sat back thoughtfully. This triggered a heated debate that continued over dinner. Virginia, Lottie noted, ate virtually nothing then removed herself at the first possible opportunity and drifted back off to her corner to read a book. Nobody commented and the wine continued to flow through the blacked-out night like a river in full bore and in the early hours, Robert played the fiddle. Everyone danced by candle light, read poetry aloud and played parlour games, except for Virginia, who slipped away, retiring early.

*

At seven a.m., Lottie was awakened with a cup of tea by Robert. A little embarrassed, she realised she'd dropped off to sleep on one of the sofas at some point and someone had put a blanket over her. She must have slept soundly as the living room was now empty. With the blackout curtains pulled back, the space was flooded with pale sunlight and, save for the bacchanalian detritus, it was almost unrecognisable from the party atmosphere of the night before. Everyone had evidently gone to their own or someone else's room and her host was nowhere to be seen. Lottie yawned and stretched.

"Gosh, I'm so sorry, I must have dropped off. Do please let me help you clear up."

Robert was busy emptying the overflowing ashtrays and removing empty bottles.

"Don't trouble yourself. Ah, you were sleeping so soundly, it would have been a sin to have woken you." He stopped what he was doing and lit a cigarette. "It was late and you'd have had to negotiate blackout to get back to your college."

"I really should make a move," said Lottie, uncurling her legs from under the blanket and getting to her feet. "I imagine everyone is still asleep?"

"They are, right enough, except for Virginia who went out early for a walk." Robert folded the blanket, with the relaxed air of a man who was comfortable around the house. "I'll be away myself, too, shortly. I have to get the train back to London."

Lottie wondered if he was married. "Is that where you have your studio?"

"Aye, Archway where the real people live! This is where I come to escape reality." He grinned. "I meant what I said last night, you should let Eleanor paint you."

"Of course, if she would like to." Lottie got to her feet. Her head felt a little fuzzy from the alcohol and she looked forward to some fresh air. "Well, goodbye, Robert. It was a pleasure to meet you. Do thank Eleanor, when you see her."

"I shall and the pleasure, Lottie, was all mine."

On the way back to college, mulling over the previous evening, Lottie decided she liked Eleanor enormously and her eclectic taste in friends.

CHAPTER 11

14ᵗʰ June 1940, Cambridge

On this day, the Germans despatch the first transport of Poles to Auschwitz and enter Paris, unopposed.

Despite her protests, Lottie had very much enjoyed her afternoon in Ely with Gareth Lewis. He was good company and made her laugh and to her surprise, he'd acted like the perfect gentleman. Since then, she'd seen him a couple of times but always in public. On Sunday afternoon they'd walked to Grantchester for tea and on Wednesday, taken a punt down the river and had a picnic on the bank. It was on that day, laying on a blanket in the late afternoon sun, he'd rolled over and kissed her and she allowed it. When they got back, he asked her to have dinner with him the next day, at his house. She agreed, as she would be going home soon for the summer. In between seeing him, she found herself thinking about him a lot, very aware he was married, wondering what to do. While she wasn't at all interested in convention, she was sure people had started to talk about them and there had been a few pointed comments in the common room. Gareth had told her his marriage was over and he was going to ask his wife for a divorce, when he could track her down, but when all was said and done, she lurked somewhere in the murky recess of the wings and Lottie's own reputation was at stake. She also knew that Gareth, being a man, would escape any blame while she would be viewed as the siren who had brought him crashing onto the rocks of seduction. Of course, she had the power to stop the affair in its tracks and quite probably should but with the future of the world as she knew it hanging by a fine thread, she really didn't feel inclined to. Closing her eyes, she could smell his cologne and feel his lips against hers and it gave her comfort in a world of uncertainty.

*

At the beginning of the week, she'd kept her promise and sat for Eleanor, in her studio at the top of House Cottage. It was a perfect English summer day, save for the intermittent roar of aircraft. The morning was fine and warm, punctuated by a light rain shower that was greedily sucked into the soil without trace, fed by the droplets that fell softly from the petals of the fragrant apricot rose that clung to the stone wall of the house, like the most perfect ornament. Lottie lay, scantily clad on a battered sofa, trying to keep the awkward pose demanded by Eleanor, who worked with languid strokes of her brushes, stopping frequently to smoke or reposition her.

"Darling, you must keep still!" she said, taking a large swig of whisky. "I need to capture you looking like Aphrodite, not a broken deckchair!"

Lottie laughed. "Sorry, Eleanor. I don't think I'm cut out for modelling."

Eleanor sighed. "You are a gift from God, sent to be immortalised! Just keep that pose. I'm nearly finished for today!"

"Have you had many lovers, Eleanor?" Lottie said, suddenly. She thought she wouldn't mind her asking.

"Of course. Many men and also a few women… Keep your head still," she said from behind her easel.

"Oh."

"Does that shock you? Why do you ask? Head up!"

Lottie spoke, afraid to move her mouth too much. "No. I just wondered. You see, there is someone I'm rather fond of but…" She paused, wondering how to put it but Eleanor pre-empted her.

"He's married, huh?"

"Well, yes. Sort of. I mean technically, yes he is. She's off somewhere and they're separated. He's going to ask her for a divorce."

"So you want to know if you should fuck?"

Lottie was a little taken aback at her directness.

Eleanor poked her head round her easel. "I've embarrassed you, darling?"

"No. Well a little, maybe."

Eleanor shrugged. "Okay, *making love* is good if you feel a… a *connection*. Who cares so long as you both enjoy it? You English are too uptight. You associate intimacy with marriage and that's where you're wrong. It leads to years of misery. What do you say? Never buy a book from a lending library?" She snorted. "Libraries exist to allow people to enrich their knowledge! What's the point in buying a bloody book unless you want to keep reading it over and over? You just become boring and damage the pages!"

"You're right, of course."

"Always! Look, go out, make love with whoever. Feel passion. That's all that matters. Make good memories!" She stood back from her work and eyed it critically.

Lottie looked at her magnificent, unconventional friend, unmistakably Jewish and suddenly she felt afraid for her. If Hitler won the war what would become of her? "Are you worried about what will happen if we're invaded?" It seemed a little pointed but Lottie needed to know.

"No," she said without hesitation. "Fear empowers… I'll be damned if I let those Nazi bastards make me afraid." She spoke softly. "They can chase me to the end of the earth but fear them for their cowardly brutality, never!"

"Will you stay here, in this house?"

"It's my home."

They both fell silent for a while. Eleanor concentrated on her work and Lottie fell deep in thought.

"My family has a house, in a remote part of Scotland, on the West Coast. We went there sometimes when we were on school holidays and when we weren't abroad. It just sits there now, empty. It's in woodland, on the coast, about five miles from the nearest village," Lottie said, eventually.

"Nice. I'm sure you had lots of fun."

"Do you have a pen and paper?"

"Somewhere." Eleanor went to a battered desk and found a sheet that was encrusted with paint and a gold fountain pen.

Lottie wrote down the address of the house and gave it back to her. "If anything happens or things look bad, you should be safe there for a while. The key is under a pot to the left of the back door. There's a man in the village called John McDonald, who runs a fishing boat. He would help you. Do you have a car?"

"Yes, in the garage."

"Try to store some cans of petrol and keep it maintained."

They stared at each other for a moment before Eleanor took the paper, murmuring, "The house at the end of the world," and put it in a drawer.

CHAPTER 12

15th June 1940, Cambridge

On this day, Operation Ariel, the Allied evacuation of military personnel and civilians from France, begins. Bread and flour are rationed in Holland.

As it was the end of term, the students were preparing to head home for the summer. Given the continued bombing of London, many of those who lived in the city sought out friends to lodge with. People cadged lifts and Lottie prepared to return to her family home, The Lindens, in Woodbridge, Suffolk. She knew it would feel odd, without the boys or her father being there. Gareth had begged her to stay on and she readily agreed but only for a few days as her mother had written to say their head gardener had been called up and she was needed to help out with growing food for the war effort.

*

As she wandered through the city, she noted as the students had begun to drift away, Cambridge had begun to look less like a university town and more like a place under siege, with its piles of sandbags and unfamiliar young men in uniform, striding authoritatively around. She wondered who would make it back in September, if any. Labour throughout the country was in short supply and given there was no sign of the end of the war, more men were being called up every day. In her pocket, she had an unopened letter from Hugh. Now twenty-three and pilot-trained, he was billeted at Uxbridge and in his letters sounded so grown-up and brave, talking about the men in his Squadron and how much faith he had in Air Chief Marshall Dowding. She knew he was a talented pilot, completely at home in the air but being gifted when being shot at, would be a wholly different thing! Lottie's godmother had given her the Tiger Moth, 'The Bee' on her eighteenth birthday and she and Hugh had spent so many hours in the air, they'd almost forgotten they had legs but that certainly was a different time and place and she now realised how much they had taken those halcyon days for granted.

Archie, a couple of years younger than her, had now been drafted too. He was training to be an Army officer at the Royal Military Academy in Woolwich. Thank God he'd missed Dunkirk but who knew what would happen next and where he'd end up. She imagined both Archie and Hugh in their different uniforms, proud and earnest, just children really but responsible for their own and other men's lives. How cheap and precarious life had suddenly become. To her surprise, she felt hot tears running down her cheeks and she wiped them away, fiercely, not wanting them to be seen by passers-by. What, she thought, was the point of snivelling when the world was in chaos? The tears turned to anger, suddenly as it seemed ridiculous and yes, *offensive* that she was prevented by her sex to enter combat as a pilot, too. Her letter to her father begging him to speak to Churchill hadn't borne fruit but if it had, she knew she'd have gone at the drop of a hat and she'd be a more competent pilot than most of the men. What right had she to be enjoying life, with her nose stuck in a book that talked only of the past, when all around her was in chaos? There must, she thought, be something useful she could do to contribute. Perhaps driving an ambulance or even nursing? But of course there was a distinct possibility she would have to take over the management of the farm with the boys and The Brig away and she'd have to content herself with digging the land. She recognised the importance and that Armies 'marched on their stomachs' but she couldn't quell the disappointment that hung around in the background, like an unrequited lover. She would see how the land lay when she got home and how her mother was coping but in any event, a return to Cambridge, however alluring, might have to wait while duty called.

*

And then, as it happened, things did change, quite unexpectedly. Without warning, a day later, a letter arrived:

White Waltham, Buckinghamshire
11th June 1940

Dear Miss Beauchamp,

I'm looking to recruit female pilots to deliver aircraft as part of the Women's Auxiliary Airforce, Air Transport Auxiliary. You have been brought to my attention as someone who holds a pilot's licence. I'm aware you are currently studying at Cambridge but I would be delighted if you would come and meet with me at White Waltham, on Friday 19th July at 13.00 hours for a preliminary discussion.

Please confirm if you are able to attend.

Yours truly,

Pauline Gower

Commander WAA

Lottie felt a tidal wave of excitement, when she read it. She'd heard about the work of the Air Transport Auxiliary, known as the ATA, through a friend of a friend but hadn't dreamed that it might be the answer for her. The fact that Pauline Gower had actually written to her, *inviting* her for an interview must surely indicate she was interested in her joining. She couldn't wait to tell Phyllis and, of course, Gareth. Dancing along the corridor to her room, she knocked on Phyllis's door and waved a letter in her surprised friend's face.

"Phil, I've news!" she said, breathlessly. "Come with me, we're going for tea at Whittard's. My treat."

"What news?" Phyllis looked at her friend from behind her spectacles.

"Just put your book down and come!"

"As it happens, I don't need an excuse. I'm just in the middle of translating a piece that's so dry I'm worried it will turn to dust before

I've finished it."

"Let it disintegrate!" Lottie grabbed her hand and pulled her gently down the corridor.

"Lottie, I need my bag," she said, laughing. "And you could at least let me change my shoes. You really are impossible. What's going on?"

"I'm not really sure but I'll show you the letter when we get to the café."

CHAPTER 13

16ᵗʰ June 1940, Cambridge

On this day – French Prime Minister Paul Reynaud resigns and is replaced by Marshal Philippe Petain. Soviet Union gives Latvia and Estonia an eight-hour ultimatum to surrender.

Lottie awoke in darkness, momentarily unaware of where she was. Then she remembered. She got out of bed, naked, and pulled the blackout curtain to one side and saw that dawn was breaking. Looking over her shoulder she saw Gareth asleep on his side, dark fringe tumbling over his forehead, the sheet loosely wrapped around his slim, lower abdomen. He looked like a sculpture, laying in chiselled perfection and he didn't stir at the gift of light. She smiled, thinking she could have stayed there forever, standing with her back to the window and would never have tired of this intimate picture of him and she watched for a while, as his broad chest rose and fell as he slept the deep sleep of post-coital satisfaction, betraying no sign of the asthma that plagued him from time to time. Leaving the chink in the curtain so that she could see her way, Lottie found his dressing gown hanging on the back of the bathroom door and slipped it on. It smelled of him and she pulled the burgundy silk collar up to her nose and inhaled the faint scent of sandalwood and tobacco and she wrapped the gown around her, excited by the feeling of wearing it. Rolling up the sleeves before closing the bedroom door behind her so as not to disturb him and making her way downstairs to his small living room, she pulled the blackouts back fully, went into the kitchen, made coffee and lit a cigarette. Had last night been reckless, she wondered, inhaling deeply and staring out of the window? It had seemed inevitable from the moment he'd stopped his car that day, that they would become lovers, but he was a married man who had not yet sought a divorce. A man who declared his love to her through poetry, while sitting on the banks of the Cam. How many, she wondered, had he courted like this and did it really matter? Eleanor would say it didn't and to just enjoy the experience. He was quite intoxicating, there was no doubt about that and a thoughtful lover, although her experience was somewhat restricted to a couple of young men of a similar age, whose gauche attempts at love-making had left them both giggling and unfulfilled. This, by comparison, felt so grown up and unlike anything she'd experienced before. The way he touched her face or stroked her skin made her desperate for him but he made her wait, prolonging the moment, making her breathless with expectation until like magic when she climaxed, he did too. The end of the cigarette began to burn her fingers and shocked her back into the moment. Quickly, she stubbed it out and lit another. Her body had become permanently aroused by him and it was both exhausting and wonderful in equal measure but within days she would be gone for the summer and she also had the interview to attend. Perhaps, she decided, it would be a good idea to put a little distance between them as surely this couldn't last. She hadn't told Gareth about Pauline Gower's letter, as maybe nothing would come of it but the thought of leaving him gave her a strange feeling in her chest and she could feel her heart aching. Was *this* what love felt like? She blew a stream of tobacco smoke into the air and considered it. Always, she'd been a little dismissive of the concept of being 'in love' and had found women dripping around over a man a little soppy and certainly not something she had time for. And yet, here she was unable to get him out of her mind. Even when she was reading a reference book, he was there, in the background vying for her attention and invariably he got it. She needed time to clear her head and although it was still early, despite her lack of sleep, she felt wide awake. Looking at the clock on the mantle shelf, she saw it was just before five o'clock. While she would have liked to have closed the curtains and crawled back under the sheet to feel Gareth's skin against hers and make love once more, she knew she really shouldn't be seen leaving his house. Ordinarily, they could have gone to a hotel, far enough away so as not to be recognised, but these were extraordinary times in which, despite what was going in the world, narrow-minded people still found time to interfere in other people's affairs and make moral judgements. Despite the thickness of the material, war-curtains still twitched and perhaps more so. Lottie decided that if she departed through the back door and made her way along the passageway where the bins were kept, she had less chance of being spotted and so, she located her hastily discarded clothes from the night before and dressed. With one last, stolen glance at Gareth and after placing a scribbled note on the pillow next to him, she left silently, to expose herself to the day.

*

As she made her way along the damp pavement, the baker's van pulled up outside Cooper's and from the back came tantalising wafts of newly baked bread. Lottie smiled and said a cheerful, "Good morning!" as though it was quite normal for a woman to be walking the streets at that time, in eveningwear.

The baker eyed her with interest, as he pulled out the trays of bread and touched his cap. "Morning, miss."

"That smells divine," she said, pausing to savour the aroma and realising she was hungry.

"Thank you," he replied, with a grin, taking some paper from a bag and wrapping a loaf in it. "Here," he said, holding it out to her. "Put a little butter on it and eat it warm. It'll taste like a bit of heaven."

"My goodness, thank you!" she said, taking it. "I'm afraid I've no change."

"It's a gift, miss. It's not often my delivery starts with such a lovely vision. The nearest I get is Charlie from the dairy and he's no oil painting, I can tell you!"

She laughed, thanked him and walked off, tearing off pieces of warm bread and eating them. At Mathematical Bridge, she stopped at a bench where she sat for ten minutes or so, watching the swans teach their cygnets how to fish, before heading back to Newnham, thinking about Gareth.

*

When she arrived back at the college entrance, the gates were open and she was relieved to see a steaming cup of tea in the Porter's Lodge but no Mr Long. Slipping past, up the staircase and along the corridor, she hoped to get back to her room without seeing anyone but a door opened and Phyllis appeared in her dressing gown, yawning. Putting her finger to her lips, Lottie grinned and signalled to her friend to go back into her room.

"Where have you been?" said Phyllis, grinning.

"Shhh!"

"Well?" She looked her up and down.

"Where do you think?" Lottie laughed. "Here, have some bread, it's very fresh."

"To the baker's?" Phyllis stared at her, in disbelief. "It's six in the morning and you're wearing your best dress!"

"I haven't been home, silly!"

Phyllis frowned. "Professor Lewis?"

Lottie nodded.

"Oh my lord! Did Mr Long see you?"

"No, fortunately."

"Sit down and tell me everything!" said Phyllis, pulling her to the chair while she plonked herself back down on the unmade bed.

"There's really nothing to tell except I really do like him," Lottie said, beaming.

"Did you… Did you stay the night at his place?" said Phyllis, looking quite excited at the intrigue.

"Yes."

"Was he…?" Phyllis struggled to find the word and they both giggled.

"It was surprisingly wonderful," said Lottie, blushing a little.

"Oh my god, you're in love!" Phyllis broke off some bread absent-mindedly and put it in her mouth.

"No! Don't be silly. At least I don't think so. I don't really know. How does one tell?"

"I don't know," said Phyllis, looking out of her depth. "I've only ever had a kiss with the son of one of my father's patients. To be honest, it was all a bit of a disappointment at the time and sort of, well… messy, like when one of the dogs licks one's face without warning."

Lottie burst out laughing and put her hand over her mouth, trying to muffle it. "I do so love you, Phyllis!"

"I love you too, darling, but you do realise he's married?"

"I know but he's going to ask her for a divorce."

"To marry you?"

Lottie shook her head. "Not specifically. I think he would have anyway but now he says it's more urgent as he doesn't want us to creep around."

"Well," said Phyllis, getting up and taking her friend's hand, "I do hope he makes you happy."

"All I can say is, last night, he made me exceptionally happy but now I need a bath." She got to her feet and gave Phyllis a hug. "I'm so glad I met you, Phyllis," she said, before opening the door and disappearing back out to the corridor, where she met Elsie.

"Good morning, Elsie," she said brightly. The girl was a year above her and a little uptight.

"Hello, Lottie," she said, looking her up and down. "Late night?"

Lottie looked at her innocently. "I was talking to Phyllis about something."

"Oh? I'm sure she appreciated you dressing up for the occasion but I could have sworn I spotted you coming into the building about twenty minutes ago."

"Bread!" said Lottie. "Can't get enough of it. Here," she said, handing what was left of the loaf to a surprised Elsie. "Do have some while it's still warm. Put a little butter on it if you have any left from your ration, it's quite divine. I'm so sorry but I have to dash." She closed the door to her room, unzipped her dress and got a waft of Gareth's cologne that had clung to her skin. Bringing her forearm up to her nose and inhaling deeply, she fell back onto her bed and closed her eyes, hoping the contraceptive cap was still safely in situ.

CHAPTER 14

18ᵗʰ June 1940, Cambridge

On this day – Winston Churchill delivers his "This was their finest hour" speech to the House of Commons. De Gaulle gives his "Appeal of 18ᵗʰ June" speech via the BBC, shortly after the fall of France and his arrival in London.

Lottie sat working in the university library, finishing an essay on modern archaeological methods when a paper plane sailed into view and landed in front of her. Looking round, she appeared to be the only one in the place and she couldn't make out from its direction, who'd thrown it. Picking it up she could see writing on the inside, so she unfolded its wings and found it addressed to 'Amelia Earhart' and invitation from 'G' inviting her to supper, at seven, at his house. She put it in her pocket and smiled. He'd been very much in her thoughts over the past two days and she'd longed to hear from him. Putting the invitation in her pocket, she stared back down at her work, but the words had become a meaningless string of letters, as her concentration waned. Shutting her eyes for a moment, she attempted to collect her thoughts and tried but failed not to think of him and his blue eyes that wrinkled at the edges when he laughed and his muscular arms that were covered in a down of black hair that met his wrist watch. Those arms would envelop her later that evening and caress her with hands that were strong, beautiful and capable of the utmost gentleness. Giving up on her essay, she put the top on her fountain pen, tidied her paperwork and with a sigh, collected her books.

*

When she reached Gareth's house, just after seven, she took a quick look over her shoulder, to check nobody was looking and knocked. As she waited for him to answer, she could hear classical music from the other side of the door. Opening it, he pulled her inside, closed the door, took her in his arms and kissed her.

"I've missed you," he said, releasing her and leaving her a little breathless.

"So it would seem," she said, grinning.

"You look beautiful," he said, taking her hand and leading her into the large drawing room where he'd set two places and put a bottle of wine on ice. "Let me get you a drink. Wine or gin?"

"Wine would be lovely. It's such a warm evening. I thought we might walk down the river after supper?"

"Really? Yes, of course, if you'd like." There was a note of disappointment in his voice.

Lotte went up behind him and put her arms around him, swaying to the music. "No! A walk is really the last thing on my mind."

"Good! And mine. Will you stay tonight?"

"Maybe? I don't want to get caught though," she sighed.

"I've thought about that."

"Oh?" She took a sip of wine. It was cold and tasted of raspberry. "Mmm, that's nice," she said.

"Come with me," he said, leading her upstairs. "Bring your glass."

"You're eager!" She laughed.

"Yes but look." He pointed to his bed where he'd laid out a shirt, tie, trousers, belt, cap and old jacket. "I got them from the costume department at the theatre. I think they'll fit you pretty well?"

She grinned. "God, you really are devious."

"Not really. It's just that Vice-Chancellor Smithson would love to have a reason to hang me out to dry. He thinks I'm too progressive and he's right of course. If he had his way, Cambridge would be a female-free city but I think that's because he likes boys a little too much."

"You mean…?"

"Of course. It's Cambridge's worst kept secret."

Lottie picked up the tie and held it up. "I always thought I'd make rather a good boy," she said, standing tall and sticking her chin out. "I was always better at climbing trees than my brothers; a real tom-boy!"

"Well, I'm very glad you're not a boy. Smithson's loss is firmly my gain. Ideally, darling, I'd take you to an hotel and we could be waited on but we can't and there's no way with your eagle-eyed Mr Long, I can come to you. The clothes are just a thought but if you'd rather not, of course…"

She sat on the edge of the bed, looking at the clothes. "It's completely genius!" she said with a smile. "If I tuck my hair up and pull the cap down low, I could be a delivery boy or gardener."

"Well, yes." He grinned at her enthusiasm for the subterfuge.

"What fun!"

*

They had dinner and made love and then, at around midnight the air-raid sirens sounded, shortly followed by a deafening explosion that rattled the windows of the house.

"We need to get to a shelter," shouted Lottie, above the noise.

"It's too late," said Gareth, putting on the beside light before throwing her his dressing gown and pulling on his trousers. "They're too close. We need to get under the table in the dining room. Quickly!"

They ran downstairs and pulled the chairs away before the sound of another explosion that made crockery fall to the floor and smash. Gareth pulled Lottie to him, instinctively covering her head with his arm.

"Christ!" he said. "That was close. How many more?"

They stared at each other wide eyed and waited, listening for the sound of aircraft but there was nothing.

"Whatever happens I want you to know, I love you!" he said, suddenly and with a sense of urgency. "I was going to tell you, I've had a letter from Sybil. She's in New York, staying with friends. As soon as she's back, I'll meet her and ask her for a divorce. There's no reason for her to refuse. She's wealthy in her own right. According to her brother, she's talking about moving over there permanently. Then I'll be free."

Lottie, however, was a little distracted, thinking about Phyllis and her other friends. The explosion sounded as though it could have come from the direction of Newnham. They wouldn't have had time to get down to the basement. She barely heard what he'd said but she nodded. "I know." She put her finger to his lips. "I'm going to get dressed and go back. I have to see if the girls are all right."

"You can't! You have to wait," he said. "There might be more. They haven't sounded the all-clear yet."

"I think it's stopped. I can't hear anything."

"If you go, I'm coming with you."

"You can't! You'll be recognised. I'll be fine in those clothes you got; I won't be noticed. Let me get dressed!" She kissed him and pulled away, making her way by the light of the torch, back to the bedroom.

He followed and pulled his shirt on. "There's no way you're going alone. I'll follow from a distance and when I know you're home safely, I'll turn back."

*

On the street, she heard shouting and saw men running in the direction of Petersfield, where the night sky was lit like a flickering beacon and the air was filled with smoke. She stared towards Newnham but it remained in darkness, so she had to assume Phil and the others were safe. Unable to continue home without seeing if she could help elsewhere, she pulled her cap further down and changed direction. Gareth, some fifty or so yards behind, followed.

*

At Vicarage Terrace, in front of the collapsed and burning row of houses, a woman in a dressing gown was screaming, "My Stan! Where's my Stan?" Others stood bewildered, one with a head injury, being attended to by neighbours. Lottie could see a body of a child lying on the ground and a young mother knelt beside it, inconsolable. People began to gather at the scene and were being shouted at to stand back, as a fire engine tried to get through, its bell ringing out urgently into the night. Suddenly, through the firelight, Lottie spotted a hand poking out of the rubble. Breaking through the crowd, she ran towards it and began pulling bricks away.

"Get back, lad!" someone shouted. "That section of roof is about to fall."

"A hand!" she yelled. "Quickly, over here!"

Gareth and a few of the men broke through and ran to help her, as cinders rained down around them like fireflies but it was no good. By the time they pulled him out and carried him to safety, contorted and injured almost beyond recognition, he was dead. With a crack and a roar, the roof rafters gave way and they collapsed onto the street. Lottie suppressed an urge to gag at the sight of the man's injuries and, with a shaking hand she reached out and closed his eyes. The woman in the dressing gown fell to her knees beside the body, wailing and cradling the broken remains of her husband in her arms. Lottie put her arm around her and gently, after a little while, she and Gareth lifted her to her feet, restraining her as she fought them to allow her to follow him into the ambulance. Gareth held her up while she sobbed into his chest until two neighbours arrived to look after her.

"Come on," Gareth said, leading Lottie away by the sleeve. "There's nothing more we can do here. I'm taking you back home with me."

CHAPTER 15

19th July 1940, White Waltham, Buckinghamshire

On this day – Hitler addresses an 'appeal to reason' to Great Britain to avert 'destruction of a great world empire.' Rejection would result in an attack with all the forces at the command of the Axis powers.

Lottie took the train from Suffolk to London Paddington and another, to Maidenhead. Outside the station, she hailed a taxi, as instructed, and directed the driver to the De Havilland Flying Club that had been requisitioned for the Air Transport Auxiliary.

*

Pauline Gower, daughter of Sir Robert Gower, was waiting for her, in full uniform, at the entrance that had the motto 'Aetheris Avidi' – 'Eager For The Air', over the large door. She immediately struck Lottie as the kind of woman who would have been Head Girl at her school. Enthusiastic, a little stiff and no doubt very capable, she briefly shook Lottie's hand and showed her into her office that, like its occupant, appeared well organised and functional.

"Do sit down, Miss Beauchamp. Can I get you some tea? The coffee's dreadful, I'm afraid!"

"Thank you, ma'am." Lottie sat in front of the desk. She looked around at the files, neatly piled on a filing cabinet and the huge, detailed map of England on the wall behind. Through the window, she could see three grass landing strips and a lot of activity.

"Pauline, please. Although we appear to be RAF we're civilians, so military greetings don't apply. As you can see, we're very busy. Now, I imagine you're curious to know why I asked you to come here today?"

Lottie nodded.

Gower interlocked her fingers and put her elbows on her desk. "I'll be brief. We need more women pilots to deliver Class One aircraft: Single-engine planes, mainly Moths, Swordfish, Fairchilds, up and down the country, to and from factories to airbases. The planes are used by the RAF for training young pilots, God help them. At the moment, I have eight women pilots and I have authorisation to recruit more. As you already have a pilot's licence and by all accounts are quite comfortable in the air, I think you'd fit in rather nicely."

"Right." Lottie, taken aback, put her tea cup down. She'd anticipated a possible role, perhaps in administration as she knew her way around an aircraft but not, in her wildest dreams, flying, straight off. Feeling a sense of utter joy at the prospect of supporting the war effort and also incorporating her passion for planes, she sat back in her seat and for a moment was lost for words.

Pauline looked at her, evidently misreading her reaction. "I do realise it would mean you putting your studies on hold for a while but in this climate everyone has to do their bit and we are desperate to recruit. I'm confident Cambridge would put your place on hold if you decided to join us."

"Of course. I wasn't hesitating. I'd somehow thought you were going to offer me a role in administration."

Pauline grinned. "No. We have plenty of ground staff. Look, ferrying planes is not without risk. We don't carry radios or ammunition to defend ourselves. We use our skills and imagination to get ourselves out of fixes but inevitably there are times…" She trailed off for a moment. "We're all a bit oddball, frankly. Most of us haven't been allowed to join up for one reason or another due to gender or on medical grounds but it's a tight family and we get the job done, to the highest standards!" She looked at Lottie. "So, what do you say?"

"Yes!" Lottie replied, wide-eyed. "Absolutely."

"Marvellous! Welcome on board, Lottie. You'll have to do a practical assessment but that's a formality." Pauline Gower got to her feet. "I'll get Kitty Farrer to show you round the base and introduce you to a few people. You'll be based at Hatfield. The Adjutant will sort out local lodging and while there is a grant for your uniform, unlike the forces, you will have to buy it yourself and claim it back. Most people go to Moss Brothers in London. They have all the details they need about design. You'll also need to pass your medical but as you already fly, I doubt there will be problem. Dr Barbour will check you out. I assume you could join quickly and start your training?"

"Yes, I just need to tie up a few things and speak to my college."

"If you give Kitty the details, I'm happy to write to the Vice Chancellor, although there won't be a problem. They've finally accepted the idea that students, however bright, are being conscripted."

"Thank you."

Gower showed her to the door. "One more thing," she said, briskly. "You'll get paid. It's not as much as the men but I'm battling to get that changed as it's nonsensical."

"Fortunately, that's not an issue. My family will be happy to continue with financial support, I'm sure."

"We're lucky the majority of our female pilots come from privileged backgrounds, else the Government would have to stump up a bit more," said Gower. "Enjoy your tour and I'll be in touch about a start date. Any questions, my door is always open. Good to have you on board."

CHAPTER 16

Tuesday 13th August 1940, Suffolk

On this day, the Luftwaffe launched a major raid of 190 aircraft which was driven back over the Channel.

Three weeks later, the village of Woodbridge was even quieter than usual, except for the continual rumble of aircraft flying back and forth and the occasional explosions from the direction of the coast as the RAF engaged with the Luftwaffe in defence of the local airbases. Lottie was tending the vegetables in the garden, with a few other village women. There were tons of tomatoes that would need to be made into chutney and plums to be harvested, stewed and stored in glass jars for the winter. Potatoes, too, needed digging up and putting into sacks and the cucumbers had just ripened. It was hard work to keep the village fed, but she loved the physicality of it and she hadn't appreciated how hard the gardeners worked all year round. Heavens only knew how her mother would cope when she left in two weeks' time to join the ATA for training. She'd managed to speak to the local Auxiliary Territorial Service woman who'd promised more help from local land girls but even so, it would be a challenge to keep on top of the gardens. Growing food required experience and they were all learning by costly mistakes. All the lettuces had been decimated by slugs and lots of the carrots had scab. Pushing the scarf back on her head, she re-tied it, noticing her tanned arms had become muscular with working in the gardens all day. How life had changed, in almost the time it took to draw breath. The job she was about to take on was dangerous but despite that, she couldn't wait. Death in itself didn't frighten her but if she thought long and hard about missing out on life, she felt a deep sense of resentment that fuelled her determination to go and help put an end to this awful war. She jumped at the sound of an explosion that seemed closer than usual and the sirens started to wail, startling a flock of crows that rose into the air making a maddening sound.

"Come on, Edith, leave that," Lottie called out to a woman who was digging at the other side of the garden to join her. There were six aircraft overhead. Leaning on her hoe, she shielded her eyes from the sun and scanned the sky.

"It's okay, they're ours!" shouted Margaret, who emerged from the shed with a sack of potatoes over her shoulder.

"We need to go into the cellar. I'm just going to check that Cook and my mother are on their way out. You know how they dawdle!" said Lottie, sprinting into the kitchen, to find them calmly putting some warm cakes in a tin, to take down to the shelter with them.

"I thought it might be nice to have a bit of Mary's marvellous fruit cake. We could be down there a while," said Lady Beauchamp.

A roar of an engine above the house sounded as though it was about to take the roof off, making them all duck and the copper pans hanging in the kitchen dance as though they'd taken on a life of their own.

"Lord, that's low! Come on, Mother. Really, we need to go now!"

Grabbing the tin and signalling for Mary to take a bottle of elderflower cordial, she followed her daughter to the cellar. "What on earth would they waste their beastly bombs on us for?" she grumbled as the three of them stumbled down the steps. "Honestly, they're reducing us to scrabbling around in the cellar like frightened mice."

"Better a live mouse than a dead one," said Lottie, inhaling as Mary took the lid off the tin and the smell of warm cake quickly filled the space. "I have to say that smells heavenly, Mary."

"Never going to be the same if the hens stop laying and we have to resort to powdered eggs, Miss Lottie," she replied as they all helped themselves to a slice, trying to ignore their dirty hands.

Lottie felt a wave of affection for the cook who had been with the family for over fifteen years. Following the death of her only daughter to scarlet fever, she had taken Lottie under her ample wing, listening earnestly to her incessant childhood chatter, bathed her grazed knees and covered up endless misdemeanours.

"Ooh that's lovely!" exclaimed Edith, taking a bite with the few teeth she had left. "If this war's done one thing, it's made us grateful for every mouthful of food."

"Eat while you can," said Margaret, darkly, through her thick Suffolk accent. "I heard Hitler was bombing all our supply ships to starve us to death."

"Well, he won't succeed!" said Lottie defiantly. "While we can dig and have a supply of seeds, we can survive." She looked up the steps towards the door. "I hope the horses are all right."

"They should be fine," said Lady Beauchamp. "They're used to it by now. I'll go and check on them as soon as we're allowed out." She picked up what she called her shelter knitting that had yet to see the light of day and began a new row by the light of the paraffin lamp.

Lottie looked across and smiled. She had no idea what it was her mother was knitting and she wasn't entirely sure her mother did, either, but any period of inactivity had to be filled, even in the half light.

*

Letting her mind drift away from the chatter of local gossip, Lottie sat in the shadows, on a sack, surrounded by the earthy smell of cabbages and onions. Her thoughts turned, as they frequently did, back to Gareth. According to his letters, nothing much had really changed for him except many of his students had been conscripted. English wasn't considered an important enough subject to keep them out of the fray so one by one, they'd disappeared as though they'd never really existed. Gareth's asthma made him unfit to fight so he remained in Cambridge for the summer, writing his novel on Keats, daily letters to her and getting involved in helping out with the war effort where he could. He admitted to feeling 'pretty damn useless' at times and outwardly 'a fraud' but his failed medical was hardly his fault and she tried to convince him of that. He said in his last letter that his wife Sybil was due back from America in a week or two and he'd finally be able to meet her to discuss the terms of a divorce. Before Lottie had left Cambridge, at a weekend together at The Lindens, he'd asked her if she'd marry him, when everything was settled and she'd agreed but she wondered, what it meant exactly? They'd both been upset when she'd broken the news to him that she was going away. But when she'd told him, although the colour had drained from his face, he'd been generous and kind and told her how proud he was of her. It occurred to her, it was possible he'd just panicked and that the proposal might have seemed like a good idea to keep them together. Of course, she couldn't think of anyone she'd rather be married to than Gareth and to be honest, she'd just assumed, perhaps naively, they'd always be together. So she'd accepted the eternity ring he'd given her as a token of their betrothal, with genuine enthusiasm and they'd made plans about their future together. However, once he'd put the thought of matrimony in her head she began, feeling suddenly very grown up, to mull it all over. There were so many uncertainties that couldn't just be ignored and the notion of a wedding with a church, venue and guests, felt quite unreal. In any case, apart from the divorce, as Gareth wasn't in a position to ask The Brig's permission, they couldn't announce anything which was a bit frustrating. The way things were going with the war, it seemed highly unlikely to Lottie that she'd return within weeks or even months to take up her studies again, let alone start married life with Gareth. When she thought of him, she missed him dreadfully but there were so many distractions that she barely seemed to have a minute to herself and when she did, with all that was going on in the world, the longings felt a bit indulgent. The "All Clear" sounded and they trailed upstairs once more, blinking like burrow animals in the sunlight.

PART 2

CHAPTER 17

2nd September 1940, Hatfield, Hertfordshire

On this day, Britain obtains 50 destroyers from the US, in exchange for land grants for US naval and air bases in the Bahamas, Antigua, St Lucia, Trinidad, Jamaica and British Guiana.

The Air Transport Auxiliary Adjutant had managed to find Lottie accommodation in a house at Coopers Green, near to Hatfield Aerodrome. It was comfortable enough, if a little small. Her landlady, Mrs Jennings, was a tall woman in her early forties whose husband had been called up to join the Army. Another young woman, also in the ATA, Emily Stanton-Thomas, was in the room next to hers. Mrs Jennings said she was a "sensible sort from a nice, middle-class family." Standing in the hallway with her bags, Lottie felt Mrs Jennings would have liked to have stayed chatting for a lot longer but she had to change into her pristine uniform and get to the airbase for her flight assessment. She made her excuses and was reluctantly shown to her room. It had a little oak wardrobe and a dressing table with three-way mirror. On the top of the bed was a yellow satin eiderdown and the window overlooked fields. There was a small chest of drawers in the corner, on which Mrs Jennings had put a vase of late summer, dusky pink roses. Taking out her uniform, and laying it on the single bed, Lottie slipped out of her dress and hung it in the wardrobe. It hardly seemed possible that she was about to enter a new world and join in the defence of her country. Once dressed, she stared at herself in the mirror and already saw a more mature reflection. Tightening the jacket belt she brushed her shoulders, positioned her cap and stood back. One hundred butterflies beat their wings in her stomach and taking a deep breath and exhaling slowly to calm them, she left the house and made her way across to the airfield, where the sound of aircraft landing and taking off made her slightly breathless with excitement.

Making her way to meet the flight instructor, Margaret Cunnison, uniformed men and women nodded to her and she felt immediately at home in this rather eclectic club.

"So you're the newbie?" The voice came from behind her.

Lottie turned and saw a woman in a Sidcot suit and leather flying cap in hand, hair billowing in the breeze.

"Margie Fairweather," she said, with a grin. "I hear you're studying at my alma mater. Well, it was until I dropped out. Way too dreary for me, I'm afraid."

"Lottie Beauchamp," said Lottie. "You were at Cambridge?"

"Briefly but it felt far longer!" Margie laughed.

Lottie noticed she was older than her and immediately she liked her. She recognised her as the daughter of politicians Viscount Runciman and his wife. Margie was the first of the eight women who had joined the ATA in January 1940. Lottie was glad she'd asked around and done her homework.

"Look, I'm parched. I'm going to sign the log, grab some tea and get out of this suit but we're having drinks later in the mess. Why don't you join us?"

"Thank you," said Lottie. "I'd like that."

"Not sure who's around today as I've just got back from Prestwick but I spotted Lettice Curtis a few minutes ago. I assume Margaret will be assessing you?"

"Yes. I'm off to meet her now."

"Good, you'll be fine, keep calm, there's nothing to it really, just the basics. Don't mind Lettice by the way, she can be a bit 'off' until you get to know her!" She pulled a face. "Honestly, she's one of our best and generally we don't bite." With a smile and a wave, she strode off and was gone.

*

That afternoon, Margaret Cunnison, Scottish and very straightforward, put Lottie through her paces in a Tiger Moth, communicating instructions via a speaker tube in the rear seat. Lottie took the Moth to a height of two thousand feet, feeling the pure joy of cold, damp air against her face, the familiar noise of the engine and propeller whirring in front of her as she flew over the golden patchwork of fields below. As instructed, she turned gently left, then right, banked steeply before Cunnison cut the engine and she was forced to make an emergency landing on the grass of runway two. It had been a textbook flight and she'd loved every moment of it.

"Don't get your hopes up to fly anything other than training aircraft," Cunnison said, unstrapping and hauling herself from the cockpit behind her. "Women aren't deemed capable of flying anything more meaty. Just remember you never fly blind or indulge in aerobatics and most of the time you'll be flying in a gaggle. That's harder than you think, as you have to keep an eye on everyone else as well as watching the ground. If the weather closes in, make for the nearest airfield. We don't take risks, our reputation depends on it. If we damage a plane, it's negligence, if a male pilot does it, it's unfortunate." She jumped to the ground with a thud. "Oh, by the way, we don't have enough maps to go round, so we have to improvise. Tomorrow, you can go solo. Well done. Now go and get yourself some tea. "

So that was it, thought Lottie. *I've passed.* It had been almost ridiculously easy. The hardest thing had been resisting the urge to demonstrate her skills by looping and spinning. She remained for a moment in the cockpit and watched Cunnison disappear into the low building, before removing her cap and clambering out of the cockpit.

"How did you do?" said a voice from behind her.

"Fine, I think. Well, I managed to pass." Lottie turned and saw a slim, fit-looking woman.

"Good. I'm Marion Wilberforce."

"Lottie Beauchamp."

"A Suffolk Beauchamp?"

"Yes. Nice to meet you." Marion, Lottie had found out through her flying contacts, was the mountaineer daughter of the Laird of Boyndlie.

"I doubt you'll remember but we have met briefly before at an agricultural do. I did some charity work with your father. You were probably around ten at the time and running around climbing trees with your brothers."

Lottie laughed. "Really?"

"Yes, you challenged me to a race."

"I did?" Lottie frowned, trying to remember.

"Yes and naturally, you won!"

"I'm sure you were kind enough to let me." Lottie laughed.

"Of course." Marion smiled. "Anyhow, must dash, I'm off to pick up a Tiger from Cowley to drop her at Sywell. Good to see you again, Lottie."

Peeling off her Sidcot suit in the changing room that smelled of leather boots and drying clothes, Lottie couldn't have been happier. For today at least, the threat of invasion and its implications took a back seat. Finally, she was about to make a small contribution to the fight for continued freedom and it felt very good.

CHAPTER 18

3rd September 1940, Hatfield, Hertfordshire

On this day Hitler postpones the invasion of Britain, as the Luftwaffe fails to break British defences. Nonetheless, fears of the forthcoming invasion continue to haunt Britain.

Sitting on the concrete terrace outside the mess, Lottie spotted Amy Johnson in her flying suit, sitting alone with a cup of tea, eyes closed, her face pointing up towards the early evening sun. Not wanting to disturb her, she tried to tiptoe past but the eyes opened suddenly and looked directly at her. Amy frowned slightly as though trying to place Lottie.

"I'm so sorry, I didn't mean to wake you," said Lottie, feeling a little queasy at coming face to face with her flying heroine.

"It's all right, I was just resting my eyes." She spoke with a soft, Yorkshire accent.

"I'm Lottie Beauchamp. I joined yesterday." Lottie said, quickly.

"Right. Pleased to meet you. I'm Amy Johnson." She smiled, disarmingly.

Lottie thought she looked younger than her mid-thirties and she was of surprisingly slight build. Somehow, she'd imagined her to be very tall but she wasn't.

"I was just on my way to get changed for dinner." It wasn't often Lottie was lost for words and she found herself wanting to escape.

Amy closed her eyes again, "Yes best get your skates on, it's Woolton Pie tonight if you're eating in and it has to be tasted to be believed!"

"Is it good?"

Amy let out a laugh. "Awful but you'll get used to it! It's served at seven in the dining room. A gin and tonic before should line your stomach, though."

Lottie smiled. "Thank you. Sound advice. Good to meet you." She felt unusually shy, so she took her leave and continued walking.

*

At 6:45, Lottie wandered into the dining room. It was furnished with two long tables that sat around twelve people with chairs that didn't quite match. A small number of uniformed men and women sat in armchairs or stood by the small bar area. To the left there was a rather battered piano. When she entered the men became momentarily distracted from their conversations. One had his sleeve pinned to his jacket and a little shocked, she realised he'd only got one arm. Cunnison was talking to Amy Johnson and another woman whom she hadn't met, under a growing blanket of tobacco and pipe smoke. They invited her over and the young girl behind the bar came out and asked her what she wanted to drink. She ordered a gin and tonic and sat down, taking everything in. Cunnison introduced her to Rosemary Rees. She had short, dark, curly hair and a pleasant face. The group were laughing about an interminable overnight train journey back from Prestwick, where a drunk soldier on his way home on leave, had kept them awake by singing and dancing in the corridor of the train until someone did everyone a favour and pushed him out with his kit bag, at Leeds Station.

*

A little later they were joined by Lettice Curtis and Margie Fairweather and Connie Leathart. Lettice, simply nodded vaguely in Lottie's direction when introduced and ordered an orange juice. Margie was, as anticipated, good company. Connie, introduced as "Con" was dressed like a man. She had short, cropped hair and ordered a double whisky. Lighting a cigar, she told Lottie that she'd only recently joined the ATA, too but it was an excellent excuse to leave Tyneside and do her bit. Between the men and women there was a good sense of camaraderie and lots of banter and it wasn't long before a young gentleman with a pipe came over and introduced himself to Lottie.

"I'm Giles Mortimer," he said, smiling and holding out his hand.

"Lottie," she said, shaking it.

"When did you join this load of reprobates?" He nodded his head towards the women who all groaned.

Lottie took a sip of her gin. "Yesterday. I did my first test flight today."

"And how did you do?" He smiled, speaking through pipe-clenched teeth.

"Very well!" said Cunnison. "She's going to give you boys a run for your money, so watch out!"

"I will indeed! Where's Pauline?" He looked around. "I thought she was here today?"

"At Waltham. She had a meeting with Pop." Margie took a large sip of her gin.

"Pop?" Lottie looked taken aback.

"Gerard d'Erlanger – ATA Commander. He's Pauline's boss. Pop's his nickname. You'll get introduced."

"He's fine. Just don't let him catch you wearing slacks when you're off duty." Giles winked.

"And that's a rule we all ignore!" said Lettice, vociferously. "We need to be practical. It's not a fashion show or a beauty parade. I really don't know what all the fuss is about, surely there are bigger things to worry the great and the good, other than a pair of slacks?"

Con nodded in agreement.

"Speaking of important things," said Amy. "Did anyone catch the six o'clock news?"

They all shook their heads.

"We know it won't be good and sometimes it's better not to tune in. Have we got a weather forecast for tomorrow?" said the man with one arm.

"Dry and clear, I think, Ronnie. A bit of low cloud in the North-East and light rain in Scotland with a light westerly," said Cunnison.

"Better have an early night, then. Looks like we'll all be in the air." Margie finished her drink and put her glass down. "Shall we go into dinner and get it over with? I want to get back for the Home Service at nine."

"Might as well!" said Amy, getting to her feet. "I need to go and give Jim a call and pen a letter to my sister."

"Where's Winnie?" Lettice said over her shoulder.

"She and Phil and Emily are overnight at Tilstock in the Crate. Lois is in her room with a headache and Audrey should be on her way back from Prestwick." Cunnison looked at her watch.

"Well, at least two of them have escaped having to endure the train," said Rosemary.

"Just think, you've got all this to look forward to, Lottie." Margie grinned. "It will make those draughty corridors of Cambridge feel like utter luxury."

"It's fine if you can sleep on a sixpence," said Giles.

"I think railway luggage racks are underrated!" Lettice chose a chair and sat down. "Things could be worse. We could all be in the world war one trenches."

Cunnison sat next to her and Margie took the place next to Lottie. "Admin does try to book us berths on the trains but sometimes they're full of soldiers going on leave and they get there first and refuse to move, ticket or no ticket. If you don't manage to get a berth, which mostly, you won't, you'll find the second major use for your parachute will be to sit on."

"Should we get Ethel to take Lois some dinner?" said Rosemary.

"No, I've checked. She just wants to sleep. In any case the food would probably finish her off. Giles, that pipe smoke is just too much at the table," said Amy to the pilot who took a seat next to her. "Honestly, it's like eating next to a bonfire."

"Sorry. Of course, I'll put it out." He smiled agreeably and pushed his chair back.

"Thank you. Lottie, I hope you can hack us all!" Amy said, turning to Lottie. "We really are like a big, eccentric family."

"I'm sure I'll fit in very well," she said, smiling.

CHAPTER 19

6th September 1940, Hatfield, Hertfordshire

On this day, the Luftwaffe bombs Grantham, HQ of No. 5 Group RAF. Fighter Command continues to attack Berlin. Thameshaven oil installation is hit and set ablaze. A huge formation of German planes are detected flying at high altitude and undetected by radar and the Observer Corps. It is a day of heavy dogfights and damage.

At Hatfield, in the wake of a distinct escalation in the fighting, there was an uneasy air. Lottie reported for duty at eight thirty a.m. and was given her first chit. She was to deliver a Fox Moth from the factory at Cowley to Desford, seven miles north of Hinkley. At nine, Margie arrived in the Anson to ferry her, Lois and Emily to the factory. From there, they were to fly Desford, in a gaggle, with Lettice leading, in a Fox.

*

The factory at Cowley was bustling with activity. Huge sheds held stocks of plane parts while others were filled with partly built aircraft that were being crawled over by teams of engineers. The factory could barely keep up with demand for new planes, all the while they were battling with continuous interruptions from air raids and parts shortages. On the runway, stood three brand new 'training' Fox Moths. Once delivered, young RAF recruits who might have never been higher in the air than a flight of stairs, would become pilots. Within a few weeks of taking their first flight, they would be signed off to fly in combat.

*

The Anson taxied to a halt and the women jumped out, eager to get going. A young mechanic took them straight to their planes and within fifteen minutes, they were cleared for take-off. As Lottie pulled back on the throttle, the aircraft drifted upwards, behind Lettice. It was perfect weather for flying and she realised how much she'd missed it when she was at Cambridge. Tonight, she would write to Gareth and let him know she'd made her first delivery. She wasn't sure when she'd see him next but in his last letter he said he had sufficient petrol coupons to drive up and take her for lunch as soon as she had a day off. In theory, it would be the following weekend, by which time Gareth should have news about his divorce. Somehow, she couldn't imagine Mrs Jennings allowing him to stay over, nor did it seem respectful to ask. There would be plenty of time after the war, she told herself and missing him as much as she did, could only be a good sign. Glancing at the control panel, her altimeter read two and a half thousand feet and she was cruising at seventy-five miles per hour with perfect visibility. Obediently she sat behind Lettice, like a duckling, resisting the urge to push the rudder left and swoop down towards earth, really putting the Moth through its paces. Instead, she busied herself with looking down on the newly harvested fields, punctuated with tiny villages, rivers and towns, identifying them on her torn, coffee-stained map as she passed overhead. Inhaling deeply, she began to sing Ferryboat Serenade at the top of her voice, confident it would be lost in the thermals. Below, on a lake, a large flock of ungainly geese took to the air, disturbed by the noise of the aircraft. Warily, she watched, aware it could prove fatal if they flew into their path but they did a short, low circuit of dissatisfaction and returned to the water. Lottie thought this was likely to be one of the shortest flights she would ever make and at this rate, she was confident they would all be back at Hatfield for lunch. Glancing over her shoulder, to her left, Emily gave her a wave before pulling back into line. Lottie had met her house mate the previous evening and liked her enormously. She was, as Mrs Jennings described her, sensible and bright with a good sense of humour and Lottie was sure that they would quickly become friends.

*

When she got back to her lodgings that evening, Lottie had two letters; one long awaited, from her brother Hugh and the other from her mother. The first was short and she could tell by the tone he was running on adrenaline.

RAF Hawkinge, Kent

Dear Lot,

I hope this finds you well and you're enjoying your new post. I can only imagine how thrilled you must be to be flying once again.

I'm fine. The men here are very busy and we have, in a very short space of time, become a tight group. We're flying as many days as the weather will allow and some under not so ideal conditions. It's exciting but also quite hairy at times but we all have each other's backs and we're determined to push the Luftwaffe back to where they belong. At least I'm clocking up flying hours and getting experience in different planes. I must say, the Spit is much better than the Hurricane. I hope you get the chance to fly one, you'd love it. They're beauties and you'd definitely want to be in one during a dog fight!

Have you heard from Archie? He's terrible at letter writing and I do worry about him.

I'll have to go as the siren's sounded.

By the way, I've started smoking a pipe. I think it suits me well!

Your loving brother,

Hugh

The picture the letter conjured up in her mind of Hugh smoking a pipe was comical. Lottie recalled the first time they'd tried a cigarette, in the field at the back of The Lindens. She'd been ten and he'd been nearly thirteen and he'd been sick as a dog. She, on the other hand had taken to it with flair, even inhaling and blowing the smoke out through her nose, which she felt to be the height of sophistication. Humiliated, he'd stomped off in a sulk and they'd had to lie to Archie about the whole thing as he couldn't be trusted not to tell their Mother. Feeling a pang of homesickness, she'd have given anything to see Hugh and Archie, just for a couple of hours to make sure they hadn't changed out of all recognition but she had absolutely no idea when she'd see either of them again and she felt her mood begin to dip.

Shaking the feeling off, she put the letter to one side and read the one from her Mother. It was longer than Hugh's and talked about the farm and the village and the letters she'd received from the boys. With the absence of her father, she said she was 'managing' with additional help from a couple of local young ladies, with the gardens and Land Girls driving the tractor and harvesting. One of the farmers was helping out the best he could, to teach them all about growing vegetables but it was slow progress with lots of unforeseen pitfalls. Her mother said she had no idea how complicated it was to grow a successful crop of carrots and the farmer must think her a very dull student. One of the helpers, the local doctor's daughter who she thought Lottie might remember as a young teenager, played bridge and they were spending a couple of evenings a week together, for company, which was very nice for her mother. The Brig also sent his love and Mary, the cook, would be sending her some biscuits as soon as she could. Her mother said, Mabel the family's beloved border collie, was missing her greatly. Her behaviour had become very strange since Lottie had left and she'd taken to forlornly sleeping on her bed on an old cardigan she'd helped herself to from the bottom of Lottie's chest of drawers. On a brighter note, she hoped Gareth was well and asked Lottie to remember her to him and to tell him she'd thoroughly enjoyed the books he gave her when he'd visited. After three pages, it concluded with, 'Take care my darling and write soon. With love, Mother.'

*

After dinner, she listened to the World Service with Emily and Mrs Jennings in the comfortable sitting room, before turning in, to write to Gareth.

CHAPTER 20

September 7th 1940, Hatfield

On this day, The Blitz commences. The Luftwaffe begins conducting raids on London and major cities, in response to British bombing of Berlin.

At nine a.m., Lottie and Emily picked up their flying chits and waited in the mess for the Anson to arrive and taxi them to Cowley, Oxford, where they would meet two other ATA pilots, Winifred Crossley and Mona Friedlander, fly to Kemble, Cirencester, and pick up more planes to ferry across to Sywell in Northamptonshire. There, they would stay overnight at a hotel before travelling north to Shropshire to drop off Moths at Tern Hill, pick up at Desford and fly back to Hatfield.

*

Emily lit a cigarette and stood watching a Hurricane land. The pilot, a man with an artificial leg, hauled himself out of the cockpit and was helped to the ground by two engineers. She turned and looked at Lottie. "Jack's back."

Lottie who was reading a paper glanced up. "Jack?"

"I suppose you haven't met him yet? Our one-legged pilot."

"No, I don't think so. I don't recall being introduced to him. I'm sure I'd remember."

"He's jolly nice," said Emily. "Very brave."

"Do you know how he lost his leg?" said Lottie, pushing the paper to one side.

"Fell off a motorbike, I believe. They had to amputate to save his life."

"Rotten luck. How did he end up flying?"

"He already had his licence and he said that in the air, he only needed one leg and in any case, it was less weight to carry and therefore more fuel efficient!"

"Goodness!" said Lottie, joining her at the window.

"He's a bit of a joker."

"Quite attractive, by the looks of it?"

Emily blushed. "I suppose."

Lottie grinned. "Are you a little bit smitten, Emily?"

"Heavens, no! He has a girlfriend. She's very rich and has a title."

"Well you're very pretty and funny and that's priceless!"

Emily's face reddened further. "You know that's not true, Lottie, and I'm not in Jack's league."

"Rubbish," said Lottie, getting to her feet. "I think that's our taxi!"

They watched the Anson land and come to a stop on runway two. Amy Johnson jumped out and gave the pilot a wave before heading towards the office.

"Don't you think it's quite bizarre to be working with her?" said Lottie. "I mean, she's so famous."

"From what I hear, I don't think she likes much attention. She spends most of her spare time here with Ann Welch. They just seem to get on with the job. Her ex-husband Jim's a ferry pilot too, which is why she flies in and out of White Waltham. He's stationed there. I gather they're still great friends. Margie Fairweather's husband Douglas is billeted there too, so they're in married quarters." Emily picked up her small bag and her maps and zipped up her suit. "He's quite a live wire by all accounts." She stopped and took a deep breath. "Come on, best get going."

Lottie followed her out of the door.

"You're such a mine of interesting gossip, Emily."

"I don't know why but people feel the need to fill me in with lots of useless information. I wouldn't mind but half the time, I don't even ask!"

"Perhaps you should be a spy," Lottie said.

"Do you think?" said Emily with a grin. "I'm honestly not that interested in detail. I'd probably forget half of what I'd been told."

"Well, I think you'd be good."

*

By eleven, they were walking across the grass, with Lettice Curtis eagerly striding ahead, to their first job of the day. The plane engines sputtered like newborns into life and within ten minutes Lettice had taxied down the grass strip and was airborne. Lottie followed Emily.

*

Visibility was again good but there was the likelihood of some high cloud further north. This morning, the plane bounced around a bit on the air pockets but on the whole, it handled well. The altimeter read nearly three thousand feet and she was cruising at ninety miles per hour. Glancing at her map, Lottie looked for the A43 road and saw it snaking through the countryside, below. She'd always found map reading easy and was good at spotting landmarks. Ahead of her, the line of the horizon looked very clear and blue. Her favourite time for taking a flight was early morning, just after sunrise, when the horizon was ablaze with golden and red light. She longed to take Gareth up in The Bee and show him how beautiful the sky could be. Perhaps they would honeymoon in Africa and fly across the slopes of Kilimanjaro, just like Karen Blixen, and watch the animals at sunrise. Gareth was travelling down to meet Sybil the next day, and Lottie hoped it would go well but there was always a chance, that when he asked, Sybil wouldn't agree to a divorce. He seemed so sure it would be fine but when push came to shove, Gareth was an optimist and Sybil might have a wholly different view. Suppose, thought Lottie, she told him she wanted them to try to save the marriage? Even at Lottie's young age, she knew people didn't always react in the way one expected or wanted. She felt a little sick at the thought, acknowledging it would be good when the meeting was over and one way or another she'd know.

Ahead, Lettice reduced altitude by a couple of hundred feet. Lottie followed suit, seeing a bank of low cloud in the distance and feeling the temperature drop as the sun slid behind it. Finding the motion of the plane soothing and her ability to control it comforting, she sat back in her seat and tried to put the meeting between Sybil and Gareth out of her mind and enjoy the flight.

*

That evening, the four had dinner together at their bed and breakfast near Sywell and listened to the nine o'clock news on the wireless. It was announced that several hundred German bombers and fighters had targeted the city of London, causing many casualties, and fire crews were struggling to put out hundreds of fires. The women sat in silence, wide-eyed with shock, unable to come to terms immediately with the announcement. When it was finished, Lettice got to her feet and turned the wireless off. "I think," she said, "we should all go to bed and try and get some sleep. It won't do anyone any good to dwell. We still have a job to do, and now it's more important than ever to get these planes delivered." With that, she turned on her heel and left the room. In silence, Lottie and Emily wracked their brains to think about who they might have known that could have been in London.

"Anyone there you know of?" said Lottie, getting to her feet.

Emily shook her head. "Not that I can think of. A neighbour perhaps? What about you?"

"My father's in Whitehall but they'd have said it on the news if that had been hit. The only other person I can think of is a friend's wife. She's staying at the Savoy." Lottie hadn't yet told Emily about Gareth.

"They'd have said if the West End had been hit; they definitely said the City."

"I guess they're targeting the docks."

"I would think so. Lettice is right. Come on, bed."

CHAPTER 21

8th September 1940, Hatfield, Hertfordshire

By midnight on the 7th September 1940, German planes had dropped 337 tons of bombs on London. The East End suffers direct hits and fires break out and spread throughout the area. 448 civilians are killed.

Lottie awoke from a restless night's sleep to the sound of aircraft rumbling overhead. She waited, trying to identify the engine and for the siren to sound but it didn't and the noise of the planes drifted off. Hurricanes, she decided, relieved not to have to decamp to the shelter, concluding it was not German Junkers that had a horrifyingly distinctive wail as they swooped low, to their targets. Downstairs she could hear the familiar sound of breakfast being prepared and the blissful normality of the sound of a tinkle of spoons on crockery. The thought of hot, buttered toast with Mrs Jennings's homemade marmalade forced her to get up and she rolled over and sat on the side of the bed, stretching, yawning and rubbing her gritty eyes. For most of the night she'd been disturbed by nightmares of London ablaze and her family being pulled from wreckage. In between, she'd woken, bathed in sweat and fretful, longing for daybreak. Immediately on waking she thought about Gareth who was due to travel to the West End that day. Unsettled by her dream and the news, she had an urge to try to call him and ask him not to go but there was no telephone in the house and she couldn't call the university and leave a message. She could just imagine the look on the secretary's face as she took down the words, 'Gareth, Darling, please don't go into London to ask your wife for a divorce today; I've got a bad feeling about it – Love Lottie.' Surely, she decided, if he was at all worried, he would do the sensible thing, stay in Cambridge and just write to Sybil. Although she didn't know the woman personally, she didn't wish her any harm and deep down, she hoped she was safe. She understood Gareth wanted to talk to her face to face but it might not be possible.

A little reassured, she got to her feet and put on her dressing gown to go to the bathroom. She was worried about Hugh and Archie too. Everything was escalating into a bloody massacre on the whim of one madman. Surely ordinary Germans must be waking up, feeling apprehensive and frightened, too. It was quite shocking how men, women and children were so easily sucked into this vacuum of xenophobia. Hatred bred hatred in a powerful upward spiral that spread like a plague and made it easy to forget what everyone was fighting for. Yet, the tribal instinct to defend one's culture, land and loved ones cut deep and was unlikely to change any time soon and Nazi rule was unthinkable. Lottie, too, would fight to prevent it while she had breath in her body.

Washing herself at the sink with her flannel and favourite soap that smelled of rose petal and lavender, made her feel a little more upbeat. Distracted from her conflicted thoughts, dabbing herself dry with the rather thin towel, she momentarily forgot what day it was, before realising it was Sunday. There were no church bells anymore and from once being a joyful sound, with the advent of war, they had become something to dread. Days of the week had become meaningless as one day simply merged into another, punctuated only by night and day. The luxury of having a relaxed day off, going to church followed by a walk to a pub or a picnic on the banks of the Cam felt like another era which, to all intent and purpose, it was. Never, she thought, would she take those things for granted, should such simple pleasures ever return.

*

Putting on her uniform and making her way down to breakfast, Lottie met Emily on the stairs who had had a sleepless night too, mainly because of an owl outside her window. They ate breakfast while Mrs Jennings told them that she'd seen the grocer that morning and he'd told her London had taken a heavy hit overnight. This did nothing to ease Lottie's anxiety but she was somewhat reassured Gareth probably wouldn't be able to get into London, although she was sure he would be worried about Sybil. In a sombre mood, discussing the implications of the raid, they walked into work.

*

Later that morning, Lottie flew from Hatfield to Sywell, dropping off a Moth at Cowley before doing the same run again. She finally arrived back at the airfield just after six p.m., desperate for confirmation that Gareth hadn't gone to London. She'd missed the news and had no idea how London was faring after the bombing the day before. She asked one of the engineers at the Cowley factory who said he'd heard a large number of enemy attacks had been directed against the docks and other industrial targets and it was too early to know the level of casualties. It was anticipated, however, to be high. He had no idea whether the bombing had started up again but he said, cheerfully, he "reckoned it was the beginning of several raids". Since it was a nice evening and wanting to stretch her legs before going back to her digs to turn on the wireless, Lottie took tea on the terrace outside the mess with Joan Hughes, a tiny young pilot who'd had her first flying lesson at age fifteen and got her licence at seventeen. She introduced Lottie to Rosemary Rees, who Emily had told her was an ex-ballet dancer with a reputation for flying all over Europe before the war to attend aero club parties. Lottie liked her sharp wit immediately and they were soon chatting away and laughing as though they'd known each other for years. During the conversation, she mentioned 'Gordon' a couple of times and when she went in to get more tea, Joan told her he was Gordon Selfridge, heir to the Selfridges department store, who it turned out, Lottie recalled she'd met once in Claridge's, when The Brig had taken her and her mother there for dinner.

*

At seven, Lottie went home. Emily was in her room and Mrs Jennings was busy preparing curried mutton for dinner. Lottie didn't feel very hungry and the smell of the curry made her a little nauseous. She mounted the stairs and sat down at her little dressing table in the golden evening light, to write a quick letter to Phyllis who had joined the Land Army and was billeted with an awful family in Lincolnshire. In her last letter she said the accommodation was a hovel and the farmer had worse table manners than his pigs. The upshot was, she would return to Cambridge and consider other options. After half an hour, she knocked on Emily's door and they both went down to dinner. Lottie sat pensively pushing the food around her plate which sent Mrs Jennings into a spin about it not being edible. Lottie then had to spend at least ten minutes reassuring her it was lovely and that she was just tired, that was all. When she went back to the kitchen, appearing at least somewhat pacified that the food was palatable, Emily put her hand reassuringly on Lottie's arm. "Gareth will be fine. The chances are the police wouldn't have let him into London anyway."

"I do hope so," said Lottie, fingering the eternity ring on the chain round her neck. She'd told Emily briefly about their affair over breakfast as she was so worried.

"He'll be in touch in the next day or so, I'm sure, and all will be well."

"Of course it will. I'm just being silly."

"No, you're not, it's natural to worry. Try and eat your dinner else you'll be starving by morning and we've got stewed apple for dessert so you'll need to coat your stomach in preparation for the onslaught of sour goo."

Lottie stared down at her grey plate of food before slowly taking a mouthful of fatty mutton and lumps of potato, going cross-eyed as she tried to swallow it, which made Emily giggle.

"Give me your napkin."

Emily looked at her. "Really?"

"Yes, I don't want to upset Mrs Jennings further."

She handed it over and glanced behind Lottie to the doorway and nodded. Quickly, Lottie put some of the mutton from her plate onto both their napkins and wrapped them up.

Emily watched in amusement. "As it's such a nice evening, we could take a stroll down to the Stone House after dinner and treat ourselves to a gin and still be back in time for the news at nine. It might take your mind off things."

"That sounds like an excellent idea!" Lottie immediately felt a little brighter. She could certainly do with something to take the edge off her anxiety.

"Ruth Lambton and Ursula Preston are bound to be in the bar, so I can introduce you."

Lottie got to her feet. "Let's go before the apples arrive. I honestly don't think I can manage one tonight."

"Quick then!" Emily grabbed her handbag and made a move towards the front door.

"We're just popping out for a bit, Mrs Jennings," called Lottie, at the door to the kitchen. "Thank you so much for dinner."

Mrs Jennings was outside the back door enjoying a cigarette but before she could attempt to inflict her stewed apple on them, the women had gone and were halfway down the street.

CHAPTER 22

10th September 1940, Hatfield, Hertfordshire

On this day, the Luftwaffe drops five bombs on Buckingham Palace. Four staff are injured.

W hen Lottie arrived back, tired, from a flight to York, she found a letter from Gareth waiting for her. Breathless and cutting Mrs Jennings short on the stairs, she ran up to her room and sat on the edge of the bed, heart thumping. Ripping the envelope open, she scanned the contents, the possibilities of several outcomes of his visit to London tumbling over themselves in her head. She caught sight of the date and to her disappointment, she noticed it was 5th September, which meant she did not yet know whether he'd made it to London or even spoken with Sybil.

5th September 1940

Cambridge

My Darling Lottie,

I'm missing you more than I can say. Cambridge feels very empty without you and I long to hold you and inhale the perfume of your skin.

On Saturday afternoon, I'm going to London to visit my brother, Arthur, at his factory before meeting Sybil for dinner at the Savoy. As you know, I haven't seen her for nearly a year and it will be good to draw a line under our marriage. I've already said but want to reiterate, we were young and had no idea of what real love or wedlock really entailed. Divorce will free us both and allow us to move on, legitimately. I do NOT want to scurry around in darkness with you, avoiding the mealy mouthed gossips, for a moment longer than is necessary. I imagine Sybil will be keen to put an end to things too, as an acquaintance from New York recently intimated about a liaison between my estranged wife and a shipping tycoon. As soon as the paperwork is signed, I hope to somehow meet with your father and ask for his blessing. After that, and provided of course that he approves, we will be able to marry. I cannot wait and I hope you feel the same? Once this dreadful war is over, we can begin to live out the life we have talked about, together. For the first time in years, I feel optimistic, despite the awful things that are happening in the world.

This afternoon, I have to prepare a lecture on Lord Alfred Tennyson. He's not my favourite poet but somehow I shall summon up the enthusiasm to recite verses of 'Charge of the Light Brigade' very loudly, to the remaining handful of my bored students. If nothing else it might keep them awake when they arrive back for the new term. I must say there are so few now that haven't been called up that it feels barely worth continuing with the course. I suppose those who graduate can go on to teach and replace those who've gone to war.

I've saved enough petrol coupons to drive down to see you, when you have some time off and I can escape from work. I understand, my love, you've just joined and are working all hours but I hope you are getting sufficient rest so as not to put yourself at risk when flying? Let me know when I can come to see you.

How wonderful that you just 'bumped into' Amy Johnson!

Must go now, my Darling. I will write on Saturday night when I get back from London. Please don't worry. This is simply an exercise in tidying the loose ends of a past life, before we can move on together. I'll let you know how things have gone as soon as I return.

With all my love

G x

Lottie skimmed through the remainder of the letter with a mounting sense of unease at the news that he'd been in London on the seventh. Perhaps she should, after all, place a call to the university and just ask to speak to Gareth and say she was a concerned relative. That way, she might at least find out if he was there. But looking at her watch she realised it was too late in the day and all the secretaries would have gone home. Hugging her knees to her, she put her head on them, thinking hard. It was now three days since the bombing started in London and she still had no idea whether he was safe or even where Arthur's factory was located but she *did* know that the most industrialised area in East London was round by the docks. She wished now that she'd asked more questions about his family and it dawned on her that there was so much she didn't yet know about Gareth. A sudden thought occurred that perhaps she could borrow a car and drive to Cambridge and back that same evening but realistically, she had no petrol coupons and people were unlikely to give any up, since fuel was so precious. In any case, she could hardly expect someone she hardly knew to loan her a car without telling them why. The only person she'd talked to about Gareth, was Ellen, and she didn't own a car. It was odd that he hadn't sent a telegram with news, following his meeting with Sybil if they'd managed to meet, but perhaps he'd been unable to get back to Cambridge and was staying with his brother. Maybe he couldn't get to a post office because of the bombings or was unable to travel home because of damage to train lines out of the city. So many possibilities as to why she'd heard nothing washed around her brain like a stormy sea that refused to calm. Finally, she resolved that she had no alternative but to be patient and wait for him to make contact like the thousands of others who would be waiting for news about friends and loved ones. Getting to her feet, she pulled a jumper on and slipped out into the garden to have a cigarette.

CHAPTER 23

12ᵗʰ September 1940, Prestwick, Scotland

On this day, a night of heavy raids continues over London. Germans claim the RAF are dropping Colorado beetles over German potato crops. Nazis confine half a million Jews in ghettos and Italian forces begin an offensive into Egypt from Libya.

Tired and desperate to get word from Gareth, Lottie boarded the crowded overnight sleeper from Prestwick to London with Lettice Curtis and Audrey Sale-Barker. Making their way down the cluttered corridor, through the Woodbine-fog, carrying gas masks and parachutes and ignoring wolf whistles from a group of sailors, they searched optimistically for a compartment with seats but there were none.

"The floor it is, then!" said Audrey, dumping her bag down. "Home from home and the office clearly hadn't managed to get us berths!"

"Bugger that," said Lettice. "I'm going to upper class!"

Lottie looked at her, puzzled.

"Luggage rack." Audrey grinned, as Lettice shoved her way determinedly down the carriage, to a chorus of, "Well excuse me, won't you?" and, "Come and sit with me, lovely."

"Unless you really *can* sleep on a sixpence, you should resign yourself to sitting on your chute, at least until Crewe, where it might thin out a bit."

Lottie dropped her bag next to Audrey's and sat down.

"How was your first flight to bonnie Scotland?" said Audrey, taking out a packet of Chesterfields and a gold lighter.

"Really good but you could feel the temperature drop once you got north of Manchester." Lottie took a cigarette and lit it. "Thanks."

"Wait till winter. By all accounts if it's as bad as last year, they'll be chipping us out of the cockpit in minus thirty and carrying us in to the bus, to thaw." She exhaled a long plume of smoke into the ceiling, where it joined everyone else's.

Lottie laughed. "I must admit, I'd hoped for a nice, warm mess building and not a disused bus."

"If nothing else, this job does wonders for managing expectations but at least we have an element of freedom." She hesitated. "For the moment at least." Audrey wriggled against her parachute, like a cushion, to get more comfortable.

"That's true. I keep wondering what a life under Hitler's rule would be like."

"It doesn't bear thinking about. One thing for sure is that it won't resemble anything like our lives before the war." Audrey yawned and put her hand up to shield her mouth. "Oh, sorry. It's so stuffy in here."

"Nothing will be the same will it? War changes everything. There will be no money to rebuild. Two world wars in twenty years…" Lottie trailed off as the singing started from further down the carriage and then Lettice's voice above them telling them to, "Do shut up!"

*

Despite being exhausted, they continued to chat for a while since the creaking and juddering motion of the train and the noise made it difficult to sleep. Above them, the dim lights cast a yellow, nicotine-stained glow and the strong smell of whisky, urine and unwashed bodies nestled into the blanket of tobacco that hung in the air. At one point, Lottie got to her feet and pulled a window down to allow in some fresh air. Outside, the calm, clear sky was filled with stars and their light cast shadows over unfamiliar, dark hills. War, thought Lottie, couldn't change that. She stood there for a while, propped against the edge of the door, lost in its beauty.

"Best shut that, love, there's a tunnel coming up and we wouldn't want you to lose that pretty 'ead, now would we?" shouted someone. There was the sound of distant laughter and coughing.

For a moment, she ignored him and continued to stare out, her hair gently billowing in the fresh wind. It had been a week since she'd heard from Gareth and each day felt slightly bleaker than the one before but she was confident there would be a letter or a telegram waiting for her on Mrs Jennings's little hall table. The sound of the train horn amplified by a rush of air made her jump and she pulled the window back up just before the train entered another sooty, black hole. Turning round, she saw that Audrey had drifted off to sleep, her pretty face with its delicate features making her look childlike. Her flying jacket had slipped down onto her knees and so Lottie went over and gently covered her. She stirred but didn't wake. Lottie found out that Audrey had been Captain of the 1936 Women's Olympic ski team but she'd grown to love flying more. She marvelled at the amazing stories all these accomplished, often very modest, women had to tell but rarely did. Who would have thought that Audrey, in her Saville Row tailored uniform with its rebellious red, satin lining would have found herself sitting on the floor of a stinking sleeper train, headed for London? War, however, was a great leveller. Sitting down again, Lottie lit another cigarette and sat, lost in thought until she felt her head begin to drop onto her chest and finally she dozed.

*

Mrs Jennings was out when Lottie arrived back at around three in the afternoon on Friday and the whole place was unusually silent. Very relieved not to have to make polite conversation, she quickly looked through her post for Gareth's handwriting but there was nothing. There was, however, one letter with a Welsh post-mark, in a hand she didn't recognise and with a rather strange feeling in the pit of her stomach, she mounted the stairs, two at a time to her room, by which time the envelope was opened and a single sheet removed. Its contents made her sink down onto the edge of her bed.

1 Crown Mews

Cardiff

10th September 1940

Dear Miss Beauchamp,

It is with great sadness that I'm writing to tell you that my brother, Gareth was killed, in London on 7ᵗʰ September while visiting my brothers factory in Silvertown. The factory took a direct hit and both my brothers lost their lives. It is thought that their deaths were instantaneous and my family will take some small comfort in this knowledge.

I believe you and Gareth shared 'an understanding' and I felt it only fair to let you know of his death. Obviously his wife Sybil is grieving and the family are doing our best to support her during this very difficult time. I trust we can count on your absolute discretion.

Yours sincerely

Gwyneth Jones (Mrs)

Lottie re-read the letter in disbelief, half expecting to find that she'd somehow misread it, but she hadn't. So that was it, within three sentences her world had been turned upside down and inside out, to the point that she didn't recognise it as her own. It felt like an out-of-body experience as though she was floating above herself, before an injection of indescribable pain made its way through her body, synapse to synapse, sapping her strength and making her fingers contract round the letter, screwing up the dreadful words in a vain attempt to make them not exist. But they did. Suddenly, she heard a sob and recognised it as her own. Falling back on the bed and curling into a tight ball, she ignored the gentle knock on the door and remained in the same position until, finally exhausted from crying, she drifted into an uneasy sleep. At seven the next morning, her alarm went off. In the few seconds between the confused state of drowsy and awake, she thought everything was normal before the awful feeling that it wasn't and the brutally dismissive words of the letter filtered back into her brain and she remembered Gareth was dead. A realisation began to percolate through her brain that in the time it took to read the letter, her private life had been obliterated while her public one would have to remain steadfastly and cruelly intact.

CHAPTER 24

13th September 1940, Hatfield, Hertfordshire

On this day, a bomb hit Buckingham Palace, destroying the Royal Chapel. In China, Japanese fighters score their first air-to-air victory.

Lottie dragged herself off her bed and staggered into the bathroom feeling wretched. Looking in the mirror, she saw she'd aged visibly, overnight. Drunk from misery, she hung her head over the sink and bathed her swollen eyes in cold water, trying to stop the tears from accumulating. It surprised her there were any left but from somewhere they kept coming. She sniffed and put the towel to her face and buried it in it, stifling a sob.

"Come on!" she whispered to herself in a voice she barely recognised. "You have to face people."

Taking a deep breath she brushed her teeth and made her way back to her room to dress. She felt as though grief had pulled a plug on her energy and left her weak and as fragile as glass. Fortunately, Emily had stayed overnight in Wales and that bought her some time as she couldn't have told her, over breakfast. Using the stair-rail for support, she made it down to the small breakfast room trying not to heave at the smell of fried tomatoes. Mrs Jennings came in with tea and stopped dead in her tracks when she saw Lottie.

"My goodness, just look at you! You look like you've had no sleep. Whatever's wrong?"

"I… think I must have eaten something yesterday." It was all she could think of. Her voice sounded thick and her throat already ached from trying to hold back tears.

"You look like you've been up all night?"

Lottie shook her head.

"Would you like some dry toast? They say that's best if you have a gippy tummy."

"Thank you." She gave her a weak smile. Under the table she dug her nails into her hand to stop herself from dissolving. Someone being nice was too much for her and food was the last thing she wanted but she knew if she was going to be allowed to get into an aircraft she had to eat and the only place she wanted to be right now was in the air, away from everyone, not having to pretend things were fine. The toast when it came was like eating large lumps of sand that stuck in her constricted throat with each mouthful. Taking it slowly and washing it down with tea, she managed a slice. By the end of it, she felt oddly disconnected from the present. Things were happening around her like a plate being cleared and her tea cup replenished but she was only half aware of it, as though her mind and body had parted company. The letter kept popping into her brain but she was too traumatised to think about it and she tried to let the words wash over her. Was this what losing a loved one really felt like? She could hear Mrs Jennings talking in the background but she couldn't concentrate. The world was moving in slow motion as though her brain had semi-shut down but hadn't notified her eyes and in revolt, they continued to well up. Lottie coughed a little to try and ease the tightness in her throat but it didn't really help. It felt as though life was being squeezed out of her. All she wanted to do was to get out of the house and be alone. With a mumbled apology, she got unsteadily to her feet and left a worried-looking Mrs Jennings staring after her, hands on hips.

*

It was raining as Lottie stepped outside but she barely noticed as she stumbled towards the airfield. Outside the office she saw Amy Johnson, who took one look at her and said, "My dear child, you look awful and you're soaked through, whatever's the matter?"

"Good morning. Nothing… really. A bad night. Eaten something. Probably. That's all!"

"Well, you don't *look* all right. Are you sure you're fit to fly?"

From somewhere, Lottie found the strength to smile and reassure her she was. "Fine now, really. I need to work."

Amy stared at her. "Well go and get dry and drink something.

Fortunately, you're down to do a couple of short runs, I believe. You take care." Clearly she was not convinced.

The last thing Lottie needed was to be grounded. "I will, thank you. Honestly!" she said, with a watery smile, before turning on her heel and making her way in to get her chit and weather briefing from Sam Swayne.

*

Fifteen minutes later, she was strapped in, doing a pre-flight check, before getting underway on her first delivery of the day to Sywell. The cold, damp air on her face as she rose up towards the clouds felt soothing. Perhaps Gareth was up there somewhere and the thought she might be a little closer to him was a tiny comfort. Was he looking down on her from a better place or was God really a construct to keep people in order and allow humans to feel better about death? Would a benevolent God really allow all this awfulness? Sadness, suddenly turned to anger. If He existed He deserved her fury for allowing this war and so, at the top of her voice she cursed her childhood God and although her words were lost to the wind and with them any faith she might have had, she felt a little better for it. Questions began to ebb and flow randomly in her brain as she sought answers. The letter said they thought Gareth had died instantly but how could they really know? The reality of being the 'other woman' had hit home like a car running full pelt into a wall. Clearly, Gareth's family didn't recognise their relationship and she had no legitimacy in his life and therefore her entitlement to grieve his death was negated too. She was irrelevant, a filthy secret to be silenced. The plane hit an air pocket and dropped twenty feet, which reminded her she was flying. Pulling the column back gently, the nose pointed up again. Wishing she'd never have to land again and face people, she noticed right ahead the cloud had thickened and she needed to lower her altitude once more so that she didn't lose visibility. Below, the fields turned a darker shade of gold as the cumulus cast its shadows on the landscape and it struck her she wouldn't after all be able to share the beauty of the seasons with Gareth and travel with him to far-flung places. She hadn't even managed to take him up in The Bee. There was so much they hadn't done in their brief time together. Doing a rough calculation, she concluded they had only really spent the equivalent of a full month in total together and yet it had felt like years. Even so, perhaps his family had a right to deprive her of a public right to grieve. She had no idea if time spent together was relevant or if you could love someone too much. In truth, she realised, she was a bit thin on experience. She wondered how on earth people coped with death of a lifetime partner or a son or daughter, if this felt so painful. Over time maybe she and Gareth would have bickered like some of the friends of her parents, and found fault in small things; a pile of unfolded clothes or the way the other brushed their teeth or ate toast. They were ordinary day-to-day things that in those early days were considered a little eccentric but still attractive, rather than down right intolerable. He'd got to her from the moment he bundled her off to Ely Cathedral that day and it was obvious they were meant to be together and it was ridiculous to question otherwise, or perhaps it wasn't…Glancing down at the river way below, she was resigned to the fact that all around the world, people were losing people they loved with the fierceness she felt she loved Gareth and those that remained behind, would have to cherish memories, pick up the pieces of their lives and be terribly brave. That, she decided, was what she must somehow do too and she was sure that's exactly what Gareth, who had so prematurely lost his life, would have wanted.

CHAPTER 25

19ᵗʰ September 1940, Hatfield, Hertfordshire

On this day, the RAF bomb German barges in ports along the French coast.

Lottie had received Gwyneth's Jones' letter just in time for Gareth's obituary to appear in *The Times*. It talked about his academic career at Cambridge and stated he would be "leaving a wife" and there was a picture of them both. It felt odd, seeing Sybil's image, as it finally brought her to life. Until that point she'd existed only in name. She stared hard at the grainy photograph, with horrified fascination. Tall, slim, dark and beautiful, it seemed Sybil looked back at her defiantly. Lottie swallowed, fighting the urge to shred the paper but she couldn't stop staring at them both. She was wearing a long fur coat that looked like mink and was holding Gareth's arm. He was dressed in a dinner suit. They looked happy and right for each other. Lottie wondered how long ago the photograph had been taken. It could have been months or years ago but it *felt* recent and she had no one to ask. A rare stab of jealousy jolted her. The photograph felt like betrayal and it made Lottie question again whether Gareth had really loved her or if she'd she been some kind of distraction for him while Sybil flitted back and forth to America. The insidious worm of doubt crept in and began slowly to feed on her confidence. Perhaps he would have had dinner with Sybil that evening and nothing would have been mentioned about a divorce. Lottie knew people had affairs and things were promised between the sheets that were quite meaningless. Just as she'd made her mind up that she'd meant nothing to him, the worm, satiated, retracted for a while. As it did, Lottie recalled things Gareth had said to her and the balance of reason tilted back the other way, making her feel that questioning his integrity was in itself, betrayal. It was all so confusing. She stared at the paper with a conflicted head and found doubting him was almost as unbearable as his death. Since the tone of Gwyneth's letter made it sound as if they were having a sordid, rather meaningless affair and demanded, yes *demanded* discretion, it clearly shut the door on any further contact with his family, whom she'd so looked forward to meeting. She'd effectively been buried with him in the rubble and was as inconsequential as brick dust. Gareth, she recalled, told her that his sister and her husband were 'High Church' so of course they would have disapproved of them. The very words 'you and my brother had an understanding' diminished their relationship, making it something sordid and socially unacceptable, like a bad smell. Closing her eyes tight, replaying their most intimate moments together, Lottie searched for even a grain of Gareth's insincerity but could find none and the pendulum of doubt once again swung back, where it hovered uncertainly.

Taking a deep breath, Lottie told herself that the only undeniable truth in all this was that Gareth had tragically lost his life and whatever the future held, he had been denied any part of it. The rest was conjecture but perhaps in death, he deserved at least to be trusted. Lottie concluded neither she nor Sybil, for that matter, had a right to waste their lives. Gareth would always have a place in her heart and she felt lucky to have experienced such love, brief though it was. Her job now, she knew, was to play her part in the fight to protect liberty. Carefully folding *The Times* so that the picture was no longer visible, she placed it in the waste paper bin for the fire.

*

She found Mrs Jennings on the landing in her flowery pinafore, vigorously dusting the bannisters, hair escaping as usual from its grips. Lottie smiled. The enemy in this house was not the Nazis but dust and there was no doubt about it, Mrs Jennings was winning her ongoing war. She stopped and looked at Lottie. "I'm making macaroni cheese tonight, Miss Beauchamp, and looking at you, you'll be getting a bit extra on your plate. You've lost weight over the last few days and all it will take is a puff of wind to snap you like a twig!"

"That sounds wonderful, Mrs Jennings, thank you." Lottie still had no appetite and she couldn't bear to even think of the pile of grey food but she was nonetheless grateful for her landlady's care.

"I'll be serving it at six prompt, mind, as I'm off to play whist at the vicarage. If you're late, I'll leave it in the oven for you to heat up."

"Of course. Thank you, I'll let Emily know."

*

The only person Lottie had confided in about Gareth's death, apart from in very difficult letters to her mother and Phyllis and Eleanor, was Emily. She had been supportive and kind and shielded her from the inevitable questions at work and from a concerned Mrs Jennings. In the evenings immediately after Lottie had been notified of his death, they had walked together, over the fields, mostly in silence to give Lottie the space to deal with her sadness. In those first couple of days, Lottie doubted she would ever feel happy again and the slow changing of the season, with the dewy lawns and spiders webs glistening in the sunshine, went unnoticed.

*

The weather was too poor for anyone to fly that day and they'd hung around in the mess waiting for it to clear, but by three thirty it still hadn't and so Lottie had taken the opportunity to be alone for a few hours as company of any sort mentally exhausted her. People constantly asking her if she was still feeling "a bit peaky" and perhaps she should see the Medical Officer for a tonic, was taking its toll as she was already battling a perpetual wave of tears that threatened to betray her insistence that she was absolutely fine. The risk of being deemed unfit to fly was all too real and with what she was going through, being grounded would be unbearable. Her colleagues were built of tough stuff and sentiment had no place in their days. Compassion existed of course but in a 'stiff upper lip' sort of way that had been firmly instilled at boarding school with cold baths and things like lacrosse injuries. They just got on with it and didn't let each other down. Showy displays of emotion just appeared weak and there was no place for weakness in a service that already sought to find any reason why women shouldn't fly. Nonetheless, their Head-Girl glances of concern were making the almost impossible far harder and so she grabbed her jacket, cheerfully made her excuses and took herself off for a walk down the lane where the leaves were beginning to turn and the wild flowers had dropped their seed. Taking solace in the cooler air, she willed the healing process to begin and little by little she regained her strength.

CHAPTER 26

3rd October 1940, Hatfield, Hertfordshire

On this day, Vichy France pass antisemitic legislation excluding Jews from most private and public occupations. Neville Chamberlain's health is failing. Warsaw Jews are moved into the Warsaw ghetto.

On the morning of Thursday 3rd October 1940, the ATA pilots were grounded in the hangars of Hatfield airfield. At around eleven twenty a.m., Lottie stood at the door smoking a cigarette, staring into the fog, wondering when it might lift. As visibility was barely ten yards, it didn't look promising. The airfield was eerily silent. She shivered and pulled the collar of her flying jacket up to shield against the damp, exhaling a stream of smoke that was sucked into the air and immediately claimed as its own. She finished her cigarette and ground the end into the 'butt bucket' by the door. Perhaps this really did signify the end of summer but if the weather turned bad it would at least slow down the air raids. On her way into work that week, she'd noticed the abundance of berries in the hedgerow. Country people always said that was an indicator of a harsh winter and perhaps they were right but she'd always thought it nonsense. She turned and went back inside and found Emily knitting, chatting to Phillipa MacMillan and Ursula Preston, while some of the male pilots were drinking coffee and playing cards. Since most of the UK was blanketed in fog, the majority of pilots were stuck somewhere waiting to fly back, so the place was relatively empty. There really wasn't much one could do when conditions were like this but for Lottie it allowed too much time for reflection. Perhaps, she thought, she should learn to knit to calm her restlessness. At least then, she could make socks and so forth to send out to the troops but she didn't think she'd be much good at it and truth be told, she'd rather have helped out with something practical like the maintenance of the aircraft.

At 11:30 there was the sound of a plane flying very low. They all looked up as if they would see it through the hanger roof and there was a moment's lull in the conversation.

"What on earth are they doing flying in this weather?" said Richard Mason after it had passed. "Royal flush!" He put his cards down and the others groaned.

"That was very low!" said Philippa. "Sounds like a bomber. I wonder if they're trying to find somewhere to land."

The noise of the engine disappeared in a north-easterly direction and faded. Emily got up and made more coffee.

"Another game?" said Sidney Cartwright, shuffling the pack.

"Go on then. Might as well make it a triple win," said Mason.

"We'll see about that. I'll bet the brandies tonight you won't make it three in a row," said, Clive Gordon.

"You're on!"

Three minutes later the 'Take Cover' klaxon sounded.

"Surely not?" said Ursula, as they all scrambled and headed out of the door for the dugouts. As Lottie ran, she could see the outline of a huge aircraft flying towards the airfield at about one hundred feet with its bomb doors open like a gaping, hellish mouth. As she entered the dugout she could hear the *ack-ack* of machine gun fire, a prelude to four loud explosions followed by anti-aircraft gunfire that made them crouch for cover in the shelter. Dust fell from the ceiling and for a moment, deafened, they were in pitch black until a voice of one of the men could be heard.

"Is everyone okay?"

There was a chorus of, "Yes," and the sound of a lighter being struck. A tiny flame danced, illuminating the wide-eyed look of fear on the dirt-smeared faces of everyone.

"They've hit the airfield!" said Ursula. "We need to get out and see if people are hurt."

"Just wait for the all-clear," said Mason. "He might do another turn."

"Shush!" Lottie said.

They all fell silent and listened but there was nothing.

"Damn it, I'm going to take a look," said Gordon. "Stay here." He crawled up the steps to the door and opened it a few inches, waited for a moment and then opened it wider. Cautiously putting his head out, he swore and ducked back down to report back.

"People are screaming and there's fire. Looks like one of the repair shops might have taken a direct hit!" As he finished speaking the "All Clear" sounded and everyone scrambled back out, into what turned out to be carnage.

Lottie stared around her trying to navigate the horror. People were running around and shouting and the air was filled with smoke and the smell of fuel. The fog had lifted a little to allow increased visibility and Lottie could see there were bodies on the ground, illuminated by the fire amid the cracking and crashing sound of masonry and metal falling and the stench of oil. She ran across the grass towards the first person lying face down on the ground, and realised, to her horror, that his foot was missing. She knelt down, trying not to look at the fraying, bloodied mass of where his foot was supposed to be, suppressing the urge to vomit and tried to turn him but he was inert and heavy. Feeling for his pulse in his neck, she could feel a viscous wetness that she knew was blood. Praying for a heartbeat, however faint, she slid her fingertips around the inside of his collar but there was nothing. It was too late. Running on to the next, she heard a groan and yelled for assistance. She recognised the man as one of the young technicians. He'd been shot in the chest and from the firelight, Lottie could see blood seeping out of the wound, fanning out across his shirt. Nobody came for several minutes and she sat by him, holding his hand, trying to stem the flow of blood with her hands, watching it bubble through her fingers, all the while trying to reassure him he was going to be just fine.

"It hurts," he said, weakly. "I think I'm going to die but if I can look at you it helps."

"I've got you," she said, squeezing his hand. "What's your name?"

"Patrick... Patrick Grove," His voice was weakening and his blue eyes were staring up into hers.

"You're an angel," he said softly. "I'm going to see my dad... Do you believe in Heaven?"

She forced herself to smile down at him and to lie, "Of course!"

"Thank you," he mouthed before slipping away.

She held his hand for a few moments longer to make sure he was gone and then gently released her bloodstained fingers and, trembling, closed his eyes. Fighting back a sob, she could hear someone calling for help, so she got to her feet and ran towards burning buildings where bodies were being dragged out from under lumps of concrete where the roof of the shelter within Repair Shop 94 had collapsed. Across the airfield, people were wandering around in drizzle, dazed and injured while a fire crew fought the flames, shouting at everyone to keep well back in case of further explosions from aviation fuel.

Someone called out, "The bastard's crash landed somewhere out near Cole Green! The police have got the crew."

"Should have let him burn in Hell!" someone else replied.

*

By the perimeter fence, Lottie found a man sitting on the ground with his hands over his ears. She crouched down and put her hand on his shoulder. In response, he raised his head up and she saw one side of his face was a mass of blood with open, charred tissue through to bone, where his eye should have been. His other eye was badly swollen and there was blood seeping through his fingers in red rivulets. Realising he couldn't see and probably couldn't hear, she just sat and hugged him to her and waited, teeth chattering, for the ambulance to arrive. She couldn't help thinking Patrick had got the better deal.

CHAPTER 27

4th January 1941, Prestwick, Scotland

On this day, Hermann Goring is appointed head of the German war economy. The Polish Government-in-exile reach an agreement with the French to establish Polish military units in France.

Three months later, weary from her flight, Lottie had a very cordial supper with Amy Johnson at The Craigmuir Hotel in Prestwick, before retiring at just before nine thirty p.m. to write to her mother. The following morning, she awoke to another bitterly cold day as low pressure dipped southwards across the United Kingdom, drawing a very cold easterly wind accompanied by snowfalls. Looking out of the window, at that time, the sky was clear blue but the trees and shrubs in the gardens were covered under a new layer of snow and she could see icicles had formed on the roof of an outbuilding in the freezing temperature, where no doubt, they would remain for weeks to come. Feeling a draught from the window and shivering a little, she thought if she had to fly a Moth today, she would have to be snapped out of the cockpit before she had even reached Hadrian's Wall. Even so, she didn't want to get stuck in Prestwick, so she'd put on an extra vest and hope for the best. When she went down to breakfast, she found that Amy had already left for the airfield. Alone in the rather austere dining room, she ate a steaming bowl of porridge before making her way to the airfield. To her relief, she found she'd been allocated a Miles Master, which thankfully had a covered cockpit and was destined for delivery to Squire's Gate, Blackpool. From there, she would await instructions, depending on the weather.

*

Around ten, following south in Amy's path, she unexpectedly hit thick, freezing fog that surrounded the aircraft like a dark grey, murderous soup. Keeping her nerve and flying as low as she dared, eyes straining, vainly trying to find a landmark and attempting to visualise the terrain beneath, she continued in what she hoped was a south-westerly direction. Below her, valleys perhaps held out the offer of a clearer passage but descending, to her dismay, she found visibility was still blocked by the dark wall of cloud that swirled around the dips in the landscape, searching for spaces to fill and obscuring the point at which the depression ended abruptly by vertical, rocky cliff-faces. Lottie knew flying in this was treacherous. Ramming open the throttles, she pulled the control column back and climbed steeply. The altimeter rose to nearly four thousand feet before suddenly she popped out into bright sunlight. She'd checked the weather before she left and there were no reports of low cloud. Glancing at the fuel gauge she found that she was unfathomably low on fuel which meant she urgently had to find an airfield or at as a last resort, a field on which to land. She could see nothing below her apart from the sea of dark grey, as she rumbled south, anxiously watching the fuel gauge. After thirty worrying minutes, waiting for the sound of the engine beginning to splutter, now devoid of fuel she had no alternative but to begin her descent, hoping she'd stayed on course and away from the corridor of the barrage balloons that ran south. By her reckoning, given her journey speed and compass reading, she should be only a few miles from the runway at Squire's Gate but given the weather, she could be completely wrong. Throttling back she lowered the nose, left the blue sky and dropped back down into the chilling darkness. The altimeter read three thousand feet, then two. She could see no further than the front of the aircraft. One thousand feet. Still dark grey. Caught in its grip, she felt the plane being buffeted by turbulence as though the cloud, having her in its grasp, was playing with her. Breaking out in a cold sweat she continued lower to six hundred feet. If she'd strayed from her course and ended up in the Lake District, she knew at any moment, at this height she could be dead. But then, to her right, there was a sudden break in the cloud and she could just make out the outline of the Fylde coast. Letting out a long breath of relief, she found she was at least, on course. The airfield was in an urban area so she couldn't afford to get her landing wrong and she would, at best, given the critical fuel situation, have only one attempt. She looked anxiously again at the gauge, tapping it with her gloved finger in the hope that suddenly it would spring up to where it should be, but it didn't move from near empty. Quickly scouring the map, afraid to take her eyes off the ground she looked for an alternative landing spot but there was nothing other than houses and commercial buildings. The fuel needle began to judder, dangerously at zero and that meant one of two possibilities, either it was faulty or the fuel tank hadn't been completely filled at Prestwick. She had to assume the latter. If she was lucky, she had possibly minutes, before the engine would fail. Sandwiched in the thin line between cloud and the heavily populated land below, frantically looking for somewhere to land as she headed in the direction of the airfield, she found herself praying to the God she no longer believed in.

*

Pulling to a stop at the end of the runway Lottie sat for a minute or two, collecting herself and staring at the dials, before easing herself out of the cockpit and jumping to the beautiful firm ground. On impact, she was surprised to find her legs almost buckled beneath her. "That," she said to the technician who met her, "was a hellish journey! Please ensure the fuel gauge is checked before she goes anywhere else. It was reading out of fuel. By the way, did First Officer Johnson arrive safely?"

He assured her she had, in an Airspeed Oxford, and that she'd immediately taken off again as a temporary window in the fog eased to complete a journey to Kidlington. The previous evening Amy had said if the weather was bad, she'd overnight at Blackpool and stay with her sister who lived nearby in Stanly Park but clearly she'd decided to continue. Lottie wondered why she'd not stayed but only someone of her calibre would even have attempted the flight and like most of the pilots, she was happier in the air. With heavy legs, and unusually happy to be on solid ground, Lottie made her way into Squire's Gate mess to get a hot drink.

*

The following morning, Lottie awoke to the news that Amy had been declared missing after her plane had reportedly crashed into the Thames Estuary, where she had ejected into the freezing cold sea. She wondered how on earth she'd ended up in the Thames Estuary and that surely there must be some mistake. But there wasn't. One of the pilots at Squire's Gate said that she'd most likely flown off course in the bad weather and no doubt ran out of fuel. It wasn't looking good, he said, "Because of the temperature of the water and strong tide. Nobody, even Miss Johnson, could last long in that!" He seemed so certain and matter-of-fact in his fresh-faced delivery, that Lottie resisted a strong urge to slap him. Instead, numb, she stood outside and looked up in the cold open sky and was reminded of just how powerful and brutal Nature was. She replayed what the technician had said, that it would have been impossible for her to last long in a freezing sea. There was, of course, the remotest chance she'd be found alive but deep down, Lottie knew it was unlikely. She recalled how she'd first met Amy and noticed, in subsequent days, how she'd hated any 'fuss' around her. Getting to know her a little had been one of the greatest privileges of Lottie's relatively short life. Wiping a tear away, Lottie did what Amy and all the others would have done, and without 'fuss', she collected her chit and amid light flurries of snow, she flew without incident but with a very heavy heart, back to Hatfield.

CHAPTER 28

23rd January 1941, Hatfield, Hertfordshire

On this day, Charles Lindbergh, Solo Transatlantic Aviator, testifies before US Congress and recommends the US negotiates a neutrality pact with Hitler.

Lottie arrived back at her lodgings cold and wet from the walk back from the airfield, wondering when the ferocious winter would end. Chilled to the very tips of her toes, she wiped her pink cheeks with the back of her hand before making her way up the stairs to towel dry her damp hair and change out of her uniform. In the living room, Mrs Jennings had set a fire and left instructions for heating up supper, before leaving for her whist evening, with the ladies from the Women's Institute. Ellen was staying overnight in Liverpool and the house was unusually silent, save for the sound of the ticking of the grandfather clock in the hall. Taking her post from the hall table, Lottie went through to the front room and turned on the wireless. She'd missed the news and Farming Today was talking about the Government's stock rationing scheme. War and more war, she thought, turning the volume down low, leaving the voices as background, just for company. She bent down in front of the hearth and struck a match, mesmerised for a few seconds by its bright yellow light and held it to the screwed up ball of newspaper, watching as it caught alight and the words were lost beneath the coal, in a sudden flare. Holding her hands out to the heat to warm them, she stayed in front of the fire until the coals glowed deep orange, before getting to her feet, yawning and stretching.

*

Over a supper of remarkably tasty egg and sausage pie, Lottie read her mail while listening to 'Howdy Folks' and the wireless programme cheered her up. There were two letters. One from Phyllis who had returned to Cambridge and the other from Eleanor who continued to paint and have wild affairs, to distract herself from the "unspeakable cruelty of the Nazis". To Lottie, Cambridge seemed a million miles away and, of course, it reminded her of Gareth. It was hard to believe his death had been over four months ago. She thought of him every day and always at the confused moment between waking and becoming fully conscious. Sometimes at night, she'd wake with a jolt and the recurring nightmare of seeing his broken body under the rubble of the factory would continue to play out. Lying there in the small room in the pitch black, she was wide eyed with terror. Concentrating hard, she steadied her breath, staring into the blackness of the room, listening to the harrowing screams of the mating foxes in the field beyond and willing herself to stay awake until dawn. Finally, exhausted and sad, she had no choice but to succumb to the heaviness of her eyelids and enter the horror of her unconscious world once again. On nights such as these, she awoke the next day feeling drained and unhappy. Clearing her dinner plate away and washing her dish and cutlery, she made a hot drink and sat by the fire in the chair next to the meagre light from the standard lamp, which made the room look more opulent than during the day, and she took up her pen and paper.

Thursday 23rd January 1941
Wisteria Cottage
Cooper's Green
Hatfield

Dearest Phil,

I know it must feel very disappointing for you not to feel useful to the war effort and Cambridge must seem really dull with half of us away but rest assured, life here isn't all about glamorous days of flying and endless parties with handsome airmen. In the main, it's long days that are frustratingly governed by the weather and fairly dull evenings. Sometimes we do go to the pub at weekends which is all rather jolly but mainly our days consist of getting up early and sitting around. If the weather's good, we get a chit to tell us where we're going and the type of plane. These are mainly Tiger Moths used for training boy pilots. As I've mentioned before, we women are only deemed capable of flying training aircraft but at least we get to fly

Masters and Oxfords, now. That is, I have to admit, quite thrilling and much warmer as it is quite possible I believe, to perish in this weather in the open cockpit of a Moth… Commander Gower is constantly and very diplomatically, I believe, trying to get women to ferry the same aircraft as the men and since the RAF have passed all transport duties over to the Air Transport Auxiliary (ATA), she may well win the day and we will realise our dream of flying Spitfires.

The atmosphere about the place is still very subdued following the tragic death of Amy Johnson, earlier this month but nobody really talks about it. I was shocked to hear one of the Pilots grumbling that out of respect, the ATA anniversary party that was scheduled for the 6th of January, had been cancelled. I accept treats are in short supply but even so! What is it about war that makes individual lives seem less important? In any case, I'm quite sure nobody felt in the party mood.

Yes, I do think about Gareth an awful lot and thank you for asking. On some days I feel very connected to him and on others I doubt whether I knew him at all. It was such a short affair and his sister's letter drove that home. I have to accept she had lost both her brothers on that night, which must have been devastating and therefore I should be charitable but I confess it's hard. What I do know, is that I shall never know Gareth any better than I did at the time he died, so I'm trying very hard to stop ruminating and just get on. There are many people worse off etc…

By the way, I've just received a letter from Eleanor. I've been thinking it would be rather nice if you both met for tea every now and again. I think you would really like each other and she'd love your dry wit.

How are your parents? I do hope your father is feeling better, after his bout of influenza. This weather can't help but doctors I hear, are notoriously bad at looking after themselves.

Do tell me more about the chap from Jesus College who's invited you for tea. I seem to recall he's a cricketer, studying mathematics? If it's the one I'm thinking of, he's quite shy but rather a dish! Please don't do your usual and think you're 'not good enough'. Any man would be very lucky indeed, to have you on his arm.

On that note, my darling friend, I'm going to shove some more coal on the fire, put my socks on (the house is as cold upstairs as our rooms at Cambridge) and take myself off to bed.

With love always

Lottie

Addressing the envelope, Lottie realised how much she missed Phyllis. Nonetheless, it was hard to imagine returning to Cambridge after all that had happened. She felt much older than her years but the war, she supposed, had aged everyone. When she looked in the mirror, she half expected to see a middle-aged woman staring back and was struck by her still-youthful image. Surely it was supposed to be the other way round but she felt as though she'd already lived a lifetime. Often she wondered what The Brig and her brothers looked like. She'd not seen any of them for well over a year and although she'd begged the boys to send her photographs of them in their uniforms, they never did. It would, she thought, be dreadful to walk past them in the street and not recognise them. The war had stolen more than just Gareth from her. A pang of loneliness brought sudden tears to her eyes and she stood up. On the radio, the orchestra began to play Glenn Miller's 'In the Mood'. Closing her eyes, she began to sway to the music murmuring, "Mister, why'd you call up, what you doin' tonight? Hope you're in the mood because I'm feeling just right. How's about a corner with a table for two? Where the music's mellow and some gay rendezvous…" For a moment she was transported to a damask covered, candlelit table, before she heard the front door open and Mrs Jennings appeared.

CHAPTER 29

20th April 1941, Hatfield, Hertfordshire

On this day: 100 German bombers attack Athens, Greece.

Hatfield ATA
20th April 1941

Baroness von Haastein
House Cottage
Kettle's Yard
Cambridge

Dear Eleanor,

Last evening, I read the tragic news that Virginia Woolf's body has been found in the River Ouse. Leonard must be devastated, poor man. I suppose that when someone is missing there's still a glimmer of hope, despite knowing, deep down they're not coming back. Now she's been found there will be the inevitable period of grief and mourning, with the wretched press speculating and clamouring for interviews. Did you see her again, after the dinner party? I'm not sure how close you were to her as she said so little that night. Even so, the news must have been terribly upsetting, if not wholly unexpected. I do hope you didn't have to read it in the papers? I believe she visited Newnam and Girton in the late 1920s and from those lectures she wrote A Room Of One's Own. I do wish I'd heard her. In homage, I re-read the book last night from cover to cover. Fortunately, it isn't very long or else I'd have had no sleep. Every woman should, of course, have their own room and one can only hope that at sometime in the not too distant future there's more equality. The very notion that women should defer to men is baseless and terribly frustrating. I sometimes try to imagine a world where there is no discrimination and women could support themselves financially, make decisions and be responsible for their own happiness. What a rich, creative place it would be! For now though, I fear we have enough of a fight on our hands for mere survival.

Thank you so much for your letter, I do love your news and I can only apologise for my tardiness in not responding sooner. It does feel a long time since Gareth's death and yet in some ways, like a moment in time. Cambridge sometimes seems like a dream as it's so far removed from what I do now. I'm quite glad to be away from it in all honesty, as this way, I don't have to revisit memories at every turn. As you very wisely pointed out, only I know the reality of how it felt when Gareth and I were together and I shouldn't let his sister's letter diminish it. I do feel stronger and that is mainly because I'm busy most of the time and the people I work with just aren't the drippy, self-indulgent sort. Mainly, they're brave, putting a smile on their faces and getting on with what they need to do, even the ones who have suffered awful adversity. On that point, at the beginning of the year we had two new recruits from Poland, one of whom managed to escape through Romania and finally got a visa for France. I gather the journey was pretty ghastly and she doesn't speak about her traumatic experience at all but there's a deep, fermenting anger that remains close to the surface and bubbles over every now and again at one of the other female pilots with whom she regularly feuds. Her other preoccupations are bridge (although she curses every hand) and several packets of Chesterfield a day, that make her fingers quite yellow.

I meant to ask in my last letter how Robert is? I do hope he's not still living and working in the East End?

I agree, the news is bleak about the European Jewish population and yes, it is extremely sinister that people are being rounded up and put into Jewish Quarters where conditions are reputedly appalling. However, someone said they'd heard there are signs of an underground resistance movement forming within these areas and I can only hope they get support. How I would love to be in the thick of trying to liberate them.

According to Phyllis, Cambridge is very quiet, indeed. I did think it would be rather good if you both met up for tea. I honestly think you'd like her. It's good to hear that you're doing lots of 'angry canvasses' and are channelling all your humanitarian fury into something creative. I very much look forward to seeing them. Do tell me more about the museum curator who is trying to woo you. Have you managed to identify the 'odd thing' he sent you as a present? You are a tease. Do send me a sketch! Perhaps he's stolen a fertility relic or something and he's hoping it has some mystical power. I think, if he's still trying to seduce you, you should at least have dinner with the poor man, for no other reason than to prevent a lot of precious artefacts from going missing.

I'm now writing rubbish and can feel my eyes are closing, so I shall sign off and go and get myself a cup of cocoa and put on my bed socks. Oh the glamour!

Do write again soon. With fondest love,

Lottie

CHAPTER 30

19th July 1941, Hatfield, Hertfordshire

On this day, Belarus is captured. The German High Command calls for the army to complete the destruction of Soviet forces around Smolensk, before heading south to tackle forces in Kiev.

It seemed like a normal summer morning as Winnie, Margie, Joan, Rosemary and Lottie filed into the office to pick up their chits. The chalkboard, however, had one word written on it, against each of their names, that would change flying history – 'Hurricane'. Stopping dead in her tracks, Rosemary saw it first and said, "Good Lord, is that some kind of joke?"

Neville grinned. "No. It's legit. They're finally letting you ladies loose on the big boys!"

Winnie let out an excited squeal and grabbed Lottie, who was standing next to her and did a bit of a jig. Margie just stared at the board in disbelief while Joan looked about her, wide eyed.

"How so?" Margie said, finally.

"I think you have Commander Gower to thank," said Neville. "I hear she worked her magic with Lieutenant Colonel Brab and the powers agreed with the way things are headed and the pressure on the Service, it was time for change. You five have won places in the beauty pageant. They'll see how it goes from there."

"Well, it's taken its time but it would appear sense has, at last, prevailed," said Margie, lighting a cigarette.

"One big step nearer to the Spit!" murmured Lottie. "I can't see how they could stop it." Her face was flushed with pure joy.

Michael Frant appeared in the office. "Morning, ladies. Clearly you've seen the board. It's your chance to impress! I'm going to run you through the technical detail, if you'd like to follow me for a briefing. After that, you'll each be doing a take-off, circuit and three-point landing. Provided you pass, you'll be authorised to fly fighters."

Lottie thought she might explode with excitement as she walked out onto the runway and stood next to the sleek, single-seater aircraft. So often she'd watched with envy, as the male pilots cruised in and out. The Hurricane was like being given a Rolls-Royce to pilot, compared to the single-engine Moths, Proctors and Lysanders. Putting her hand on the body of the plane, she could feel the warm metal and her pulse beating against it. This was a proven line of defence against the enemy, both easy to manoeuvre and deadly and she was about to pilot her.

*

At the end of the morning, all six of the women pilots had passed without fault. They knew, with absolute certainty, there could be no fails and as soon as the last pilot landed they went inside for a celebratory tea.

"I have an idea," said Winnie, looking animated. "Who has petrol coupons?"

"I have two." Joan poured some more tea.

"Rosemary?"

"Yes, in a drawer, I think."

Margie shrugged. "Must have one somewhere! I'm not in charge of coupons in our house, they just appear when one needs them."

"In that case, who fancies dinner in London tonight? We need to celebrate. I don't mean just by going to the pub. This is far more important!" Winnie looked at each of them, expectantly.

"I agree," said Lottie. "Let's party, for once, in style!"

"Marvellous, I need to make a call," said Winnie. "I know it's a Saturday but I think I can pull a few strings and get us into the Ritz."

"Dust off your frocks, girls, looks like we're about to hit the capital!' Rosemary grinned.

"I can already taste oysters!" said Lottie.

"Do you think they'll have them?" said Joan.

"I'm sure they will. Good restaurants and hotels don't go short, believe me."

"Steak!" Joan said suddenly looking as though she'd gone into a trance at the possibility.

"My mouth is already watering," said Margie. "I'll contact Douglas and let him know I'll be late home and get the Anson to drop off my glad rags."

"You can share my room, Margie," said Winnie. "There's a spare bed."

"Even better!"

*

At six o'clock that evening, the pilots drove south, crammed into Winnie's car as she navigated her way through Marble Arch and Piccadilly. Inside the car there was the aroma of Guerlain and there was a distinct whiff of party atmosphere.

"This is what I miss!" said Winnie, driving too fast and narrowly missing a drunken soldier who was wielding a bottle of beer in the road outside a pub on the corner of Green Street.

"What? Indiscriminately running people down?" said Rosemary.

"No! *This!*" She took her hands off the wheel and gesticulated. "London and a good old night out."

Lottie laughed. "It seems so long ago, now, and the days of afternoon tea at The Savoy, followed by and theatre in the evening." As they sped down the roads, she looked around. The buildings were still mostly intact but the atmosphere had changed. Gone was the relaxed playground atmosphere of the West End. War had put paid to that, replacing once bustling pavements with sandbags and semi-deserted streets. It was a London she recognised and yet did not.

*

The Ritz, was busy, despite the constant threat of air raids. At seven they were seated in the elegant restaurant, at a table set with a starched linen tablecloth and napkins folded into cones. People looked at them as they passed by, as it was unusual to see a table of six women dining together but in their excited state and quite used to attention, they didn't really notice or care. Waiters with slicked-down hair, in black shirts and white aprons moved expertly through the room, under glittering chandeliers, with trays of oysters on beds of ice and domed silver platters held aloft. This was, thought Lottie, as she sipped champagne and looked around, as if she had been transported back in time to when war never existed. From the street, they'd floated through the grand entrance to an entirely different world and the only telltale sign that the country was at war, were signs on the walls that gave instructions about what to do if there was an air-raid. Looking around her, she noticed the couple on the table next to them were holding hands, clearly in love. He was an Officer in uniform and she was dressed in satin with a string of pearls around her perfect neck. They made her think of Gareth, his last day in London and what they'd missed. In her mind's eye she pictured them both like that couple, perhaps celebrating their engagement. Aware that this was the first time in a few days she'd actually thought about him, she immediately felt guilty but was determined not to let her mood dip. She pushed the thoughts away and forced herself firmly back into the moment, nodding her agreement to oysters to start before an entree of beef with dauphinoise potatoes and vegetables.

"Ah," said Margie, "you're back, Lottie. I thought for a moment we'd lost you."

"Not at all. Just taking it all in." She smiled.

"Champagne, please!" said Winnie, to the waiter.

"Of course, madam," he said.

Joan inhaled and closed her eyes. "I simply *cannot* believe we're here!"

"At one time we'd have all taken this for granted," said Margie.

"Some might," agreed Rosemary, raising an eyebrow, "but not all of us."

"You know full well what I mean."

"Yes," she agreed with a grin, "I do."

At that moment the waiter returned with a glistening bottle of Moët and five glasses. All the women watched, mesmerised as he teased out the cork with a very satisfying pop and poured the golden liquid.

"Right, I propose a toast to Winnie for coming up with a blinding idea, working her magic to get us a table and driving us here!" Rosemary raised her glass, its bubbling contents catching the light from the chandelier, above.

"To wonderful Winnie!" Margie took a large sip. "And of course to the Hurricane gals!"

CHAPTER 31

14ᵗʰ August 1941, Hatfield, Hertfordshire

On this day – The Atlantic Charter joint declaration is released by President Roosevelt and Winston Churchill, following a meeting of the two heads of government in Newfoundland.

New ATA recruit, Mary de Bunsen, daughter of Sir Maurice de Bunsen, 1ˢᵗ Baronet and a British Diplomat, limped through the door of the Ferry Pool Office. With a cheerful greeting, she glanced myopically around her as she fumbled with her glasses that had slipped off and edged forward determinedly, towards the desk.

"Made it, finally!" she said, pausing for a moment to catch her breath. "The train was late. I'm looking for Pauline Gower."

There was a moment's silence, as from behind the desk, Lenny Carmichael appraised her.

Lottie, who was handing in her chit, turned and said, with a broad smile, "You must be Mary?"

"Yes, that's me. And you are?" Re-securing her glasses behind her ears and pushing the bridge back up her nose and into place, she blinked and looked around her like a newborn who had arrived into a strange but rather exciting world.

"Lottie Beauchamp. I'm one of the pilots."

"Very pleased to meet you, Lottie." Mary eased herself forward and shook Lottie's hand firmly.

"Welcome," said Lottie. "I spotted Margie speaking to Pauline a few minutes ago outside one of the hangars." She deduced, given the heat and evident lack of fitness, Mary would probably be more comfortable taking a seat than a tour of the airfield, so she steered her next door to get a cup of tea while she went off to find Pauline.

She was, thought Lottie, a funny little creature to be piloting a plane but as she had found out in her time with the ATA, it took all sorts and having a physical disability was not necessarily a drawback, if one was a reasonable pilot and already held a licence.

*

Unzipping her Sidcot suit, Lottie made her way to the hangars noticing how the heat haze distorted the view of the end of the runway and thought how pleased she would be to get out of her thick suit and boots. Above, there was a loud roar of a Merlin engine as a Spitfire came into sight, plopped gracefully onto the grass and came to a halt, some fifty yards from her. Stewart Keith-Jopp pulled himself out of the cockpit with his one good arm and jumped from the wing onto the parched earth, calling out to Flight Engineer Janice Harrington that the altimeter wasn't working correctly. Lottie had her test flight in a Spitfire the day before and was still reeling from the excitement. It had handled like a dream, dancing through the air and responsive like no other plane she'd flown. She had the greatest respect for Pauline, for her ceaseless efforts in turning the establishment on its very chauvinist head where it had finally capitulated and allowed the women pilots to fly fighter planes. Lottie had thought, from the moment she sat, heart pounding in the compact cockpit, it was simply the most perfect aircraft and, as she rode through the air, barely having to touch the stick to make the aircraft respond, her opinion strengthened. The experience had been nothing less than glorious and she couldn't wait for her first ferry job.

*

At six, while she was walking back to her lodgings, the sky suddenly grew dark and the heavens opened. Putting her jacket over her head, she ran under a tree and waited. The deluge hit the dry, ungiving land, bouncing back up with force and an earthy fragrance filled the air. Lottie inhaled deeply and smiled. Mother Nature's perfume, she thought; as familiar and wonderful as the smell of bacon and freshly laid eggs. It reminded her too, of walks through Suffolk woods, in the rain where, as children, she and her brothers had built camps at the bases of great oaks. Like gypsy children, their hair curled by the damp, their shorts grew muddy. Long socks with over-stretched elastic tops allowed them to slide down stick-thin legs and ruck into grey wrinkles, like old elephant trunks but they were always too absorbed in their task to notice such trivia. The rain subsided as quickly as it began and Lottie's reverie was broken when Lettice's treasured Lancia Augusta overtook her and pulled to a stop, swerving to avoid a large puddle. Ursula Preston was in the passenger seat.

"Gosh did you get caught in that?" she said, winding down the window. "We're going for a quick drink in Trewin. You might like to join us?"

Lottie hesitated. She really wanted to write to Eleanor and Archie.

Ursula sensed her reticence. "Come on, don't be a bore, Lottie!"

"I could do with freshening up," she said, running her fingers through her wet hair.

"You look lovely as ever. Bedraggled becomes you. One drink. Lettice will bring you back on her way home, won't you?" Ursula looked at Lettice who was fiddling with a knob on the dashboard.

Lettice nodded. "Sure."

"All right." Lottie laughed.

"Jump in," said Lettice. "Let's get going before the heavens open again. I'm not sure how long these wipers will hold out."

*

Two hours later and feeling a little light headed from drinking two large gin and oranges on an empty stomach, Lottie was delivered at the end of the road leading to Mrs Jennings's house. Her supper would have to be re-heated but she'd become used to that. She thought she might sit in the garden as the heat was stultifying and the rain had stopped and given she'd abandoned the thought of letter writing. In any case, there seemed so little to say other than to talk about the war and at times, it felt that's all everyone did. Perhaps Emily would be home, she thought idly as she made her way towards the house. Later, they might listen to the news together and she could tell her about her test flight.

As she opened the gate, Mrs Jennings appeared in the doorway, gravely waving a telegram at her.

"I wondered when you'd be back, Lottie. This came for you."

Lottie's heart stopped for a moment and within an instant, she was sober. Telegrams these days never brought good news. Taking it, she opened it, hands shaking and while still walking towards the house, she read the words.

'*Hugh shot down. Badly injured but alive. In hospital. Call when you can. Mother.*'

*

Coming to a standstill, she could feel the blood begin to drain from her face. Her mind posed one hundred questions but the loudest was how 'badly' injured? She was vaguely aware of Mrs Jennings scrutinising her face and of the hand on her arm as wordlessly, she began to mount the stairs to her room.

"Is everything all right, dear?"

"No, Mrs Jennings, I'm afraid it isn't…" was all she could manage to say as the hand reluctantly released and allowed her on her way.

*

The only telephone box in the village was in use when Lottie arrived and there was one other person waiting. The middle-aged man in front of her, puffed away on his Woodbine and intermittently stepped forward and tapped impatiently, on the small glass window. Turning to Lottie, he looked her up and down and smiled appreciatively, showing three stained, yellow teeth.

"You women really know how to gas!" he said. "She's been in there for over fifteen minutes and never mind there's a queue."

Lottie just glanced at him but didn't answer.

"Local are you?" He coughed, turned and spat into the hedge. Moving towards the box, he banged loudly on the glass. "Come on! I've got pigs to feed."

Lottie stared into the distance, imagining Hugh lying in a hospital bed with bloodied bandages and his life hanging in the balance.

The noise of an aircraft drowned out the man, momentarily, but he pointed upwards. "Now there's planes, it's a different ball game to the first war." He lit another cigarette with dirty hands and black fingernails. "To think we've got women pilots billeted just over there!" He nodded in the direction of the airfield, tutted and shook his head, "What's that going to lead to, I'd like to know? Chaos, that's what! Women need to have their feet firmly on the ground and in the house, not gallivanting around. It's not natural."

The door of the telephone box opened and a young woman emerged.

"About time!" said the man.

"There's no law about how much time you can spend in a phone box, as far as I'm aware!" she retorted, "And it's bad manners to keep banging on the glass!"

"Well, it's bad manners to keep gassing when there's a queue!" he said, in a loud voice to her back as she walked off up the street and he eased his large frame into the small space and the door closed.

Lottie paced up and down on the verge outside until finally the man vacated the box and sauntered off down the road, whistling. She dialled the number of The Lindens, hoping her mother would pick up. Very often she didn't hear the bell if she was upstairs and Mary, the housekeeper, would have gone home by now. She wasn't even sure if her mother would be there. Perhaps she was with Hugh, wherever he was. Another thought occurred to her that he might not even be in hospital in England. The phone rang for a very short time and to her relief, she heard her mother's voice. Putting a penny in the slot, she pressed button 'B', to allow her to speak.

CHAPTER 32

August 23rd, 1941, Southampton

On this day the German 2nd Army heads south as Hitler postpones drive on Moscow to take Kiev.

Margie Fairweather landed the Anson at Hamble airfield, humming a song from The Mikado, to herself. Her passengers, Lottie and Philippa, unbuckled and jumped to the ground.

"Hope all goes well," called Philippa to Lottie, as she broke away and jogged to the office where a car was booked to take her to Southampton's Royal Victoria Hospital. In reply, Lottie waved over her shoulder. She had no idea really what to expect. Her mother had said Hugh was alive but he'd injured his eyes and leg, but that it was virtually impossible to get information out of the busy hospital staff. The Brig said he would get him moved nearer to Suffolk, when he was well enough to travel, which would at least be closer to The Lindens. There was no timescale, though, as her father was, as Lady Beauchamp put it, "In the thick of it with Churchill."

*

The taxi driver was chirpy. Making small talk was really the last thing Lottie wanted but she remained polite while barely listening to his rant about the war. The trouble was, everyone had an opinion and they were about as useful as dust.

"Have you got a relative at the hospital, then?" he said, as he ran out of steam and they finally pulled into the grounds.

Lottie stared at the red-brick building. It seemed vast but not unattractive, with its turrets and arched stonework. It looked solid and capable and irrationally, comforting.

"Yes," was all she could muster.

He turned and looked expectantly at her as she delved into her pocket and brought out a shilling tip.

"Miss!"

What now? she thought. Unnerved by what lay ahead and irritated with him, she turned. "Yes?" Her tone was short.

"You don't want to be forgetting this, do you?" Scrabbling to get out of the door as quickly as possible, she'd left her gas mask on the back seat.

"Thank you." She turned back and as she went to take it from him, he held on to it for a moment.

"I hope he's all right, miss."

"Thank you." The sudden kindness from the stranger was almost too much to bear and, feeling a prickling sensation in her nose, a prelude to her eyes filling with tears, she turned and fled into the building.

Inside, there was an air of organised chaos. Ambulances were bringing the wounded in on stretchers, while nurses triaged and doctors flitted about, conducting cursory examinations and directing orderlies to wards. People were moaning, barely conscious and one young man was calling for his mother, his face blackened and body swathed in grubby bandages, stained ruby red.

"Help me!" he said as Lottie passed, holding out a bloodied hand. She paused for a moment and took it.

"You're safe now," she said. "The doctors will soon have you patched up, and you'll see your mum." Her words felt hollow. She gave his hand a reassuring squeeze and moved on, wiping the traces of blood from her fingers and stopping briefly to ask a porter for directions to Gladstone Ward. The air of the long corridor was filled with the smell of Dettol, which barely disguised the pervasive and acrid odour of fear and death. People in civilian clothes made their way towards the hospital exit, faces hallmarked with the grey pallor of bad news and eyes deadened by grief.

*

After what seemed like an interminable walk, Lottie saw a sign to Gladstone Ward. At the entrance she paused and collected herself.

She knew she had to be strong for Hugh and not allow herself to shatter into one thousand pieces when she saw him. Taking a deep breath, she propelled herself forward and found a nurse, just by the entrance.

"Good morning, nurse. I'm looking for Hugh Beauchamp," she said, unbuttoning her jacket.

"And you are?" said the nurse, looking her up and down.

"His sister."

"He's at the end, to the left. Don't expect too much. He's not having a good day and he's had a lot of morphine. There's only half an hour left of visiting time, by the way."

"Thank you." She tried to keep her eyes ahead, concentrating on moving her legs that had turned to lead. What did she mean by 'not having a good day'? Someone coughed, making a deep, wracking noise that made her walk faster. As she approached, she could see a figure propped up by pillows in the end bed but his head was bandaged and from a distance he could have been anyone. Lottie slowed, trying to prepare herself.

*

He was lying still when she arrived, arms by his side, sheet turned tidily down, making him look like a corpse. It seemed likely he was asleep but she couldn't tell as both his eyes were bandaged. Looking down at the sheet she could see the outline of his left leg but on the other side the sheet was flat from about halfway down. By the side of the bed there was a pair of tell-tale wooden crutches. Reality finally dawned. Sinking onto the chair next to the bed as her legs began to give way, Lottie gently touched his hand. He moved his head and murmured, "Nurse?"

"No, darling, it's me, Lottie."

"Lottie." He formed the words but his voice was hoarse. It was a man's voice, unfamiliarly deep. She didn't know what to say.

"Do you need a drink?" she said, finally.

"Yes…" He moved his hand out to feel for the glass on the side cabinet. She passed it to him and guided his fingers around it. "How are the rest of the men?" He tried to push himself up, "We have to get back!" His head moving from side to side with agitation.

"Are you in pain, darling?" She stroked his dark hair tenderly, above the bandage. Tears were falling down her face but it didn't matter as he couldn't see them and he didn't seem aware that he was in hospital. Through the blur, she could see the residue of dark bruising and a cut running vertically down his cheek before it disappeared into the growth of his beard. If she hadn't been directed to his bed, she would have walked on past, thinking he was a stranger. Only the Cupid's Bow of his lips told her it was unmistakably Hugh. Ironically, he'd grown to hate his perfect mouth as he believed it made him look effeminate and yet it seemed it was the one thing that had survived, unblemished.

"No...." he said, after a while. Speaking seemed an effort and he trailed off. "Tired... We can't stay here," he whispered, suddenly, putting his hand out and finding her arm. His grip was vice-like. "It's so dark but they're all around us, listening... watching."

"It's Lottie, Hugh. You're in hospital but you're safe," was all she could think of to say as her brain tried to process what was left of her brother and what this all meant for his future. He seemed to drift off momentarily and his head fell slightly to one side. She'd expected him to be more awake. Gently she removed his hand and went to find a nurse and located one tending a patient who needed a bedpan, so she waited patiently outside the curtain that had been hastily drawn round.

"I need to speak to someone about my brother Hugh Beauchamp, please," she said, when she re-emerged.

"Doctor's doing his afternoon round in about an hour, so you might catch him then," she said, "but visiting time ends in ten minutes, so you might have to wait downstairs or you could try Matron. She's in her office over there." She pointed to a door.

Lottie nodded. "Thank you."

*

The ward Matron was brisk. "He got an infection. He was operated on again yesterday but there was no way of saving his leg and the surgeon had to amputate above the knee. It was very sudden but he deteriorated quickly. He's sedated from the anaesthetic and he's had a lot of pain relief."

It dawned on Lottie that none of the family would have known and it was impossible to imagine breaking the news to them.

"Is… is he going to live?" It was the question she didn't want to have to ask.

The Matron frowned. "It's too early to tell but the best thing for him is rest."

"What about his eyes?"

"Again, difficult to tell. We'll know more in a week or so. He's definitely lost sight in one eye and there's significant scarring. The second, we're not sure about. There's still a lot of swelling. To be honest, he's lucky to be alive."

The word 'lucky' seemed misplaced to Lottie, at that moment. "He loves sport and flying." she murmured more to herself than the Matron.

"Well, he'll have to adapt and it will be hard, there's no denying it but there's plenty who have lost their lives. I see it, every day. At least this way, he has a chance."

"But he's only twenty-five." She got to her feet, unsteadily. She understood it was difficult for the woman to become consumed by the fate of each of the wounded patients who transitioned through her ward but she appeared so detached.

"Indeed. Now, if you'll excuse me, Miss Beauchamp, I really have to get on." Her expression softened slightly. "He's in the best hands. My advice to you is to go home and await further news."

Lottie wandered back to Hugh's bedside. He was still fast asleep, his chest rising and falling steadily. The sun had come out and it cast its rays through the window above the bed and fell on the empty space where the outline of his left leg should have been. Perhaps, once he'd recovered physically and if he regained his sight in one eye, he might still have some quality of life but his battle had just started and even if he survived, he would face a very long road ahead.

CHAPTER 33

29th September 1941, Hatfield, Hertfordshire

On this day, the SS commence the slaughter of thousands of Jews at Babi Yar ravine, Kiev.

On the twenty-ninth of September, Lottie and twelve of the other women pilots moved from Hatfield to a new headquarters, at Number Two Women's Ferry Pool, Hamble, under the command of Margaret Gore and her deputy, Rosemary Rees.

*

Lottie walked out of the gate of her lodgings at Hatfield before stopping suddenly, putting her suitcase on the path and running back to give a surprised Mrs Jennings a hug. After a moment, still in her housecoat, the older woman put her arms around Lottie and patted her on the back, saying, "You girls are welcome back any time, you hear, but you need to take care flying those planes!"

"We will! You look after yourself, Mrs Jennings."

Ellen, who had already done her brisk and rather more restrained farewell, was waiting for her at the end of the row of houses. "Come on, Lottie, we'll be late for The Anson. You know how Margie hates to be kept waiting!"

"I know, I'm coming! I do feel sad at leaving Hatfield, there are so many memories."

"I agree. I'm not sure it'll be the same at Hamble but at least there are more than a dozen of us and a change of scene might be fun." Ellen smoothed her jacket collar with her free hand.

"True." Lottie wondered why her suitcase always felt heavier whenever she left somewhere. "I think Margot will be a good Commanding Officer."

"And we get to fly Spitfires nearly all the time."

Ellen, Lottie noted, seemed to be striding forth, carrying her belongings with great ease but then she didn't really own very much. She'd said shortly after they'd met, one good dress was all one really needed and that people didn't really notice what she was wearing anyhow, as she didn't have a face or for that matter, a body that people found terribly appealing. It was true, she wasn't beautiful but Lottie had told her that she was being ridiculous and she thought she had a rather interesting face. Ellen with raised eyebrow responded that 'interesting' was generally used to describe odd, scientific specimens and they'd both burst out laughing. Lottie was glad she'd be billeted on the Solent, with strong, dependable Ellen and at least she'd be much nearer to Hugh, who was still in hospital in Southampton, awaiting his move to convalesce.

*

Hugh and his future were constantly on Lottie's mind. His eyesight hadn't returned and he was left with only a vague sensation of dark and light and bad headaches. He was unable to do much at all really and he sat, for most of the time, according to the nurses on the ward, in the chair next to his bed, mute and coldly resisting all efforts to try and encourage him to use his crutches or even sit in a wheelchair. In between bouts of sleeping, he'd told Lottie when she'd been to see him at the end of August, that they should have left him for dead and the doctors were negligent for not letting him die. They had, he said bitterly, "No damn business playing God!" She'd fitted in another visit ten days ago, on a brief trip to Southampton, to pick up some papers for Pauline Gower but the pain she felt whenever she saw him, almost sucked the life out of her, like she too, was drowning in his anger and needed to fight just to come up for air. Barely recognisable when the bandages were removed from his face, she found it difficult to look at him and he'd sensed it.

"I know, I'm a bloody freak!" he'd said, his mouth twisting and displaying a little droplet of white spittle on the right side.

The Matron had been right, the scarring was significant around the empty socket and he was wearing a patch. The other eye was open but unseeing.

"No, Hugh, no!" Horrified that he'd sensed her recoil, she'd put her hand on his and he threw it off as if she'd scalded him.

"Why have you come, Lottie? I told them I didn't want any visitors. Just forget me and get on with your life." His voice had changed, she noticed, and not just in tone, as he was unable to control his speech as though he'd suffered a stroke.

"How can I forget you, Hugh? I love you, you're my big brother." She said it quietly and as calmly as she could, trying not to stare at his missing limb.

"What use is a damned, miserable, blind cripple to you? Your brother's gone, do you hear? I'm changed. Just GO, will you?"

"You *will* get better!" She stood her ground but realised how weak that sounded and almost plaintive.

"How?" he retorted, coldly. "It's fine for you, off flying your Spitfires, doing what you love! Much better to throw what's left of this useless battle fodder to the farm pigs!"

Suddenly a childhood scene from the riverbank slipped into her memory. He'd been upset because The Brig had given her a pony while he'd got a new bike for Christmas. "It's all right for you!" he'd whined. "You're the favourite because you're a girl!"

"But you don't even *like* riding!" she'd retorted as he gave her a shove down the bank. "You *wanted* a new bike, which you got and I'm not the favourite! The Brig loves us all the same! Why do you have to be so beastly?" She'd got to her feet and gone and punched him as hard as she could on the arm and he'd fallen on the muddy ground, groaning as if she'd killed him and then, as always, anger dissipated and they'd giggled.

Now, nobody was laughing and he had every right to complain. Listening to him and hearing his self-loathing, she wanted to fiercely hold him tight to her, taking on his pain as though it were her own and relieving him of it. His sense of hopelessness was unbearable. It burned into her like the fire that had left him a molten, distorted husk of a young man. On that same visit, the nurses intimated he was rude, demanding and uncooperative and as a result, they let him be for most of the time until he asked civilly for something. Looking around the ward, Lottie realised they were run off their feet, relentlessly spinning plates until one dropped and shattered and was swept away and another immediately put up in its place. Perhaps, she thought, convalescence would be better for Hugh and he might be encouraged to get up in the morning. He could meet other men with life-changing injuries and perhaps learn new skills and they might give him a reason to live because it seemed, at this time, nobody else could. When she'd tentatively put it to him, he'd said sarcastically, of course that was the answer and that he could take up basket weaving in 'mutilated camaraderie with the other walking dead'. Nothing she said was right. She'd wanted to run away then and never come back but she didn't, she remained rooted to the linoleum floor, trapped and at a loss. Acknowledging the hospital had done what it could for Hugh, she realised listening to the sounds of death and suffering in the beds all around him couldn't be good for him. She had a deep, sickening fear that his road to recovery would be interminably long and to be honest, if she was in his position, she'd have felt terribly angry, too. If she survived the war, she made a silent promise that she would set up home and dedicate her life to looking after him.

*

Ellen stopped at the entrance to the airfield and waited for her to catch up, leaving Lottie slightly out of breath with trying to keep up and having to stop frequently to secure the strap to her gas mask, as it worked its way off her shoulder, down her arm and banged maddeningly against her leg as she walked.

"You have too many clothes in that case!" Ellen exclaimed, shaking her head.

"This blasted mask! Is it even possible to have too many clothes?" said Lottie, laughing, her cheeks red with exertion. Temporarily, the omnipresent nightmare of Hugh retracted as they made their way along the runway, towards the Anson and the next chapter in their lives.

CHAPTER 34

September 29th 1941, Hamble, Southampton

On this day and the next, at Babi Yar ravine, Kyiv, Ukraine, the Nazis slaughter approximately 33,771 Jews. It is possibly the largest two-day massacre carried out during the Holocaust.

To Lottie, Hamble village seemed a million miles away from its battered neighbour Southampton, where buildings rose up like a mouth full of rotten, broken teeth against the backdrop of the docks and where cranes moved in a slow-motion dance across the skyline, unloading provisions from across the Atlantic from dawn till dusk. Since the outbreak of war, every minute of daylight had become as precious as a gemstone.

*

Hamble Airfield was functional. Besides the two runways it contained a long, low building that housed a number of rooms including offices, a signals and map room, parachute store, dining room and kitchen. Adjacent to the runways on this grey morning, was a line of tantalising Spitfires, waiting to be taken to the Airspeed factory in Portsmouth or to Colerne, Wiltshire. What the place lacked in elegance, it made up for in importance to the war effort and for the women, it was to become home for the foreseeable future. Lottie, as much as the other pilots, longed to get settled in and get on with the job.

*

During their initial briefing from Commander Margot Gore, the new arrivals were told to pack an evacuation bag with a few essentials, in case they were ordered to evacuate, at short notice. It was something Lottie tried not to think too much about. If it happened, it meant they'd been invaded and she wasn't at all confident they would survive, in spite of a good woollen jumper and some chocolate. It felt a rather futile gesture but of course, she would do as she was instructed. Fortunately, her mother had progressed with her knitting and had sent her a rather gorgeous, green cardigan. If it came to it, she would be rather proud to be wearing something created with love.

After the briefing, they were shown to their billets in some very sweet cottages on the riverbank. Most of the women pilots stayed with local families that were more than happy to take them but for the remaining few, the Adjutant had rented empty properties. There was a general feeling of excitement, like the first day at boarding school, as they bagged bedrooms and squealed with delight at the views of the river. It felt to Lottie, as she unpacked her case in her tiny bedroom with its sloping ceilings and lattice window, as if France couldn't possibly be only twenty or so miles across the Channel.

"I think we should celebrate our first evening with a trip to one of those pubs we passed in the village," Lottie called out to her new housemates, Ursula, Mary and Ellen.

"I agree," said Ellen, appearing in the doorway. "Perhaps the others would like to come? We could go en masse. Gosh these floorboards are very creaky. I think we'll have to have an agreement that nobody uses the lav' after ten, unless it's an absolute emergency!"

Ursula appeared behind her. "Well that won't work! I have to go at least twice a night but don't worry, I'll jump over the worst ones. I was rather good at long jump, at school."

They laughed.

"Where's Mary?" said Lottie, trying to close her stuffed wardrobe door and having to put her shoulder against it.

"I'm in the kitchen," she called. "What on earth are these strange pots with handles?"

"Saucepans!" they chimed.

"It's a completely new world, this kitchen... I shall be using the mess!" she announced.

"Can you fix a gin?" called Ursula, over the stair-rail.

"Well, of course I can, I'm a De Bunsen! I'm looking for glasses as we speak."

"Well that's fine then. None of us can cook, really, can we?"

"No but so long as there's bread and gin, we'll survive. I must say those three pilots the air ministry has kindly left us with, seem very accommodating," said Ursula, making her way down the narrow stairs.

"Yes, I thought the one called Bruce was rather sweet," said Ellen.

"He was! What was the name of the one who has lost his arm?" said Lottie, brushing her hair.

"Charles. His brother's George."

"I think they'll be fun to work with. I wonder how he lost it?"

"Lost what?" Lottie had gone into the bathroom to do an inspection and was no longer listening.

"His arm!" said Ursula, rolling her eyes.

"Oh, I've no idea."

"Which pub shall we go to?"

"The Bugle's supposed to be nice," called Mary from below as they heard another cupboard door bang as she continued her investigation of the kitchen. "I've got glasses for gin but they're quite inadequate."

"Well, we'll have to buy some. There's certain things we can't do without. Let's try The Bugle. If it's full of dreadful, inebriated sailors, we'll move on to one of the others," said Ellen. "I'll swing by and see if the others want to join us. We might as well make a bit of a party of it."

*

Once she'd finished unpacking, Lottie went outside and had a look around. Above the Solent, the gulls called out to each other as they scoured the sea with beady black eyes. It reminded her of holidays with family friends in Devon. As she turned inland, in the direction of Southampton, she decided she would go and visit Hugh on Saturday. Gareth drifted into her mind. It troubled her that when she thought of him now, that his face didn't seem quite so distinct in her memory and she wasn't sure if that was normal and she was worried the essence of him would fade away completely over time and she would be left with just a vague outline. Coming to a standstill with the onshore wind blowing her hair back, she closed her eyes and concentrated and she found him again, on the bank of the River

Cam, heard his voice and his laughter and, comforted, she smiled and continued.

*

On Saturday, when she arrived at the Royal Victoria Hospital and made her way to the ward, she experienced the familiar feeling of dread at seeing Hugh. It wasn't that she didn't want to visit him; on the contrary, she longed to walk along the beds and to find him sitting up and giving her a cheerful wave but she knew deep down it was as likely as finding fairies at the bottom of the garden. The ward was at capacity as usual and the nurses were preoccupied with other patients. She couldn't see anything because the green curtains were drawn round a patient's bed and there was a metal-ringed whoosh as nurses purposefully came and went. The man in a nearby bed was calling out, asking if the man behind the curtains was dead. Another patient, who had two relatives with him, shouted across and told him to shut up and give him some peace and quiet. Lottie tried unsuccessfully to blot it all out. The time it took to walk along the rows of beds felt like a lifetime. She couldn't see Hugh, as his curtain was drawn one side. Perhaps he was trying to get some rest, although it was difficult to see how one could sleep with all the activity on the ward. It must, she thought, be incredibly disturbing without eyesight, to make sense of the endless, plaintive calls for 'Nurse' or 'Doctor'. When she reached his bed, she was quite unprepared for it to be empty and freshly made for an occupant who was clearly no longer in residence. The small bedside table was empty too and all his belongings had gone. Her heart began to beat faster as she turned and looked for a nurse but there was nobody available. The last time she'd spoken to her mother, she'd been told he was improving and the infection was under control. What if it had come back and he'd suddenly died? She'd heard sepsis was quick. A wave of panic overtook her as a doctor in a white coat emerged from behind the green curtain at the other end of the ward, shaking his head.

"Well, looks like he's a goner, then!" said the man in the bed opposite. "Poor fella."

Lottie turned, having no spare capacity for sympathy. "Excuse me, the man in *this* bed," she said, pointing to where Hugh was. "Do you know where *he* is?" Her mouth had gone very dry.

The man removed his glasses from the one ear he had left and the makeshift ribbon tie that went around his head to hold them in place. Lottie saw that the side of his face seemed to have been melted into a featureless mass of scar tissue. He peered at her, as if trying to focus. "You mean Hugh? He's been moved, Love."

"Moved?" She felt relief clatter, uncontrolled, around her head.

"This morning. Going to convalesce, I believe. They couldn't do any more for him here, see?"

"I do see. Moved, where? Do you know?"

"Near to Cambridge, I think."

"Right. Thank you, so much." Relieved, she turned to make her back down the ward. "I'm sorry to have disturbed you."

"Are you his sweetheart?" He called after her. "If not, I've got a vacancy."

"No. His sister. I'm so sorry, I have to find out where he's been taken." She turned and began to walk, unsteadily to once again face the Matron.

CHAPTER 35

January 6th, 1942, Hamble, Southampton

On this day, in his State of the Union speech, President Roosevelt promises more aid to Britain including planes and troops.

Diana Barnato, daughter of the owner of the Bentley Motor Company, arrived at the ATA with panache. Lottie spotted her from the far end of the runway but in truth, wearing a leopard skin coat, she'd have been difficult to miss from the air. Although she'd never met her, Lottie, through a friend of Hugh's, had heard of Diana's reputation as a pilot and debutante. She was reputed to have an insatiable appetite for good living and Lottie couldn't wait to be introduced. Margie had said she'd been due to arrive months before but a bad equine accident had prevented her from flying. The word on the block was that Diana had suffered major facial injuries, after which, her society boyfriend left her just before he was shot down and lost his life. Diana, thought Lottie, straining her eyes as she approached, would need to have a lot of spirit to overcome all that. As it turned out, although short in stature, she made up for any loss of height and the scarring of her face, with personality. On introduction, she greeted Lottie with a giggle and took her arm.

"You must tell me, darling, where all the fun is around here. I mean, all right, there's a war on but for God's sake, it shouldn't stop a party."

Lettice, who was in earshot, looked her up and down disdainfully, before heading off in the opposite direction, muttering something about them being there to work.

Lottie smiled, immediately warming to Diana. "Well, it's a bit limited but we try to make our own fun."

"Any lovely chaps? They are a key ingredient, after all."

Lottie noticed she smelled of Chanel. She'd almost forgotten what it was like to wear scent and she inhaled. "We have three and they're all lovely in their own way."

"I'm reading between the lines. How terribly diplomatic!" She turned to face Lottie who tried hard not to look for signs of scarring beneath the makeup. In the event, she looked fine; not a beauty in the conventional sense but she was blessed with high cheekbones, lustrous dark hair and eyes that sparkled with humour.

"No, I didn't mean they aren't at all attractive, it just depends on what type of man you like."

"Well, I'll check them out for myself and in any case, since the Japs overstepped the mark at Pearl Harbour, the Yanks are on their way and they'll add a bit of glamour." She looked hard at Lottie. "How is it we haven't run into each other before? Were you presented?"

Lottie smiled. "No. I ended up with chicken-pox on the day."

"Oh, bad luck!"

Lottie wrinkled her nose. "Not really my thing."

Diana burst out laughing. "Nor mine, although I do love a good ball with badly behaved people. By the way, what's the food like here?"

"In all honesty, dreadful."

"Oh Lord, I'll have to send an order in to Fortnum's. I'm too long in the tooth to put up with terrible food. There is a limit."

"Good idea."

"Right, I shall go and unpack and perhaps we should catch up properly later, if you've got nothing better to do and maybe go to the pub? I assume there's a decent place for a girl to get a dirty martini around here?"

Lottie nodded. "Of course, I'll happily show you round Hamble when I finish work but first I've got a delivery to make. I'll be back around three, weather permitting."

"Of course, don't let me keep you! Lovely to meet you and all that." With that, she waved her hand and disappeared towards her lodgings. Lottie retraced her steps, smiling and shaking her head, knowing, without a doubt, first impressions from the other pilots about Diana would be polarised.

Lottie arrived back at the airfield later that afternoon, having delivered a Spitfire to Chattis Hill, Hampshire, and picking up another. The sky looked very much like snow and she'd just made it back in time, flying low to avoid the accumulating dense clouds. January was notoriously hellish: short days and bad weather left the pilots small windows in which to get the aircraft to and from the factories. She strode into the office, the tip of her nose red, looking forward to a hot chocolate. When she pushed the office door open she was immediately presented with a telegram. Quickly taking her gloves off, she frowned and put it in her pocket, not wanting to open it in front of Bruce and George, who were animatedly discussing the US's intervention and its likely effect on the war. She got her chit signed and was informed there would be no more flights that day. Making her way back out into the cold wind, she felt in her pocket and pulled out the small brown envelope. Hugh was now safely at The Lindens but she wasn't sure about Archie. As far as she was aware, he was on a troop ship, heading for Borneo. Her heart sank and then leaped as she remembered the date and realised with a start, it was her birthday. Breathing a sigh of relief and thrilled that someone at least, had remembered, she slid her finger under the flap of the envelope and opened it. It did not however convey the good wishes she'd anticipated. Instead, it just said:

Lottie, Please call home immediately. Father.

Stuffing the telegram back into her flying jacket, feeling uneasy, she ran back into the office.

*

The telephone rang ominously at the other end for a long while. Eventually she heard The Brig's voice but it didn't sound like him. It was strained and it sounded as though he had a cold. There must, she thought, be something wrong with her mother. Why else would he be at the farm?

"Brig, it's me."

"Lottie!" He sounded relieved.

"I just got the telegram. Is everything all right?"

There was a pause and a muffled sound as though he had his hand over the mouthpiece.

"Father?"

She began to panic. Instinctively she knew something was terribly wrong.

"Yes, I'm here. Lottie… It's Hugh."

"What about him? He's at the farm, isn't he?"

"He… Lottie… He's… Hugh's taken his own life." He could barely articulate the crushing words.

Lottie sank into the office chair, like she'd been punctured.

"Lottie?"

"He can't have!" Her mind was in overdrive.

"He…" She heard her father swallow and what sounded like a stifled sob. "He took himself off to the barn…"

"But he couldn't see and his leg…" she interrupted. "How?"

"He took himself off to the barn, in his chair, when your mother was at church and he…"

Lottie could hear him sigh.

"He shot himself."

There was a silence.

"Are you there, darling? I'm so sorry we have to do this by phone but I wanted to tell you myself, before anyone else did.

"I—" she began but he interrupted.

"You see, he couldn't face life crippled."

It was as though someone had injected her with ice and it was trickling its way through her veins, slowly paralysing her. She recognised the feeling as similar to when she heard about Gareth's death but this, if anything, was worse.

"How's Mother?" she found herself saying, weakly after a few moments.

"Oh, you know…"

"I'll speak to the CO and I'll come straight home."

"No. We want you to stay put, darling girl."

"But I should be home with you. What about Archie?"

"I've contacted his unit. He was due to go to the Far East but there's been a delay. The vicar's been here and we've arranged for Hugh's funeral to be on the fourteenth. Come home for that. You really can't do anything and it's better for you to keep busy."

"Can I speak to Mother?"

There was an uncomfortable silence until at last, he spoke again.

"She's gone up for a rest. Dr Curtis has given her something to help her sleep." He sounded hollow, as though he'd had the life scooped out of him.

Lottie couldn't think of anything to say. She'd always dreaded getting the news that either Hugh or Archie had been killed in action but not this. There'd been an assumption that he was improving, albeit slowly. But while the rest of them had been getting on with their lives, between them they'd not kept him safe and he'd died in the care of the family. Finally she managed, "Goodbye, Father," before replacing the receiver and putting her head in her hands. After several minutes, she got unsteadily to her feet, just as Mary De Bunsen limped through the door.

"I say, Lottie, they're setting up a cinema in the mess this evening so we can have a private viewing of the 'Ferry Pilot' before it gets released. I can't wait to see Audrey and Joan in action. Of course, Lettice thinks it will be a travesty, just showing women pilots as 'totty', when the real flying is done by men. I don't care though. It'll be such a treat and we owe it to the girls to watch it."

Lottie put her head down. "I'm sorry, Mary," she mumbled, "I have a terrible head. I'm going back to my room." She edged past her, face averted, towards the door. "Please give my apologies."

"Oh, poor you. Yes of course!" Mary called after her. "Do you need anything?"

There was no reply.

CHAPTER 36

14ᵗʰ January 1942, Suffolk

On this day, off Antarctica, German auxiliary cruiser Pinguin captures fourteen Norwegian whaling vessels without a single shot being fired.

Hugh was buried on a freezing, sunny day in the middle of January, at St Mary's Church, Woodbridge. A dusting of snow lay on the ground and on top of some of the ancient grave stones, covering inscriptions, long ago obscured by lichen. Snowdrops with their heads down sat above the earth, punctuating the thin, white blanket with tufts of emerald green that glinted in the sunlight and brought a dash of colour to an otherwise monochrome landscape. Lottie watched as her brother's coffin was lowered into the family grave, adjacent to her grandparents, disrupting the correct order of death.

*

The vicar said, "For as much as it hath pleased Almighty God in his great mercy to take unto himself the soul of our dear brother here departed.."

*

In His great mercy? she thought, bitterly. There was no evidence of mercy, that was for sure. Archie stood to attention next to her, staring into the distance, jaw set as though he wasn't really part of what was happening. Always the cry-baby of the three of them, she'd somehow expected him to break down sobbing but he didn't. He'd no doubt been trained for death and had absented himself to another place where raw emotion was not admitted. She noted how he seemed taller and more muscular than the last time she'd seen him, nearly two years ago. In that time he'd grown different, with his dark-shadowed jaw and deeper voice. He didn't really look like her and Hugh and she found herself trying to work out who he resembled; her father, perhaps but on closer inspection, not really. More like their grandmother in colouring. Lottie noticed there was an impatient air about him, as though he wanted all this to be over and he could get away from them all. Lottie had hugged him to her when he picked her up from the station but there was an awkwardness of strangers that hung between them and it was unbearable, as though he too was slipping away from her. The Brig looked grey with unspent grief and her mother diminished, standing there in black, staring uncomprehending into the grave as though she wished she could be buried with her first-born. As none of them wanted to share their loss publicly, they waited, dignified, until they could close the front door to well-wishers and retire to separate rooms. Lottie had an uneasy sense that as a family they would never recover from Hugh's death and the process of destruction of the erstwhile tight unit had begun. Some families became closer in the face of adversity but unfathomably there was no sign of this happening with her own. She felt sure there would never again be the happy family picnics or Christmas mornings full of laughter round the tree. War had snapped its ugly fingers and in an instant, all that joy was gone, leaving fractured families for whom the very act of congregation just served to highlight distance.

*

"We therefore commit his body to the ground; earth to earth, ashes to ashes, dust to dust; in sure and certain hope of the Resurrection to eternal life, through our Lord Jesus Christ."

*

Lottie watched as first The Brig, then her mother scattered earth on the coffin. It made a light thud. People were looking at her, expectantly, waiting for her to do the same and she followed suit, stiffly followed by Archie. The whole service seemed a pointless, primitive gesture, ritualised by time and lacking in any substance. It meant nothing to her.

The family trailed in silence back to the house, heads down, and the mourners followed at a respectful distance, exchanging glances and looking forward to getting back into the warm. The Brig tried to take his wife's arm but she shook it off, albeit gently and discreetly, unable to stand physical contact. Once inside, they became dutiful hosts, handing out glasses of sherry and making small talk, counting the seconds until everyone left. Offers of condolence were received stiffly but gratefully, nonetheless. Lady Beauchamp distracted herself with handing out sandwiches and making cups of tea. At one point Lottie saw her legs begin to buckle with the strain of it all and she quietly went to her assistance.

"Can I help, Mother?"

Lady Beauchamp turned her head away and waved her hand in a dismissive gesture. "We have to get through today, darling. Please don't fuss. My goodness, we've run out of tea. I shall go and make some more."

"Why don't you let Mary do it?"

"Because I *need* to. Please, sweetheart, go and speak to Mr Williams. He looks awkward."

She did as she was asked and they talked woodenly about the price of corn and the wheat crop and not at any point of the elephant in the room. Already, it seemed the world was moving on.

*

After everyone left, the washing up was done, more logs were put on the fire in the drawing room and The Brig had taken her mother up to bed to get her settled, Lottie asked Archie if he would go with her to the barn.

"Why," he said slowly, putting the tea-towel down, "would you want to do that?"

"Because I need to see it. If I don't do it now, I'll never go in there again."

"Would that be such a bad thing?"

"Yes, it would."

He shrugged. "All right. Now?"

She nodded.

As they walked away from the house in silence, it began to snow again, leaving a telltale trail of their footprints behind them.

"When do you go back?" said Lottie, breaking the silence.

"Tonight."

"So soon?"

"Yes. What about you?"

"On Friday. I work thirteen days on and have two off. My CO let me take an extra day. I'll work it when it get back. It doesn't seem long, does it? I feel bad about leaving Mother and The Brig."

"Hitler won't wait for families to mourn their dead."

His tone seemed too matter-of-fact to Lottie and she glanced at him in surprise. On arrival at the door, they hesitated at the entrance.

"Shall I go first, then?" he said, suddenly taking charge.

"No." Pulling the door back, the gloom drifted from outside into the space, throwing the weak winter's light on the outline of The Bee. Lottie edged forward waiting for her eyes to acclimatise. On the face of it, everything looked the same but in reality, nothing *was*. She stopped holding her breath and found the place smelled of dust and ancient hay, just as she remembered it and not, as she'd expected, of death. She looked around wondering where Hugh had pulled the trigger but secretly dreading the thought of finding any evidence of it. There was none. The place had been thoroughly cleaned and tidied by soldiers billeted nearby, once the police were satisfied that Hugh had taken his own life.

"I still can't quite believe he…"

"Well, he did. He's gone, Lottie."

"You know Mother went into labour in here with Hugh?" Lottie found herself whispering.

"No, I didn't," he replied. With a sigh, he bent down and picked something up from under some bits of old straw. As he dusted it off, she saw was an old metal plane with its red paint chipped away."

"This was his!" said Archie. "I coveted it when I was little but he wouldn't let me have it."

"Well, have it now… if you still want it." Her tone sounded sharper than she meant it to.

Archie shook his head. "It belongs here." He put it on a shelf. "You know he hated me," he said suddenly, with his back to her.

"Who did?"

"Hugh."

"Don't be ridiculous, Archie! What on earth makes you say something like that?"

"He resented me. It was just you and him. I was just the annoying third child."

Lottie was staring at his at his back, aghast. "No!"

"Yes," he said matter-of-factly. "The sad thing is, I worshipped him." He gave a little laugh.

Horrified, Lottie grabbed him by his shoulders and turned him round. She was momentarily distracted by the size of them. He didn't even *feel* like Archie who she used to tease for having thin arms. "You mustn't think that!"

"No, it's *true*."

Lottie took a deep breath. "Hugh loved you. The last time I saw him he was so worried about you joining the army. He wanted to protect you."

"It doesn't matter, really, not now." For the first time since seeing him again, she recognised her small brother in his expression.

"Archie, it *really* does." And then a terrible thought struck her. "Do you think I don't love you?"

He thought for a moment. "I honestly don't know."

A huge sense of dismay and guilt engulfed her and she pulled him to her. "Well let me reassure you, I *absolutely* love you, more than I can say." She felt his shoulders suddenly sag and he let out a sob.

"I'm so sorry," she kept saying, over and over, tears running onto his rough uniform. "What did we do to you?"

"You were so close," he said through his tears.

"We were just closer in *age!* We never meant to shut you out."

"It's fine," he said, gently extracting himself.

"No, it's not at all fine. This has to change, starting now."

He blinked and rubbed at his eyes with the back of his hand.

She took the plane back off the shelf. "You take this and

whenever you have any doubt about Hugh or me, you remember what I've said. I *promise* you, Archie, he would have given you the world and I would too. The tragedy is that now, as an adult, he can never tell you himself that he loved you but I can, do you hear? Wherever we are and however long we walk on this earth, rest assured you are the most important person to me and don't you *ever* forget it."

CHAPTER 37

18th April 1942, Hamble, Southampton

On this day, sixteen U.S. Army Air Force B-25B bombers launch from USS Hornet, approximately 600 miles off Japan.

Despite being tired from her flight, Lottie breezed through the door of the dining room and found Ellen staring at the notice board. "Guess what?" she said, grinning.

"What?" Ellen said, turning.

"I'm off to Luton to do my class four training!" She waved a piece of paper in the air.

"Twin-engines! Well done, you." Ellen gave her a friendly punch on the arm.

"Yes, Wellingtons here I come. I think you'll be next. Lettice has already done hers ages ago. She said flying a bomber's a whole new experience. I expect it will be like flying an elephant after the Spit but I can't wait."

"It's bound to feel enormous! When do you go?"

"A week, tomorrow."

"Gosh, I hope they let you come back."

"I expect so. They just want to broaden the experience of the pool. We'll probably all have to do it now the Americans are joining. What were you looking at on the board?"

"Another invitation," she said with a chuckle.

"Who from?" said Lottie, looking over her shoulder.

"The RAF Officers at Stoney Cross, to drinks, next Saturday. They'll send cars if we let them know how many of us!"

"They must have heard about the new arrivals," said Lottie, pulling off her flight jacket. "Talking of which, are they here?"

"No. They're due shortly, I believe."

"It'll be nice to have a few more of us."

"Yes, I suppose so. I hope they have a sense of humour. Have you met any of them?"

Lottie frowned. "Just Mary Wilkins. She's nice."

"The place is going to feel positively crowded," said Ellen, picking up *The Evening Standard*. "'Darlan To Inherit Petain's Job'," she muttered reading the headline aloud. "Where are they staying?"

"Who?" Lottie was stretching the stiffness out of her neck.

"The newbies."

"Bursledon, I gather."

"When I spoke to Lettice earlier, she seemed very happy to be at White Waltham," said Ellen, from behind the paper, "and she'll be very glad to have missed the new influx, I dare say."

"I suppose it suits her better. She hated Leicester. Also Frankie Frances is heading up Ferry Pool One and I hear she's got an awful crush on him." Lottie grinned. "I honestly can't imagine her swooning over anyone."

"Indeed! I do know she didn't want to come back here."

"Well, the rumour is, she might have to, for a while at any rate."

"Oh? And by all accounts, the American intake has descended on Luton. Jolly good of them to join in the war, finally!"

"Well, I don't believe they're enjoying it. Lots of complaints apparently about the food and nobody turned out to meet their ship when it docked at Liverpool," said Lottie, perching on the arm of the chair, next to Ellen.

"Really?"

"Yes. According to Con they're in a tight band with their mentor, Jackie Cochran."

"I've heard that name being bandied about. Do you know anything about her?"

"Only that she's massively rich and very influential over the pond. Hugely well connected and I mean *really* well connected. She knows the Roosevelts and I believe, Churchill." Lottie was rubbing her feet to improve the circulation. "She's married to a cosmetics mogul. A little brash, I believe, and a bit of a busybody, according to Charlie Oliver."

"Pauline must hate her, already."

"I doubt Jackie's spending much time at White Waltham. Charlie said Mayfair is more her thing although she does drop in to the Air Ministry a couple of times a week. On the plus side, she is, I gather, very pro-women pilots and she really hates the Army Air Corps. She blames them for sabotaging the American pilot Betty Taylor Wood's plane."

"I thought that was just a rumour. Do you think she's right?" Ellen was quickly thumbing through the final pages of the paper.

Lottie thought for a moment. "Anything's possible, isn't it? She got killed. They don't want women anywhere near aircraft so the word is, they tried to make it look like pilot error. If they can make women look incompetent, they've got a stronger argument to stop us flying."

"But to deliberately sabotage a plane?" She folded the paper and put it down.

"I know. To prove a point, Jackie Cochran flew a bomber solo across the Atlantic in a sort of recruitment campaign."

"Oh that was her, was it?"

"It was, indeed. Claimed her plane was tampered with but she finally made it to Prestwick."

"Good for her!"

Lottie stood up and stretched. "Aren't you glad we don't have to do the Scotland runs anymore?"

"Absolutely! We really ought to at least try to make the new pilots feel at home, don't you think? I know we're busy and tired most of the time but I do think we should make an extra effort this evening."

"I agree. We'll ask Cook to do something edible and arrange a welcome drink or something?" Ellen yawned. "If I can stay awake, that is. I'll speak to Margot."

"I'm going home to have a bath," Lottie announced, getting to her feet. "Shall we meet back here at seven for drinks?"

"Sounds like a super idea."

*

The new intake, fresh out of training school seemed young and enthusiastic and despite only being a few years younger than Lottie, they seemed like schoolgirls.

"What are all those names on the curtains?" said Jackie Moggridge, in surprise.

"Visitors sign them," said Ellen, matter-of-factly. "It's all very relaxed here. A little like a mad boarding school when we're off duty."

"Sounds like fun," said Doreen Williams.

"It is, I suppose," said Lottie. "Everyone's very friendly. Come and meet Con, Lois and Audrey."

Con stubbed out her cigar and turned to face them. Doreen looked a little taken aback at her masculinity but recovered quickly.

"Hello," she said.

"Hello, I'm Connie, Con. Pleased to meet you."

"Yes, and you. I'm Doreen."

"This is Audrey," said Lottie.

"Oh, I remember you from the film. You looked very glamorous."

"Well, forget the glamour. It really doesn't exist." Audrey pulled a comical face.

"Obviously Audrey is beautiful. She just prefers not to be defined as such because more importantly, she's an adventurer," said Lottie, proudly.

Audrey laughed. "Quite right about the last bit!"

"Get her to tell you, one day, how she and her friend ended up in an air crash near Nairobi and wrote an SOS and gave it to a passing Maasai warrior, for delivery to the nearest town."

Audrey rolled her eyes.

"Really?" said Doreen, wide eyed.

"Absolutely true," said Lottie. "And she was captain of the women's Olympic ski team in 1936."

"Lottie, do stop, won't you?" said Audrey, laughing. "Come and say hello to Lois," she said to Doreen. "She's a damn fine skier, while we're on the subject. She represented Canada."

"I'm feeling a little out of my depth," said Doreen. "You're all so accomplished by far! What's your claim to fame?" she said to Lottie, with a look of panic.

"I don't have one but I suppose, there's still time. I'm working on just surviving the war, at present."

"Her current claim to fame is that she's a favourite with all the male officers. They positively swoon when she walks in. They've all been desperate to date her but she ignores all advances." Lois put out her hand to greet Doreen.

"Utter nonsense!" muttered Lottie.

"Would someone please turn off 'The Band Played On'?" Margot Gore called from across the room. "Honestly, there is a limit to how many times one can listen to the same gramophone record. Do play something else."

"Actually, I'm off home to bed," said Con, finishing her whisky.

"Me too," said Ellen. "We need to be up at six thirty. Let's hope the Hun give us a peaceful night. Did anyone check the weather for tomorrow?"

"Fine but a bit of low cloud at noon," said Audrey.

"We have several Spits to deliver from Chattis Hill to Brize Norton for radio and gun fitting so we shall start early," said Margot. "Please collect your chits by 7.45 a.m. Sleep tight, everyone."

CHAPTER 38

10ᵗʰ June 1942, Baker Street, London

On this day Nazis burn the Czech village of Lidice as a reprisal for the killing of Reinhard Heydrich. All male adults and children are killed and all females are taken to concentration camps.

W hen she'd been asked to drop in and see Pauline Gower at White Waltham, on her way back from delivering a Wellington to Lyneham, Lottie had no idea it would be to ask her to report to the War Office. Pauline had not given her much detail, she'd merely sat with an embossed letter in front of her and said, "The Whitehall lot want to see you, Lottie. Don't ask me why, they haven't said." Lottie noted that she didn't look overly pleased and unusually, avoided eye contact. It had been disconcerting and intriguing at the same time and she couldn't imagine what they'd want with her, unless they thought she knew something or even someone of interest. She couldn't for the life of her think that she did. As she rose to leave, Pauline had passed her a separate piece of paper with the address, date and time of the meeting and the name Miss Atkins. She told her she wasn't to say anything to any of the others. If they asked, she was to tell them she'd been granted leave for family business. It was just, Pauline said, 'protocol in these situations.' Lottie nodded, unsure of what 'these situations' could be.

*

It was raining in London as Lottie got off the tube at Westminster. Avoiding puddles and sand bags piled across pavements, she walked down Baker Street, looking for a block of apartments called Orchard Court. She had no clue as to who Miss Atkins was, or the reason for the meeting. It was all very strange. The train journey had been tedious from Southampton and she was too curious about what Miss Atkins had to say, to concentrate on her book. Two army soldiers had sat in her compartment, smoking heavily. One, who had rather a rough accent, had tried to engage her in conversation even though she'd made it perfectly clear she wanted to read her book. She'd answered politely but she'd been glad when they got off, heaving their kit bags onto their shoulders, smelling of stale sweat and laughing as they made their way along the platform.

*

Lottie arrived on time, outside the elegant townhouse, just off Baker Street at number 6, Portman Square. She rang the bell and stood back, her eyes taking in every piece of detail. A young man in flannel trousers and casual jacket opened the door. For a moment, Lottie thought she must have got the wrong place.

"Oh," she said, taken aback. "Is this number six?"

"Indeed it is," he replied, smiling. "Miss Beauchamp?"

"Yes. I'm here to see Miss Atkins." The whole thing was getting curiouser by the minute.

"Do come in." He opened the door wider and glanced past her as if to see if anyone was looking. "Awful weather. Let me take your coat and I'll show you through."

She'd expected to find a busy office within but was taken aback by the half-panelled hallway that had a rather worn carpet with a large grandfather clock at the end. Several rooms led off it and mostly the doors were closed and there didn't seem to be anyone else around. She handed over her coat and followed the young man through the second door on the left. Opening it, he stood aside to let Lottie past.

"Miss Beauchamp, lovely to meet you. I'm Vera Atkins and this is Captain Jepson. Thank you for travelling from Southampton to meet with us." The woman, dressed in civilian clothes, unfurled her tall, slim body from an armchair and rose to her full height, holding out her hand. She was attractive, perhaps mid-thirties, with dark hair and a rather deep, soft, upper-class voice which was clipped but with a very slight trace of foreign accent. The man, standing with his back to the tall window, was of indefinite age, dressed in army uniform. He had a small, military-style moustache and dark hair.

Lottie shook hands and looked around, expectantly.

"Do sit down. You must be wondering why you're here?" There

was a buff-colour file on a small side table, with the initials SOE and a number but no other writing on it. "I'll explain but first, can we get you a tea or coffee?" Jephson smiled and held his hand out to a seat.

The young man was standing in the doorway.

"Coffee, please." Lottie sat on the sofa. The furnishings she noticed were unremarkable but comfortable.

"Leon, would you be so kind?" Miss Atkins said, over her shoulder.

"Of course," he said, before closing the door behind him.

Vera Atkins picked up a silver cigarette box, opened the lid and offered one to Lottie.

"We work for a branch of Government called Special Operations Executive," said Jephson, sitting down opposite Lottie. She glanced at the older woman who held her cigarette right at the bottom of the V of her right hand between her index and forefingers and lit it, her mouth obscured momentarily by her manicured hand. Immediately she tilted her head towards the ceiling and blowing a stream of smoke into the air, Vera took a seat at the opposite end of the sofa and crossed her long legs. Lottie had no idea who or what Special Operations Executive was or what it had to do with her. Looking back at Jephson, she remained quiet.

"We work in intelligence. I'll cut to the chase. Your work in the ATA has been exemplary but more importantly, I understand you can speak fluent French and German?" Jepson's hand rested temporarily on the file but he didn't open it.

"Well, yes, my grandmother lived in…" Lottie frowned, wondering where this was going. Perhaps they were looking for translators. If so, she couldn't think of anything worse and she would have to somehow, politely decline.

"Strasbourg," Miss Atkins interrupted, regarding her. "And you had a German governess for many years."

Lottie was taken aback. How on earth did Vera Atkins know that and more importantly, why? Vera exhaled before stubbing out her half-finished cigarette in a rather full ashtray. A thousand questions ran through Lottie's mind but she stayed silent and waited.

"We need your help, Miss Beauchamp." Miss Atkins immediately lit another cigarette.

This, Lottie felt, was about to become awkward. "My help? Sorry, who is 'We'?" She wished they'd get to the point.

"The Department, moreover, your country. We need bright, resourceful women who can speak French and German, to join us. It's important work but dangerous. You need to understand that, and think carefully about it. If you agree to join, you'll be part of an elite group who will contribute significantly to us winning the war." Jephson stared at Lottie enigmatically. Leon tapped on the door and entered with a small tray containing two cups of coffee. He set them down and, wordlessly, left the room.

It sounded rather grandiose. Lottie wondered fleetingly what part Atkins and Jephson played in the Special Operations Executive.

"Milk?" asked Vera.

"A little, thank you."

"Tell me what you're thinking?" she said, passing her a cup and saucer.

Lottie took a sip and found the coffee was tepid. "I'm not really sure what to think. What exactly do you want me to do?"

"I can't tell you too much at present but the work is linked to overseas intelligence. First you will need to be assessed for your capability to do the kind of work we feel you are capable of undertaking. If you pass, we'll go on to discuss your role in detail and you can make your decision about whether or not to undertake the work we ask you to do. I'm sorry it's not very clear at the moment but the work of our department is, by necessity, top secret. For your own safety and that of others we limit information to a strictly need-to-know basis."

"Well, obviously if I can help in any small way," said Lottie, doubtfully.

Jephson and Vera Atkins exchanged glances.

"We hoped you'd say that," said Miss Atkins with a smile. "You've already signed the Official Secrets Act for the work you currently do. I'm sure I don't need to tell you it will apply to our meeting today and any further communication between the Department and yourself. To all intent and purpose, this meeting did not take place.

Do you understand?"

Lottie nodded. "Of course."

"We'll be in touch after I've made contact with your Senior Commander." Jephson got to his feet, signalling the interview was over. "In the meantime if you could keep a low profile. No press calls for photos, etcetera. I know they're intrigued by you ATA ladies but we need to keep you as safe as we can. I can tell you that all your details will be removed from ATA records, if you move across to the Department. For the rest of the war, you will be given a new identity and Lottie Beauchamp will disappear for the duration. As far as your family and friends are concerned, you will be working for the Civil Service on secret work that means you won't be contactable for long periods of time."

"Right." Her heart missed a beat. A new identity?

"Good to meet you, Miss Beauchamp," said Miss Atkins, showing her to the door.

"You too."

"We will be in touch in due course with details of when and where to report for assessment. Until you hear from us, continue with your day-to-day life as though nothing has changed."

Except, thought Lottie, her head spinning, it sounded as though everything had.

*

Behind the closed door, Jephson walked back to the window and looked out. "Ideologically she should be quite sound and by all accounts she's fearless and very mature. I see she lost her elder brother recently and her married lover before that."

Vera nodded. "Her father's a close aide to Churchill. I take it he won't try and block recruitment?"

"I gather not. He's in favour of his children making their own decisions." He sniffed. "The only question in my mind is the way she looks," he said, thoughtfully. "She's so fair skinned and blue eyed; the archetypal English Rose. I'm worried she'd stand out too much."

"We can tone down her hair. Make her mousey. Perhaps give her spectacles."

He turned. "Yes. If she passes assessment, The Firm can send her to Paris. She'll blend in more there. It's more glamorous. If we sent her south, to a small town, she'd stick out like a sore thumb." He took out a white handkerchief and blew his nose. "Sorry, damn hay fever season. We'd have to give her a solid cover story."

Vera nodded. "Fine, I'll let Buckmaster know."

"We have seven possible women recruits then?"

There was a knock on the door and they fell silent. "Come in," said Jephson.

Leon arrived with an envelope. "This has just been delivered by courier," he said, passing it to Jephson." He took it and read the contents quickly. "Right, Vera, I need to go. Get me a taxi would you please, Leon?"

"Yes of course, sir." He turned and closed the door behind him.

"Including Beauchamp, we have Borel, De Baissac, Sansom, Herbert, Aron and Nearne," continued Vera.

Jephson turned at the door. "Once we have the nod from Buck, we can get things organised. Borel is ready. If the rest prove themselves, which I have to say, I very much doubt and I'm still sceptical we should be sending women at all, but as we have no choice, we need them operational by late summer."

PART 3

CHAPTER 39

19th August 1942 – Hampshire, England

STS 31 Party No. 27 OB School 6

On this day, Operation Jubilee, a British/Canadian raid on Dieppe, France, ends in disaster. Most are captured or killed by German defence.

Shortly after her interview with Captain Jephson and Vera Atkins, Lottie got the call for her assessment. She left her ATA colleagues with little notice, explained away by family commitments at the farm. Hugging Ellen, she took the first, difficult step in her new covert life and lied her way out of the world she had come to love so much. Over the summer, she'd attended Special Operations Executive (SOE) Preliminary School at Wanborough Manor, where her character and potential to be a special agent were assessed by a series of tests and interviews but it was at Paramilitary School, in Scotland, that the fun had really begun. The physical training had been gruelling and was designed to get the recruits to a stage where they could credibly learn and execute unarmed combat, including the art of silent killing with a small knife, training to shoot a Colt .45, .38 and Sten Gun, 'killing' targets that appeared as life-sized figures set on winches to come at the trainees at high speed from behind trees, field craft, demolitions and basic radio communications. As it turned out, her tom-boy childhood on the farm had been excellent preparation and she relished every moment of her training, longing to share the experience with her closest friends and family but it was impossible. Having written to them all before she went 'off grid', she told them she'd been asked to join a Government team in London and that she'd not be in a position to contact them for a while. Reassuring her mother she'd be safe and requesting help from Vera Atkins to arrange assistance to Lady Beauchamp for the day-to-day running of the farm, she effectively put her life on hold and hoped that, if she didn't make it back, her family would understand and forgive her. Several of the original recruits with whom Lottie had started her training, hadn't progressed that far. They'd disappeared suddenly and were most likely on their way to what was known as The Cooler, to de-learn what they'd been taught, before being sent back to civilian life. The sense of failure was something everyone dreaded but in any event, to her relief, Lottie's report had been satisfactory and she'd gone on to the next stage.

*

Parachute training at Manchester, Ringway, had been exhilarating. The rush of adrenaline when Lottie had done her first jump from the aircraft had been second to none and it was quickly followed by another from a static balloon. The low heights of the jumps had been a little unnerving. It seemed the parachutes had only just opened in time, as the ground rushed towards her at deadly speed but thankfully she'd landed well both times. The next time she dropped out of a plane she realised, as she gathered up the white silk on her final jump and removed her 'striptease' jump suit, was likely to be under cover of darkness, in occupied territory.

*

By the middle of August, the weeks had passed quickly and Lottie suddenly found herself at what SOE called 'Finishing School'. Here, she would learn how to successfully play the part of a secret agent. Both male and female trainees arrived at the location, in darkness, in covered wagons to disorientate them. Immediately, they were split up and sent to different 'Houses' where they were given Security Talks by the House Commandant. He stood at the front of the room, legs slightly apart, hands behind his back, bespectacled and unsmiling as they filed in and quickly took their seats.

He waited for silence. "Good evening. This is the most important part of your training. You will therefore, in your own interest, be subject to strict security rules." His voice had traces of a northern accent.

Nobody moved. The mere thought of breaking a rule at that point, was beyond imagination. Lottie noticed the dull ceiling lights reflected on his Brylcreamed head as he addressed them. "I'm going to begin with General Security Precautions and Local Security Rules that must be followed at all times while you're here," he said. For the next fifteen or so minutes, he spelled out that trainees would be required to stay on site, hand over any identity documents and valuables.

Pacing back and forth at the front, he continued, staring at them through eyes as clear as his message: "You will not use the telephone while you're here and any letters sent to you or from you will be checked and censored. When you leave, if you ever recognise anyone from this course you must not acknowledge them, unless it's in a business capacity. You have been allocated quarters for sleeping. In a few moments, you will be shown to your rooms. Breakfast will be served at seven promptly and we will reconvene in this room for a further briefing at eight a.m. Now, I will bid you all goodnight." With that, he turned and left.

The men and women began to stir and look around at their colleagues. Lottie found herself scanning the room and making rapid judgements about who she immediately felt an affinity with. She judged those who were likely introverts and the more outgoing; the ones whose eyes darted nervously around and people who looked her in the eyes; fellow trainees that showed warmth and those who were of a different class. They weren't left alone for long, however. After a few minutes, the door opened again and a young man arrived to show them to their rooms.

*

Setting her case down on the now familiar military bed that seemed to follow her with rather comforting familiarity wherever she was sent, Lottie politely introduced herself to the other women who were billeted with her. Everyone had been told on arrival, to speak French at all times and that none of them were to divulge their personal details. The less they knew, the better it would be if ever they were interrogated in the field. It had been a rather sobering instruction and left little to talk about, other than the moment. It felt strange to Lottie that she would be spending time with people she was actively required to work with but not to get to know. It felt like she had entered a theatre where characters were assigned but the script withheld. Of the six of them sharing, three were considerably older: Lise had white hair, pale eyes and a quiet, pleasant manner. There was nothing about her that stood out as extraordinary except her apparent calmness. She and Lottie hung back and waited, politely, for the rest to choose which beds they wanted. The others had dark hair and eyes and looked plausibly French, unlike Lottie. Mary was tall with a rather handsome, angular face; Odette, vivacious and rather beautiful was perhaps in her late twenties and Jacqueline, she deduced, was more her own age and had a determined look about her. Only Helene looked strikingly different because she was, unmistakably, a Jew.

CHAPTER 40

23Rd September 1942, RAF Tempsford, Bedfordshire

On this day the Soviets go on counter offensive in Stalingrad.

The dull lights in the Nissen hut adjacent to the runway flickered occasionally and the place felt chilly. Lottie and her two fellow agents, Lise de Baissac and Andree Borrel, stood waiting in their jump suits, for their final briefing from Ernst Van Maurik. Operation Whitebeam was finally on and they were about to parachute into France. Vera Atkins was the epitome of reassurance. She reiterated HQ were there for them, always working behind the scenes for their safety.

"Empty your pockets," she said, quietly to Lottie. "We need to do a final check. It wouldn't do to find something that might cost you your life."

Lottie obliged, removing the gold compact, pencil and cigarette case filled with Gauloise cigarettes. They were the presents given to all of them, not merely as farewell gifts but practical things of value that could be sold or traded in an emergency. In addition, she had a box of French matches, some centimes and a money belt containing two hundred and fifty thousand Francs. In her sleeve pocket was a folding switchblade knife for cutting the parachute and in her leg pocket along with her flashlight, some rations in case she had to spend the night in the forest.

"Good, Lottie. All set. Now Lise."

Lise stepped confidently forward for her final inspection although her face was pale and lined under the light.

"Excellent. Finally, Andree?"

In silence, Andree emptied the contents onto the table. Neither Lise nor Lottie had met her before now. She'd been due to go to France weeks before but fate had intervened in the form of weather and she'd missed the last two full moons. Both of them immediately took to the beautiful, young Parisienne as she was full of fearless enthusiasm and vocal disgust for the Nazis.

"I want to get out there and get on with it," she said with a determined grin, making a pretend gun gesture. "Bang, bang!"

Lise raised an eyebrow and laughed. "Well, fingers crossed you will be rewarded, sooner rather than later."

Lottie perched herself on a table, moved her shoulders to loosen the growing tension and lit a cigarette. She wished they could get going. Weeks of intense agent training had changed her mentally and physically and while she was excited and nervous, she had matured beyond her years and had learned how to control her emotions. Vera looked over at her. "All good, Heloise?" She nodded. She'd gotten used to her new name and her transformation was complete.

"Yes, thank you. Just keen to board the aircraft." She thought about her cover story as a governess, brought in to teach the children of a family in Chantilly. The details of her new life had been drummed into her relentlessly over the final weeks of training and she barely felt like 'Lottie' any longer. The family she would be working for had become so real that she felt she had known them all her life and her fake identity made her feel like a lizard who had shed its original skin and grown a new one. England had become foreign and leaving her natural family and the memory of Gareth and Hugh behind, Lottie felt she was on her way home to France. Being Heloise was all consuming and she would deal with coming back to Lottie Beauchamp, the trainee archaeologist, if and when it happened. Outside on the concrete path, she heard footsteps as the door opened and Van Maurik arrived.

"Ladies, we've had a final weather report. We should have you underway shortly. Firstly I need to issue you with these." He divided three lots of pills and put them on the table. "This," he said, holding up the first, "is Benzedrine. Take one with a swig of cognac or coffee and it will keep you awake for several hours." He held up the second. "If you need to induce cramping or diarrhoea take one of these. And these are sleeping pills. When mixed with coffee or cognac, it will render someone insensible for up to six hours. Finally," he held up single tablet in a small rubber cover, "this is 'L', commonly known as cyanide. It's a suicide pill. If you bite on it, you'll be dead within fifteen seconds. One of these is sewn into each of your jackets, here." He gestured to Andree's right sleeve. Through the fabric Lottie could see the outline of a small round object. Do not confuse the tablets." A self-congratulatory smile played on his lips as though it was a favourite line he'd delivered time after time and it still amused him. "Is that clear to everyone?"

"Yes," they replied in unison.

Lottie tried not to dwell on the scenarios in which she'd willingly take cyanide.

"Right, let's get you into your harnesses."

They fell silent. Vera helped, checking and re-checking everything, like a school matron. "Identity papers, shovel, torch, compass, loaded revolver, additional cigarettes, matches, a small sum of local currency…"

Revolver. The word that would once have filled Lottie with unease was as now as common-place to her as 'nail-file' or 'lipstick' and she was quite certain she would use it, if she had to. She looked at Lise, the star of Beaulieu. She appeared, as ever, unruffled as they tightened the straps to her parachute harness.

"Do I look good in this?" Andree turned to her and struck a comic pose.

"Delicious," said Lottie. "An angel falling out of the sky! The reception committee will be swept away."

"Tres bon! To the Nazis I will be the angel of death!"

"I'm sure you will!" said Lise. "Are we ready?"

"Yes." Vera looked at Van Maurik and he nodded.

"Let's go and as we say in the department, 'Merde Alors!'"

"Fuck it then!" the women repeated.

CHAPTER 41

23rd September 1942 – RAF Tempsford, England

Also on this day Transport Number 36 departs with French Jews to Nazi Germany.

The three women shook hands with Vera Atkins and walked out of the Nissen hut to the Whitely on the runway, to begin their journeys. It was a perfectly still night, illuminated by a bright, full moon that cast its silver light over the otherwise deserted airstrip. Falling silent, they climbed into the back of the aircraft and sat on the sleeping bags that had been provided to enable them to get some precious rest on the journey. Sleep, however, was the last thing on Lottie's mind. Vera gave a wave, her expression reassuring like that of a mother dropping her children off to school for the first time and she stood watching until the door of the aircraft was closed. They couldn't see outside from within, as the windows had been blacked out. As the anonymous pilot started the engine and began to taxi down the runway, Lottie's life as a secret agent felt suddenly very real.

*

The Dispatcher was a man of about forty, balding with a cheery demeanour and a cockney accent. He shouted above the noise of the engines, "Good evening, ladies. I'm going to be looking after you for the duration of the flight. When the time comes for you to jump, I'll be responsible for ensuring your safety. When the pilot signals we're in the correct position and at the right altitude, I'll shout 'Action Stations'. The hole will open." He signalled down at the bomb hole in the floor of the fuselage. "Just as you were briefed at Manchester, I'll double check your harness, connect you to the static wire and the first of you will sit with your legs dangling over the edge. When I raise my arm you will go, immediately. You first," he said, pointing to Andree. "You second," to Lise, "and you, third," to Lottie. For security, he was not allowed to know their names. All women agents were known simply as 'Janes' and all men as 'Joes'. "My recommendation is that you don't look down until your chute opens. Don't hang around to think about it, as we need to drop you as close together as possible and on target. Any questions?"

"What are those?" said Lottie, pointing at piles of what looked like pamphlets.

"Propaganda leaflets. We call them 'Mein Pamph'! We'll be chucking those out over Orleans to make the Jerries think that's why we're flying over. It's a decoy, that's all. They won't twig we're dropping agents at the same time. It's also designed to let the locals know they've not been forgotten and to remind them that De Gaulle is beavering away in pursuit of their liberation, in London."

The plane hit an air pocket and dropped suddenly, making them jump. "You might want to hang on just while we're going over The Channel," said the Dispatcher. "It could get bumpy. Nothing to worry about. Anyone hungry? We've got an assortment of in-flight treats, including sandwiches and chocolate and if your nerves are getting the better of any of you there's a tot of rum. If you can manage something, please do. You don't know when you're going to get your next meal."

"I'll take some chocolate," said Andree, wriggling her bottom half into a sleeping bag. "I would much prefer having my feet on the ground than in this bouncing, windowless tube!"

"I think I'll start with a cigarette," said Lise.

"It will be fine. It's just turbulence. Really nothing to worry about." Lottie wrapped the sleeping bag round her feet. The temperature had dropped due to altitude in the back of the plane and there was the slightly sickly smell of newly printed paper pamphlets and gasoline. She would have much preferred to be up front, flying the thing, but those days were behind her for the foreseeable future. There was, though, something quite comforting bobbing about in the air, once again. Had she made the right decision to give up flying and throw herself into darkness, she wondered? The answer came back immediately that she had. This was her chance to make a real difference and avenge the deaths of Gareth and Hugh.

It was hard to chat freely above the noise and in front of the Dispatcher, so one by one, they fell silent. Lise sat with her back against her parachute with her eyes closed but Lottie sensed she wasn't asleep. Andree was staring ahead, eating her chocolate as the aircraft gently rose up and down as it encountered air pockets. A random vision of her mother sitting in the cellar of the house knitting, drifted into Lottie's head. She must worry endlessly about the safety of her remaining two children. In lots of ways and given the state of the world, it must be better, Lottie thought, not to have any. Since Hugh's death her mother had become increasingly diminished as though her spirit had been drawn away into darkness and couldn't find its way back from the unbearable loss. Lottie made a silent apology for causing her further anxiety before forcing the thought away and replacing it with the practicalities of the next few hours. If the reception committee made one small error or the plan had been leaked to the French Militia, it would all be over in a heartbeat and the chances were that she would be dead this time tomorrow. Considering the odds, she put success at no more than fifty-fifty but there was no point in dwelling on it as she wouldn't know anything about it. If it happened, she just hoped it would be over quickly. From now on, her life and that of others would depend on their wits, with no room for errors of judgement. Instinctively she felt for the reassuring outline of the revolver in her pocket. Across the gangway, she could see the metal containers containing guns, ammunition and a wireless that would be parachuted in with them. Once again, she ran over the procedure, in her head. On landing, everyone would move fast, under cover of darkness and within a few days of her arrival, she'd be expected to start work, delivering messages for Michel Dechanel, the head of Waterman Circuit. She looked over at Andree and Lise and wondered what they were thinking and if they were scared. Apprehensive maybe but it would be impossible to do this job if one was really frightened. Assessment and training had done a thorough job of removing the ones without the appetite for a high-risk, clandestine existence and Lottie knew the jangling of the nerve endings in her own stomach was nothing more than sheer excitement.

CHAPTER 42

24th September 1942 – Blois, France

On this day, German forces in Stalingrad cut the 62nd Army in two, at the Volga River.

Lottie could feel the rush of cold air on her legs as they dangled over the gaping mouth of the fuselage. She watched as Andree and Lise released into the darkness and disappeared silently. The dispatcher, illuminated by the green light, shouted, "Action stations!" and she closed her eyes and tipped forward, into the abyss. For what seemed like eternity, she free-fell through the sky until her chute opened and jerked her back from death, like an adult pulling a child to safety on a busy road. The ground slowed its rapid approach as she floated down, towards the red lights and flashing white light of the reception committee. *So far, so good,* she thought, listening for dreaded gunfire but there was nothing except the noise of the aircraft moving off into the distance. The harvest moon glowed orange in contrast to the night sky and on the ground, Lottie could see the outlines of spent parachutes on the grass, a hundred or so yards apart. Small figures worked quickly to release themselves and gather in the billowing evidence of their landing that had, for a short time, been a life-saver before turning instantly into a betrayer. Suddenly, Lottie was down with a thud, pulled forwards by the silk balloon as it flapped, reluctant to be restrained and eager to dance back up in the air and announce its presence. The last to jump, she saw she'd landed in an adjacent field, just short of a wooded copse. Working quickly, she released herself from her chute and listened but there was no sound, save for the breeze trying to reclaim the silk for the air. Sprinting forward, she began to gather it into a bundle, at the same time looking around for a suitable place to bury it. She didn't have time to wait for the reception committee to find her and help. The grass beneath her feet was dry and baked hard and the warm earth smelled deeply organic, of cut straw and wild mushrooms. To dig it would take up valuable time. She chose instead to give it a woodland burial, where the soil was more giving. Breathless, she removed her suit, finished her task and crouched on her haunches, like a wild animal on high alert.

*

She didn't have to wait long. The crack of twigs gave the person away, as they moved tentatively through the trees. She stiffened, hand on her revolver and listened.

"Heloise?" The whispered voice of a man cut through the undergrowth.

Standing up, she emerged from behind the tree to greet the shadowy figure, wiping the soil from her hands.

Shaking her hand, the young man asked her to come quickly and she followed. At the road, he put his arm out, gesturing her to wait while he checked for any movement before waving her forward into the next field where several men were loading the dozen metal canisters onto the back of a farm truck. He didn't stop but carried on walking, beckoning her towards the trees beyond, where there was a small hut in the woods. "Please wait in there. Your comrades are already waiting. At first light, we'll come back and take you to Avaray."

*

Andree and Lise welcomed her with a hug and a sense of barely contained euphoria passed between them at having arrived safely. Dressed as French civilians and now unarmed, if caught, the three of them would have to explain the reason for being out past curfew, hiding in a rundown building and they would feel more secure, once they were at the safe house. For the next few hours though, there was a feeling of comfort in still being together and, unable to sleep, they sat talking in hushed tones, falling into silence at the sound of a fox calling or the rustle of a nocturnal animal. Rural France was asleep behind its battered shutters, oblivious of the beginning of a new dawn.

*

As soon as the shadows began to fade and the birds began to stir, they were collected by horse and cart. Ordered to lay low in the back, cocooned by freshly harvested hay bales, the horse plodded forward along the lanes with his visibly innocuous load and brave driver. If the local police stopped them and carried out a search they would all be arrested and likely executed. Still running on adrenaline, Lottie looked forward to getting some rest. It was impossible to see which direction they were travelling in or to know how long the journey would take, as they wound their way down the country roads. Andree had drifted off to sleep with the motion of the cart but Lise was awake. Every so often they mouthed short sentences to each other but it was too dangerous to speak. The cart was uncomfortable and each time the horse hit a rut, it jarred Lottie's bottom and her leg was becoming cramped where Andree's arm rested heavily on it. Just when she thought she could bear it no longer, the horse stopped with a jolt. Lise looked across at her, the whites of her eyes flecked with the pinkness of a night without sleep. They listened for voices but there were none and finally they heard the sound of a door or gate being moved with hinges that needed oiling. Lise mouthed the word, "Here?" as the horse began, without warning, to move forward again. Lottie shrugged, making a crossed finger sign. Andree stirred and Lottie reached out, covered her hand gently over her mouth, lest she spoke and gently shook her shoulder. She woke with a start and Lottie put her finger to her lips. The young woman nodded. The cart came to a stop once again and this time there were voices, a woman and a man talking to the driver. A moment later, the bales of hay were being pulled away to reveal them.

"We have arrived," said the driver. "Please come quickly."

CHAPTER 43

24th September 1942, Avaray, France

Also on this day, over Stalingrad, Soviet pilot Olga Yamschchikova becomes the first female pilot to shoot down an enemy aircraft.

The elderly Bossards, fish merchants by trade, hated the Nazis. They had been easy recruits for diminutive Yvonne Rudellat, SOE Agent, code name Jaqueline, who had arrived early in France, by boat. As soon as she saw Lise, Andree and Lottie, she hugged each of them, fiercely.

"You will stay here with my friends for the next few nights, so you can rest before continuing on to your assignments."

Mme Bossard, dressed in her night garment and shawl, was stirring a pot of stew on the range, a satisfied smile playing on her lips. Every now and again, she glanced shyly over at the four women and nodded. Monsieur Bossard, stick thin with patches of walnut-weathered skin visible beneath grey stubble, pulled a bottle from a mahogany dresser and poured thick, amber liquid into small glasses. He toasted them and they all drank. Lottie shivered as the alcohol burned her throat and made its way down her chest and into her bloodstream. As soon as they put the glasses down, they were refilled.

"Here's to the King of England!" said Jaqueline, downing hers.

"The King of England!" the rest chimed.

"Where will we sleep?" asked Lise.

"There is only one spare bedroom so it will mean sharing and you can't leave the room unless told otherwise. You will have to be very quiet. Other villagers call in during the day and it's important that everything appears normal. Few people in the area support the Allies and there's a high chance of you being arrested. Now, there's a cellar beneath our feet. If anyone unexpected comes to the house you will be told to hide down there. Remember not to leave beds unmade or personal items anywhere."

Monsieur Bossard pointed under the huge table. "That's the trap door."

"Unfortunately, being on the border, the area is well-policed and there are a lot of checks," continued Jaqueline.

In the half light, Mme Bossard, her grey hair escaping slightly from the restraint of its grips, began to ladle stew onto plates and placed a large loaf of bread on the table. It smelled, to Lottie, divine. Rubbing her eyes, she dipped a slice of freshly baked bread into the rich gravy, not realising just how hungry she was. The clock on the kitchen wall chimed seven a.m.

"Delicious, thank you," she said to Mme Bossard who beamed with pleasure. Fleetingly, Lottie thought about what the Gestapo would do to this sweet couple if they were found to be shielding spies. Undoubtedly they would be shot. She stopped chewing for a moment. The reality of the risk they were taking made her shudder.

"Are you all right, Heloise?" Lise looked across the table at her.

"Yes, fine. So, Jaqueline, how is everything going?"

Jaqueline scooped a black and white cat up and held it to her, lovingly stroking its head. "Well, it's true that nothing happens quickly," she said cheerfully as the cat rubbed its face into her neck. "Pierre and I seem to spend most of our days looking itinerant and trying not to attract too much attention. I've taken some messages to Paris but we've been waiting for arms. The drop that accompanied you should help but…" she shrugged, "it's simply not enough."

"What happens from here?" said Lottie.

"Tomorrow I will see a man about train tickets for you all. In a day or two, you'll be dropped at different local stations at staggered times to avoid attracting attention. By the way, the Gestapo are stopping trains frequently and running spot checks, so make sure all your papers are handy. After that, you're on your own until contacted by the circuits at your destinations. For now, you might as well get some rest. People rise early here and it's not safe for you to go out." Lottie could feel her eyes getting heavier as the hot food and alcohol subdued her adrenaline and she became sleepy.

"Our lovely Mme Bossard will show you to your room." Jaqueline looked over at her fondly as she put the cat gently on the floor and got to her feet. "I'll be back tomorrow. Sleep well." With a grin, she was gone.

*

The room was small but comfortable with a double and single bed crammed in. Mme Brossard pointed to a chamber pot, under the large bed.

"Who wants the single?" said Lise.

"Well, given we all must smell like the farmyard, it hardly matters." Andree pulled a face.

"I really don't mind." Lottie felt at that moment she could have slept standing up.

"Well, in that case, if neither of you mind, I'll take it. My back is aching a bit and I don't want to keep either of you awake, tossing and turning." Lise stretched and winced.

"Nothing bad?" said Lottie.

"No, just landed awkwardly."

"Do you want me to rub it for you?" Andree held out her hands, eyes wide. "Look, very strong fingers."

"Bless you, no. I just need to lie down."

"Does anyone know where our cases are?" Andree looked round the empty room.

"Under the kitchen floor, I would think," said Lottie. "The Bossards won't want us unpacking."

"In which case we'll have to sleep in our underwear."

"Looks like it… It was good to see Jaqueline… Sweet dreams," said Lottie, flopping onto the soft mattress in the airless, shuttered room. Within seconds, darkness descended, taking her down to a different place and she was asleep.

CHAPTER 44

26th September 1942, train north to Paris

On this day senior SS official August Frank issues a memorandum detailing how Jews should be "evacuated".

Lottie sat in a compartment at the rear of the crowded train as it chugged its way through the flat countryside of the Loire, en route to Paris. On her lap was a battered copy of *Les Fleurs du Mal*, by Charles Baudelaire. She didn't feel at all like reading poetry but it would be a useful deterrent should someone want to strike up a conversation with her. No longer blonde and with her features partially covered by a large pair of spectacles, she looked very plausible as Heloise Fournier. There wasn't much of Lottie's own past she could use apart from her love of history and literature and so, she had to create Heloise from scratch. At SOE Finishing School, she'd spent hours getting to know her character and being tested time and time again on the details surrounding her birth and childhood, deceased parents and lack of siblings. She'd been woken suddenly at times, in the middle of the night and random questions fired at her about Heloise's past. When half asleep, agents were most likely to make mistakes. If she was caught and interrogated, Lottie could not afford to get any of the details wrong. She'd had it drummed into her that 'dropped guard' could result in capture, torture and death and she had no intention of experiencing any of those.

Her new charges were two children from a wealthy Chantilly racing household. Monsieur and Mme Toussant, the parents of the children, had lost their fortune to the Nazis, who had stolen and shipped their thoroughbred racing stock to Germany and requisitioned the stables to house their own injured horses. As a result, the Toussants were sympathetic to the Resistance and clearly judged the risk to their family of having a member of the Resistance under their roof was an acceptable one. Whatever happened, fundamentally, she would always *be* Lottie. Her true identity mattered. It was like words running through a stick of rock and couldn't be changed. By the time she left for France, the role of Heloise had become Lottie's alter ego and she took her over in the way she presumed happened when an actress stepped onto a stage. She now thought and acted like her, even she realised, eating differently and walking with more measured steps. Unlike Heloise, fun-loving Lottie would not have blended happily into the background and noticed things like the man currently standing on the station platform with rather obvious British cufflinks or the way that someone smoked a cigarette. Her brain had been changed with SOE training into something that now relentlessly processed the smallest of details around her. The words of the SOE Manual were imprinted on her brain – 'Like a primitive man in the jungle, the agent must always be alert. This is all he has…' Vigilance meant survival and her senses had been honed. There was, she admitted to herself, a sense of pleasure in getting one over on the Germans, although not, she concluded, as much for her as for the feisty Andree Borrell. She reluctantly rested her head on the rather grubby train headrest that had traces of grease from previous heads and stared out of the window. She hoped Andree had reached Paris safely. Lottie sternly reminded herself to forget her real identity and to always think of her as 'Denise' and of Lise De Baissac as 'Irene'. She shouldn't have even known their real names but she'd heard two officers at training school talking as she'd passed one of the offices. She yawned and closed her book, avoiding eye contact with the woman opposite her and the bodies wedged against the glass of the compartment window, unable to move. There was no sign of any delay to the trains, which suggested the Gestapo hadn't bothered to stop and search along the line but that wasn't necessarily a good sign. Thinking about her final destination, she wondered when the head of the Waterman Circuit, French vet, operating under the name Michel Dechanel, would make contact with her, hoping she would hear soon so that her real work could begin. She envisaged it might be difficult to juggle her duties as a governess with her job as a courier for Waterman and there would be times it would inevitably take her away from her base in Chantilly. Children noticed these things and asked questions, so for their safety, she would have to be very careful. The train suddenly veered to the left as it went over a set of points, making the crowd mutter apologies as they lost their balance and crushed the person next to them, even more. Grateful for having a seat and for the open window that allowed a little air to circulate, Lottie took out her powder compact and applied a little to her cheeks, idly wondering what Michel would be like. London had not given her a description. Tall, short, blonde, dark haired or perhaps red, it mattered little. The important thing was that they would work well together and get things done.

*

The train slowed and pulled into a station and suddenly the atmosphere changed. On the platform stood six German soldiers, steely blue eyes scanning each compartment until the train drew to a halt. Uneasily, Lottie mentally visualised the contents of her suitcase and hastily ran over her story once again. As they started to open the doors they shouted orders at the passengers to get out with their luggage. Heloise lifted her brown suitcase from the luggage rack and stepped down to the platform, keeping her head low.

"Quickly!" they shouted. "Stay with your luggage!"

Sun glinting off the butts of their Mauser rifles, they pointed them at several young men and barked an order to open their bags and briefcases. With a sense of dismay, Heloise immediately identified the one they were searching for by his body language. He was standing a few feet from her. Beads of perspiration began to develop on his forehead as bit by bit he lost his composure and his eyes, magnified by his spectacles, searched frantically for an escape exit from the station but there was none. By now the platform was teeming with soldiers and they were belligerent and efficient in their search. His silent panic was infectious and she looked away, not wanting to draw attention to him, hoping that something would divert the search party but nothing did. As one soldier caught sight of him inching away from his bag, he sounded the alarm and like a pack of adolescent jackals they sniffed the air, smelt the scent of their quarry and bore down on him as he was ordered, protesting, face down on the concrete in front of her, hands behind him. Heloise flinched, as his arm grazed hers as he was forced down and the crowd shrank back. Suddenly the stark reality of her role was laid out before her, pleading his innocence to boys half his age. To the right of them, a young child began to cry loudly, no doubt sensing the anxiety of his young mother who kissed his head and shushed him. Within seconds, the man was dragged to his feet and taken off with his bag, leaving behind his wire-rimmed spectacles now bent and lenses smashed, on the concrete platform floor. Two soldiers remained, faces impassive, commanding the passengers to re-board the train in French but with distinctly German accents. Nobody paused lest it be construed as defiance and there was a scramble back into the compartments. A whistle blew and the train began to move slowly off once more, to the sound of a single gunshot.

*

Paris was still recognisable amid the austerity of war, although its striking façade did not completely disguise the changes. Ornate, wrought-iron balconies were no longer decorated with the final flush of bright, trailing geraniums. Instead they became home to pots of sickly vegetables and the odd scrawny chicken, rendered barren by lack of food. Heloise negotiated the pavements of Austerlitz, on her way to the bus that would hopefully take her to Gare du Nord and on, from there, to Chantilly. At one time she would have just hailed a taxi but there weren't any, only pedi-cabs, ridden by men demanding a high tariff and the only cars on the road were for the exclusive use of the Nazis. Swastika flags billowed confidently in the late summer air giving a stark flavour of what occupation looked like. It was true, life continued with a veneer of elegance but under an atmosphere of subdued anxiety that made her shudder. This, she thought, could be London if things went wrong.

*

The bus arrived on time. People waited patiently for passengers to alight at the back. A well-dressed woman with a small dog picked her way carefully down the staircase that curved round, from the open seating area at the top, like a mini helter-skelter. The driver waited while a man retrieved his prized bicycle from the rack at the back, which would have cost him a month's salary. When it was her turn to board, Heloise held her case aloft and climbed to the seating area above.

"Mademoiselle, can I help you?"

The man was about her age. He was smartly dressed but she

noticed the knot in his tie was stained and his suit a little threadbare round the cuffs.

"Thank you but I can manage," she said, not meeting his eye, wanting to avoid any opportunity for conversation.

He shrugged and slid into the seat in front of her. Lottie watched Paris from above, as the bus made its way down the streets, now devoid of traffic, punctuated by cafés that no longer spilled out onto the pavements filled with happy pre-war people taking long lunches. Nonetheless the streets were busier than Lottie had expected, since the Parisiennes had drifted back into the capitol following occupation but the people, she noticed, now walked like aliens in their own land.

CHAPTER 45

26th September 1942, Chantilly, France

Also on this day the submarine H.M.S Thorn is reported missing, considered lost.

Maurice Toussant, a stocky, ruddy-cheeked gentleman, with an imposing moustache and cheerful disposition, picked Lottie up from the station in a horse-drawn cart. His car had been stolen by the Nazis, he said, along with his horses. When she asked about the children Lucien and Sylvie he shook his head sorrowfully, saying they were 'monsters' and that his wife Margot had aged considerably since his daughter, who was now eight, had started to talk. Lottie, who had limited experience of young children other than her brother, Archie, when he was little and a few cousins, felt disconcerted. In reality, she'd given the actual job of governess very little thought, her mind having been occupied with the more risky business of being an agent. But it was suddenly dawning on her that controlling two unruly children might prove quite tricky. As the horse trotted confidently home and Maurice chatted as though they'd known each other for decades, she wondered what she'd let herself in for.

On meeting however, the children could not have been sweeter. Sylvie had insisted on taking her hand and showing Lottie to her room and Lucien, aged six, took her to see his pet rabbit. Maurice introduced Margot as his 'beautiful wife', to which she responded with a rebuke and blushed deeply.

"You will have to excuse Maurice, Heloise. He's a terrible joker. Don't take anything he says seriously!" She looked at him affectionately. "I suppose you told her the children are badly behaved?"

All at once he looked wounded. "But of course. That way, Heloise will be pleasantly surprised."

Margot shook her head and Lottie laughed.

"They seem adorable."

"Well, not always but I think they will enjoy having you to stay with us. The war has limited their social interaction."

"I do hope so."

"If you will excuse me," said Maurice, "I have spinach to plant. The war has turned me into a reluctant gardener. Please make yourself comfortable."

"Thank you," said Lottie. She looked round to make sure the children were out of earshot. "Please rest assured I will do my very best to keep you and your family safe."

He nodded, his expression suddenly serious, as he turned on his heel and left.

"What have the children been told about my work here?" Lottie asked Margot.

"That you are a friend of the family and you'll sometimes help them with their schoolwork and give them lessons in German and French."

"What about routine?"

"You mean, their day?"

"Yes," said Lottie. "Sometimes I'll be required to go off and work at odd times and at short notice."

"Don't worry. I'll distract them. Despite what Maurice told you, they're very obedient."

Lottie nodded.

"Tomorrow, Maurice will call the vet out to see to the pony. He will be invited to stay to supper. His name is Michel Dechanel."

Lottie nodded. Margot looked away quickly, distracted by the sudden sound of running footsteps.

"Now, as my children have returned we should leave you in peace to unpack and have some refreshment."

"Thank you, Margot, for your hospitality."

"It's our pleasure."

*

Lottie's brightly lit bedroom in the large house overlooked the Chateau and the racecourse in the distance. She placed her suitcase on the wrought-iron bed and began to unpack. On the dressing table, Margot had provided some homemade lemonade and bread and cheese. As she had been travelling for most of the day, she suddenly realised how hungry she was, so she sat in the old armchair in the corner of the room and ate. When she finished, she got on with unpacking the few things she now possessed. They hardly filled one drawer but it was essential to have as little as possible when she might need to leave quickly. Taking out her food coupons, she put them to one side to give to Margot, determined to be as little of a financial burden on the family as possible. If food had been scarce in Britain, it was even worse in occupied France. The Germans sent whatever fresh produce France grew, back to Germany and the country had turned from a sophisticated culinary cornucopia, to an unwilling exporter. People were hungry, Lottie knew, and there was now a thriving black market for goods. Hunger was very slowly fuelling anger at occupation like a spark against slightly damp wood but it would be hard in the face of starvation for the French to remain passive for ever.

CHAPTER 46

1St October 1942, Chantilly, France

On this day the P-59 Airacomet US Jet fighter makes its maiden flight.

As he entered the room, Michel Dechanel, was unexpectedly arresting. At over six feet tall, he was broad-chested with high cheekbones and brown eyes that in the light of the Salon, appeared golden. Lottie thought he looked more like a Hollywood film star than a French vet who specialised in equine health. When they were introduced by Maurice, he didn't smile but simply nodded, tight lipped, eyes barely registering her, as if he was brought there under duress and was really too busy to hang around.

"I'll leave you to talk," said Maurice.

"So?" said Lottie, breaking the awkward silence in the room.

Michel cleared his throat. "I did not ask for a woman courier." He sounded petulant.

For a moment Lottie was taken aback before her mouth opened. "There's a war on. It's not Christmas. You don't get to choose!"

He glared. "Can you read a map? Fire a gun? Slit a German throat?" He made the motion with his finger.

"Yes, to all. Can you?" She spoke quietly and confidently despite feeling her blood rapidly heating.

"Well, we shall see. Don't mess up. I haven't got time to look after you."

Lottie took a deep breath and glared at him. "As half your countrymen are busy, passively turning a blind eye, you might be pleased to be working with an English woman!" She could feel a rash of anger developing around her neck at his breathtaking arrogance

181

and an uncharacteristic flash of temper got the better of her.

Looking her up and down, he murmured with a look of surprise, "Well, thank goodness the British have arrived."

Lottie could barely contain her anger but she held back and said coolly, "Now our mutual disappointment has been aired, perhaps we can get down to work?"

He thought for a moment then said, resignedly and with less aggression in his voice, "We still have no wireless operator so our progress is woefully slow. I have a message for you to take to Prosper during the day on the sixth. There have been a few problems with his arrival." Michel looked disdainful. "You will do this via your colleague, Denise, in Paris. Her address is 51 Rue des Petites Écuries, 10th Arrondissement." He held out an envelope. "If you find yourself about to get stopped and searched, open the envelope and put the message in your mouth. The paper is very fine and you should have no problem in swallowing it."

Lottie gave a curt nod.

He looked awkward for a moment. "By the way, I will be invited here for dinner on Saturday the tenth. It will be easier to operate if we have a legitimate reason to be seen together in public. The Chantilly people will be treated to a sham romance between us. I hope you won't find that idea too repulsive but I have to protect this family." His eyes appraised her, with evident distain.

Lottie felt herself recoil as the film star image he arrived with, morphed into something quite repugnant. "I agree, it's an act, like all of this. Our personal objections are not relevant."

"Fine, I'll come round on the evening of the sixth to see if there's a response. If you need to contact me in the meantime, tell Maurice. I'll see myself out. Goodnight."

Lottie felt the urge to walk over and slam the door behind him, but she didn't. Who on earth did he think he was? She paced across the kitchen, fuming. Could she read a map or fire a gun? She hadn't come all this way and endured all the SOE training to be treated like that. She would show him just how competent she was and *he* would choke on his words.

Maurice knocked on the door. "I saw Michel leave," he said. "I assume he chose not to stay for dinner?" He raised an eyebrow.

"No." Lottie forced a smile. "Have the children gone to bed?" She felt quite shaken by the immediate degree of animosity between her and Michel and how badly their first meeting had gone.

"They have but they would like you to say goodnight, if you don't mind?"

"Of course not. I'll go up now." She brushed past him and made her way up the stairs.

"Heloise…" Maurice was standing in the doorway.

She turned and looked at him. "Yes?"

"He's a good man."

"I'm sure he's passionate about his cause." She continued up the stairs and found Margot reading a bedtime story to Lucien, hair falling over her face as she pretended to be a lion. Lottie smiled at the sound of him giggling as his mother tickled him, one hand trying to pull her hair back behind her ear. Making her way to Sylvia's room, she found the young girl talking to her favourite doll, Catherine.

Lottie sat on the edge of the bed. "Where's Catherine going?" she said. "She's looking awfully smart in that dress."

"She's going to a party, just like Mother and Papa used to, before the war."

"Well, when she comes back, I'm sure she'll tell you all about it."

"Yes, she will. I'm her best friend." The child looked thoughtful. "Did you go to parties too?"

"Not often, no. I looked after my mother."

"Did you have a husband?" She remained looking at Catherine, fiddling with her hair.

"No. Now young lady, too many questions. It's late and you need to go to sleep and let Catherine go out or else she'll be late." She stopped and listened. "Can you hear that?"

"What?" said the child, wide eyed.

"I can hear a carriage arriving for Catherine."

"May I look?"

"No, I'll escort her to the front door."

Sylvia kissed her doll on the cheek. "Please be back by midnight or your prince will turn into a frog." She passed the doll to Lottie.

"Have you said goodnight to your mother?"

"Yes. Goodnight, Heloise."

"Goodnight, Sylvia, sweet dreams."

Lottie put out the little light and waited until Sylvia was asleep before tucking the doll under the blanket next to her and making her way downstairs to dinner.

CHAPTER 47

6th October 1942 – Chantilly, France

On this day, the Queen Mary, carrying thousands of US troops, slices HMS Curacao in half, killing 239.

Lottie sat down to breakfast of freshly made bread and damson preserve. There was no butter but it really didn't matter. The children, who were sitting quietly opposite her, were always well behaved at the table and had nice manners. When they were finished, they were excused to get ready for school. Lottie had had a disturbed night, thinking about her meeting with Michel, asking herself over and over, how it had got off to such an awful start. She was cross with herself for snapping at him. It had been rude and offensive to say that about his countrymen but she hadn't expected him to dismiss her so readily. As she tossed and turned she asked herself if she'd been stupid to expect a warm welcome. She hadn't, by any stretch of the imagination thought there'd be bunting and a band playing but neither had she anticipated outright hostility. It knocked her off guard and she needed to be more measured in future as there was no time for ill feeling. However, she drew the line at offering an apology and decided she would just have to prove her worth at the end of the day. Their lives and others within the Resistance, including those who sheltered them, depended on Michel and her working well together.

"Please can Heloise walk us to school?" said Sylvia, sliding off her chair.

Margot looked at Lottie.

"Of course, if you would like me to?"

"Yes!" cried both children.

"Then you had better go upstairs and brush your teeth," said Margot.

They ran off and Lottie heard them arguing on the stairs.

"I need to go into Paris after I've dropped the children off."

Margot nodded. She didn't question why. "There's a seamstress on Rue Lafayette, opposite St Vincent de Paul Church. She's closed between one and three. If you get questioned at any time, tell the police you're collecting a dress. Here's the invoice." She pulled a small piece of paper from her skirt pocket. "The woman is a sympathiser. She will understand but be careful, Heloise, the Gestapo are all over the city."

"I know. Thank you." She took the ticket, gratefully.

Suddenly, they were interrupted by the sound of small footsteps running through the hallway. Margot turned. "Did you brush your teeth properly?"

"Yes, Mother," they chorused.

"But I did mine for longer," said Lucien, glancing at Lottie for approval.

Lottie looked down. "Open your mouth," she said, sternly. The small boy immediately obliged. "They look very good."

"Mine are good too, Heloise!" said Sylvia, opening her mouth wide, unsolicited, for inspection.

"They are! Well done both of you."

"Now get your coats and put on your shoes. Sylvia, put Catherine down." Margot began to clear the breakfast away.

"But she wants to tell me all about her evening."

"She can do that when you get home at lunch time, now please do as I say."

"Yes, Mother." The young girl sat the doll on a chair and told her to be good. It made Lottie smile to herself. She couldn't really remember playing with dolls. She'd had them, of course, but they had remained largely ignored in the corner of the playroom at the farm, unworthy of attention. Instead, she'd played checkers, jacks and dominos with her brothers. Hugh always seemed to win and generally Archie ended up in tears. How she missed them both and suddenly she felt a little homesick, small and irrelevant in this place. It seemed impossible that Hugh was gone. She wondered how Archie was doing and if he was well. It was hard not knowing. She thought about her mother too, trying to keep the farm going and wondering where on earth her daughter was. Vera Atkins promised to send agents' families 'vague updates', about their offspring from time to time, just to try to reassure them that all was well. Her mother though, was no fool and she imagined her father being interrogated by her about what he knew.

"Heloise, we're ready!" Sylvia's voice broke into her thoughts, which was no bad thing.

"Good, let's go. You'll need to show me where your school is." She pulled on her coat. Through the window, the sky was grey, threatening rain.

"I can tell you," said Lucien, slipping his small hand into Lottie's.

"We will *both* show you," said Sylvia, asserting her seniority.

*

On her way, Lottie passed the Mairie where the day after her arrival she had duly presented her identity papers as required by the Germans, to keep track of the population and their movements. She had been asked, politely, why she was in Chantilly and she explained about her new post as a live-in governess to the Toussant children. It went smoothly and the middle-aged registrar who reeked of garlic had stared over his spectacles at her then back at her picture and with a bored sigh, nodded and told her she could go. She'd been pleased to get back out into the air. Any formal scrutiny of her paperwork raised her anxiety and she imagined it would continue to do so all the while she was serving in France.

*

At Chantilly Station, she sat in the empty waiting room for half an hour before the train to Gare du Nord arrived. Lottie thought about the man who was shot a couple of days ago and wondered what he was carrying and if he had a family. She concluded he must have been shot trying to make a run for it or perhaps the power-crazed soldiers had just wanted to make an example of him. Today, though, the journey was mercifully without incident. The train snaked its way south and before she knew it, she had reached her destination. The platform was busy and she was jostled as people attempted to board the train before the passengers got off. Glad to be out in the air, she straightened her brown beret and made her way out onto the Boulevard de Magenta, where the elegant cream stone buildings with their grey domed roofs, resolutely lined the road. Buildings had no allegiance and they didn't care who occupied them and what language was spoken within. For centuries they'd seen change and absorbed it into their walls. Lottie glanced at the people as she passed them on the pavement. Nobody really looked or stared at one another, afraid of attracting attention. Mostly, they made their way, looking down or purposefully ahead of them. Occasionally a car would pass, filled with German soldiers but in the main, there was little traffic except for bicycles and the occasional bus or delivery truck filled with turnips and carrots. The air carried on it the odour of manure, oppression and bad drains.

CHAPTER 48

6ᵗʰ October 1942, Paris, France

Also on this day there is an allied assault on oil installations at Bula Ceram, Indonesia.

From Gare du Nord, Lottie walked down Rue La Fayette past L'Église St Vincent de Paul. She paused for a moment and looked at the church. The imposing building was, she felt, rather incongruous, with grand entrance columns and Greek-style portico. The recent rain had rendered the stone a dark grey and the trees that flanked it dripped dismally from leaves that had begun to fade. She walked across the square and found the seamstress's shop quite easily, at the top of Rue d'Hauteville on the Place Franz-Liszt. The window at the front contained a rather battered sewing machine and a cobwebbed mannequin. Inside, the place looked deserted but she could see a dim light at the back. Rue de Petites Écuries, the street Denise had moved to on her arrival in France, was a very short walk from there, in the heart of the less chic, 10ᵗʰ Arrondissement district. The area was home to the poorer elements of Paris and working-class bordellos. The cobbled street was dirty and quiet, with shabby, shuttered windows closed against the daylight. Inside its occupants slept off the excesses of the night before, when they had entertained the Aryan occupiers in whichever way they desired, in exchange for alcohol, chocolate, Francs and cigarettes.

*

Number 51 was above a small café. The greasy concierge appeared from nowhere and Lottie enquired which apartment Mme Monique Urbain occupied. This was Denise's public identity. He looked her up and down lasciviously, the whites of his eyes tinged liverish yellow. She eyed him with barely disguised revulsion but thanked him politely as he directed her up the stairs to the first floor. It wouldn't do to make enemies of these people who were the eyes of the city. She knocked and waited and after a few moments she heard movement from within.

"Hello?" Denise's voice was cautious.

"It's me, Heloise." Lottie kept her voice low, certain the concierge was listening from below and her voice would echo back down the well of the staircase.

Denise opened the door. She looked well rested. "Come in."

Lottie found herself swept into a tight hug.

"It's good to see you, Denise, but this doesn't feel like a good area to rent?"

Denise waved her hand dismissively. "It's better to be somewhere like this. Nobody asks questions and they don't want paperwork. The men spend their money getting drunk at night and the girls entertain the bastard soldiers while I'm under the radar." She laughed. "You look so worried! Don't be. I like it here. I'm used to living among the working people; I prefer it. Do you want a drink? I have wine. It's from downstairs. It's good, black-market stuff."

"Thank you. I have a message from Waterman." Lottie extracted the slip of paper from the false lining in her handbag and passed it to her.

"Yes. We were expecting it."

"I think he's keen to meet up with Prosper."

"Everyone wants to meet but it's tricky, the Gestapo are everywhere."

"How's it all going?"

"Slow," said Denise. "But Prosper finally arrived a week ago and now he can take overall control of the local network and we can start to get things moving." Denise sighed. "Except he hurt his knee on landing and the packages dropped with them weren't what they expected, so he had no other clothes than those he landed in. I've managed to sort that but he still needs support to walk. How are you finding your new home?"

"I'd heard there was a problem with his arrival. The Toussards are lovely people." She didn't want to go into her initial difficulties with

Michel Dechanel. Sipping her wine, she found Denise was right, it was very good quality.

"What about the people living here in the street or the concierge?"

"What about them?" Denise poured more wine.

"Aren't they curious about where you're from?"

"Nobody asks questions, people come and go all the time. I haven't been here a lot so you're lucky to have found me in. The women are mainly whores which is one of the only ways to get fed and I pay the concierge to keep his mouth shut. Do you have any cigarettes? I've run out."

Lottie opened her bag. "Here," she said passing her the packet.

"Thanks." Denise tapped the end and helped herself. She passed the packet back to Lottie.

"Keep them," she said. "Do you think you can trust him?"

"The concierge?"

"Yes." Lottie looked doubtful.

"As much as anyone. Provided the money keeps flowing... He knows nothing of importance and the Nazis just come to the area for pleasure."

"How will I contact you in future?" said Lottie.

"There's a beekeeper on the edge of the forest in Chantilly. He's a member of the Resistance. He'll get basic messages to you, through the Network. You can meet with him on the pretext of buying honey or perhaps even to learn beekeeping?"

Lottie's eyes widened. "We used to keep bees, before the war. It would give a perfect cover."

"His name is Bernard Aubert. Talk to Waterman."

"The next meeting we arrange will be at the Cinema Studio Twenty Eight, on Butt Montmartre. The matinee begins at three. I will sit in the back row. If I'm not there, watch the film and come the following week at the same time. Sometimes I will be away at short notice on business with Prosper. In any case, until the wireless operator arrives and we can communicate with London, our activities will be restricted."

"Do you know when that will be?"

"Perhaps the end of the month."

Lottie looked at her watch. "I'd better be on my way." She swallowed the rest of her wine and got to her feet. "You take care of yourself, Denise."

"You too, Heloise." She kissed Lottie on both cheeks and showed her to the door.

"I'm sorry, I forgot to ask," Lottie said. "Have you had word from Maurice?"

Denise's eyes seemed to darken. "No, other than he's somewhere in the south. It's too dangerous." Her voice softened. "Perhaps once all this is over…"

Lottie touched her arm. "Don't give up."

"Never."

*

The street had begun to awaken. On some stone steps outside the building opposite to Denise's, two women stood talking. One had a baby on her hip, his tiny hand held tightly onto the collar of her coat as she talked to the other, hips swaying him from side to side in an attempt to keep him quiet. The other woman wore a floral house coat, which she wrapped around her to preserve her long departed modesty. Her make up was smudged slightly, her lips a dull red and her hair, pushed back by a band, was piled onto the top of her head like scribble and the daylight was not kind to her face. She shivered a little as she talked, sucking intermittently on her cigarette, her calf muscles defined by her high-heeled shoes. As Lottie passed them, she caught the smell of stale perfume and as the women glanced in her direction, she nodded and pulled her coat collar higher.

CHAPTER 49

10th October 1942, Chantilly, France

Also on this day, a revolt in the Bowmanville prisoner of war camp, Ontario, Canada, breaks out.

Lottie was playing with the children when Maurice Toussant arrived home from the stables. Since the occupation, having had his own stud stolen, he'd been forced to manage the welfare of fifty horses under German 'ownership'. In spite of everything, he worked with remarkably good humour.

"Bonjour, Heloise," he said, scooping up his son and daughter and twirling them round, making them giggle.

"More, Papa," they laughed and he did it once again before setting them down, dizzy and thrilled.

"I saw Michel earlier today."

"Oh?" said Lottie, casually.

"He seems quite smitten with our new governess."

Lottie nearly laughed aloud. "Is that so?" How could she tell Maurice she thought Michel had all the charm of an un-lanced boil and that it was all part of a ruse to give them reason to meet?

"Apparently so, I didn't hear it from him. The grooms are all gossiping. He's coming round later today to help me with a tree I need to fell."

"Can we play ball before dinner, Papa?" said Lucien.

"Ask your mother, but I think we can," he said, looking down at his son and tapping him affectionately on the nose.

"Perhaps you will take a glass of wine with Michel, before dinner?" Maurice said, turning to Lottie.

193

Lottie nodded. "Of course, it will be an absolute pleasure to meet with him again." She hoped the sarcasm wasn't evident in her voice but Maurice glanced at her, with a slightly puzzled expression.

"I said I would go and help Margot. She's stewing apples," said Lottie, smiling at the children.

"Did you hear that, you two? Stewed apples from our tree for dinner! How lucky are we, eh?"

"Very lucky, Papa," said Sylvie.

Lucien wrinkled his nose in disgust before going back to his toy soldiers.

*

An hour later, Michel arrived carrying an axe over his shoulder. "Bonjour, Heloise," he said. "How are you today? I trust you've settled in well?"

Lottie was certain he hoped she hadn't and had written to London, demanding that she be sent back. Well, he could think again. "Very well, thank you."

The exchange was cordial but there was no warmth.

"Can I offer you wine?" she said, turning her back to him. They were alone in the kitchen, Maurice and Margot having discreetly moved into the cavernous salon.

"Thank you." He took a seat at the table. "Just a small glass, I may need to operate on one of the horses later."

"I delivered your message to Denise."

"Okay." He looked at her expressionless as if she'd met the expectations, no more, no less. He began tracing the grain of the oak table, lightly with his index finger. "Is there a date for meeting?"

"No."

"Merde!" he said under his breath.

"Prosper has just arrived and he's been held up. He had an accident when he parachuted in."

"I'd heard. He's still out of action, then?" There was a note of impatience in his voice.

"I believe he's still limping, which will, naturally, draw attention to him and slow him down. Denise is sorting out logistics and they're still waiting for the wireless operator. By the way, I need to make contact with Bernard Aubert, the—"

"Beekeeper," he interrupted.

"Yes," she said. "The beekeeper." She felt irritated that she'd felt the need to defend her colleagues to him.

"We need leadership from the centre and there needs to be co-ordination. We're wasting time." He continued to air his complaints. Lottie ignored him. "Fine, all I can do is manage this end and as courier, you will need to make contact with Aubert."

"It was suggested, I might learn to keep bees with him as a sort of apprentice. It would give me a reason to meet regularly with him, without arising suspicion, locally. Here's your wine." She set it down firmly in front of him, like a publican who had called 'last orders'.

He thought for a moment and shrugged. "All right."

"All right what?"

"The beekeeping. I will speak to Aubert and if he's willing to teach you, we can arrange it." He took a sip of wine and wiped the edges of his mouth with his thumb and index finger. His nails, Lottie noticed, were clean. That was one thing in his favour and at that moment there was little else to commend him.

"Tomorrow morning, we'll walk to church together. I want you to meet Abbe Charpentier."

"What's his role?"

"We use the church to store guns and ammunition. He's a little outspoken against the Germans for my liking but he's well respected."

"And we can trust him?"

He sat back, resting his arm across the adjacent chairs and looked at Lottie, his eyes widening. "Are you questioning my judgement, already?"

"I'm just asking a question. I don't think that's unreasonable given all our lives are at stake."

Was it always going to be this difficult, Lottie wondered?

"Yes, we trust him," he said, head on one side and in a tone that would be used to pacify a child. They stared at each other in silence for a moment, eyes locked in battle, during which Lottie suppressed an almost overwhelming urge to reach across the table and slap his face. Instead, she pushed her chair back with more force than she'd intended. It made a clattering noise on the flagstone floor as it fell backwards. Wordlessly, heat rising in her face, she picked it up.

"Is that all?" she said. "If so, I have things to do."

"Sit down, I have a job for you," he said.

Lottie remained standing, hands on hips. "What?" Perhaps, she thought, he wanted her to iron his clothes for him or maybe do a little shopping.

He sighed and shook his head a little, as if she was being unreasonably difficult and reached into his pocket. "Here," he said, putting a piece of folded notepaper onto the table and pushing it towards her.

"What is it?"

"A message for a man known as Laurent. He has some new recruits for us. You will need a bicycle. Margot has one, so ask to borrow that."

"And where can I find 'Laurent'?"

"You won't. There's a dead letter box. We use a well at the edge of the hamlet Mont-L'Évêque. It's dried up. Put the message in the bucket which will be near but not right at the top. Cover it with leaves and lower the bucket right to the bottom."

"Where's the well?"

"Take the road east to Senlis. You'll see Mont-l'Évêque signposted at the centre of the village. It's about fifteen kilometres each way. On the edge of the hamlet there's a farm called Le Rosingnol on your right. The disused well is directly opposite the entrance, across the road. It's in the undergrowth. Make sure nobody sees you."

"What's my cover story if I get stopped?"

"Go and find Aubert after church and get some honey. It will be a good excuse for you to meet him. If you do get stopped, tell the police you're delivering to Le Rosingnol farm. They won't check." He got to his feet, towering above her. "Have you got all that?"

"Yes," she said.

"Good. There may be a message for you to pick up. If so, the bucket will already be at the bottom of the well."

She nodded.

"Now, if you'll excuse me, I'll see you tomorrow," he said with sudden politeness, giving her a curt nod.

Lottie said nothing as his tall frame stooped slightly and disappeared through the doorway.

CHAPTER 50

11th October 1942, Chantilly, France

On this day, the US Navy ships intercept a Japanese fleet on their way to reinforce troops on the coast of Guadalcanal. With the help of radar, they sink one cruiser and several Japanese destroyers.

"The body of Christ," said the Abbe, placing the Host on Lottie's open palm.

"Amen," she said, closing her eyes and taking it into her mouth. She wondered if Abbe Charpentier would disapprove of her taking the Host as a Protestant, turned atheist. If she had remained seated, while others trailed to the front, she would have stood out too much, so she joined them all in the ritual, feeling nothing. Michel kneeled next to her, in his brown suit, his eyes staring devotedly up at the figure of Jesus as he crossed himself. Above the pervading odour of incense, she could detect he smelled faintly of thyme and his thick black, curly hair was still, even on a Sunday, untamed. It was a shame, she thought, that so handsome a man could be so objectionable. The feel of his arm accidentally touching hers, as he got to his feet, made her shudder but she smiled across at him and accompanied him back to their seats under the keen eyes of the congregation. The service seemed to go on for hours and Lottie began to feel trapped in a ceremony she could barely relate to. Distracting herself from her boredom, she watched the dust swirl in spirals through the beams of the sun that radiated from the beautiful stained glass of the dome above, reflecting in the gold pillars behind the altar.

"Go in peace," said the priest, finally, his doleful voice echoing through the church.

"Thanks be to God," said the large congregation.

Finally, it was over and one by one, they filed out. Michel put his hand on Lottie's arm to slow her and they hung back waiting for the Abbe to finish his prayer.

"Michel," he said, turning with a smile.

"Father, I would like you to meet Mademoiselle Heloise. She's staying with the Toussants as their governess."

"Bless you, my child," said the Abbe. "You are most welcome." The elderly man nodded and eyed her with myopic interest. He was in his late fifties or perhaps even sixties, Lottie surmised. His eyes had a slightly opaque colour to them and his hands were blue veined.

"She'll be joining us for Friday prayers," said Michel, glancing round, to check that no one had lingered.

Charpentier looked at Lottie. "I see. By the grace of God, we will put right the injustice of this invasion," he said quietly so that the echoes of the church could not betray him. Glancing at the figure of Christ on the cross, "God will guide us in this fight."

Michel nodded. Lottie watched in surprise as he pulled a gold crucifix from around his neck and kissed it.

"Are we still waiting for our delivery?" said the Abbe, ushering them towards the door.

"Yes. The next full moon."

"Then I will see you both at confession when you have information to communicate. It's safer that way. This is too public. You must go now or the town will be expecting a wedding!"

Lottie recoiled at the thought. The Abbe, picking up her alarm, smiled, showing a graveyard of teeth.

"Of course, Father. We would not want to give the wrong impression," said Michel, quickly.

Lottie nodded. "Indeed not!"

"But we need a reason to be seen together."

A slight smile played on the Abbe's lips. Perhaps he sensed the tension between them. "I hope you can pull off this ruse."

Michel shrugged. "There is no choice."

That, thought Lottie, was the first thing they had agreed on.

*

Bernard Aubert's white house sat neatly on the edge of Chantilly Forest. A sign outside, painted in yellow and black said 'Apiculteur'. Lottie knocked on the wooden door and waited. Rounding the corner of the building, a slight figure emerged in a hat and veil and leather gauntlets on his arms.

"Hello?" he said, peering through the netting at his unexpected visitor. "Do you want to buy honey?"

"Yes, please," said Lottie, moving towards him. She could see through the veil he had rather large ears and a small head with tiny features and was rather like a bee, himself. He looked back, shyly.

"How many jars do you want, Mademoiselle? I have limited supplies."

"Four?"

He frowned. "Please come this way." He pulled the veil back like a bee-bride and turned and went back down the side of the house.

Lottie followed.

The back garden was set out as an orchard with gnarled trees whose leaves had turned wonderfully rich autumn colours. The grass was left long except for a path mown between them that wound to the end of the long garden. It reminded Lottie of a fairytale grotto. Aubert walked past the path towards some sheds that were padlocked. Of course, thought Lottie, honey was liquid gold in these lean times. He took out a key from his pocket and drew the large bolt back, with his small, smooth hands, which had nails like shells. They were, thought Lottie, the hands of someone used to delicate work.

"I've been sent by Waterman," she said, as the door swung, noiselessly closed, its hinges no doubt eased with wax.

"Of course. You're the governess?" He smiled.

"Yes, my name is Heloise." She held out her hand and he took it with a slight bow.

"We thought I might be able to assist you in some way and to learn the art of beekeeping." She wondered how he would react to the suggestion. The beekeeper on the farm had been solitary and, more often than not, he'd ignored them as children. When Hugh was about eleven, he had lifted the lid of one of the hives and as a result had been badly stung. When The Brig heard about it, he was furious and threatened to ground Hugh. Much to their surprise, the beekeeper defended him, saying, "The lad would have learned his lesson." And referring to Hugh's swollen face he said, "The bees have their own way of meting out punishment."

"You would be most welcome," she heard him say, breaking her train of thought.

"I'm sorry?"

" I said, it would be my pleasure, to teach you."

Lottie nearly hugged the little man.

"Just now though, I'm shutting the hives up for winter. There is still work to do, such as cleaning the old frames, making new and feeding them. I also have a lot of wax that needs to be strained to make candles and so forth."

"Perfect. How many hives do you have?" Lottie smiled warmly at him.

"Twenty but I must take care to ensure I lose as few colonies over the bad months, as possible. Last year was a very good harvest but the spring can have a sting in her tail." He chuckled at his joke and Lottie smiled. "If the Melice come to buy, I tell them the harvest was poor. I will not have my bees working for them." With that, he knelt down and pulled up a couple of floorboards and reached down into a hole that must have contained several dozen jars of honey. "This is my secret store," he said, triumphantly. Pulling out three he handed the honey-filled jars to Lottie. When he got back to his feet, he took one from her and held it up so the light gave the honey a tawny glow. "What do you think?"

"Just wonderful," said Lottie, her mouth watering. "How much do I owe you?"

"Who are they for?" he asked.

"Nobody specific; I have to collect a message. They're insurance, in case I get stopped."

"Then they are on loan. Bring them back if you don't use them."

"I will. Thank you, Monsieur Aubert."

"You are most welcome and if you are to be my apprentice, please call me Bernard."

Lottie nodded. "Thank you, Bernard." As she turned and walked back towards Rue de Chantilly, clutching the liquid gold, she began to feel more at home in her new world.

CHAPTER 51

12th October 1942, Chantilly, France

On this day Red Army methods of ferrying troops across the Volga into Stalingrad appear to be a success, as German advance is halted.

The next day Lottie set out on the road to Senlis. It was flanked by trees and round every corner, she anticipated a road block but in the event, there was none. In the basket of Monique's old bicycle, there were the four potentially life-saving jars of honey, covered by an extra jumper for if the weather turned colder. Lottie had immediately liked the little beekeeper who was passionate about his bees and she was pleased to find that not every member of the circuit was as rude as Michel. She calculated that if she cycled at a leisurely pace, the whole mission would take her around three to four hours to cover the thirty kilometres and it felt good to get some exercise. Training in England had made her extremely fit and she wanted to maintain it, without drawing attention to herself. In France, women didn't run through the forest carrying heavy rucksacks, they worked in the home and a little on the land, mainly tending to children. She pedalled faster, pushing the muscles in her legs and after several minutes she could feel dewy perspiration on her lip and her lungs working. Removing her hat she let the cool, autumn air run its fingers through her hair as she cycled. She would have liked to have jettisoned the awful spectacles in a hedge too, to give her a true feeling of freedom but she didn't. In the distance she could see the gothic steeple of Senlis Cathedral. By the time she reached the outskirts of the town, she was thirsty and so she stopped in the square to drink water at the fountain. Around her, the population were going quietly about their business, seemingly untouched by the invasion and glancing round, there was no evidence to suggest the town was occupied. People smiled and said, "Good Day," as they passed. She looked casually for the signpost to Mont-l'Évêque and saw it ahead of her. Doing a quick calculation, she was happy she was being directed east. The French had a habit of changing the signposts to confuse the German troops in a small attempt at defiance but on the whole, most conformed and simply got on with their lives. Mounting the bicycle once more, she exited the town and continued her journey.

*

Four kilometres later, the bicycle started to judder and drag and she found to her annoyance she had a puncture. Pulling over, she looked for a source of water but there was nothing. With a sigh, she began to wheel the bicycle towards Mont-l'Évêque, estimating it would take her an extra hour to get there unless she could mend the dratted thing. There was a small bag attached to the back containing some rubber strips, adhesive and a lever to remove the tyre, along with a pump clipped to the bar under the seat but it would take time for the patch to dry and get her back on the road again. Still, she decided she had no alternative as pushing the thing for nearly twenty kilometres there and back was really not an option. Looking into the distance she could see no farm vehicles to flag down and ask for a ride so she pushed on, for a bit, her mood changing. Eventually, she found a convenient place at the edge of the forest that flanked the road and turned the bike upside down. The tyre came off easily but it wasn't in the best shape. The tube inside was 'as flat as Lincolnshire', a saying Mary the cook used on the rare occasion her Yorkshire puddings didn't rise. The memory of that, at least, made her smile. Holding the tube up to the light she inspected it but there was no obvious tear. She pumped it up and spat on it, smearing saliva around until she could see where it bubbled. When she located the pin-prick hole, she dried it with her coat sleeve, and applied the patch. She was just putting the inner tube back inside the tyre when she heard a vehicle, travelling at speed, coming from the direction of Senlis. There was no time to pull the bike into the forest so she stayed where she was and waited.

*

The truck full of German solders pulled to a stop next to her and the one in the passenger seat got out.

"Good morning," said Lottie confidently, counting six of them in the back and two in the front, including the driver.

"Good morning," he replied, his white-blond hair slicked back under his cap. "What are you doing?"

"My bike has a puncture."

"I see." He walked around it, his head tilted on one side. "Where are you going?"

"I'm delivering honey to a farm at Mont-l'Évêque."

"Can I see your papers?"

"Of course." Lottie felt inside her coat pocket and brought out her identity card.

He looked at the card and back at her. She could feel the soldiers in the back of the truck staring at her but she ignored them. It was likely they would drive off after asserting their authority by checking her papers. The soldier gave her back her card. He was barely more than twenty, she thought.

"What is the name of the farm?"

"Le Rosignol."

"Where have you come from?"

"Chantilly."

"That's a long way. What is your address?"

"8 Avenue de la Plaine des Aigles."

"What is your occupation?"

"Governess but I am also apprentice to the local beekeeper."

"Okay," he said, waving at the solders in the back. "Klaus," he said in German. "Come and take the bicycle."

Lottie stiffened. Surely they weren't going to confiscate it. On the face of it, she'd done nothing wrong but the message for Laurent burned in her pocket.

He turned to her, his blue eyes cold. "As your bicycle is broken, we will give you a lift, Mademoiselle Fournier."

"Thank you," she said, her mind racing ahead. She couldn't refuse. If she did, they might become suspicious but if they dropped her at the farm and stayed with her there was no guarantee the farmer wouldn't give her away. She went towards the back of the truck, following Monique's bicycle that had been carefully lifted, its newly repaired inner tube lolling out like entrails as it was hauled up and put between the men. She waited to be handed up into the sea of fresh-faced solders but the Obergerfreiter stopped her.

"Mademoiselle, please take my seat. I will ride in the back." He walked her to the passenger door and held it open for her, his polished boots gleaming in the sunshine.

She nodded and smiled in a display of gratitude, clutching the jars of honey that she'd wrapped in her jumper. She glanced sideways at the driver who looked her up and down then stared straight ahead, waiting for the command to continue. There was a knock on the roof and he pulled away while Lottie worked out possible solutions to the likely scenarios. Her mind working at speed, she barely noticed the rest of the journey, punctuated with the chatter of German voices above the roar of the engine.

*

Presently there was another urgent thump on the metal roof, making her jump. To her left was the sign 'Le Rosignol'. The driver who was about to overshoot it, put his foot hard on the brake. There was a protest from the back and dust flew up from the road as he skidded to a stop. Lottie heard the sound of boots making their way towards the passenger door. She could see him in the round wing mirror, strutting forward. It was positive that they'd stopped but the next bit could be tricky. She looked out of the window for any sign of life in the yard but the farm buildings were set back. The passenger door was opened and the Obergerfreiter put his hand on the door and leaned in slightly.

"Here we are," he said. "Please get out."

Lottie swivelled round and did what he asked, avoiding any lingering eye contact. She heard what sounded like her bicycle being unloaded from the rear of the truck and one of the soldiers wheeled it round to her.

"We've finished the repair," announced the Obergerfreiter.

"Thank you," said Lottie, a little taken aback but for all the solders' apparent chivalry, she knew she wasn't out of the woods yet. The situation could turn in an instant and at that moment he was staring at her as though trying to recall something at the back of his mind but after a moment he averted his eyes and handed her the bicycle. Holding the other side of the handlebar, in silence, she began to put the honey back in the basket.

"Good day, Mademoiselle," he said, suddenly and moved aside to let her pass.

"Thank you," she said again, taking her time to cover the honey, waiting for the truck to move off but it didn't and she was forced to wheel the bike slowly into the farm entrance.

They waited until she had made her way towards the buildings before driving off. Looking around, she could see a man on a tractor about three hundred yards away but he had his back to her. The farmhouse door was open and somewhere close, a dog barked. Quickly, Lottie returned to the entrance and stuck her head out cautiously onto the road, but the truck had turned round the bend up ahead and was no longer visible. Breathing a huge sigh of relief, she pushed the bicycle over the road and into a clump of trees, in search of the well. She found it easily. Michel's directions had been precise. The bucket wasn't visible but someone had oiled the mechanism and it rose noiselessly to the top. Sure enough there was a message at the bottom, covered with dry leaves. Putting it into her inner coat pocket, she exchanged it for Michel's and let the bucket descend fast, wanting to get away from this place. Squeezing the punctured tyre, she was relieved to find that it was firm to the touch and would hopefully get her home. She contemplated burying the jars of honey near the well, in case she saw the truck again, but it seemed unlikely. Instead, she tied them back up in her jumper and put them at the top of her basket, ready to jettison into the verge. The honey was just too precious to leave behind and luckily she met no one on the winding road back to Senlis, apart from an elderly man on a horse and cart.

CHAPTER 52

9th November 1942, Chantilly, France

On Sunday 8th November, Operation Torch, the Allied invasion of Vichy-controlled Morocco and Algeria began.

The news on the street was that the Nazis were to invade France once again and take control of Vichy to prevent the Allies from making gains via North Africa. There was a sudden flurry of outraged young men wanting to join the Resistance and Michel, keen to recruit as many as possible while their blood was fired with patriotic indignation, was busy arranging training, deep in the Forest of Chantilly. He had no alternative but to involve Lottie, albeit in a passive role, as organiser. Her days were suddenly filled, working in haste to get groups trained as daylight hours grew shorter, passing on messages about where to meet and briefing the men on their alibis if they got stopped when they were not where they should be. She finally felt as though they were making some progress and it excited her. Although she'd grown very fond of the Toussant children over the last six weeks, she yearned to do what she had been trained for. Her relationship with Michel had not improved much and wherever possible she knew he sidelined her. Now, with men in short supply, she felt she had an opportunity to make him include her and her chance came sooner than she thought.

*

A dozen young farm labourers stood in a line in a small clearing of the dense forest, listening to Michel speak to them about why they were needed and the importance of covert working. He stood on a fallen tree, his gun slung round his neck and spoke passionately about a free France and how the Nazis were taking all the food and sending it to Germany, leaving nothing but cattle feed and disrespect for the French. Their mothers and sisters were slowly starving, he said, and it was time to do more than just passively watch. If the Germans invaded France for a second time, the French must not sit back and allow it. They all nodded in agreement. They would, he told them, be heroes when France was liberated and bread and meat were back on the table. When he finished, he allowed them to ask questions, filtering out those who might waiver but none did. His speech was rousing and lit up their anger like a match to a trail of gasoline. Lottie watched them become energised and ready to die for their cause and, standing watching from under a nearby tree, she had to admire Michel for his skill. Wrapping up his introductory speech he divided them into groups of six to practice combat. It was essential, he told them, to be able to kill silently with a knife.

Lottie watched, frustrated, from a distance at their incompetence. At Inveraray, in Scotland, she had completed her paramilitary training and while she didn't share Denise's lust for German blood, she did envy the men's automatic right to combat. Having been taught by the best, she itched to walk out and take over the session. At this rate, they would be lucky to have these men adequately trained before Christmas. The clumsy proceedings were interrupted by a low whistle from one of the lookouts. He'd either seen or heard something and Michel silenced the men and made a motion for them to lie down. Lottie, who had not been given a gun, felt vulnerable. She dropped down behind a tree trunk and listened for the sound of voices or twigs cracking underfoot but there was nothing apart from the patter of rain on leaves. After a few minutes, he sounded the all-clear and the men were allowed up. Lottie had had enough. She brushed the leaf mould from her coat and strode over to Michel.

"There aren't enough men to train these boys," she said in a low voice, "Within forty-five minutes we'll be in darkness and no further forward. It will be quicker if you let me help."

He stared at her. "You want to show these men how to cut throats?" he said, eyebrow raised.

"Yes."

His eyes still on her, he called out, "Caspian, come here!" The largest of the new recruits left his group and lumbered over to them. He was a tall, thickset farm hand, known locally for his immense strength.

"Comrade Heloise will show us how to *properly* use a knife to kill," he said, with a barely perceptible hint of sarcasm, holding out his knife to her. The dozen faces turned to her and she knew she had only one chance with this. If she messed up, she would lose any vestige of credibility and worse, would become a laughing stock.

"Right, act as though you are on watch," she said to Caspian. "Over there, where the tree has fallen."

Caspian looked doubtfully at Michel for validation of the order.

"Come on, what are you waiting for? Do as you're told!" he barked.

Lottie took the knife Michel held out to her and disappeared among the trees. Caspian grinned at his friends.

"Why are you pulling faces?" Michel glared at him.

"Sorry sir... I'm not."

"Keep your eye out for the enemy. Your life and those of all your fellow men could be compromised. This is not a game!"

"Yes, sir!"

Concentrating, Lottie circled the group and got down low, approaching from a thicket behind the tree. She watched the young man for a while, learning about where he was looking and when before she moved in. She took her time. Invariably, there was a pattern and frequency that dropped when there was a presumption that there was no immediate threat. She found a stick and surveyed the ground. It was wet and silent underfoot. Waiting until she was ready, she suddenly hurled it in the opposite direction to her line of attack, it clattered through the trees, onto the forest floor. His body turned in response and in an instant, she was on top of the log, his mouth covered from behind. Immediately he went to throw her off.

"Don't move," she whispered in his ear.

The point of the knife was angled precisely in his neck so that she could, in a swift, inward and upward motion, dispatch him. There was a moment of stunned silence before the men started to clap. She released the red-faced Caspian and handed the knife back to Michel who did not meet her eye.

"Quiet!" he said. "We have thirty minutes before dusk. Divide yourselves into groups of four. Comrade Heloise will supervise one group and you will continue to pay attention and learn knife combat."

CHAPTER 53

16ᵗʰ November 1942, Chantilly, France

On this day, the naval battle of Casablanca ends in American victory.

"We need more guns," announced Michel. He was meeting with Lottie in the Toussants' kitchen at lunch time. "I'm not sending men to receive drops unless we have them. It's too dangerous."

"I agree," said Lottie. Since she had proven herself in the forest, Dechanel had changed a little towards her and had become more respectful and inclusive.

"Heloise, I need you to take a message to Denise, asking her to arrange a meeting with the Monkeypuzzle Circuit. They have guns and ammunition. We need to borrow some for the twenty-second. If London actually manage to deliver anything, we might get *something*, at some point, to protect ourselves with," he grumbled. "That should make things a whole lot easier."

"As far as I'm aware, Denise is away with Prosper. Are they back?"

"So I hear." He drank the last of his lemonade. "I'm due to meet with him on the boat on Wednesday night." The boat, *Le Mirage*, was an old barge, moored on the River Oise at Parmain, west of Chantilly and licensed for transportation of raw materials on the stretch of river where it joined the Seine to the west of Paris. A tiny room behind a false partition in the hull, gave the Resistance a secure meeting place. Michel looked tired, Lottie noticed. Two days before, they'd lost two of the new recruits at a road block at Écouen, on the outskirts of the city. The Gestapo had stopped them and they panicked, running off, under fire. They were gunned down and luckily for them, they were killed outright and not dragged off for interrogation, before facing a firing squad. In truth, thought Lottie, under torture they were too young to rely on, although in reality, they had little information that they could impart. Still, they knew members of the circuit and that exposure in itself was an enormous risk. If they'd been captured alive, Waterman would have been compromised and would have had to close down for a while, going dark, until or unless it could be safely resurrected. It was widely known that Sergeant Hugo Bleicher of the Abwehr who had responsibility for flushing out and crushing the French Resistance, was relentlessly stepping up his operations like a starving fox pursuing any scent it believed might lead to a decent meal. To both Lottie and Michel, the thought of Waterman being closed down, just as they were starting to grow and make progress, was unthinkable and made them even more vigilant.

Michel rubbed his eyes, and looked at his watch. "I have to get back to the hospital. They'll be wondering where I am and I have to administer pain relief to a few of the horses the Germans have run into the ground."

"Poor things," said Lottie.

"Yes," said Michel. "Not their war." He looked saddened, getting to his feet. It was the first time Lottie had noticed any softness in him. "Let me know how your meeting with Denise goes."

"I will," she said.

Suddenly he turned to her. "Do you like horses?"

She looked at him, surprised. "Of course. I used to ride when I was growing up. I miss it." She was reminded of their pony, Rowan. Lottie had been the only one to ride him bareback and shoeless in the summer, across the hay meadow, telling him about all her childish troubles. Back then, she'd honestly thought he'd listened and perhaps he had. It had been one of her worst days when he had been found dead in his stable one morning at the grand age of twenty-four. Lottie was suddenly aware that Michel was looking at her.

"The grooms are told to gently exercise some of the horses who are rehabilitating. I go with them sometimes to check how they're recovering. Perhaps you'd like to join us sometime?"

Lottie was taken aback before deciding the invitation was merely part of the ongoing campaign to publicly demonstrate their growing 'friendship'.

"Good idea," she said. "It would be a good opportunity to be seen together publicly."

He looked confused for a moment, then nodded. "Oh, yes… that. I'll contact you to arrange a day and time." His tone had become a little stiff and businesslike, once more.

Lottie nodded. "Fine."

With that, he turned and was gone, leaving Lottie wondering if she'd somehow offended him.

*

Clearing away the plates and cheese, Lottie put on her coat and went to find Bernard who was happy to have her offer of help to clean the sticky propolis from his hive frames. There was a definite chill in the air and the fog that covered the town that morning, had not long lifted. Most of the avenue of trees that lined the Rue L'Anglais were nearly bare, day by day unveiling their twisted skeletons. Lottie sniffed; her head was aching and her throat a little sore and she wondered if she was coming down with a cold. Perhaps Bernard would let her buy a jar of honey.

On arrival at The Apiary, she could smell woodsmoke from the house. When he answered the door, he smiled, clearly happy to see her.

"Heloise, come in! Will you take a little absinthe?"

"I will, Bernard, thank you." The cottage was neat, like him. Lottie wondered if he had ever been married but there was no evidence of a woman. She made a mental note to ask Margot.

Bernard was regarding her with concern. "You look pale. It's cold and I'm not sure you should be working outside, today."

"I'm happy to be in the fresh air," she said. "I'm fine." He was so thoughtful and sweet it was tempting to give way to his care.

"It's a hard and dirty job trying to get the propolis off the frames," he said, unconvinced, looking at her clean clothes. "I will have to give you an apron."

She did feel a bit lethargic. "Thank you. How are you, Bernard?"

"I'm fine. I have been getting rid of old frames that had Wax Moth." He looked pained, his ears moving slightly as though independent of his head, which made Lottie smile.

"I'm glad you've come, Heloise, as I have a message for Waterman." He dropped his voice despite it being impossible that they could be overheard. "Things are getting busier, since the invasion of the South, like the country is stirring from a deep sleep. I'm excited now for the future but you must be careful. Things are becoming more dangerous by the day." He was looking at Lottie, earnestly, through his round glasses.

"So I hear. Bernard, I do need to meet with Denise."

"Can you get a message to her quickly?"

"Of course."

"As I understand it, she's staying away from her flat at the moment. She's worried the Carlingue Gang is getting a little too interested in her comings and goings." He handed her the absinthe.

"Where is she?"

"In a flat, south of the Seine. Everyone is steering clear of Monmartre at the moment, there's too much... activity." He hesitated, looking for the right word. "Too many Germans."

"I need to meet her on Wednesday, if possible. We have an agreed meeting place in the event she can't make contact."

"Okay but as things have changed, so will your agreed location. I'll get a message to her to tell her to meet you at Le Deux Magots café, 6 Place Saint-Germain des Pres, at around midday?"

"Thank you."

She downed the absinthe; its aniseed taste reminded her of the candy twist sweets they had a boarding school and as it came into contact with her sore throat, she winced.

He noticed at once and regarded her, his head on one side. "You really don't look well, Heloise."

"Just a bit of a head cold, I think. I'll live." She grinned.

"I shall make you honey and lemon and give you a theory lesson on the bees rather than cleaning frames," he said, getting on a chair and putting his hand right to the back of a small cupboard that was obscured by a small watercolour painting of a house, cypress trees and mountains somewhere in the South of France.

"You have lemons?" Lottie looked surprised, then smiled as he brought out a jar of preserved lemon in brandy.

He clutched the jar as though it was a treasure and put it on the table, before hurriedly reaching behind the gingham curtain below the sink to get her a clean glass. "I promise you, this will cure everything in hour. My mother swore by it."

Lottie watched as he poured it before adding a little hot water and a large spoon of honey, concentrating, like an alchemist.

"Voila!" he said, finally, holding it out to her like a doctor to his patient. "Sit by the fire."

Lottie did as she was told and she sipped the drink watching the flames in the hearth lick gently at the wood before devouring it. The next thing she knew, she woke up two hours later, covered in a blanket and feeling much better. Bernard was nowhere to be seen but she could hear him working in the yard. Getting to her feet and folding the blanket, she could have hugged the man for his kindness.

CHAPTER 54

18th November 1942, Paris, France

On this day, President Roosevelt orders registration for Selective Service of all youths who had turned 18 since July 1st 1942, making 500,000 more Americans eligible to fight.

It was drizzling when Lottie emerged from Gare du Nord Station. Calculating the walk would take her around forty-five minutes, she pulled the collar of her brown promenade coat up as far as it would go, her scarf more tightly round her neck and her hat lower to keep it from fogging up her spectacles. She could have taken the metro to St Germain Des Pres but chose instead to walk to get fresh air. The previous day she had spent in bed with a pounding headache and temperature but overnight it had dissipated leaving her with raw skin around her nose that she had covered with a magic bee balm that Bernard had insisted she took home with her. She inhaled deeply and her breath exhaled a plume of white smoke as it came in contact with the cold air as she walked purposefully down Boulevard du Strasbourg. She continued past the Theatre Antoine-Simone Berriau and the omnipresent bread queues and into the wide, tree-lined Boulevard Sebastopol and as she did so, she experienced a sudden, profound wave of love for the city. It occurred to her how wonderful it would have been to have shared Paris with Gareth. Suddenly a large motorcade approached and as it passed, swastikas dancing triumphantly in the wind, she recognised Hermann Goring, Reichsmarschall and Commander of the Luftwaffe in the back seat, talking to another high-ranking officer she did not recognise. How she wished she had a machine gun at that moment. It passed quickly and turned left into Rue Rivoli on its way, no doubt to Nazi Headquarters or perhaps to Rue Royal where he would enjoy a lunch of oysters and prostitutes. Quickening her pace, once again fired up by the business in hand, Lottie crossed over the Seine and turned right into Boulevard St Germain.

*

Les Deux Magots was busy inside. Lottie pushed her way through the carousel door and looked casually round for Denise but could not see her. A waiter in a white apron showed her to a seat and took her order for coffee. She took her hat and coat off and removed her glasses to clean them, setting them down on the tablecloth. On the table next to her, a group of four men sat, talking loudly, deep in debate. One of them glanced over at her and smiled. Nodding politely, she looked away and when she looked back, she found he was still staring at her, pipe in mouth, as though scrutinising every inch of her face. Uncomfortable at the attention, she quickly put her glasses back on and looked down at her watch, wishing Denise would arrive soon. The waiter returned but before he could deliver her coffee, the man stopped him in his tracks and pulled him down to whisper something in his ear. He nodded and straightened. Putting the coffee cup down in front of Lottie, he bowed and said, "The gentleman would like you to have this with his compliments. He wants you to know he thinks you're very beautiful but you should um…" he faltered, reddening, "change your spectacles."

Lottie didn't know whether to laugh or be affronted. "And who is the gentleman?"

The waiter looked at her embarrassed, lowering his voice. "Mademoiselle, he is the famous artist, Mr Pablo Picasso."

"Please thank Monsieur Picasso for the coffee and his advice on style," she said, straight faced.

The waiter bowed again. "Yes, Mademoiselle, of course."

She watched as he went back to the table and delivered her message, to which Picasso threw his head back, laughed and raised his glass to her. A few moments later, Lottie was happy to see Denise walk through the door and the three men get up to leave.

"I must hurry, Picasso," said one of the men who resembled a toad. "I'm meeting Simone for lunch."

Picasso hesitated as they passed by Lottie. "Don't you think she's got the perfect face, Jean-Paul? Does it not move you at all?"

Sartre looked at Lottie and muttered an apology for the intrusion.

"Beauty like art, Pablo, is meaningless," he said on their way out. "Look, it's raining. We will get wet and already I have a cold."

*

Lottie stood and kissed Denise on both cheeks.

"What was that about?" Denise stared after the men as they clattered round the carousel door before being delivered onto the pavement.

"That was Pablo Picasso and Jean Paul Sartre!" said Lottie leaning forward, whispering.

"Oh, they're always in here," said Denise. "Picasso is on the Gestapo's radar; they can't understand his art and therefore can't tell if he's a supporter or anarchist. Sartre's a Marxist of course. Either way, the Nazis don't trust them and by and large, just leave them to their art." She sounded dismissive. "Now, how have you been, Heloise? You're looking very white." She held both Lottie's arms and regarded her.

"I'm fine, just a cold. What about you, Denise?" Lottie's small bubble of excitement at seeing Picasso and Sartre had been well and truly burst.

"It's been a busy few weeks travelling around," Denise said, ordering a coffee and looking around her. Satisfied they were not going to be overheard, she said, "I saw Jaqueline on Monday."

"How is she?"

"She's good, very busy running messages across the Loire. Since Vichy was occupied, recruitment has shot up. It's a pity we haven't got anything to arm them with. Are you all set for Sunday?"

Lottie shook her head. Denise sounded ten years older than the last time Lottie had seen her. Under the weight of responsibility, she'd quickly lost the youthful exuberance she'd displayed on the journey over to France.

"That's what I need to speak to you about." She drank the rest of her coffee.

Denise frowned. "More guns?"

"Yes, we have the recruits now but not enough Stens and ammunition."

"How many do you need?"

"Ten, maybe? If the Gestapo turn up we'll have to leave whatever's dropped and we can't afford to do that."

"No. There's so little to go around but a wireless operator is due to arrive with supplies and a wireless this week so if all goes well, at least we'll be able to get messages to London more easily." Denise thought for a moment. "The drop zone is between Senlis and Barbery?"

"Yes."

"There's a derelict blacksmith's forge on the road to Barbery, just as you turn off D44. We'll deliver them there on the night of the twenty-first. At dawn on the twenty-second, you need to get them picked up."

"That will be no problem," said Lottie. "The farmer is harvesting swedes in a nearby field. He's one of ours. I will have the truck pick them up."

"Where are you storing the delivery?"

"The church."

Denise wrinkled her nose. "The Abbe needs to curb the content of his sermons. His views are being talked about."

"I know. I hear you're staying away from your flat for a while?"

"Yes, someone in the flat below was asking questions."

"About you?"

Denise stirred her coffee. "Yes. One of the Carlingues. Jaqueline and Irene use the flat whenever they come to Paris and I think it got noticed so I went to stay with my sister for a few days, then joined Prosper to work."

"Will you go back?"

"Yes, probably, when things cool down."

"Isn't that a risk?"

Denise shrugged. "Maybe but I've made friends with a couple of the prostitutes in the street. After a few glasses of wine, they're more than happy to tell me what they know and some of the information about troop movements peppered with stories of perversion, is priceless. Their network is like a brothel telegraph!"

Lottie laughed.

"Seriously, Heloise, you'd be amazed what the stupid Nazis tell them when they're banging away!" She shook her head disdainfully.

"But the Carlingue," said Lottie, "they're as dangerous as the Gestapo, perhaps more so."

"For sure. French bastard traitors! Last week, in Tenth Arrondissement, they pulled a Jewish family from a basement and shot the father in front of his two young daughters."

"That's just awful, the brutality is unfathomable!" Lottie felt an overwhelming sadness, picturing it.

They both sat in silence for a few seconds, contemplating the depths to which humanity will go.

"How are you getting along with Waterman?" Denise said suddenly, changing the subject.

Lottie swallowed and thought for a moment. "Well… I think he's beginning to realise that a mere woman can be an asset." She was careful, not knowing how well Denise knew Michel.

Denise snorted. "Is that so?"

"Yes, it's taken some effort, though."

At that moment, the waiter came to ask if they would like anything else. His black waistcoat, Lottie noticed was missing two buttons a metaphor for life now. Denise thanked him and pulled out her ration book. She looked at Lottie. "Have you settled already?"

"No, mine was complementary."

"Complementary?"

"Monsieur Picasso."

Lottie detected a hint of disapproval.

"He sent it over with his compliments." Lottie shrugged. "It was easier to accept than make a fuss."

"Of course." She stood up. "Is there anything else you need?"

"Yes, I'm running out of hair dye. I can't easily shop for it as I'm supposed to be a natural brunette and I doubt London will remember to send any. I have enough for one more application and I can't risk blonde roots emerging."

"I'll speak to my sister. She can get anything. By the way, I've put a message in your pocket from Prosper to Waterman." As the waiter returned and stood near, she said to Lottie in a louder voice, "It has been so lovely seeing you, Heloise. Give my love to your mother."

"Thank you," said Lottie. "I will." She gave Denise a few minutes before she put on her coat and left.

CHAPTER 55

22nd November 1942,

Barbary, near Chantilly, France

On this day the Red Army secures the vital bridge over the Don River at Kalach-na-Donu, west of Stalingrad.

Lottie crouched in a freezing cold ditch at the edge of the field, on the opposite side of the road to the tiny village of Barbary, listening for the sound of an aircraft or the more ominous sounds of the Melice. Yesterday evening, she had waited in the Toussants' kitchen with Michel, listening intently to the BBC World Service broadcast for a coded message of confirmation that the drop would take place. Among the seemingly random sentences, they finally heard the phrase they wanted, "The black cat is sitting on a wall." Before leaving shortly after, Michel had told her to meet him at nine the following morning, at Bernard's house. Ordinarily, Michel wouldn't have sanctioned her joining the men but two had gone down with influenza and since her display of competence in the forest, like an untrusting animal reluctantly walking towards an outstretched hand, he began to treat her with more respect. She'd expected they'd make the long journey to the drop site by bicycle but instead, to her joy, he'd arrived with two horses.

"You said you could ride," he said. "We'll be faster on horseback."

So they had ridden softly, along winding forest paths, hooves muffled by the carpet of leaves, the earth's heady perfume of rotting leaf mould, mingling with horse-breath. Either side of the narrow paths, skeletal trees that clung onto their few remaining leaves flanked them as their legs whipped through the wet undergrowth that had grown limp in the autumn rain. Lottie, cantering behind Michel, felt at one with the forest.

*

It was a light, cloudless night, with a large bright moon which was just perfect for a delivery. They left the horses in the forest and walked to the drop site. Lottie blew on her fingers that were going numb. Across her chest, she had the strap of a precious Sten gun, plus ammunition. She could hear Bertrand, fifty or so yards away, stamping his feet to keep the circulation going. Something moved in the undergrowth and she swung round and aimed the gun. A fox or a wild boar, perhaps? Suddenly it stopped. She looked at her watch. It read twenty minutes past midnight. The aircraft was late. Raising her head above the wall of the ditch and tracing her eyes along the field, she couldn't see any of the others and everywhere was silent. Feeling her nose run, she fumbled for her handkerchief but couldn't locate it so she wiped it on the back of her already damp glove. At least, she thought, wriggling her toes to keep the circulation going, the ditch was dry. Suddenly, there was a distant rumble that built until it was approximately two or three miles away. Three figures ran into the field, took up their positions and signalled to the plane overhead with torches. The aircraft continued past the field, before banking and turning sharply, coming in at around five hundred feet and spawning a dozen or so white jellyfish into the sky, before it turned again and accelerated up and away.

The metal canisters landed around the field and the men scrambled to remove the chutes and bury them. The truck arrived at the side of the road but it was too risky to bring it onto the field as the tyre marks could betray them. Instead, the men had to carry all twelve to the road. It was heavy work and Lottie could hear them breathing heavily and talking in low voices as they rushed to get them out of the field and loaded into the back of the truck. She scrambled out of the ditch, signalled to Michel and re-positioned herself at the roadside, a little way away from the men in the direction of Senlis. If anyone came, she would see them and raise the alarm. This was the most tense part of the operation but the men worked quickly and efficiently. Within half an hour the field was cleared and the truck, filled with canisters and men, drove the short distance to the farm where the contents could be temporarily stored in the hayloft. Over the next few days, they would be transported to the care of Abbe Charpentier, in Chantilly, where the contents would be stored in the church crypt.

*

Lottie waited for Michel. He emerged from the back of the truck, his gun slung over his shoulder, looking satisfied with the night's work. Time was passing quickly and he needed to return to Chantilly and get the horses back into their stables fed, watered and all telltale sweat brushed away, before the grooms started their day at dawn. Lottie had to be in her room at the Toussants' too, before the children awoke and came to knock on her door. Together, feeling exulted by the night's work, they disappeared once again into the forest, like ghosts.

CHAPTER 56

22ⁿᵈ January 1943, Chantilly, France

On this day Australian and American forces defeat Japanese army and navy units in the Battle of Buna-Gona with heavy losses all round.

Michel and Lottie were sitting in Bernard's living room, huddled round the fire with Prosper and his long-awaited wireless operator 'Archambaud', code name Glazier, discussing their plan to de-rail a train en route from Spain. It was carrying wolframite, for steel production in Germany. On the table, a map was unrolled and they all poured over it.

"The train is due to reach Gare du Nord at sixteen hundred hours tomorrow. From there, it continues its journey via Belgium to Cologne," Michel said, tracing his finger along the line. "We plan to set the explosives here." He tapped his finger on the map. "Where the line goes through the Bois de St-Laurent."

"You seem to have done your homework. What are the risks?" asked Prosper, his piercing blue eyes staring at Michel.

"Patrols?"

"Yes."

"We can never be sure but none so far."

"What about on the train?" Lottie broke in. "There are likely to be soldiers on the wagons. It's a precious cargo."

"I don't think they'll be expecting anything. There may be half a dozen guards but we can deal with them. We've not sabotaged anything at that location before and it's perfect for us to set the explosive and get out through the woods. If we're lucky, we can get the line out of action for several hours, if not days, and spread the consignment over the countryside." Michel made a booming noise.

"It will need a lot of explosive and long fuses for you to get clear before she goes up," said Prosper, taking a deep breath. "And stocks are running low."

"I thought you'd messaged London?" said Michel. "Where are the drops?"

"I'm constantly messaging London but that doesn't mean anything's forthcoming. I was hoping for something tonight but what with the weather, it isn't looking promising. Don't get me started, I'm angry enough as it is."

"So, what do you want to do about this?" Michel looked at the map then back at Prosper, who got to his feet and stretched.

"How many men have you got?"

"At that time of day, six, seven with Heloise."

"Guns and ammunition?"

"Just about enough," said Michel. "But I'm planning not to use them. The main risk is detonation but there's enough cover along the track to get us out safely and the men are experienced lookouts. I *have* done derailments before." His tone was slightly resentful.

"I'm not suggesting you're inexperienced, Michel, but this is a big job. I want it checked properly." He got to his feet and walked around a bit, flexing his knee and wincing.

Michel looked away and Lottie could detect his frustration at his competence being questioned.

"Okay, let's do it," said Prosper, suddenly. "Send word via Bernard when the job's done. Right, Archambaud, let's get going."

The man got obediently to his feet and stubbed out his cigarette. "Denise sends her best wishes, by the way," Archambaud said, pulling on his coat.

"Please return mine," said Lottie, smiling. "I hope you've settled in well?"

"Well, enough." He grinned, put on his cap and, winking at her over his shoulder, followed Prosper out of the door to an old truck they'd borrowed.

*

After they'd gone, Michel sprang into action. "Heloise, I need you to go to Confession."

"What?" Lottie looked at him, taken aback.

"If you go now, you can tell Abbe Charpentier to leave the church unlocked tonight. I need access to get the guns and ammunition. While you do that, I'll go and pay a visit to Guillaume at the forge and Benoit. We'll meet tomorrow at the southern point of Étang de Vallière. We'll use Guillaume's truck and hope we don't get stopped."

*

Lottie entered the cold church and lit a candle, bobbing at the altar and making the sign of the cross. An elderly woman sat hunched over in one of the pews, her eyes screwed up with concentration, rosary held close to her chest as she fervently prayed for something Lottie felt sure wouldn't be delivered. She crept past, trying not to disturb her as her heels clicked over the polished tombstones, as she made her way to the wooden confessional. Knocking quietly, she was admitted and she heard the unmistakable voice of the Abbe behind the grille.

"Father, I've brought a message from Waterman."

There was a short pause before he spoke. "Heloise?"

"Yes, Abbe."

"What's the message?" he said quickly, his voice lowering, barely audible through the grille.

"He'd like you to leave the door to the church open tonight."

"Of course. Please tell him that will be done. Is that all?"

"Yes, thank you."

"Nothing to confess while you're here?"

"No, Abbe."

"Not a believer, then? Or just not Catholic?"

"Neither." She sounded apologetic, not wanting to offend him.

"In which case you should go back out and take a seat in the church for a few minutes and pretend to contemplate your sins and make peace with my God. If anyone is watching, it will at least look correct." His tone was not reproachful, just matter-of-fact.

"Of course. Thank you."

Lottie did as he suggested, looking up at the statue of Jesus bleeding on the cross, feeling nothing except that the whole thing might benefit from a clean. She was, however, suddenly preoccupied with Michel. She found, to her consternation, that even when she was thinking about mundane daily tasks, his face appeared, like a figure in a renaissance painting that had been illuminated by light. She shook her head slightly as though to try and rid her head of this image but it returned as obstinate as the man himself.

"Merde!" she said aloud and left the church.

CHAPTER 57

23rd January 1943 – Bois De Saint Laurent, Nr Paris

On this day the British capture Tripoli, Libya.

The truck rumbled along the back roads, smelling of rotten eggs as coal burnt in the cylinders at the front was converted into methane gas to drive the engine. Guillaume never seemed to tire of proudly explaining the physics and how they'd thwarted the Germans in their attempts to keep ordinary people off the roads. The odour made Lottie feel a little nauseous and being sandwiched between Guillaume who smelled of stale sweat and Michel whose thigh was pressing, unavoidably, against hers, was making the journey almost intolerable for different reasons. In the back, buried under a tarpaulin were Benoit, Bernard and Caspian. The farm hand, Pierre, would meet them at the lake. Michel looked at his watch, checking once again they were on time to rendezvous at three o'clock.

*

It was raining heavily when they parked off road, under trees, at the southern point of the Étang de Vallière. In the far distance, the turrets of the Chateau de Vallière rose up over the tree canopy. They pulled dead branches over the truck and walked the last few kilometres through the woods, to the railway line carrying guns and equipment. If they got caught, the plan was to split up and try to get back to the truck. It wasn't, Michel acknowledged, the best idea to do this in daylight but they had no choice. They moved forward with stealth, on full alert, Michel signalling to them when to move and where.

The line ran straight through the forest before winding north to Belgium then Germany. Michel positioned Caspian, Lottie and Bernard at various points in the undergrowth beside the track, but where he could still see them. Then he, Guillaume and Benoit fixed the explosive to the rails, fitted the detonators and unwound the fuses well back into the trees, where they hid and waited. At four, the train had still not arrived. For many minutes, there was no sound except for the soft patter of ice-cold rain. Lottie pulled her beret down at the side to stop the water from filtering through the wool and running into her eyes. She was cold and wet and her boots were by this time, heavy with mud. With the low cloud, darkness was descending quickly.

*

Out of nowhere, the rails seemed to twitch, almost imperceptibly at first, as though waking from a coma and coming to life. Michel signalled to them to get down as the movement was soon accompanied by the distant sound of the locomotive. Lottie's heart began to beat faster as the train rumbled towards them and within a minute it was there, a massive lump of hissing iron, wheels bearing down on the rail. The engine rolled over the rails set with explosive, followed by the first couple of trucks. The fuses, now lit, snaked their way to the detonator. The comrades turned and ran back into the forest as a deafening explosion filled the air along with debris, the wheels of the train squealing as the rail beneath it buckled and disintegrated, derailing the open coaches behind the locomotive. One by one, like dominos they rolled with a terrible roaring sound, snapping trees like twigs as the cargo spewed out. Someone shouted in German and from the locomotive, four soldiers emerged with a dog and began to give chase, the dog barking as it raced in the direction of the fleeing gang. Lottie ran, stumbling in the half-light, as her foot caught on a root. There was a stab of pain in her ankle that made her want to cry out as she began to hobble. Michel was ahead of her but he turned when he saw her slow down and he stopped.

"Go!" she called. "Don't wait!"

But he *was* waiting, gun aimed at the direction of the barking that was getting closer.

"Come on, Heloise!" he shouted. "Just keep going!"

There was no sign of the others but she could tell, by the dog's bark, raised voices and the sound of intermittent gunfire, that the soldiers were rapidly closing in.

Rising above the pain, she ran for her life. Just when she thought she couldn't go much further, she saw the lake ahead of them. Michel was making for the water and to her astonishment, he jumped in, gun above his head, waving at her to follow him. Entering the ice-cold water took her mind momentarily off her ankle. She pushed against the resistance of water, moving forward, dragging herself through roots and floating reeds and forcing her feet out of the silt at the bottom. She wanted to swim but she'd lose her gun so she persisted, her lungs screaming for air. Michel, fifteen or so yards in front of her, was making his way towards the upper lake, and a small bridge. He waited until she was level with him and pointed down into the brackish water and a large drainage pipe that was gravity fed from the lake above. There was a tiny section of the pipe above water but surely it would be impossible to survive in there. She stared at it for a split second, terror taking hold of her, before hearing the sound of the soldiers getting nearer, she took a deep breath and went under, following Michel into the body of the pipe. She couldn't see anything and she could feel herself panicking, unable to hold her breath any longer and ready to push back up, preferring to face death by bullets, than by drowning. But a hand came out and held her down, pulling her forward against a strong force of water before choking, she was dragged up to the surface. Her nose she found, to her horror, was only an inch or so above the water level as she struggled to stifle the noise of her lungs expelling water in exchange for air. Michel had found a lead pipe to hang on to and he clutched Lottie's jacket and kept her with him, as she felt herself being pushed back out into the lake by the force of the water. She held her head as far up as she could against the top of the pipe, as he forced his mouth to the surface and whispered in her ear to 'breathe'. The stinking water frothed around her upper lip, dancing capriciously around the entrance to her nostrils. She strained upwards towards the limited airspace, commanding herself to be calm in the face of panic. Michel held her tight to him, his chest heaving and she could feel his breath as they waited for what seemed like several lifetimes. The excited barking grew close with more gunfire and it appeared the soldiers were on the bridge directly above them. She could hear them shouting to each other and the dog.

"We've lost them!"

"They must be around here somewhere."

"If they were, the dog would have found them."

"It's getting dark. We need to get back to the train."

"There's no point. First we should inform the station, there will be other trains coming through. Let's go to the Chateau. They'll have a phone."

The dog had stopped barking, suddenly. Something moved in the water, next to Lottie's head. Swivelling her eyes towards it, she could tell by its shape and size it was a rat. Her body jerked, arms flailing and Michel held her tighter. She shut her eyes, digging her nails into his arm, trying to avoid inhaling any more water or crying out in terror. Seconds later she opened them again and it was gone. The soldiers' voices were getting fainter as they moved off in the direction of the Chateau. When they could hear nothing more, Michel said, "Ready! Just relax and go with the current." Without more warning, he loosened his grip and they were ejected unceremoniously, into the lake by the force of the water and back up to the surface. Dragging themselves out against the mud, on their stomachs, they made their way, exhausted, back into the trees and followed the road to where the truck was parked and the men were waiting.

"We thought you'd never come!" said Benoit with a grin, spitting on the ground. "And you've had time for a swim?"

Michel looked at him, unsmiling and shook his head. "That was too close."

Lottie sat on the ground shivering and emptying her boots, pretending to examine her ankle. Michel bent down and put his hand on her shoulder. "Heloise, are you okay?"

She looked up at him, the whites of her eyes contrasting with her mud-splattered face and nodded, unable to speak. Tenderly, he reached out pulled a strand of pond weed from her hair and helped her to her feet.

CHAPTER 58

7th March 1943, Paris

On this day the Polish Government-in-exile reports for the first time, the executions of prisoners in Auschwitz

Smoke swirled around the Hot Club de France at Rue Cardinet, in a jazz haze. The place was crowded as Lottie, Michel, Prosper, Archambaud and Denise pushed their way through to a table in the shadows. On the low stage at the front, the band played Sweet Georgia Brown and couples danced like there was no war and the members of the Resistance had cause that evening to feel optimistic over the Russian victory in Stalingrad.

"Where's Reinhardt?" said Prosper, looking at the quartet line up.

Michel sniffed. "Probably dining with Oberleutenant Dietrich Schulz-Kohn! In German eyes, the 'Gypsy needs to stay in favour'."

"No doubt," said Prosper. "Still, I was hoping to hear him play."

"Maybe he's too good for us, now?"

"Forget Reinhardt. What shall we drink?" said Denise, looking for a waiter, her shoulders moving to the music.

"Whisky, if they have it?" said Archambaud. "Better than the wine, I think?"

Across the room two drunk, off-duty German soldiers, sat with prostitutes who draped themselves over them like cheap curtains, eyes hard and louche, loose lips, playing them for a good tip.

"We should dance," said Archambaud. "Denise, will you?"

"Why not?" she said, getting to her feet.

She looked very pretty, thought Lottie, her hair now dyed blonde and piled high on top of her head. She sported a pleated dress, pinched at her sparrow waist in 'zazous' style. Lottie knew she'd made a special effort for the handsome new wireless operator with whom she seemed quite infatuated. They looked good on the dance floor as they span around energetically to the music, laughing. Lottie sat back and watched, slightly envious. She wished Michel would ask her to dance but she knew he wouldn't and there was no way she'd contemplate asking him as the inevitable rebuff would hurt and she was too proud. Sometimes over the past few months, something passed between them but it was almost imperceptible, like a tantalising moment's breeze that came and went in a heat wave, a look or a light touch that made her think he cared for her but then things would return to normal and he'd treat her once more, like one of the men. But, as that's exactly what she wanted, she knew she couldn't then expect him to treat her as a desirable woman. She now believed she'd misinterpreted the subtle signs of interest and he'd just been playing the role of 'Michel and the Governess'. Above all though, she absolutely didn't want to desire him.

Archambaud and Denise came back to their seats, breathless, to find Michel and Prosper deep in discussion about horse racing.

"You must be so bored, Heloise," Denise said, flopping down next to her, taking a sip of whisky, "listening to these two."

"Not at all. I like to watch the dancing and listen to the music." Lottie thought she sounded like a maiden aunt, brought out for the evening for an airing, to watch the young enjoying themselves.

"Then, we should dance?" said Archambaud, holding out his hand to her.

"Yes, Heloise, you must, he's not bad!" said Denise.

"I think that's a compliment from Denise!" said Lottie, getting to her feet.

"Perhaps the nicest thing she's said to me," said Archambaud with a grin.

Lottie had to get past Michel to get out and he moved back politely, to give her space.

"Sorry," she said, not looking at him as she inadvertently brushed against his leg and moved out onto the dance floor, where the tempo had picked up. They began to touch step and triple step, moving their hips and swirling around to the band's version of Limehouse Blues. Lottie was loving it and at the end of the song, they turned, laughing, to make their way over to their seats. It was then Lottie noticed Michel staring at them, his dark eyes taking it all in but he wasn't smiling. It looked for that moment like sadness and as soon as she made eye contact with him, he looked quickly away.

Denise was clapping, cigarette between her teeth. "Bravo, you two!"

Archambaud sat down heavily. "I'm absolutely exhausted!" He put his arm across the back of Denise's chair and lit a cigarette. "I'm done with playing the gigolo for these women," he said, exhaling. "Michel, you'll have to take a turn, next."

"Shall we get some more whisky?" said Michel, pointedly ignoring him.

Denise looked over at him and grinned, enjoying seeing him out of his comfort zone. "Don't you ever dance, Michel?"

"No," he muttered, getting up. "Excuse me, I'm going to the toilet."

"Let him be," said Lottie. "Dancing and fun isn't for everyone."

"He needs to be more loose," said Denise, wriggling in her seat by way of demonstration. "Come on, old man, get back on that dance floor!" She got up and pulled a protesting Archambaud to his feet and they disappeared into the moving mass of people.

"How is everything?" said Prosper, leaning forward on his elbows and regarding Lottie with a paternal smile.

"Good," she said, nodding, "but it would be nice to be busier."

"February was diabolical," he agreed. "There are men in here that want to join us but it's pointless training them when we have no supplies. By the time they arrive, they'll have forgotten what they've been taught. But things *have* started to pick up." He looked past her as he caught sight of Michel returning. "Michel will brief you."

Lottie wondered fleetingly if Prosper missed his young family. She didn't imagine sitting in bars at night was his 'thing' either but it was something for the four of them to do to kill time, between recruitment and small acts of sabotage, given there had been no successful drops in February. The war was dragging on longer than any of them had imagined and plans were constantly being put back.

There was a sudden commotion as one of the German soldiers got to his feet, listed to the right and fell onto the table, sending glasses skittering across it and onto the flagstone floor, where they smashed.

"Disgusting!" said Denise, with a low growl, sitting back down and throwing the rest of her whisky down her throat and jabbing her finger on the table. "Look at those bastards with their full stomachs and warm clothes! There's no escape from them and they're treating our city as a playground at our expense!" They all turned and watched as the other soldier, a little less inebriated, hauled him to his feet, placed his cap back on his head while apologising to the waiter who assured them all was, "Fine," while turning his head away, muttering with exaggerated camp, "Heil Hitler," and rolling his eyes. His compatriot put his arm under him and staggering under his weight, half carried him out into the cold night air, followed by the giggling women.

"We just need to bide our time," said Prosper. "One day, Paris will be back where she belongs."

CHAPTER 59

5th April 1943, Paris, France

On this day Americans bomb the town of Mortsel, Belgium.

On the 8th of March Denise had returned to her flat and found the police had been snooping again. Bomelburg, the Nazi Major responsible for stamping out the Resistance, was said to be casting his net wide and deep through the city. Rather than 'going dark', as Baker Street demanded of Agents suspected of being under Gestapo surveillance, Denise became, if anything, more determined to continue with her work. However, her one concession was to keep herself off the radar of the Nazi collaborator Carlingue Gang by spending her nights with Archambaud. It was not as it turned out, much of a sacrifice, as he had quickly become her lover. Lottie worried about her but it was pointless. Denise was fearless and that made her, to some extent, reckless. Prosper did his best to reign her in but she was on a mission to win the war, single-handedly, if necessary.

*

On a sunny spring morning, Lottie walked to meet her at a café on Rue Saint-Maur. She noted the city looked more Germanic than ever, with Swastika flags seemingly on every road and street signs increasingly turned from French to German to emphasise occupation. As if anyone needed reminding, thought Lottie as she buttoned her coat against the cold wind, but she comforted herself in the knowledge these things were only 'window dressing' and could be torn down in an instant. Now and again there were meagre but still joyous signs of rebellion where someone had taken their life in their hands and daubed 'Fuck the Nazis!' in red paint, in large letters on a wall. Fuck them, indeed, she agreed. But, there was no denying at that point, the identity of Paris was fading and the French, she knew from the amount of young men now wanting to join the Resistance, were feeling increasingly displaced. Images of Buckingham Palace and the Houses of Parliament covered in the aggressive black red and white bunting infiltrated her mind and she blinked several times to rid herself of them. The war had begun to take its toll on her too, physically. Like many other women, her periods had gradually stopped as she grew from slim to thin and while she didn't miss its messiness, she still experienced a monthly cycle of headaches and abdominal cramps that threatened but didn't deliver anything, like a drought teased by a far-off rumble of thunder. Everyone was constantly hungry and the bread queues just got longer as the tide of food grown in France, flowed relentlessly to Germany. The only things becoming fat in Paris, apart from the Nazis, were the buds on the avenues of trees that stood, carelessly defiant in the early spring sunlight above the anti-aircraft artillery positioned in virtually every elegant square across the city. In her mind, as she walked past, Lottie blew each one up.

*

By the time she reached the café, Denise was drinking coffee. She was glowing. Clearly being in love or at least taking a lover like Archambaud, suited her. Lottie sat and the waiter took her order, flirting a little with them.

"You look well, Denise. That colour suits you." She was wearing a small, red scarf.

"Thank you. How are you, Heloise?"

"I'm fine."

"You seem a little," she put her head on one side, "sad?"

"Not at all, I was just reflecting on things as I was walking here, that's all."

"Well, according to Prosper, we have every reason to be upbeat."

"Oh?"

"Let's have our coffee and walk through the park? It'll be easier to talk."

"Yes. Now tell me," said Lottie, smiling. "How things are going with Archambaud?"

"He's nice," said Denise. "A little posh but handsome and lots of fun but I think it's best not to get too intense!" Her brown eyes softened. "But, you know…"

"Yes, I do. Well, that's lovely."

"What about you?"

"Me?"

"Oh come on, you and Michel?"

"There's no me and Michel." Lottie was caught off-guard and she blushed.

"It's obvious he likes you."

Lottie was surprised but she couldn't help feeling pleased. "I think you're mistaken. We have to pretend but that's all."

Denise shook her head. "No, *trust me*, he likes you."

"Well, if he does, he's a funny way of showing it!" She laughed and drank her coffee, wanting to change the subject. "Shall we walk?"

*

The watery sun poked through the grey clouds in a desperate attempt to get noticed. In the borders of the park, plants were beginning to unfurl their leaves, stretching up skywards and Lottie found the early signs of spring and the dependability of the seasons, comforting. Denise linked her arm and they followed the paths, away from the man who still found crumbs to feed the birds and the rough sleepers who had lost everything.

"Have you heard from Irene and Jacqueline?" said Lottie when there was no chance of them being overheard.

"Yes, but they can't come to the apartment any longer. Jaqueline is busy acting housewife to Pierre in Romorantin. Like us, they're waiting for supplies. It's bloody shit, frankly. Prosper is being called back to HQ in London. He's being picked up in a few days, so it will be a perfect opportunity for him to," she hesitated for a moment, "what do the Yanks say – kick some ass?" Her French accent made the phrase sound practically poetic and Lottie laughed. Denise looked round to make sure they weren't being followed. "In the meantime, as you know, we have plans to blow up some power stations around Paris. Here is your location and the date." She handed Lottie a small piece of paper with pencil map references. "Can you memorise them to pass on to Michel?"

"Yes, of course." Lottie already had.

"Good. I'm doing Chaingy and I'm taking Worms with me. He and I shall go for a picnic with a bag full of explosive. It's the perfect cover and it doesn't get more romantic for a Jewish boy than the sound of a German-controlled installation exploding!" She threw her arm out, opening her hand, wide.

"Sounds perfect!" Lottie grinned.

"By the time the Gestapo arrives, we will be cycling happily away through the lanes to a backdrop of black smoke."

Lottie looked at her fondly. "It's quite marvellous how the movement's growing, isn't it? We had another four join up, last week, all terribly young but strong and passionate and ready to die for France."

"Yes, things are finally gaining momentum. If the Allies land soon, as we think, we need to be able to support them."

"Yes, and we know it's possible for local people to fight back and make gains," Lottie said, eagerly. "Look at Karditsa."

Denise nodded in agreement. "The Greek Liberation Army fights well and they can hide in the mountains and shoot traitorous Italians, what could be more perfect?" She glanced down at her watch. "I have to go, Heloise. I've new recruits to train in combat at four and I'm playing poker at seven."

They kissed on both cheeks, said farewell and a little more upbeat, Lottie turned and began to walk back in the direction of Gare du Nord.

CHAPTER 60

5ᵗʰ April 1943 – Paris

Also on this day, the German submarine U-635 is sunk in the North Atlantic by the RAF.

L ottie reached the outer edge of the Tenth Arrondissement, after meeting Denise, her head full of ideas to put to Michel for the sabotage of the power station. The drizzle that had begun as she left her in the Jardin Villemin and walked down Rue des Recollets in the direction of Gare du Nord got heavier and she pulled her hat down low and collar up. It had been another long, cold winter, during which nobody had fat reserves to keep them warm, leaving bones aching and skin cracked and open to the elements. The buildings she passed had seen better days and happier people. It wasn't the most prestigious area of Paris and only a short walk to Denise's, largely now abandoned, apartment. It was, however, away from any of their usual meeting places and it was good practice to make changes. People got to know faces and there were still many people in Paris who would, out of desperation, inform for money or food and opportunist eyes were, it seemed, everywhere. She looked at her watch and hoped her train was on time. Ahead of her, at the far end of the road were a couple of soldiers busy checking papers and so she slipped down Passage des Recollets to avoid the checks which, if slow, might cause her to miss her train.

The Passage was quite narrow and deserted with one car parked but just as she reached the halfway point, a truck driving at speed pulled in, mounted the pavement, drew to an abrupt halt just behind her and two German soldiers jumped out. Instead of putting her head down and walking on, as her training would have mandated, Lottie slipped into a dark doorway, curious as to what was going on. She watched as three Gestapo officers emerged further down the street, roughly pulling two women from a building, one by her hair. From where Lottie was hiding, she could clearly see gold stars roughly sewn onto their jumpers. One was carrying a basket, the other was trying to fight the men. Both were shouting. Lottie felt sickened. She fought an overwhelming urge go to their assistance but they would all probably end up getting shot and the Resistance would be one trained agent down, which they could ill afford. The woman with the basket was screaming, "My baby! Don't hurt my baby!" It was then she caught sight of Lottie pressed into the doorway and dropped the basket at the side of the road. The Gestapo officers didn't notice and having done their dirty work they jumped into the parked car and sped off, leaving the two soldiers to try to get the frightened, flailing women into the truck. Both were now wriggling and fighting and screaming. As the flaps were pulled back, Lottie could see an array of stars as the faces of other rounded up Jews, gaunt and pleading, held hands out, trying to help the women who continued to put up a good fight. One of the solders lost his hat and it flew into the filthy gutter on the other side of the road. Unable to gain control, he resorted to pulling out his pistol which he aimed it at the women. "Get into the fucking truck!" he yelled. The other had picked up the woman who was carrying the basket and threw her over his shoulder. She paused before delivering another onslaught against his back with her fists, looking in Lottie's direction, eyes pleading, mouthing silently, "Take my baby! Please, please take my baby!"

Lottie nodded, pressing back against the door, praying the soldiers continued to be distracted. The scene unfolding in front of her was no more than a minute or two but it seemed like hours. She was well aware the women would be sent to a camp and would probably be shot or die from starvation. The basket and its surprisingly silent contents was no more than ten yards away from the doorway and in the scuffle, the soldiers ignored it. At the back of the truck, one was preoccupied with trying to stay upright as he heaved the resisting mother of the baby, into the back. She had hold of his collar and was pulling him in with her, swearing. Lottie realised then, she was probably buying her a few moments to get the child. The second soldier made his way across the road at a fairly leisurely pace to retrieve the cap, his face scratched and expression surly. He was not in a hurry, it seemed, to get back to the seething vehicle as he picked up the light grey cap and began to brush the dirt off it with evident distaste. For a moment both soldiers had their backs to her and she sprinted out, grabbed the basket and returned to the cover of the doorway, praying the sudden movement wouldn't make the child cry out and it didn't. Not daring to look out she held her breath, heart leaping out of her chest, waiting for the truck to pull away, leaving her with the infant.

Looking down into the basket, the child's face, thin and pale looked back up at Lottie and the small mouth opened into a perfect 'o' and yawned. It couldn't have been more than a few weeks old. Discarding the basket, she wrapped the child up and hugged it to her, talking softly to it and looking up and down the road which had now fallen back into a dirty silence. She had to get out of there quickly in case the soldiers realised they'd left the baby and came back. Opening her coat, she tucked the child that felt no more than a few pounds in weight, inside to keep it warm and began to walk in the direction of the station. If she was quick she'd still make her train and they'd both be safer out of Paris. As she walked, she concocted an albeit weak story about looking after the baby for a friend, knowing if she was stopped she had no identity documents for it, there would be a problem but she couldn't just leave it somewhere. She didn't even know if the baby was a girl or a boy. The main thing was that it remained mercifully quiet. If by some miracle, she made it to Chantilly, she would have to try to get from the station to the Toussants without anyone from the town asking her questions. She doubted the Gestapo would bother looking for the child and if the soldiers admitted to leaving it at the side of the road, they'd be disciplined.

*

On the train, Lottie relaxed a little when nobody seemed interested. A man did get up and offer her a seat, for which she was grateful, as her legs had begun to feel weak from shock. The motion of the train seemed to lull the baby back to sleep and she looked at its innocent face, its big eyes flickering under the blue-veined lids as it snuggled into her, its mouth making a sucking motion. It was probably hungry and if it woke up, Lottie was certain it would wail like a siren, drawing attention to them. If that happened, she would have to try to act naturally, putting the tip of her finger in its mouth to try and pacify it, as she'd seen mothers do with their babies. She wondered how the

Toussants would react to her bringing an infant home and what on earth she would do with it. It really wasn't ideal as they were already taking enormous risks in having her there and now this. She just hoped, they would understand. A huge wave of sadness engulfed her as she realised the child would probably never see its mother or father again and he or she would be lucky to survive the war. She hugged it tighter, feeling obliged to silently apologise for the horrific world it had been brought into.

CHAPTER 61

5th April 1943, Chantilly, France

Also on this day, docks and shipping at Brest are raided by the Royal Air Force.

Margot was doing some washing when Lottie arrived home with the baby. When she opened her coat, knowing she was stretching the support of the couple to beyond its limits, Margot remained calm and took it from her, while she removed her coat and hat. The child awoke and began to cry softly. Lottie winced, wondering what Margot would do when it filled its lungs and really let the world know it was there. She explained what had happened and the somewhat more experienced woman rocked it from side to side and suggested it would need feeding and probably changing. As luck would have it, she said she still had some baby clothes put away from Sylvie and Lucien and some towels that could be cut up for nappies. Before the war, she told Lottie, she and Maurice were planning another child but not now, not like this. Food, Lottie was told, was more of a problem. Margot said she couldn't trust the exhausted women, undernourished and breastfeeding in Chantilly to act as wet nurses, so the only thing she could think of was to dilute some cows' milk and a little evaporated milk and feed the child that way. It wasn't the best for the gut but hopefully the baby would keep it down. At that moment, looking at Margot's natural ability and struggling with what could be viewed as her own ineptitude, Lottie could have hugged her. The baby let out a wail and Margot passed her back to Lottie to rock her while she sorted things out.

"What about Sylvie and Lucien? They'll be home soon," Lottie said, swinging the baby from side to side in an attempt to pacify it.

Margot stopped and scratched her head and thought for a moment. "When I pick them up, I'll tell them that we have a wonderful surprise waiting for them when they get home but that it has to be a family secret..."

"Because?"

Both women looked at each other wide eyed, racking their brains to think of a plausible excuse.

"Because... your friend in Paris is unwell and you have taken the baby for a few days until she's better."

"But why the secrecy?"

"Because the father of the baby mustn't know where it is?"

Lottie puffed out her cheeks, mulling over the story. "Why? They're bound to ask."

"They don't have to be told everything. All they need to know is that they must do as they've been asked and not keep asking questions."

"And after a few days?"

The baby was now screaming at full capacity.

"We must get it fed. Is it a girl or boy? We can't keep calling the poor darling, 'it'."

"I don't know. We'll find out when we change it," said Lottie.

Margot seemed to shock herself back into action and ran up the stairs. Within minutes, she was back down with an assortment of towels, flannels, small, lovingly crocheted blankets and a bottle.

"My goodness, you're an absolute angel." Lottie stared at her with complete admiration.

"Do you know how to change a baby?"

Lottie shrugged. "I watched our nurse do it years ago."

"Your *nurse?*" Margot grinned above the noise that was filling every nook and cranny of the kitchen.

"Yes, I have a younger brother," she said, quickly, annoyed at herself for imparting personal information.

"Oh, well let's hope you can remember. Let me give you a head start." She folded the large square and laid it on the table. "There!"

Right, this, thought Lottie, couldn't be difficult. She laid the child, whose face had turned crimson with sudden rage, on the table and removed the layers from it. It was a bit like unwrapping a Christmas gift but more difficult to handle as it kept moving. "Come on, little one," she said as the baby's arms and legs flailed around. Eventually she managed to get the woollen clothes off and she could tell by the smell, it badly needed changing. Wincing and holding her breath, leaning over it, she removed the heavy, noxious padding from around its bottom and as she did so, a jet of urine caught her in the face.

"Arrgh!"

Margot who was busy mixing milk with boiled water turned and laughed. "It's a boy!"

"Yes," said Lottie, wiping her face with the back of her hand, barely controlling her gag reflex as she pushed away the napkin and its weighty contents. She looked frantically around for somewhere to put it, not wanting to leave it on the table.

"Put it on the floor, we'll deal with it in a moment." Margot brought over a bowl of warm, soapy water and soaked the flannel in it before handing it to Lottie. "There, we'll clean him up and feed him. That should make him happier."

"What shall we call him? I wish I knew what his mother named him."

Margot looked at him, hands on hips. "'Yves'. A good French name. You don't want anything that stands out."

"Yes, Yves it is. What on earth am I going to do with him, Margot?"

Margot tested the temperature of the milk on her wrist. "I think I might have an idea. There's a young family who lives on the outskirts of Barbizon who have ten or eleven children and one infant who has just passed. It was stillborn, poor thing. The man is a woodcutter and they're very poor but they're good people and I think for a sum of money they would take him with no questions asked."

"How would they register him?"

"They live remotely, I think if they do it soon, the Germans wouldn't find out. One of the local doctors not far from there is sympathetic to the Resistance and we could get an identity card or use the one of the dead child. They would be around the same age."

"Wasn't there a funeral?"

Margot shook her head. "They don't have the money. I doubt many people even knew of the death."

"How did you know about it?" Lottie was wrestling with the baby and the nappy pin. "It doesn't seem the most watertight plan and could put the woodcutter and his wife at risk." Finally it was fastened and she wrapped the baby Yves in a towel and looked down at him. Already his cries had subsided and she scooped him up and passed him to Margot, who sat down with him in the crook of her arm and offered the bottle to the hungry lips that opened immediately and began sucking.

"The doctor's wife was trying to get some clothes for the older children and she asked me."

"Shall I go and see the family?"

"No, let me get a message to them and test the water."

"I can get money."

Margot nodded. "Heloise, we need to think of another plan in case this doesn't work."

"I need to talk to Michel too."

"Good luck with that." Margot looked up at her.

"Just when things were going well. He's going to be furious."

"Probably!"

"What about Maurice?"

Margot shrugged. "I'll deal with my husband, don't worry."

"I'm so sorry, Margot, for bringing trouble to your door. I know it's an enormous security risk."

"Life is full of risk but it isn't worth a thing if we can't protect innocent children." She looked down at Yves and smiled as he guzzled the remainder of his feed, staring up at her earnestly, his hands with tiny pink nails, clasped round the bottle.

"Here," said Margot, when he'd finished. "Take a cloth and put him over your shoulder and rub his back, he'll need winding before we put him to bed in one of the spare rooms."

"Perhaps he'd better be in with me?" said Lottie. "So if he wakes in the night I can try to pacify him."

Margot nodded. "Maybe. I will show you how to prepare a bottle for if he wakes."

"Right." Lottie frowned. This wasn't exactly how she'd expected her day to end but looking at the baby and recalling the mother's pleading face, she couldn't regret her actions but she'd have to work hard to mitigate the consequences.

CHAPTER 62

6th April 1943, Chantilly, France

On this day, the British and US Armies link up in Africa.

"A baby?" Michel repeated, quietly as if he couldn't quite believe what he was hearing.

"Yes, Michel, a baby." Lottie closed her eyes and sighed. She'd sent a message to him to meet her in the woods.

"Did you just forget all your training?" His dark brows narrowed over his eyes.

"With respect," she began, "you weren't there. Under the circumstances, I'm sure you'd have done the same."

"With *respect*, you're presuming to tell me what I would or wouldn't have done?" His curly fringe fell over his eyes and he flung it back. "Have you *any* idea what this could mean?"

"His life is saved?" She felt herself getting defensive.

"What this could mean to the whole Circuit and to the Toussants?" He turned and walked a few paces, fists clenched. "We could be closed down if London gets to hear about it."

"He's an innocent child!" She almost shouted at his back.

"And your reckless action could have cost the lives of many people," he said, turning. "I thought you were more…"

"More what?"

"Responsible!"

"And it would have been *responsible* to leave the baby on the pavement or let the soldiers take it to the camp?"

He didn't answer. Lottie sighed and said more calmly. "Look, Michel, I don't expect you to understand about how precious a child's life is but to that baby's mother..."

He interrupted, pointing at her. "You don't think I know how precious a child is, huh?"

"Well, you don't have them, so how could you? How could I? But I was the one that saw her face when she was fighting the soldiers and pleading with me to save him!"

"What the Hell do you know about me?"

Lottie stared at him. "I beg your pardon?"

"I *had* a child," he said, after a moment, taking a step towards her, his eyes now wild and she took a step back.

"What?"

"I had a child," he repeated, his face now contorted with pain.

"You *had* a child... When?" She went to take a step towards him, to reach out but an impenetrable barrier, invisible but very present, stopped her.

He turned his back to her and said, barely audibly, "Just before the war."

"Oh, Michel, whatever happened?" whispered Lottie, feeling as though someone had run into her with a car and driven off. When he turned back she could see he was crying, silently, his eyes now red raw and filled with anguish.

He sniffed and wiped his eyes, roughly, with the back of his hand before looking beyond her. "In January 1940, my wife and I had been married for a year. Our baby girl, Hannah, was one month old..." He stifled a sob and took a moment to collect himself. "My wife's name was Keturah. She was Jewish. We lived in Poland, near to her parents. In April 1940, Keturah, my daughter and her parents were taken to the Lodz Ghetto and by the end of the month, it was sealed off from the outside world. There were thousands of Jews inside. Most, if not, all perished. I was away with my work, in Vichy. A friend told me my wife had argued with the German guards because they beat an old man and she and my daughter were... executed." He was sobbing now, his shoulders heaving with grief and anger. Lottie went towards him to comfort him but he held his hand out in front of him to stop her. "So Heloise, when you say I couldn't know how precious a child is, you couldn't be more wrong!" He paused for a moment to collect himself. "You should get the baby to safety without compromising our operations any further."

"Michel, I'm so sorry! I had no idea…"

"Why would you?" His expression told her it was none of her business to know anything about him.

"Nobody said…"

"Why would they? Nobody knows but I have made a pact with God to avenge their deaths! We have the opportunity to save hundreds of babies, Heloise, not just one. Don't you see, we can't afford to be… impetuous? Let me know when you have dealt with things." With that, he turned and walked away through the trees and feeling helpless, she watched him disappear into the twilight.

*

Back at home, Margot had returned from a visit to the woodland family with the doctor and had somehow managed to convince them to take Yves in return for a sum of money to feed their hungry children. Out of necessity, things moved rapidly. Two days later, Lottie kissed him goodbye, silently wishing him well and Sylvie, who had been told he was going back to his parents, gave him one of her treasured teddy bears. They bundled the baby and as much cash as Lottie could muster, into a large bag and Maurice delivered him on horseback, with his new identity papers, in the darkest of nights, to the bereaved mother whose breasts were full but her stomach empty.

CHAPTER 63

19th May 1943, Chantilly, France

On this day, Winston Churchill addresses a joint session of the US Congress and praises the partnership of the two allies.

After Michel told Lottie about his wife and daughter, he became distant with her once again and avoided eye contact. It was like she'd rolled the dice and slid down an enormous snake on a Snakes and Ladders board. She hadn't told anyone what he'd said but she'd thought about it a lot and could only imagine his pain. She'd long put out of her mind any thought of romance and stopped subconsciously looking for signs of his interest in her and just focused on the job. In some ways, his revelation had helped her to understand him a little better and she no longer misinterpreted his brooding moods as him being simply an arrogant, middle-class Frenchman. Her own losses weren't diminished by his of course but she felt further down the path of grief than Michel and she was so immersed in playing the part of Heloise it was as if she'd had to let go of Hugh and Gareth who didn't belong in her new world. Eventually, if she survived the war, she was afraid that as soon as she set foot back in England and became Lottie Beauchamp once again, the buried memories of her brother and lover would come flooding back to her on a rip tide and sweep her away. For now though, that seemed far off and England now felt like a foreign country. Sometimes she wondered if there would be any point in her returning home. Perhaps, after the war, someone would save Michel, if ever he wanted to be rescued from the past, but it wouldn't be her and for now, as comrades in arms, they had a job to get on with.

*

Since the beginning of May, the Physician network under the leadership of Prosper who had by then returned to Paris, from

London, had as expected complained loudly and bitterly to HQ about the lack of supplies. He had been assured that an Allied invasion was no longer imminent but something he said must have been heard, as London spurred into action, making half a dozen successful drops to the network over the month and by all accounts, this was set to continue.

*

On this particular evening, ten of the Waterman Circuit, whose members now included three generations, were staked out at a camp, deep in the woods. Under the light of the full moon the night was sultry and warm and the air was fragranced with wild garlic. To pass time while they waited for the drop, they smoked and talked about the land and of fighting and families, while they shared a delicious picnic made by Monique. Lottie sat quietly at the very edge of the group, listening and wondering if in Germany or Italy, similar conversations would be taking place in woodland, houses, bars or shelters. Regardless of war humans, whatever their nationality, really weren't very different. Whichever side they were on, they all loved, laughed, cried, fought and died and, as individuals she felt, they were really terribly insignificant. Looking up through the tree canopy to the heavens where tonight, the stars' brilliance competed with the moon and lost, she contemplated what life would be like on another planet and whether they did things better in a different world.

"What are you thinking about, Lottie?" Michel came over and helped himself to a bottle of Monique's homemade lemonade. It was strange for him to ask a personal question and it threw her.

"Oh nothing, really."

He sat down next to her and lit a cigarette. They were silent for a while and she felt a little awkward at the close proximity as they listened to the newly recruited Clement teasing his gentle-giant of a father, David, about forgetting his wife's birthday. He'd managed to do so for a second year in a row and she was so annoyed, she chased him round the farmyard with a pitch-fork. Next year, if he did it again, she told him she would run him over with the tractor. They all laughed and it broke the tension.

"I'm sorry," said Michel, quietly.

Lottie turned and looked at him, surprised. "About what?"

He looked to make sure nobody was listening. "The baby... the boy."

"Oh, that..."

"I shouldn't have taken things out on you. It would have been my Hannah's third birthday."

"There's really no need to apologise, Michel. I truly understand why you reacted like you did." Lottie hugged her knees to her.

"I want... need to make things right between us." He looked down at his boots.

Lottie nodded and smiled looking down at the grass. "It's fine, really."

He nodded and got to his feet. "We need to bury this stuff," he said, addressing the men, pointing to the food papers and bottles, "and get into position. Clement, please go and tell both lookouts to stand down and join us for a final briefing."

*

The aircraft rumbled towards the field. When Michel gave the signal, three men ran out and shone their torches, guiding it in. The parachutes opened and one by one the canisters dropped to earth. Michel waited for all of them to land before giving the signal for everyone to move into the drop zone and start to clear away the chutes. They had a short window of ten minutes before the transport arrived and they could begin loading.

As soon as they began to run from their hiding places to retrieve the delivery, shots rang out into the night as the ambush announced itself. The lookouts sprang into action and began to fire back randomly in the direction of the gunshots, in an attempt to provide cover for their comrades. Lottie threw herself into a ditch and returned fire, before ducking back down. Clement joined her and followed suit. Not more than twenty yards from Lottie, one of the men ran through the trees to try to get a better position but a burst of fire felled him to the ground. The sound of furious retaliatory fire rang out.

"Cover me!" Lottie shouted at Clement before rolling out of the ditch and, commando style, made her way to the casualty, under a barrage of fire. She identified him as Jean-Luc, one of the new recruits. Groping inside his jacket collar for his neck, she held her fingers against where she should have felt his pulse but there was nothing. Michel was frantically waving at her to get back down. A bullet ricocheted off the ground in front of her in a firefly of light, kicking up dust and missing her by inches. With a massive push backwards, she was back down in the ditch. There was a moment's lull. Michel looked over and signalled behind him to a dead tree.

"Follow me!" Lottie pulled Clement's arm. "Stay low. We're making for that tree over there. Michel will cover us."

Michel opened fire and they ran, zig zagging before diving over the large log as bullets rained down around them.

"Keep firing! Cover Michel. He can't go anywhere. I'm going to circle round to see if I can flush them out into the open." She was breathless from the sprint and adrenaline rush.

"Okay, Heloise. Be careful."

She waited for her moment and bent double, ran further back into the depths of the forest before banking right towards a narrow road. The gunfire was coming from that direction and the Gestapo or soldiers must be parked somewhere there. She ran from tree to tree for protection anticipating being showered with bullets but nobody appeared to have spotted her. About one hundred yards to her left, she could see the outline of a car. There didn't appear to be accompanying vehicles which meant, at most, there were four soldiers, including the driver. Reloading her Sten gun, she moved forward to the rear of a thicket and lay down flat. Her deduction was correct. The soldiers were spread thinly out with no more than thirty yards between the four of them. This wasn't a planned ambush. They must be soldiers on their way somewhere and had spotted the aircraft. She calculated from where she was positioned, she could take out two of them, with no trouble. Waiting for her moment, she opened fire, spraying them with shot as they cried out in horrified surprise before crumpling and falling to the ground. The other two guns immediately turned on her and she rolled back under cover. Michel and the men continued shooting to take the pressure off her until it stopped again, suddenly. There was an eery silence of anticipation. Lottie could no longer see the other two figures who had disappeared. She slowed her breathing. If they were trying to work their way round to her, she would see them before they caught sight of her but she couldn't work out why her comrades had stopped shooting. Unable to break cover and move, she had no alternative but to watch and wait. Then, after what seemed like hours, she heard the sound of the engine of the car being started before it accelerated and raced off down the road. The men began to shoot again in the direction of the noise but this time nothing was returned. Evidently they had gone. Lottie got to her feet and cautiously began to work her way back to the men. Within a few minutes she was nearly back to where she started. She gave a low whistle to identify herself and it was returned. Moments later, the woods began to stir as the men came out of their hiding places.

"Four soldiers, two down. They've taken off in a car towards Chantilly."

"They'll be back. We need to get the truck over here," said Michel, running towards Jean-Luc's body. "We can't leave him here. When they return they'll eventually identify him and we need to get him back to his family. Clement, go and let Claude know."

Clement immediately turned and sprinted off.

"What about all this stuff?" said David, looking dismayed at the field of bounty that was about to land in enemy hands.

"Forget it. We don't have time. It's gone. We have to get out of here and quickly!" Michel looked around at the men. "Let's get Jean-Luc to the road."

As he passed Lottie he stopped and put his hand on her shoulder and stared into her face. "You were very brave. Well done, Heloise."

She shrugged. "It makes the training worthwhile." The lingering feel of his hand sent a frisson of electricity through her that made her shudder involuntarily. Misreading it, he pulled it away as though he'd accidentally put his hand on a hot range. "Come," he said, gruffly. "We need to leave."

She picked up her gun with a sniff and, slinging it across her chest, she put her shoulders down and strode behind him, mulling over the fact that she had just taken two lives and far from being shocked or disgusted, she was rather triumphant. She felt a bit like a child at their first hunt where blood is smeared on an upturned face to signify a rite of passage. In this case though, the quarry was not a benign, innocent creature killed for entertainment. She watched the men load Jean-Luc into the back of the truck, his arm hanging at the side, hand trailing in the dirt, the elixir of life oozing from a chest wound and forming a dark patch on his shirt. Perhaps, she thought, war really had changed her.

CHAPTER 64

22nd June 1943, Paris

On this day, the US Army Air Force carries out the second heaviest bombing of Germany. It drops 422 tons of bombs and loses 16 aircraft.

June had been a busy time for the Prosper circuit. They had taken part in several successful acts of sabotage and it felt to Lottie as though they were finally making some headway in support of the long anticipated Allied invasion. Drops had become more frequent and, in turn, the Gestapo were increasingly frustrated at the growing number of acts of sabotage. Hugo Bleicher was ever more determined to catch and publicly punish enemy agents.

*

Lottie sat in a stuffy Parisienne cinema, watching the film 'Adrien'; a comedy about a man who had invented a motorised roller skate. It was somewhat ridiculous. If the French had them, like everything else, the Germans would have doubtless requisitioned them. She had a sudden vision of Hitler and his terrible entourage being propelled round the Arc de Triomphe on electric roller skates and she suppressed a sudden urge to laugh out loud. As the German Official Censorship Bureaux forbade anything even vaguely controversial, the public were left with undemanding cinema. Nonetheless, she'd sat the film out and waited patiently for Denise who had an urgent message for her. In order to attract minimal attention, she'd taken her usual chair in the darkest recesses where there were fewest people and finally, Denise slid in behind her, whispering in her ear, making her jump.

"God, you startled me!" she mumbled, without turning.

"Sorry."

"Luckily for you, you missed half of the film."

"There's a problem."

Lottie stiffened. "What kind of problem?"

"Jaqueline has been shot and Pierre's been arrested."

"Is she alive?" Lottie was thinking fast.

"We don't know. Shot in the head, we think. If she's lucky, she'll be dead. Two Canadians they had picked up near Dhuizon have also been arrested."

The image of Jacqueline with a bullet in her forehead made Lottie recoil. "Did they have anything on them?"

"We think Pierre's briefcase is missing and there's no knowing what was in it. There was a parcel on the seat of the car containing radio crystals and encoded messages for the Circuit. On that basis alone, there's no way they'll let Pierre go."

"Shit!"

"Shit indeed! Everything's on hold. We need to lay low for a while and be extra careful. Prosper's waiting for more news. As soon as we hear anything, we'll let you know."

"Okay."

"I have to go, Heloise."

"Stay safe."

"You too."

With that, she was gone and the film came to an end.

Lottie held back until the jumpy credits and music had finished, pretending to fiddle around in her bag under the dim light of the cinema, while the audience queued to leave, before she made her way to the exit, glancing round, to check she wasn't being followed. Satisfied, she turned in the direction of Pigalle Metro when the air-raid siren sounded. She quickened her pace but only slightly. Paris was rarely hit and people were generally laissez-faire about the whole thing but it was best to blend in and so she followed the growing tide of the general public who were heading for the Metro.

People poured down the entrance, like liquid being swallowed by a dark mouth. Lottie got swept in too and disappeared into the hot, dim light of the subterranean world. People were calling out to friends and family, trying to keep them together in the crowd, as they looked for somewhere to sit in the miserable oven. The platforms were soon covered but most tried to accommodate others and reacted good-naturedly to being trodden over. Lottie sat, legs tucked in, thinking about the terrible news about the competent, likeable Jaqueline and the possible repercussions from Pierre's arrest, as she waited for the sound of bombs or an all-clear. It would be ironic, she thought suddenly, if she were killed by a bomb delivered by plane she'd once flown. She looked about her and saw, adjacent to her, a swarthy, well-dressed gentleman with a guitar and next to him another with a clarinet. She was sure she recognised them but didn't want to stare. The one with the guitar made eye contact and he smiled and nodded. It was then, with a stab of excitement she realised she was sitting next to the famous Django Reinhardt, from the Quintet du Hot Club who she had never yet had the privilege of seeing play live. She smiled back, feeling herself blush. From a few yards away, a young man called out, "Play for us, Monsieur Reinhardt?" The man looked a little embarrassed but the young man had betrayed his identity and his name spread like a wave that gathered momentum along the platform and 'Reinhardt' filled any spare space. At the end of the platform, a group of German soldiers, one an officer, stood deep in conversation under a light and they turned sharply to see what the disturbance was about. Lottie put her head down. The officer picked his way through the people, politely waiting for them to make space and stood above Reinhardt and his band member, Hubert Rostaing, regarding them from beneath his cap. "Monsieur Reinhardt?"

"Yes."

The officer looked around. The place had fallen silent. The crowd were wary and on edge, always anticipating trouble.

"The people would like you to entertain them, so while we wait, please do as they ask."

Reinhardt and Rostaing got to their feet and began to play Nuages. The atmosphere changed in a heartbeat as the crowd visibly relaxed and began to sing softly along, swaying from side to side to the beat.

I'm leaving, I'm much better off without you
Your memory pierces my cold blood
I want to believe you when you cry
But the more I hate you the less time passes, yeah
Fractured your life now is just a thought
My soul is at war, I would like to leave the trench
The shadow of your body appears on the floor
Your smile and your lips in my eyes are foreign
I write our history, I read in your voice
I'm afraid she'll collide when she thinks of me
I'm in quicksand, I look at the sky and I fly away
Anger shares my life, the more I blame myself, the worse I am
I'm lost, I'm alone in the dark
The heartbeats are violent
She flees, hatred takes place
I don't really like you
Without you I feel free, without you I feel alive
I face the immense night, I ask forgiveness it made me jump into the void
In the clouds
In the clouds
In the clouds… etc.

The voices of the crowd rose up and disappeared down the tunnels and Lottie found herself, too, mouthing the song that had become the anthem of the Resistance. Momentarily, it took her mind off the news about Jaqueline and Pierre and reminded her that even war had its magic moments that were so rare and precious, they had to be taken.

At the end, as if on cue, the all-clear could be heard above the sound of applause. People struggled to their feet and, lifted by the impromptu recital from the Gypsy King of Jazz, they spilled back out onto the street.

CHAPTER 65

24th June 1943, Chantilly, France

On this day, there are continuing attacks against the Ruhr industrial valley. Large numbers of German civilians are evacuated from the area.

"Heloise?" Something in Margot's voice sounded urgent.

Lottie, who had been putting fresh linen on her bed, opened her bedroom door. "Margot?"

She was standing at the top of the stairs, looking pale.

"Michel's here. Please come quickly!"

She dropped the sheets and raced down the stairs after Margot. Michel was in the kitchen with Maurice, standing with his back against the range. He looked like he'd seen a ghost.

"What's going on?"

"We have a problem. Denise and Archambaud were arrested by the Gestapo last night."

Lottie's whole being seemed to go into freefall and she felt momentarily dizzy. "Are you sure?"

He nodded. "Completely."

"Where?" She tried frantically to understand what this meant for her friends and for the rest of the circuit.

"They were staying over at the Laurents'. At midnight they came for them and caught them making false papers."

Lottie's mouth went dry. "And Prosper?"

Michel shook his head. "No news yet but if they have Denise and Archambaud, they'll be after him. We have people watching his apartment at Rue Mazagran."

"The circuit is compromised!" Lottie gripped the back of the kitchen chair, her knuckles white.

"Yes. Collect your things, we need to leave." He said it calmly but with an unmistakable note of urgency.

"What about Maurice, Margot and the children?"

"They need to go too. The price for harbouring you, Heloise, would be… execution."

"Come, Margot," said Lottie, springing into action. "I'll go up and pack small bags for the children. You go and collect them from school. It'll be their lunch in twenty minutes and it will look absolutely normal. Tell them you're taking them on holiday." She took Margot's hand and squeezed it. "It will be okay, trust me." She turned to Maurice. "We need to get you away from here, now. Feed the animals but give them extra. I'll put a few clothes into a case and when Margot returns she can take it with the children to the station." She span round and addressed Margot. "If anyone asks you'll say you're going away to spend a few days with an old school friend. You'll then catch the first train to Gare du Nord and wait for Maurice near to the seamstress's shop." Lottie was thinking on her feet.

Margot nodded. "I'll go for the children."

Michel, arms folded, was listening, intently. "Do you have anywhere to go? Somewhere as far away as possible from Paris, where you would be safe?" he said, finally.

Maurice shook his head. His eyes had become sunken and his face had aged ten years with fear for his family. Michel thought for a moment. "Put together whatever money you have and take a train south-east to Dijon. Travel in a different compartment to Margot and the children and give her some cash. Have your stories tight. Don't deviate. Head for a village south of the Dijon, called St-Jean-de-Losne. I have a friend who lives at number 6 Quai de la Hutte. His name is Alain Boucher. Tell him I sent you and explain what's happened. He and his wife are members of a guerrilla group called the Marque. They will look after you until we can arrange new identities for you. Wait to hear from us. Let's go, my friend, we will do everything we can to keep you and the children safe." He went over and hugged him.

Lottie thanked Maurice and wished him well before turning to Michel. "I'll wait here for Margot and meet you at Bernard's in no more than an hour? Once we're satisfied they're on their way, we can decide what to do from there."

Michel held her by both arms and stared into her face. "We need to leave Chantilly as quickly as we can. I'll make arrangements. Be careful, Heloise, I couldn't..." He trailed off.

"You too." With that, she turned and ran back upstairs to pack for everyone, making sure each child had at least one favourite toy.

*

By the time Margot returned, she had finished packing for all of them and started on her own, concentrating on making sure she left nothing for the Gestapo that could implicate anyone.

"How wonderful you are going on holiday!" she said, beaming at the Lucien and Sylvia when they ran through the door. She ruffled Lucien's hair affectionately, her throat tightening as she realised this would doubtless be the last time she ever saw them.

"Are you coming too?" said Sylvia, frowning. "We would like you to, Heloise."

"Darling I can't but you will have a lovely time. I've packed Catherine as she wants to go too!"

"Why aren't you going with us?" Sylvia was not being fobbed off that easily.

"Because I have to stay here and look after things."

"Come along, both of you, enough chatter, we need to get the train." Margot looked at Lottie. "You both go downstairs, I will be down in a moment, I just need to speak to Heloise."

"But Mother, I want to choose more toys to take." Lucien's bottom lip started to protrude and far from excited, he looked about to cry.

"Lucien, be a good boy and soon you can make sandcastles which will make you forget about all your boring old toys. Now, go downstairs." Her tone was uncharacteristically sharp and Lucien began to cry as he stomped off.

"They're never like this!" Margot put her hand to her forehead.

"They can sense your anxiety. Once you're on the train it will be better, I promise."

"But where will we end up?" Her eyes were wide with fear.

"Listen to me." Lottie put her hand on her shoulder, staring into her eyes with a false reassurance. "Remember, you're off to stay with a school friend for a few days near Dijon. Think of a name that you'll remember, if questioned. Maurice will meet you outside the seamstresses. He'll be on a late train from Chantilly so just wait for him. Make it a big adventure for the children. If you get separated or something happens, the address is St-Jean-de-Losne, 6 Quai de la Hutte, Ask for Alain Boucher. Maurice will carry the bulk of the money. All you need is enough for the train fare into Paris. I have put a little more in, just in case one of you is delayed. Make sure you have all your identity documents. Okay?"

Margot nodded.

"I've packed some things for you including your jewellery."

Margot looked a little upset by this. "What I can't even pack for us?"

Lottie looked into her face and shook her head. "There's no time. I'm so sorry you've been caught up in this, Margot!"

"It was Maurice... It was *our* choice to help the Resistance."

"And now, we have to help *you*. It's time to go..." Lottie said gently.

"What about you, Heloise?"

"I will be fine. Goodbye, Margot, and good luck." She kissed her on both cheeks and eager to get them on their way, she helped her downstairs with the suitcase.

CHAPTER 66

24th June 1943, Chantilly, France

Also on this day, the Battle of Bamber Bridge, Lancashire, takes place. The US demand racial segregation of black soldiers in the town. The town's people oppose it and refuse.

O n arrival at Bernard's cottage after she'd seen Margot and the children safely off to the station, Lottie was told by the beekeeper, he'd just heard that the concierge to Prosper's apartment had gone missing and it was presumed she was being held by Gestapo. Prosper was supposedly on his way back from Normandy and, in any event, there was no sign of him in Paris. Bernard had been reliably informed the Gestapo were indeed waiting for him, at Rue Mazagran. It was impossible to warn him and to make the situation even more bleak, there was a rumour of additional arrests in Oise, of the Meru Resistance. The net, he and Lottie agreed, was rapidly closing in and once Hugo Bleicher and his henchmen began to torture the members of the circuit, it wouldn't be long before someone caved in and they arrived in Chantilly, to round them up.

*

As he gathered a few belongings together, Bernard looked very sad about leaving his hives. "Merde, next month I would have had *kilos* of honey and now, all that work for nothing!"

"I'm so sorry, Bernard…" Lottie knew how much the bees meant to him. "But at least they'll have food for winter, if nobody tries to take it."

"It's not your fault, Heloise," he said with a sigh, taking a small family photograph out of its frame and putting it in his pocket. "I doubt we'll be back any time soon to check."

Lottie shook her head. "Not until France is liberated."

"Best go and get the new papers for us all."

Several months ago, Lottie had suggested the three of them should have a spare set of identity papers made, paid for from the money sent from HQ in London, as insurance for a moment such as this and Bernard had duly arranged for them to be produced through one of his contacts and had hidden them in one of the hives. "The bees," he'd said with a chuckle, "will stand guard and God help any Nazi that tried to get them!"

He still seemed reluctant to accept they had to leave.

"You go and do that, then," she said, gently, to allow him a moment with the bees. "Michel will be here shortly. Let's hope he's managed to arrange transport out of Chantilly. If we don't leave today, we'll have to camp in the woods. We can't risk staying here now."

"No, we can't," he said resignedly.

"What food do you have in the house?"

"There's bread and a little cheese and of course honey. I also have a bottle of Cognac for emergencies," he said, looking over at his tiny larder. "And now appears to be that time."

"I'll parcel up the food. I don't know when we'll next get to eat."

"Okay." He disappeared through the back door and Lottie glanced out of the front, to see if she could spot Michel but all was quiet except for the sound of chickens squawking from a smallholding, far into the distance.

She glanced at her watch. It was nearly two pm. He was already half an hour late and she began to feel twitchy. If he was much longer, she and Bernard would have to wait in the woods and watch the house from there until he arrived. What, she thought, if he'd been stopped and arrested? It didn't bear thinking about. She tried to distract herself by doing something positive and so she ran through what was in her suitcase: Identity papers, money, scissors, soap, a headscarf, clean dress and underwear, pair of sensible shoes, make up, a couple of pairs of different designs of spectacles containing clear glass and hair dye. In case they had to sleep rough, she'd changed into trousers and boots before she left the Toussants and had brought the thick, moss-green jumper her mother had knitted for her, during her time in the Women's Auxiliary Air Force. She'd also packed the Colt .45, bullets and knife she'd hidden in the rafters at the family house. In her new identity photograph, she was blonde again and going back to her natural hair colour was the one small thing that she was looking forward to. She went to look out of the window again for Michel but to her relief, the door opened and he came in with Bernard.

"Michel, thank goodness, I was getting worried," she said, trying to sound perfectly calm.

"I'm sorry. Getting things organised took a little longer." He'd visibly aged too, thought Lottie.

"What have you managed?" said Bernard, putting the crumpled sets of identity documents, neatly tied with string, on the table. They had been intentionally made to look well used, so as not to arouse suspicion.

"In about an hour, there's a truck making a delivery of machinery to a rubber factory in Montargis, one hundred and seventy kilometres south-west of here. The driver has agreed to take us to the house of his friend. He'll collect us en route in one hour on the other side of the forest at Mongresin. From there we'll make our way further south to where I know people who can hide us for a few days. I'll tell you more when we're on our way."

"Can we trust the driver?" Lottie looked up. She was finishing wrapping the cheese into a square of paper.

Michel shrugged. "I think so but we don't have much choice. He's a relative of Claude's."

"Any news on the other men or of Prosper? I take it you've heard they're looking for him?"

He nodded. "There are people out trying to find him and warn him but it's likely the Gestapo will get there first. As far as the others from here are concerned, if they keep their heads down they should be all right. Nobody will have their names and I've never kept a list apart from in my head. I doubt any of them would be openly associated with me. We've been careful. Our names, on the other hand, we have to assume are now in the hands of the Gestapo."

"It's time to get rid of our original papers," said Lottie.

"Yes." Michel reached inside his jacket and pulled out his ration books and identity card and put it down on the table.

Bernard followed suit and, in silence, Lottie pulled hers from her case. Gathering them up and putting them in the grate, she bent down, lit a match and as the flame that licked at Heloise's photograph quickly enveloped the others, the three of them looked on in silence as their previous lives turned to ash.

"Here," said Michel, holding out her papers. "Celeste Durand, schoolteacher, and for you," he looked at Bernard, "Clement Simon, agricultural labourer. From now on, I will be Etienne Moreau, agricultural labourer. Heloise, Bernard and Michel are no more. Now we must look to the future and continue our work."

CHAPTER 67

25th June 1943, Montargis, south-west of Paris

On this day, Dwight D. Eisenhower becomes the Supreme Allied Commander of World War 2.

The journey to Montargis had been long and terribly uncomfortable. The bed of the truck had been hastily covered in a thin layer of straw and the centre lined with bales to "prevent the machines from moving about". It had a narrow corridor in the middle, just wide enough to hide the three passengers, sitting one in front of the other. The whole cargo was then covered with a heavy tarpaulin that reeked of gasoline oil. The effect was a dark, airless coffin that would more than likely become a real one, if the Malice stopped it and did more than a cursory search. Lottie hid the loaded revolver under the straw, next to them, just in case.

The driver was jovial and stopped a couple of times along the road where it was quiet, to allow them out to take a comfort break. Apart from that, the only thing they could do was to try to sleep as the noise of the engine made talking almost impossible and they had no idea when they would next be able to rest. A few hours later, they were stopped at a road block. Lottie had just drifted off and had fallen back against Michel, who was seated behind her. As the truck jolted to a halt the sound of voices woke her. Michel tensed and she touched Bernard on the shoulder to make sure he was awake.

"Get out of the truck, please." The muffled German accent was only feet away from them. Lottie felt for the pistol. She could feel sweat running down her back in the heat, as they listened intently and awaited their fate.

"Where are you going?"

The voice was polite.

"To Montargis."

"What are you carrying?"

"Machinery."

"What kind?"

"For the rubber factory. I have a permit." The driver appeared to remain calm. He had as much to lose as the three of them if they were caught, unless he could convince the soldiers that they'd somehow stowed away.

"Show me your papers."

"Of course." There was a moment where nobody said anything but the cab door was opened and then closed.

The three remained deadly still.

"Open the tarpaulin."

Lottie cocked the gun as she heard the sound of ropes being loosened and the tarpaulin moved above them and sagged a little, potentially betraying the void in the middle. Any moment, she expected to see daylight appear and she readied herself to begin shooting. The only thing they had, was the element of surprise but it would be difficult to move out of this space and in reality they were sitting ducks. She swallowed, barely daring to breathe as the sound of footsteps could be heard walking round to the other side of the truck. The tarpaulin flapped again but stopped short of being completely removed.

"What are those straw bales doing?"

"They stop the machines moving while in transit. They have very delicate instruments and I would be in trouble if they got damaged." The driver was doing his best.

"You may secure your load and proceed," said the soldier, after a moment, apparently satisfied. "You'll need to drive quickly to get there in time for curfew."

His French accent was poor and he struggled for words.

"Thank you." The tarpaulin tightened again as the ropes were re-secured and Lottie felt able to breathe.

"That was close," murmured Bernard.

Michel's chest was against her back and she could feel his heart banging.

"How many lives do we have left?" she whispered.

"Enough for us to make a difference, I hope," he replied.

*

The safe 'house' on the outskirts of Montargis was basic but Lottie was just happy to be able to get out of the truck and stretch and rub her limbs that felt as though they had atrophied on the journey. It consisted of one room next to a barn and appeared to have been used at some point for saddles and tack. Rotted remains of leather were scattered over the cobbled floor with the odd rusty, broken buckle and one end of the room was covered with fresh hay. At the other, there was a basin with a tap that when turned, reluctantly dispensed brown water that gradually turned pale orange, before finally, clear. They didn't see anyone after they were dropped off but the driver promised to return the next day to help them move on. Someone had left a bag with some stale bread and some apples, for which they were grateful and they sat eating the bread with Bernard's cheese, washed down with the Cognac. After this, Lottie took the scissors out of her suitcase and cut the men's hair short. As Michel's dark, curly locks fell to the ground, she realised this was indeed a new beginning. Even within a day, a dark shadow of growth had begun to form round his beard and he was transformed, still handsome but now he resembled a peasant. Bernard took some soap and she shaved the rest of his head, taking care not to cut him with his razor. She then made a reluctant Bernard cut her hair shorter. From the light of the rays of evening sunshine that found their way through the cracks in the old oak door, she then dyed it blonde, putting her head under the tap to remove the residue of the bleach, while Bernard shaved his beard, leaving a small amount of growth for a pencil moustache. When they finished, Lottie handed Michel a pair of wired spectacles and the transformations were complete. Regarding each other and laughing, they awarded one another points for their new looks which Bernard won and got an extra swig of Cognac as a prize.

"We need to make plans," said Michel with a sigh. "I have contacts from long ago in the Haute-Loire, a small band of Maquis living in the mountains. I think we should make for there and try to make contact with London. We can then try to get Celeste back home perhaps through Spain, when things quieten down."

Lottie was combing her hair which had gone a little brittle with the dye. She stopped. "What do you mean, *home*?"

"Back to England. We'll all be recalled now the Circuit has failed."

"What about you?"

"I'll stay on and fight, of course."

"As will I!" she said, firmly.

"The mountains are no place for a woman, Celeste." His voice was confident as though there was no sense in questioning what he was saying.

"So you don't think I'm *man* enough?"

"It's not that. I wouldn't dream of questioning your competence but the winters are brutal, minus twenty at best and the men are rough."

"I'll make that decision, Etienne. Do I need to remind you that you're no longer in charge?"

He held his hands up in defeat. "Okay, I'll leave it to you. I'm just trying to be practical."

"Well, don't!" she said, lightly. "I'm more than capable of looking after myself, I think you'll agree?"

"Look, we need to decide what happens tomorrow, forget about the winter," said Bernard, intervening. "Etienne, as you have the contacts do you have any *suggestions* about how we get there?"

Michel looked Lottie straight in the eye. "As a matter of fact, I do have some *ideas for discussion.*"

"Of course you do! Let's hear them, then," said Lottie, in a slightly patronising tone.

Michel ignored her. "Okay, we need to split up. It's too risky travelling together. I'm hoping the driver will have contacts going further south. We," he looked at Bernard, "should try to go by truck. Labourers would be expected to travel that way but Celeste, I think you should go by train. A teacher going to a new post would arrive by public transport."

She thought for a minute and couldn't argue with his logic. "And where is this 'new post'?"

"A place called Le Chambon-sur-Lignon, a small town, high in the mountains of the Haute-Loire."

"If I get stopped, the Melice will want proof of a job offer?"

"Well, we haven't got that. You'll have to make up a story. Maybe your letter got lost? I don't know."

"And if they check?"

"We have to hope they don't. It's the same for all of us. If Bernard and I get stopped, the chances are we'll be shipped off to a labour camp or to Germany to work. Once we get into the mountains, we should be safer. It's easier to hide. I suggest we try to meet in Le Chambon within a week. If I don't get there, ask in the bookshop for John-Baptiste and say the phrase, 'The mountain air is good for one's lungs but not in summer.' That was the code two years ago. I just hope he's survived."

"And if not?" said Lottie.

"I'll find other contacts when I get there. In the meantime, perhaps you could try to find out about vacancies at the school?"

"Yes, I'll talk my way into something." Lottie had calmed down but could see by Michel's eyes that he was irritated and hurt by her sharpness. She could have dealt with his over-protectiveness differently but it irked her and now she felt guilty that she'd snapped at him. She didn't have the energy to tiptoe around him and for that reason, it would indeed be sensible to get some distance between them for a few days.

"Good, is that agreed, then?" Michel looked at them both, warily, no doubt expecting her to be difficult again but instead, Lottie nodded.

"Look, now we have some form of plan, we need to get some rest," said Lottie, stifling a yawn. "I'll take the goose-feather mattress, with the fine linen sheets, if you don't mind?" she said, trying to lighten the mood that had darkened, walking over to the thin pile of hay that was to be their bed for the night. "Cocoa, anyone?"

CHAPTER 68

29ᵗʰ June 1943, Auvergne, Haute-Loire

On this day, Benito Mussolini falls and the construction of the Death Railway in Burma, is completed.

The cart made its way along the back roads from St Julien Chapteuil to the remote town of Le Chambon-sur-Lignon. Although it was only just past six a.m., already the heat was building but with luck, they would arrive by midday. Everywhere was quiet, save for the sound of the horses' hooves, rhythmically plodding along the road, as the farm cart moved in and out of the shade to the frequent sound of the farmer spitting as he chewed on tobacco. In the distance, were the dormant volcanoes of the Massive du Meygal and Mont Mezenc that had once fashioned the dramatic landscape, spewing lava and boulders high into the air, sculpting the land where they fell, into deep valleys and beehive-shaped craters, as far as the eye could see. At any time they could re-awaken and on a whim, destroy what they had made but for now, in this untameable land, man was forced to work around the landscape, in order to make a meagre living. Here, the pace of life was necessarily slow and old fashioned. Hardy trees grew, where they could, and tenacious roots could penetrate and exploit weaknesses in the grey rocks. Although it had a dramatic beauty, it was an alien terrain to Lottie and yet, she thought, she was about to fight for its liberation. Looking around her, there seemed little to fight against, apart from the elements.

She also thought of her friends, Denise, Prosper and Archambaud languishing in jail if, indeed, they had survived thus far under interrogation. Lottie knew from her training exactly what they could expect: humiliation, physical and mental discomfort, relentless questioning, isolation, beatings, sleep deprivation, exhaustion… The list was endless. She recalled the horrifically real, mock interrogations and the debriefings during training: keep denying, if you contradict yourself, blame the interpreter, pretend to tire before you are, avoid replies that take you down cul-de-sacs, don't admit to understanding German, be measured in responses, beware of 'friendly warders' etcetera, etcetera. Of course there was only so much preparation they could give you and under torture, who really knew how long you could hold out? Lottie didn't think for one moment that feisty Denise would give in, even under intense pain but she couldn't know that for sure. She felt too, with a heavy heart that it was too late for the Allies to save any of them, as the long-awaited invasion still hadn't materialised. The balance between life and death was so fragile, it made Lottie more determined to avenge their inevitable deaths. So what if she died too? It just didn't seem to matter anymore. The only thing that counted was freedom and she would continue to fight in their names. She was sure Denise's legacy and passion would sustain her through whatever the future held and she was damn sure she wouldn't be returning to London until France was liberated.

*

The farmer was a man of few words and that made the ride a little more relaxing, although he did glance back at her slyly from time to time and when he did, she made quite evident she'd seen him looking and he quickly turned away as if he'd been caught with his hand in a forbidden jar. They passed nobody until they reached the signpost for Fondernaud, Ronservaux and Le Chambon and the horses, so used to the route, turned off without so much as a tug on their reins. High above them, Lottie could see forests of fir trees that doubtless were home to the partisan guerrilla force known locally as the Maquis. Lottie wondered if she would arrive first at Le Chambon and she was eager to get there and find both Michel and Bernard safe and sound. It had been a long journey by train and bus to get to Le Puy-en-Velay and it had taken her nearly five days. Twice she'd been stopped and questioned by the Melice but she'd managed to charm them and they allowed the pretty schoolteacher on her way without too many questions. In Moulins-sur-Allier a middle-aged man had persistently tried to engage her in conversation on the train but she feigned illness and he finally removed himself from the compartment, in case whatever she had might be contagious. In Clermont Ferrand, as she weaved her way slowly south, she booked into a small hotel and in the evening ate in the restaurant. At eight p.m., two high-ranking

German soldiers arrived and sat at a nearby table. Lottie had no alternative but to remain seated with her book and when they began to look over in her direction, the wife of the owner quickly showed her into the back room, to finish her meal in peace. When they asked who the attractive mademoiselle was, they were told she was a friend of the family and when the complementary wine began to flow, the soldiers lost interest.

*

By the time Lottie arrived among the grey, stone buildings of Le Chambon-sur-Ligne, it was closed for lunch. Lottie thanked the farmer and made her way into the centre of the town where she hoped she would find the bookshop in Rue St Agreve and somehow get word about Michel and Bernard.

In the meantime, she would find somewhere to stay overnight, postponing, until the last possible minute an approach to the school, with a fake letter of introduction she'd fashioned on her journey. She walked past Hotel Central and Hotel Du Commerce where a couple of German solders hung around outside smoking, leaning on crutches, with heads and arms bandaged. They ignored the young woman with a suitcase who walked past, head down and she continued to the end of the road until she saw two women standing talking in the street.

"Excuse me, Mesdames, I'm looking for somewhere to stay."

One of the women looked at her and nodded. "You need a room? Where have you come from?" She smiled reassuringly. "It's okay, we can look after you." Her voice was quiet, confidential.

Lottie was taken aback.

The dark-haired woman looked around before lowering her voice even further. "Are you a Jew?" She frowned, scrutinising Lottie's face and fair hair. "You don't look like one but if you are, you can't stay on the street, it's not safe. We've had a raid this morning and the police will probably come back."

"No, not a Jew," she said, quickly, wondering if this was some kind of trap. "I'm looking for work. I'm a schoolteacher. I heard there might be a position here."

Both women looked relieved. "Oh, well, in that case, try Hotel de

La Place on Rue de La Grande Fontaine. The school is École Nouvelle Cevenole." She pointed towards the river. "The Principal has gone away with my husband, on business. Speak to his wife, Mildred. She's the English teacher. Tell her Magda sent you. I'm the Pastor's wife."

Lottie nodded and thanked her and walked on, puzzled. These people were sheltering Jews? When she thought about it, it was probably the perfect place, tucked away here in the mountains, but they mentioned there'd been a raid. If the police did come back, she needed to be prepared for them asking questions about any new arrivals. As she walked she went over her story, checking once again for consistency. She'd deliberately chosen a small, obscure village as the location of the fictitious school she'd worked at before. If she did get caught and taken in while they checked, it would all fall apart like a house of cards but nothing was watertight and she was aware that rather more depended on her plausibility at the time of being stopped.

*

The Hotel du Place had vacancies and she gave her details, with a confident smile. The elderly gentleman who checked her in, showed her to her room, unusually without questions about where she was from and why she was here, so she volunteered the information, anyway. He smiled and with a shrug left her to it. The room was clean but otherwise unremarkable and spartan and had a bathroom at the end of the corridor that was shared by three rooms. Dinner, he had told her would be served at six. Lottie could smell mutton stewing somewhere and its distinctive smell permeated through the dark corridors with their closed doors. Lottie wondered who was behind them. Checking windows and convenient routes of escape was so natural to her that she barely noticed herself doing it. She'd requested a ground-floor room, facing the street and she was pleased to find the windows opened wide enough to climb through and exit down the side of the hotel. A teacher, new to the town, would no doubt want to go and look at the school and it was a perfect excuse to have a look at the place, so she smoothed her dress and tidied her hair, before going back out again.

She found the École Nouvelle Cevenole easily. Outside, the boys and girls were clustered in small groups, chatting in the sunshine but there was an atmosphere of unease that spread beyond the school playground. The air, Lottie noticed, was agreeably fresher on the high plateau than it had been elsewhere on her journey. Continuing slowly past, so as not to draw attention to herself by stopping and staring, she made her way down to where she could see an old stone bridge over the River Lignon. She stood on it for a while, watching the clear water cascade over rocks, until it was time to make her way back up to the bookshop.

*

When Lottie tentatively gave the bookseller the phrase Michel had told her to use, he smiled and told her that 'Etienne had arrived that morning and would return at around five'. There was no news about Bernard but he did say the townspeople were deeply shocked by the sudden arrest of a man called Daniel Trocme, who was the manager of a refuge for 'displaced people'. Some of the 'residents' of the refuge had also been taken. That, she thought, must have been the raid the women were referring to. She wondered who lived at the refuge and whether they were Jews. The bookseller advised her to go back to her hotel and wait there until Etienne came. She thanked him, told him she would do as he suggested and left.

*

Michel, to her relief, turned up at five thirty, now with a full beard, looking tired and his skin rather more tanned. He'd made the journey in the rear of three trucks and his back, he said was aching, badly. Despite this, he looked relieved to see her, and they walked separately away from the hotel, down one of the roads, where they found somewhere secluded to speak.

"We need to be careful," he said. "There's been an incident."

"I know. Where are you staying?"

"In a barn four kilometres away, further up the mountain."

"Did you find your contact?"

"Yes, he's there, with other Maquisards. Have you managed to visit the school?"

"No."

"Leave it to me, I'll speak to the Headmaster but you need to lay low for a few days as the man arrested was the cousin of the Pastor and the town is angry and suspicious. This is the worst time for a stranger to arrive."

"I stopped two women and one of them asked me if I was a Jew. She offered to protect me. What's going on, here?" Lottie felt uneasy.

"They're pacifists, protestants. They don't believe in what the Germans are doing but they won't fight. They're good, brave people who will take anyone in and protect them."

"And the police?" This strange place was sounding less and less safe, to Lottie.

"Generally they leave them alone, up here. Something must have happened. Don't worry, the Principal's away but I'll find his deputy, tomorrow."

"I don't need you to speak to anyone on my behalf, thank you, Etienne. I haven't come here to teach, I've come to do what London trained me for, so it would be preferable for you to take me to your friends and I can get on with the job!" She found herself raising her voice and despite her mounting irritation, controlled herself and lowered it.

"The men are living at a camp about an hour's walk from here and it's too primitive and dangerous for a woman. You would be the only one there. They have no weapons and they're frustrated and bored. Some are on the run from prison for God knows what! Murder, rape… who knows?"

"And you think I can't handle that?"

"I think," he said, his pupils fixed on hers and dilating with anger, "you overestimate in this situation, what you could handle! Do you really think these men would accept and recognise your 'training'? You have absolutely no provenance here!"

"Don't patronise me!" Her face was close to his, her voice now trembling with fury.

"I'm *trying* to protect you!" he growled.

"Why? You aren't responsible for me. I thought I'd made that abundantly clear!"

"Because," he said, glowering down at her, "I'm in love with you and for that reason, I want to look out for you but do what the hell you like!" He spat the words out with contempt as though it was the worst possible thing, before turning on his heel and walking off up the road.

Lottie stood, her legs rooted to the spot and watched him walk away, replaying what had just happened as if to double check she'd heard him right. Then, something, long-forgotten, flooded through her that she recognised from the dim and distant past as an overwhelming feeling of happiness.

"Celeste?" The low voice was familiar and shattered her moment like a stone through a pane of glass. She turned and saw Bernard a few metres from her, his face too, burnished from the sun, clothes dusty with his bag slung over his shoulder.

"Speak as though you're asking directions," she said, pulling herself together.

Bernard pointed vaguely towards the centre of town. "It's good to see you. Have you seen Etienne?"

"Yes. It's a relief to see you too, Clement! He left a moment ago. Follow the road to the right. He's no more than one hundred metres in front of you. Ask him to meet me at ten o'clock tomorrow morning at the back of the hotel. Tell him it's really important, I have some news for him."

"Of course. Good day and thank you, Mademoiselle," he said loudly, with a grin, touching his cap.

"Clement?"

He turned. "Yes?"

"Be careful, there's been a raid here, earlier today."

CHAPTER 69

30th June 1943,

Chambon-sur-Lignon, Haute-Loire, France

On this day Allied troops land on the islands of New Georgia and Rendova in the South Pacific Ocean.

Lottie barely slept in the shuttered room, despite the mountain night being cool and the bed comfortable. Michel's words ran round her head like a marble on an uneven, polished floor. Several times she got up and stood at the open window, watching the outline of bats catching insects in flight. Somewhere, up high, a mountain cat cried out like a baby and an owl hooted. Apart from the animals, the town was as silent as if it did not exist. She inhaled deeply, hoping the fresh air would give her some peace and allow her to rest but it didn't. For want of some distraction she walked over to the mirror on the small dressing table at the end of the bed and regarded her shadowed image. Since Bernard had cut it, her corn-coloured hair was of varying lengths and needed some drastic action. She held clumps up and regarded them critically. Opening one of the shutters that had blown half closed, she allowed more moonlight into the room and taking her scissors she cut it shorter at the sides, leaving the top longer. Despite Michel's obstinacy about allowing her to join the Maquis, she was equally determined to do so and if she was to live in the mountains and fight with the guerrillas, long hair would not be practical. It would also portray her femininity which she was now keen to disguise. When she'd finished, she stood back and regarded her handiwork and felt that with her high cheekbones, tanned skin and tall, slim body, from even a short distance, she could pass for a fine-featured, young man. Sill unable to quieten her brain, she got dressed, slipped out of her window and went for a walk up the mountain, until the light of dawn broke and, with the stealth of a cat burglar, she returned.

*

At ten thirty, Michel was standing at the rear of the hotel, with his back to the door, arms folded, waiting for her. Lottie was surprised he'd even come after yesterday's revelation but she was pleased he had. When he turned, he did a double take at her hair and frowned but refrained from comment.

"Etienne, I…"

"I should never have said anything!" he interrupted.

"I was going to say that I think the reason I get so heated with you is that I feel the same… I had no idea you felt anything for me," she added.

"You *love me?*" He was thrown for a moment.

"Yes," she said quietly and held out her hand to him and after a moment, tentatively he took it and gently pulled her towards him, looking into her eyes before taking her in his arms and kissing her. Finally they broke apart and stared at each other, smiling and shy like two children who had never touched and didn't quite know what to do next.

"What now?" said Lottie, eventually.

"I don't know. Do you want to take things slowly?" he said, wide eyed.

"Do you?"

He shook his head. "No."

"Me neither."

He thought for a moment. "Look, I'm not happy about it but if I take you to the camp, it must be as my wife. The men will respect you, then."

Lottie laughed. "That's not the most romantic proposal I've received!"

He looked shocked. "No… I'm so sorry, I didn't mean it to sound like that!" He dropped down on one knee. "I love you and I want to spend the rest of my life with you, so would you do me the honour of becoming my wife?"

She looked down at the earnest, handsome face that stared up at her through the fake spectacles and beard and felt as though she would burst with joy and she too got down on one knee and accepted.

Getting to their feet they held each other until the hotel proprietor came out and interrupted what he felt was a very private moment and he apologised profusely. Still holding her close, Michel smiled and said, "There is no need to be sorry, Monsieur. This beautiful schoolteacher has just agreed to become my wife."

The elderly man beamed showing a gummy mouth where once teeth would have been. "Then let me be the first to congratulate you both! Please come in and have some wine. We must celebrate! I will call my wife, she's out feeding the chickens."

Arms still round each other, they made their way into the small salon and the proprietor toasted them. When she heard the news, his tiny wife clapped her hands with joy. Perhaps sensing these visitors to this town of secrets were not what they imagined, they asked no questions but wished them well.

*

"Getting married is a lovely idea but where will we do it, without risking our necks?" said Lottie when they were finally alone and sitting on a rock at the top of the village, looking down on it, drinking lemonade from the picnic prepared by the wife of the hotel owner.

"The Protestant preachers around here are sympathetic to the Resistance despite preaching against violence. I'll find someone, don't you worry, although it will have to be a quiet affair."

She laughed. "Not exactly what my mother had in mind."

"Will she mind? Should we wait until after the war?" He looked worried.

Lottie sighed. "No. I want to do it soon. Have you thought though, it can't be legal?"

He frowned. "Of course, we have fake identities!"

"Yes." She shrugged. "So… let's do it anyway. They're just fake names. They don't matter. They don't change who we really are or what we feel for each other. We can do it properly after the war but here, at this time when we speak aloud, we are Celeste and Etienne."

He laughed. "Yes! We'll have two weddings," he agreed. "I think God will not mind, under the circumstances."

"No, I'm sure God won't mind," she said, giving his hand a squeeze. "But you're a Catholic."

"Yes."

"There are no Catholic churches around here, I'll bet."

"No. But we share the same God as the Protestants."

"I suppose you do."

"You don't believe?"

"No. Not anymore." She got to her feet and brushed the dust from her clothes. "I'll tell you one day but now we have a wedding to plan."

CHAPTER 70

July 9th 1943, Fay-sur-Lignon, Haute-Loire, France

On this day, a German air raid kills 108 people, many of them children, in a cinema in the British town, East Grinstead.

In the tiny chapel of Fay-sur-Lignon, Etienne Moreau and Celeste Durand married, in a low-key ceremony witnessed by Clement Simon and Albert Camus, a writer friend of the local Pastor Daniel Curtet. Camus was staying nearby in Panelier, while writing his novel, *The Plague*. Michel presented his new wife with a beautiful ring made by a Maquis carpenter, out of birch bark. After signing the register, the couple left with their friend and comrade, Clement, to begin their marital life in a disused barn, high on the plateau, above Le Chambon-sur-Ligne.

*

"I should," Michel had said, doubtfully, eyeing the open oak door that was flanked on one side by a water barrel and on the other by four Maquisards playing cards, "Carry you over the threshold."

Lottie smiled and replied, "Perhaps that wouldn't be the best way of introduction?"

"I think it would!" he said, scooping her up as more men gathered to see who the stranger was. "This," he said, in a loud voice, to get everyone's attention, "is my beautiful new wife, Celeste who I have just had the privilege to marry. She has come to join us."

The men cheered and clapped and came over to shake hands.

"At last," one shouted. "Someone to cook for us!"

"She's not a cook, she's a trained killer." Michel looked at them, one by one, his face now serious. "Do *not* underestimate Celeste. She's as much a fighter as you," he pointed, to one, "and you!" to

287

another. "She's dispatched more Germans than any of you so, if you value your lives, treat her with respect!"

They nodded, not quite knowing what to make of the woman being presented to them.

"Tonight, before we retire…" Michel was interrupted by whistles.

Lottie rolled her eyes.

Michel held up his hands. "We will toast my new wife with a glass… or two of wine."

There were more cheers.

"But for now, get back to what you were doing. We'll be back after sunset."

With that, he took her deep into the forest and they made love, until the view of the volcanoes in the distance had faded into darkness and it was time to return to the farmhouse where the men had made them a straw bed in the hayloft, strewn with wild Verbena and blue Gentian. At midnight the Maquisards tactfully departed for a night under the stars, mellowed by wine, leaving the newlyweds alone.

*

The next morning, the brief honeymoon was over as the men returned at daybreak and married life began for Lottie.

"I'd like to introduce you to my wife, Celeste, Leon," said Michel, proudly to Eyraud, the leader of the local Maquis, who was scrutinising a map.

"Pleased to meet you," he said, turning, clearly preoccupied. "Congratulations on your marriage," he said, as an afterthought.

"Thank you. As I told you, she's fully trained in combat and sabotage and will be a match for the best."

Leon Eyraud looked doubtfully at the tall, thin, woman in woollen britches, who looked like a pretty German boy but he nodded and said, "You must excuse our lack of ceremony. We have a long-awaited drop of arms due today. We're just running over the plans once again."

"Did you hear the coded phrase last night?" said Michel.

"Yes but we need to be cautious." He frowned. "Something doesn't feel right. I think we might be being watched."

"Let's stake out the drop zone?"

"I've already sent men down there. If there's any activity in a five-mile radius, we'll know about it."

"Okay, we wait?"

"Yes."

One of the men turned from the map and stubbing out his cigarette, he looked at Michel and grinned. "So this is the unlucky woman?"

"Yes, Celeste this is Marek. We've known each other for a long, long time."

"Years ago, in Poland," Marek said quietly, sensing Lottie's confusion.

"Oh?" She'd known Michel had a connection in Haute-Loire and she hadn't really questioned it but here, in front of her was someone who knew Michel before the war. Her first thought was that he must have known Michel's first wife, Keturah, and perhaps his child, Hannah. It struck her for the second time in her life, that she knew so little about the man she loved but as they needed to protect each other's safety. If they were caught and tortured, they would genuinely know nothing that could betray the other. Until now, it had been as if someone had come along and erased their pasts but she felt a sudden longing to sit down with Michel and talk to him about his childhood, parents, siblings and yes, his wife and daughter. The list was endless and this open-faced stranger, Marek, who was now standing perfectly at ease with his arm slung familiarly around Michel's shoulders, knew her husband's story, like a library to which, at present, she had no access. At that moment she felt keenly the distance between her and Michel and it seemed like an bottomless gorge. Who really knew what might be lurking down there? But she felt so bonded to this man in the present, that nothing in the past could be shocking enough to break it.

"Celeste?" Michel was looking at her. "Are you okay?"

"Yes," she said, staring at him, forcing herself to reconnect.

"You look pale," he said.

"I'm fine, really." She smiled. "Good to meet you, Marek." She nodded politely. "Michel, brief me about the drop?"

Eyraud, who had gone back to the map, looked up as they approached and went to cover the area with his hand.

"It's fine, Leon. You can trust my wife with your life and at some point in the future, you may be glad to do that."

He relaxed a little at this and gave a curt nod.

"Where's the drop zone?" she said, leaning over to look. "How many men do we have?"

Eyraud was still reluctant but he told her around thirty and outlined what little ammunition they had and said that if the drop today was successful, they should have enough to make a difference. When she began to ask intelligent, informed questions, he was surprised and began to relax, realising he could speak to her like a man.

Listening to what he said, it seemed to Lottie, that they would have to go a long way further than an assortment of men without proper combat training, whether armed or otherwise, living up a mountain, to "make a difference" but she listened politely, if with a sense of growing disappointment, at the prospect of what could be achieved. When Eyraud had finished, she looked round at the ramshackle group who were staring at her with a mixture of curiosity and a few with barely disguised hostility, wondering how loyal they were and how readily they would accept orders.

*

As it turned out, as they waited with men stationed at various points across the mountain, Eyraud's instinct had been right and the Gestapo had somehow found out about the drop and were ready to ambush the Maquis. Luckily, one of the men on reconnaissance saw them and sent word back and the reception was reluctantly abandoned. Fortunately, the plane didn't arrive, either. Eyraud and the men were bitterly disappointed and some of them ended up drinking, well into the early hours. Lottie was glad to crawl under a blanket with her new husband where she lay awake in his arms, listening to his soft breathing against the creaking of the barn and the noise of the men sitting round the hearth in the adjacent room, until finally, she drifted off to sleep.

CHAPTER 71

21ˢᵗ July 1943

Maquis camp above Le Chambon-sur-Ligne, France

On this day the Battle of Roosevelt Ridge begins in the Salamaua region of the Territory of New Guinea between the US and Japanese forces.

Lottie was standing in line with two new recruits to the Maquis, one a French-born Jew called Charlie and the other, a young Frenchman who was on the run from German-imposed Compulsory Work Service. Leon Eyraud held a piece of well-worn paper in front of him with the Maquis 'Oath of Allegiance' printed on it, which he read out to them in a sombre voice, carefully modifying it to include reference to Lottie's gender.

Every Man [or Woman] seeking admission to the Maquis is not only a defaulter from German occupation but a volunteer partisan and an auxiliary soldier of the French Army.

He [She] forfeits the right to communicate with His [Her] family or friends until the end of the War.

He [She] will observe absolute secrecy as to His [Her] hiding place and the identity of His [Her] leaders and comrades.

He [She] knows that any violation of these rules are punishable by death.

He [She] knows He [She] cannot receive any assurance of regular pay and even His [Her] food and weapons are not guaranteed.

He [She] will respect the life and property of French, Allied or Neutral Citizens, not only because the Maquis depends for its existence on its good relations with the population but also because the men [women] of the Maquis form an elite and because it is their duty to prove by example that courage and honesty go together in all true Frenchmen [Frenchwomen]. It goes without saying that no distinction of religion or politics is made among would-be recruits. All who are ready to fight the craven enemy are welcome.

A wounded man [woman] must never be abandoned. The dead must be taken away and buried, wherever humanly possible to do.

The Maquis volunteer will not be armed until he had proved himself [herself] worthy by His [Her] toughness, training and discipline and therefore receiving one of our precious weapons.

The penalty for losing a weapon is death. The penalty is severe but essential for the safety of all.

Every Man [Woman] is an enemy of Marshal Petain and the traitors who obey him.

France lives and will live!

"Celeste Durand, do you swear, upon this oath, to be bound by these rules?"

"I do," she replied.

"In that case, it is my duty to welcome you to the Maquis."

The men clapped but some, more heartily than others.

Eyraud jumped on a hay bale to address the men. "As you are all aware, Comrade Celeste is fully trained in combat and sabotage and you will all treat her with the utmost respect. While we continue to await supplies of arms, Celeste will help with weapons training and run English lessons. I have it on good authority she speaks both English and German, fluently. It was unfortunate that the drop on the tenth of July was unsuccessful. Time is not on our side and it is of great importance that we don't waste it while we wait. As our oath states, we'll continue to train and build our physical strength as well as increasing our members so that when the time comes we're ready to fight. Autumn is nearly upon us and winter won't be far behind it. As most of you are aware, only the physically and mentally strong will survive in the mountains. I would also like to advise you that from today, Etienne will be my second in command. When I'm not present, you will all take orders from him. Any questions?" He looked at them and waited. Most shook their heads, someone coughed and spat. "Good! In that case, comrades, I'm going for a meeting with Bonnisol and Fayol in Yssingeaux."

"Right, we'll now split into groups and do some unarmed combat training." Michel took over and looked at Lottie. "I need to talk to you." He steered her out of earshot of the group, looking worried.

"What's the matter?"

"Clement's gone."

"Gone, where?"

"Left the camp. He's had enough. He had an argument with Leon earlier this morning."

Lottie was shocked. "But surely he's coming back?"

"Not according to Charles. He packed his bag and said he was leaving."

Her heart sank. "Without telling us?"

"He didn't have time. Charles said he asked him to pass this to one of us." Michel held out a scrap of paper with characteristically neat handwriting. It simply said, 'To my friends Etienne and Celeste, I'm sorry to leave but I'm going back to the bees. Merde alors! With love, Clement.'

She read it twice while a sense of deep loss engulfed her. "Perhaps we should go after him?" she said, folding it and giving it back to Michel but as she said it, she knew it was pointless. He'd made no secret of the fact he'd hated it at the camp and that he'd felt like an outlaw in his own country but she would miss him so much. He was one of the few constants in their lives and she had difficulty quelling the urge to run towards the village, find him and beg him to stay.

"No. It's the right thing, for him," said Michel, putting the note back in his pocket. "In any case he left a couple of hours ago." He touched her gently on the arm. "We need to get back."

*

Lottie turned to the men who were getting restless. Looking at them she felt an overwhelming sense of discontent that she realised had been bubbling away for the last week. The news of Clement's leaving threw a match and ignited it at that moment and the sight of all of them suddenly disgusted her. It was true that the recruits were mostly willing and above all, passionate about a "free France" but without weapons, it really was no better than training boy scouts. At most there was one Sten gun between six and no detonators, explosives or machine guns. It was hard for Michel and her to feel motivated, let alone keep the men occupied. Regarding them one by one she saw how thin and hungry they were. Their clothes were worn and in need of repair and some of the men wore clogs rather than boots. They were a dismal rag-bag of men playing at being guerrilla fighters on a mountain, where it was difficult even to believe there was a war going on. In Paris, at least it felt real and there were reminders on the corner of every street. Despite being deeply in love and happy on one hand, on the other, she felt completely 'wasted' up here among the barren rocks preparing for battle, a few kilometres above a brave but secretive village, wondering every day, when the next drop might be and the fighting could commence. A week? A month? Never? Would the war be over before the fighters of the plateau would see any form of combat? In such a short space of time, she found she missed the thrill of action and a feeling of purpose. For two pins, she'd have grabbed her bags and joined Clement but not without Michel. With a resigned sigh, she vowed to do the best she could to stave off boredom, in the unlikely event the time did come for the Maquis to make a difference.

CHAPTER 72

22nd January 1944

Maquis camp above Le Chambon-sur-Ligne, France

On this day, the Battle of Anzio begins in the region Anzio and Nettuno, Italy.

It had been an uncompromising autumn and winter on the plateau. Lottie awoke when it was daylight to yet another day of freezing temperatures that made her head ache. She huddled closer to Michel under the pile of blankets that had seen better days. Through the broken glass in the window of the tiny room in the farmhouse they'd occupied, the wind projected a funnel of icy air that announced its unwelcome presence with a continual, low wail. Michel stirred and instinctively drew her in. Like all of them, his face had become wind-burnt from days of high-altitude exposure, which etched out fine lines around eyes and desiccated lips. His beard had grown full and he was thinner too and she could feel his ribs against her own, putting her in mind of a pair of chicken carcasses, laid side by side, stripped of their meat. She buried her head in his thick hair that had, over the months, once again become unruly. He smelled musky and feral, like the mountains. She rolled over, trying not to wake him and steeled herself. The worst part of the day was getting out of bed and lighting a fire. Outside, in the relentless, unbearable whiteness of the snow and temperatures that made them all breathless, she could hear men clearing their lungs in a routine that preceded getting dressed and lighting the first cigarette of the day. Even the cockerel it seemed, now routinely slept in; the hens scrawny and barren were barely worth his energy.

Reluctantly, Lottie extricated herself from Michel and got out of bed, her prematurely ageing joints stiff from the cold. In the next room she could hear Marek snoring. Over the months, he'd become like a brother to her and his quick wit sparked something in her personality that had been buried under war. Knowing he was there gave her comfort in the knowledge that the men were safe and there was still such a thing as 'normality', even up there. If truth be told, she had grown terribly fond of all the Maquis men, bar one or two who thankfully she had little to do with. Changing her socks and pulling on a thick jumper made from the greasy, impenetrable wool of plateau sheep, she made her way through the house, passing the gun and ammunition store which, thanks to a drop last August, was now reasonably well stocked and entered what they laughingly termed the 'kitchen'. It was fitted with a sink and one tap that was frozen for most of the winter and a long table where she, Michel and the ten other men who were under their command, took their meals.

*

Jean Bonnissol, area leader of the Maquis, had been arrested in December by the Gestapo and subsequently of the other regional commanders, Pierre Fayol had taken greater charge locally. He arranged the Maquis into 'siziaines': five men, each with a leader. Both Lottie and Michel had been given 'leader's' roles but only after Michel had refused unless Lottie, a mere woman in Fayol's opinion, was given the same. Neither of them warmed to Fayol nor agreed with all his ideas but recruitment to the Maquis was now reaching hundreds as people felt the Allies were finally making progress. At least, under his leadership, the local Maquis groups were less fragmented. Still, Lottie and Michel felt things were happening too slowly and this was made worse by the fact that the Allied invasion had yet to start. The Maquis' first serious sabotage on the railway line at Vauvre Bridge between Beauzal and the River Lignon way back in August, led by Bonnissol, before his arrest, had been successful. Casualties had been high for the Germans but since then, apart from an attack on a dairy supplying the enemy, in nearby St Agreve in November, there had been little advancement. Lottie had smiled through clenched teeth and said, "The war will not be won by depriving the Nazis of custard!" Meanwhile, they waited in anticipation in the mountains, living in frozen filth, as the autumn turned into deep winter. Lottie felt every day that had she not been in love and, equally passionately hated the German occupiers, she'd have left in the early autumn and tried to make her way across the

Pyrenees, to Portugal, where she might have got a boat back to England. But she adored Michel and there was no place in the world for her without him and morally, she was unable to desert France.

*

Charles, one of the men under her command was in the kitchen building the fire, when Lottie entered, running her tongue along her flaking lips and wincing as saliva burned on contact. He sat on his haunches in front of the tiny embers, nurturing them like a newborn and blowing on his swollen hands in a vain attempt to warm them. Above the fire, a large pot of beef offal hung in anticipation of the heat, so it could be made into a broth and eaten later that day, with boiled potatoes. As technically the Maquis didn't exist, they had no legitimate rations. Unless they were able to get their hands on a forged ration card, they were dependent on the generosity of the locals, primarily farmers, who would lie about how much they produced to the authorities and sold, or in some cases 'donated' food to them. Lottie vowed never to eat beef again, once the war was over although she was grateful for whatever they were given.

"Good morning, Charles, I'll go and get fresh snow for water," Lottie said, stretching and yawning.

"Okay. Did you sleep well, Celeste?" Charles turned and smiled up at her.

"Yes, I did thank you. What about you?"

He shrugged and laughed. "The freezing air knocks you out but if that doesn't work, Thomas farts all night!" The flames began to devour the kindling as it gained energy. "Here we go!"

"It must be hard, all of you in two rooms, with no privacy."

"I must admit I dream of sleeping alone someday, or better still, with my girlfriend."

"Hopefully sooner than you think, Charles. There's a rumour that the Allies are close to taking Rome and that Berlin has been blitzed."

"I heard that too. Do you think it's true?"

"Well," she said, "Fayol seems to think it's happening and he has access to a working wireless." She stood with the bucket by the door and hesitated before going out. "I often worry the war might have come to an end, and we'll be the last to know and come blinking out of the forest like an Amazon tribe, months after it's over!"

He laughed. "It's entirely possible."

"How's Matthieu this morning?" she said. The young man, who had recently joined them, had been suffering from a swollen leg.

"I don't know. I think he's still asleep."

"If his leg hasn't gone down this morning, we will send for Dr Forestier," she said, over her shoulder, disappearing into the frozen courtyard, closing the door quickly behind her.

There had been a fresh fall of snow in the night and in places it had drifted to over two metres high. Training exercises would once again be limited to yet another session of physical combat and stripping and cleaning rifles as this was all the weather permitted and there was no spare ammunition to practice with. Lottie longed for a sign of a thaw, to alleviate their boredom, but there was no prospect of one for days or even weeks. In the bright blue sky which she sometimes felt was the only thing that kept her sane, a long-tailed black and white eagle searched for prey, its head moving from side to side, in wait for a movement in the snow, that might signify a meal lurking beneath.

"Good luck," she whispered, shielding her eyes before taking a spade and shovelling the virgin snow into the bucket.

*

When she arrived back inside, Michel had come downstairs and was joined by Albert, a capable man of around thirty-five, who was originally a car salesman from the Dordogne.

"Here, let me help with, that!" said Michel, moving towards her.

"It's fine. Please go and get the bread out. If it's a bit stale, we can toast it over the fire," she said, gently. He'd never lost the desire to jump in and protect her and she had learned to soften and meet him halfway. When the war ended, and they were living in London or Paris, or wherever, she had a feeling she might be sorry she'd railed against his gallantry but here there was so much heavy work to do and she had to prove herself as capable as every other Maquisard.

"There's cheese in the outhouse," said Albert, "Olivier delivered it yesterday. I'll go and get it."

"You do that and I'll make some coffee and there should be a bit of hot water for those who want to wash," she said, doubtfully. It was perhaps understandable that washing had become an exception, rather than the rule among the men and only a handful seemed to bother to brush their teeth even once, let alone twice a day. Personal hygiene was about the only thing that Lottie was strict about and she clung to her 'routine' like a limpet to a rock in a stormy sea and the occasional gift of a bar of lavender-scented soap was to her, just heaven.

CHAPTER 73

27th April 1944

Village near Le Chambon-sur-Lignon, France

On this day, hundreds of American soldiers and sailors are killed over two days, in a D-Day training exercise at Slapton, Devon, England.

Lottie and her men waited in a ditch at the side of the road, having turned the signpost to Puy-en-Velay in the opposite direction. The motorcade was due at any time. From the hills above, a mirror was used to signal that it had been spotted and its arrival was imminent and sure enough, less than five minutes later they heard the sound of two scout motorbikes checking the route. As they reached the crossroads, instead of turning in the direction according to the sign, they stopped in the road just above the ditch where the Maquis were hiding.

"I thought Puy was that way," said one of the riders.

"Do you think the signpost has been altered?" replied the other.

"I don't know. Something doesn't feel right. I think it's to the right. Do you have the map?" He looked around, uneasily. They were less than ten feet from the Lottie and her men.

"Yes." He pulled a document from inside his coat.

Lottie pulled out a knife and motioned to Matthieu to do the same. She pointed to him and at the first rider and to herself to the other one. Holding three fingers up, she waited until they were both looking at the map and she saw their opportunity to take them by surprise. Two. One.

The German soldiers barely had time to look up before Lottie and

Matthieu were behind them, silently despatching them in two swift movements.

"We need to get them out of here!" Lottie shouted to the other men. "Come on, quickly, before they bleed onto the road!"

They emerged from the ditch, wide eyed, and began to drag the men into the undergrowth.

"Get the uniform off that one, now!" Lottie called out. "Hurry, before the blood stains get visible."

"Why?"

"Because the motorcade will expect to see the scout bikes waiting to confirm the route has been checked." Lottie had begun to pull off her jumper and trousers.

"What are you doing?" said Charles, doing a double take.

"Get me one of the uniforms and move one of the bikes into the undergrowth."

"You can't! If they see you're a woman you'll be shot. Let me do it, Celeste."

"No and they won't. Who else among us speaks German and for that matter, has blonde hair and blue eyes?" She began to put her legs into the tailored, grey wool trousers that were still warm from the previous occupier. "I'm just going to point them in the direction we want them, that's all. I'm not going to let a wrong turn fuck this up. Get that other bike moved out of sight! At most, we'll have ten minutes before the convoy arrives. The rest of you get back in the ditch and cover me if anything goes wrong. Don't do anything stupid. Take your orders from Charles. All I'm aiming to do is keep them on the wrong road."

The jacket smelled of body odour and of the ferrous odour of fresh blood that had dripped down inside of the collar but was not yet visible on the outside. Fuelled by adrenaline, she pulled the belt tight, the cap down low and donned the gloves and boots. This, she thought, was more like it. Striding over, she sat on the bike and waited until the sound of the motorcade came echoing through the valley like the noise of an avalanche gaining momentum.

The first car drew to a halt next to her and the driver wound down his window. Behind there were several more bikes and three more cars. Lottie saluted, "Heil Hitler."

"Is everything okay?"

"Yes, sir!"

"Where's the other bike?"

"Gone ahead, sir, to check the road."

She could see the two targeted, high-ranking Nazis in the car behind, looking out of the windows. Keeping her head low, she said, "Turn left up here towards Yssingeaux."

The driver nodded and began to wind up his window and prepared to move off. Then she heard the door slam. The passenger had got out of the second car and began walking towards her.

"Stop!" He held his hand up. "Come here," he said, addressing Lottie, who got off the bike and strode towards the Lieutenant, hoping the men would hold their nerve and not begin shooting. They were hopelessly outnumbered and it would be a blood bath. "The General thinks Le Puy is that way," he said sharply demonstrating left with his hand.

"I'm sorry, sir, the General is mistaken. Le Puy-en-Velay is definitely in that direction." She pointed to the signpost that directed them to the right. "We checked the map."

The driver, who towered above her, looked down at the top of her cap and thought for a moment, before turning back to his vehicle and stiffly imparting what he'd been told. There was an exchange that Lottie couldn't hear, before he returned.

"The General wants you to ride with us and escort the convoy." He was now staring at her, his cold eyes meeting hers. She looked ahead avoiding meeting his stare, in an attempt to act subordinate.

"Of course." Lottie hadn't bargained for this. She wasn't sure if the General was suspicious or whether he just wanted someone who purported to know the road, riding ahead. Either way, she had no choice but to do as she was told. The one thing she did know for sure, was that the Maquis ambush would take place five kilometres down the road near La Chambertiere and her men wouldn't have time to alert the waiting party. At this rate, it was highly likely that she would be shot by her own comrades, even her own husband. Saluting once again, she turned and climbed back on the bike, hoping the key was in it and it would start. Both her brothers had had motorbikes and had thankfully taught her how to ride them around the farm but she hadn't ridden one for nearly ten years. Feeling herself breaking out into a cold sweat, she squeezed the clutch and made sure it was in neutral before turning the key and frantically surveying the machine. On the first determined kick-start, the bike roared into life. Squeezing the clutch, her foot located first gear and she let the brake off, accelerating smoothly out in front of the motorcade. Riding slowly, she waited for the cars to follow, which they did in a deadly crocodile. If she suddenly drove off, the chances were the other bikes, whose riders were far more experienced, would follow and as she had no gun and was greatly outnumbered, she had no alternative but to wait. She changed into second and then third gear as they all gained speed. Sweat was running down her back and face. If she drove too slowly, to give herself time to think, they would suspect something was wrong. Either way, it was looking increasingly likely she would be shot by one side or the other and this felt disturbingly like she was escorting her own funeral cortege.

*

Frantically, she thought about the geography of the road ahead. She knew it well enough to know there were no side roads she could suddenly take. Then, with less than a quarter of a kilometre to go to the ambush, she spotted the narrow track up ahead, not more than one hundred metres in front of her and less than two metres wide. She had no idea where it led and for all she knew it was a dead end but It was her only option. Keeping her speed steady, she prepared to peel away. If this came off, the cars would hit the ambush before they had time to stop and pursue her. It was perilously close to where the Maquis were hiding. She waited until they were almost past the entrance to the track before she turned sharply right and accelerated hard into it. Nearly losing the rear wheel as it slid in the wet mud, she managed to somehow right the bike and climb the fifty or so metres of rough ground into the hillside before she heard the sound of gunfire as the cars were caught in the trap. Jamming on the brakes she flung the bike down and sprinted into the undergrowth, jettisoning the cap and tearing off the jacket, to reveal her tatty, now bloodstained, wool shirt. The trousers and boots would have to remain, until she could make her way back to camp but for now, from a distance, still at risk of being mistaken for a German soldier, all she could do was hide.

CHAPTER 74

10th June 1944

Maison Forestiere, Mont Mouchet, Haute-Loire.

On this day, at Oradour-sur-Glane, Haute-Loire, France, 642 men, women and children are killed in a German response to local Resistance activities. In the Distomo massacre in Greece, 218 civilians are killed.

In a hide-out at the top of Mont Mouchet, over two and a half thousand Maquisards, led by Colonel Gaspard, lay in wait to stop the Germans on their way north, to meet the Allies. Celeste, Ettiene and their men, requisitioned from the Maquis of Le Chambon, set up camp under the trees and, like the rest, they waited as the mountain air filled with tension, like a pan of red hot liquid, simmering so close to the top that everyone waited in tense anticipation for the overspill. At Clavieres, one of the entry routes to the mountain, the Maquis had erected a sign that said, 'Here Begins Free France!' The day before, the Nazis attacked three nearby villages, defended by Maquisards, causing heavy losses for the Germans, who promptly sent for reinforcements.

Michel had long given up his own battle to stop Lottie from doing as she pleased and she now fought, ate and slept side by side with the men, her face smeared with grime and hands now rough as any labourer's. Each day, skirmishes broke out at the foot of the mountain as the Maquis tried to cut off key, winding roads that passed through the region, flanked by rocks and trees and the Germans relentlessly fought back. The advantage the Maquis had in their knowledge of the terrain was matched by the superiority of the Nazis' equipment and each dawn was followed by a day of increased violence and casualties on both sides.

Lottie awoke to the noise of a small creature scurrying around near to her blanket and the sound of one of the men urinating in a nearby bush. The acrid smell reached her nostrils and she turned her head away, eyes gritty from lack of sleep and her back aching from yet another night on the uneven, damp ground. Running her fingers through her short hair that had now lost its lustre and become brittle, she dreamed longingly of a hot bath and soap made from rose petals and for a split second, once the aroma of piss had subsided, she thought she really could smell its sweet perfume. She got to her feet and looked across the field to see if she could spot Michel and his men but he was nowhere to be seen. On makeshift wood fires, food was being prepared but it was the same soup of lentils every meal, getting thinner and less substantial as supplies depleted. Nobody had expected the fighting to continue for over a week and Lottie wondered how long they could hold out. Each day, the German fighting force seemed to swell like dough left to prove and from the mountain top, their convoys looked like trails of indestructible ants, making their way determinedly through the countryside with their artillery. Every so often, there would be an outbreak of fighting and machine gun fire would echo through the valleys, followed by another temporary lull.

Someone called out to her, "Celeste, get your men! Thirty of you are to go down to Paulhac to defend it. A German troop is heading there. Gaspard's put you in charge!" Immediately she sprang into action.

"Charles," she said, shaking him awake. "Come on! We're on the move. Jean-Luc, get ammunition!" The men were sluggish and she had to hide her impatience, knowing they were exhausted. When they were all on their feet, rubbing sleep from their eyes, they were ordered out of the camp, one or two grumbling at the lack of food. It was true, they were so thin, some of them seemed almost opaque and Lottie worried about their lack of energy. Grabbing some bread, and grey-looking cheese, she dished it out as they filed past her, with the command, "Eat!"

And so they made their way down the mountain towards the village of Paulhac to the sound of machine gun fire. Lottie wondered where Michel was. She looked around at the thirty men but none were under his command and now she had little time to think about him. Her own men needed to be organised. From one hundred or so metres above, she could see the turrets of the small chateau and the pink terracotta tiles of the roofs of the dwellings and then smoke curling upwards from one of the buildings. She dropped down low and ordered the men to do the same. Through the trees, the German soldiers were visible, setting fire to anything flammable and executing the villagers. Lottie felt a sense of outrage and disgust so huge that it seemed to flow like a toxic sweat out of every pore in her body but there was no time to indulge in outrage at the barbaric scene that was unfolding below them and getting worse every second. They needed to try and stop it. Looking quickly around, she positioned the men behind rocks and immediately they opened fire from above, in an attempt to at least slow the carnage. It appeared to work as attention was turned away from the innocent and machine guns were aimed at the Maquis and a bloody battle commenced. German soldiers started to fall from sniper fire but it was too late. The village was burning to the ground, its occupants either murdered in cold blood or rounded up and taken away. Two of Lottie's men were shot dead before the Germans moved on. By the time the Maquis entered the village there was little left that was recognisable from the charred, bloodied remains of men, women and children and eventually, they returned to the camp in traumatised silence, taking their own dead back for burial.

*

Throwing her rifle on the ground, unable to rid herself of the images of what she'd witnessed, Lottie wiped the sweat from her forehead and went to find Michel. Pushing through the hundreds of faces, most of whom were strangers to her, and feeling sick and angry, she searched for someone she knew but it took some time to locate anyone. Now physically indistinguishable from the men, she had no fear of being assaulted in their midst and, shoulders forward, she pushed through until she thought she saw Marek but it wasn't. Finally she found a man named Pierre and asked him but all he knew was that Etienne had taken his men down to Clavieres and was trying to hold the Germans back. So, she returned to her men and waited. But neither Michel nor Marek returned and finally someone found her and broke the news that both of them had been captured and were last seen being loaded into a truck, at gunpoint.

CHAPTER 75

11ᵗʰ June 1944, Mt Mouchet, Haute-Loire, France

On this day, Commonwealth troops advance south of St Aubin-sur-Mer in the Mue Valley, France. The men of the 46 Royal Marines Commando liberate the city after furious fighting with the German 12ᵗʰ SS Panzer Division.

Lottie didn't sleep. Instead, she prowled around by moonlight, looking for her husband and Marek, crouching on her haunches to study sleeping bodies covered by blankets in the foetid camp. She looked too, at the dead, checking they weren't among the many brought back but she couldn't find them. For every hour, a grain of sand slipped through the hourglass from hope to despair at the growing probability that what the soldier had witnessed must be true but she couldn't find him to ask. She knew only too well, Maquisards caught by the Germans were publicly executed as a lesson to the French not to support them. The only hope was that the Nazis would assume they were villagers and they would be sent to a camp. Now that the Allies had landed in Normandy, the war should be over in a matter of weeks if not days and that might mean the Germans wouldn't have time to deal with the volume of prisoners. On the other hand, they might just execute them all in an act of revenge, before they could be saved. The scales of probability kept madly see-sawing from one side to the next from hope to complete hopelessness. Lottie kept imagining what had happened to Michel and Marek. Perhaps they'd been beaten or held somewhere with hundreds of others, waiting to be put onboard a train or maybe their bodies had been thrown on a rat-infested pile, like a discarded carcasses, where arms and legs appeared to have no owner and bloodshot eyes stared into nothingness like bloodied mannequins. Her beautiful, brave husband and his best friend, extinguished. She stumbled blindly into the trees to find a small space to be alone and found some bracken where she hid, among the fronds, curled up on the dry soil and wept until there was nothing left inside her. At dawn Charles found her and half carried her back to camp.

*

By nightfall, under a barrage of sustained fire, the Maquis began to retreat from Mount Mouchet, taking many of their dead, according to their oath and burying the rest. Lottie hadn't wanted to leave as she felt it was too soon to abandon the wait for Michel and Marek but in the end, she had no alternative but to accompany what was left of her men. Reluctantly, with the support of Charles who somehow managed to convince her that the mountain top was no longer safe and if Michel was able to return, he would find a way back to Le Chambon. Finally, in the middle of the night, she was ordered into a crowded truck, bound for Yssingeaux.

*

Fayol, who had been ordered to stay in Le Mazet, was unhappy at being excluded from the Mount Mouchet battle. More interested in indulging his own anger than showing much interest in his missing leaders, he raged that none of it had been his doing, and if he'd been there Michel and Marek would certainly have come home. In disgust, Lottie turned her back on him and walked away, afraid she would be unable to control herself and she would take a gun to him. By the time his rant was over, he barely noticed she'd gone. The meeting had, however, served a purpose and Lottie knew she had to get back to her men and reassume command. They were exhausted and hungry and they needed her to show strength and courage. Convincing herself Michel might still return to her, she held on to that glimmer of hope like a woman clinging to the side of a boat in a storm and she vowed that for as long as she lived, she would keep searching for him until, one way or another, even if she had to tear France and Germany apart, brick by brick, she found him and brought those guilty, to justice.

CHAPTER 76

17th June 1944, Le Chambon-sur-Lignon, France

On this day the British 41 Commando, Royal Marines, secure the surrender of the German garrison at Douvres-la-Delivrande, Calvados, Normandy, France.

"I've just spoken to Fayol," said Charles, sitting down on a tree trunk. Lottie was busy skinning a rabbit and she immediately looked up, hearing an unusual note of excitement in his voice.

"And?" For a moment, she held her breath, thinking there might be word about Michel.

"Three nights ago, he claims he had a visit from Bohny the schoolteacher who took him, during curfew, to a meeting with a couple of women, a Madame Marcell and a Madame Boitier in Le Chambon. Madame Marcell claims she can get us arms via London." He scratched his head, frowning.

"She's in contact with *London*?" Lottie's attention was immediately re-focused.

"He took her to view the possible drop zones yesterday morning, first light."

Lottie stared at him, slightly horrified. "Sounds like a trap!" But as much as she detested Fayol she knew he wasn't a complete fool and above all, he was paranoid about everything.

"Possibly but somehow she convinced Fayol. She claims she came from Cosne-sur-Loire where she's armed some eight hundred partisans. She told him she received a message from Allied Command, via BBC broadcast, to say D-Day was finally happening and since then, hundreds of action messages are being broadcast telling each Resistance circuit to begin their planned harassment and sabotage." He was gabbling.

"What's she offering us, though?" Lottie wiped the blood from her hands and put the pink carcass to one side.

"Fayol was reluctant to believe her at first because as we know, he thinks war is for men and what would a mere woman be doing out here, but she gave him one hell of an interrogation before passing over one hundred and fifty thousand Francs from a money belt inside her dress!"

"One hundred and fifty thousand Francs?" she repeated.

"It's true, he showed me the cash! Then the two women left to return to Cosne to 'finish off some business'," he made quotation marks in the air with his hands, "and to speak to Allied Command to see how she could help with supply of ammunition and to request a wireless operator! She asked him if he had forty good men who would execute her orders." The words were tumbling from his mouth as he became more animated.

"Her orders?"

"Yes. I truly thought we were done," Charles said, pacing around. "After the Germans massacred Saint Agreve and the killings in Le Puy but now…"

"If this is legitimate, we might be able to fight back at last," Lottie said, finishing his sentence for him.

"Wouldn't it be wonderful, and if it's true that the Allies are finally about to land?"

Lottie's eyes were darting around as her brain sprang into sudden action. "If we get supplies, we might be able to slow the Germans moving north through the valleys and prevent them from torching everything in their path but when?" Through her misery, a glimmer of excitement reluctantly forced its way out. "When will we know?"

"Know what?"

"If she can deliver. You said, she'd gone off to speak to London?"

He shook his head. His eyes, Lottie noticed, had suddenly come alive with the prospect of purpose and revenge. "I don't know. She didn't give a timescale. Hopefully days but there are no promises. Other resistance groups also need arming across the country."

"So we're competing for a handout, like in a beauty contest?" Suddenly, the excitement drained away like a plug that had been removed from a sink.

"Yes but if she didn't think we're worthy, surely she wouldn't have given over that amount of money?"

She thought about this. He had a point. "Who knows? I wonder who she is?"

"I've no idea, Fayol said she had a shockingly bad French accent."

Lottie wondered if she'd trained with her, in England. "Did Fayol describe her, other than that?"

"Yes, tall, attractive, red hair. Oh, and she walked with a strange gait."

Lottie looked over Charles' shoulder, deep in thought. "No, that doesn't ring any bells. You?"

"No but there was talk of a woman who was based in Lyon but don't know if it's her…"

"Oh, well, let's see." Lottie looked up at the sun that had reached its full height. The news had been interesting but all she really wanted was word of Michel and Marek. "I need to go. We're doing some more orienteering this afternoon, and yet another five-kilometre run but on the plus side, it sounds like we might, at last, have a reason to train." She looked at him. "The sooner we can give the men some good news, the better. Motivation levels are somewhere below sea level."

"Yes, I know."

"Still, at least with the money rolling in, there should be some decent rations." She picked up the rabbit and said, "See you later."

CHAPTER 77

15th July 1944

Le Chambon-sur-Ligne, Haute-Loire, France

On this day the British continue attacks directed south and east of Caen, Normandy, as part of D-Day 'Operation Overlord'. The Germans refuse to abandon their positions.

Virginia Hall, code name 'Diane', the tall American woman with the rich copper hair, swept into the plateau in early July, like a Provencal Mistral, wearing an army jacket and orange neck scarf. Khaki trousers hid the wooden leg sustained before the war in a shooting accident, while out hunting at her home in Baltimore. They couldn't, however, hide her distinctive limp. Well-connected but with talents woefully under-appreciated by SOE, she was finally dispatched to Le Chambon to get things organised for the Allied invasion and to act as wireless operator. It was a mammoth task. From her arrival, she and Fayol did not see eye to eye and it wasn't long before he began to discredit her to the local Maquis. He accused her of an inability to deliver what she promised until, she promptly did so, and the long-awaited delivery of three tonnes of supplies floated nonchalantly to earth, into the desperate hands of the local Maquis. Credibility restored, 'The Madonna' as she was also known, managed the pickup and store the stash at a local safe house, leaving no trace on the mountainside. After that, the drops continued one after the other as though Christmas had arrived late but made up for its tardiness in both the volume and quality of gifts. Shortly after Diane arrived, a message was sent to Lottie, inviting her to go and see her, at her hide-out at a barn, not far from Le Chambon, in Vilelongue.

*

"Do come in, Celeste" she said, getting up from the battered oak table to greet them. "I'm Diane." She turned to the young man behind her. "Dede would you be so kind as to get our guest a drink?"

As she moved into the light, Lottie could see she was indeed attractive and exuded an air of matronly competence. "Now, do come and sit down. Excuse the state of the barn but I need to move around to do my transmitting and it doesn't leave one time to make oneself at home. The Germans are now very good at locating our signals but fortunately, as I'm sure you're aware, it's taken them until they've all but lost the war." She smiled with satisfaction. "Right, to business. We're at the start of something big and I'm looking for the most capable among the men and of course," she looked approvingly at Lottie, "women, to help me. You come highly recommended but…" she hesitated, "there can only be one local person in charge to make this a success, and that will be me and not that fucking arrogant idiot, Fayol! Do you get my drift?"

Lottie practically fell off her chair in astonishment at the outspoken woman, and found herself nodding.

"Look, at this point I'm not interested in who you are or where you've come from," Diane continued, waving her hand in the air, dismissively. "And although I'm sure it would be a delight to trade stories over a whisky sour frankly, at this point, we don't have the time. Men are pouring through my door in droves to join the Maquis, many of whom are serving or have served under Fayol but who have become disillusioned. Again, I don't give a damn what their motivation is, so long as they are willing to follow my orders to the letter. I have to organise hundreds of men in a very short space of time and that's where you come in." She lit a cigarette and threw back the contents of the small glass of spirit, pausing for a moment to savour it. "Alcohol is truly appreciated when liberated from one's enemy don't you think?"

Lottie swallowed hers and tasted the familiar, illicit apple flavour that she had shared, as a dare, with her brothers, while staying at her grandmother's in Strasbourg.

"Schnapps?" she said, surprised.

"Yes, we managed to *purloin* a few crates after a shootout, near Cosne, and I can tell you the odd glass has sustained me through many a sleepless night. Anyhow, I digress, I want you to join me to lead much bigger groups, train the men and manage receptions for drops. You'll get uniforms and I'll pay you a reasonable amount to do it. Our job is to oversee drops, sabotage railway tracks, power lines, roads etcetera, all the usual stuff you've already been involved with but we're about to really ramp up operations and slow the damn Germans in their tracks to buy the Allies time. Are you in?"

"Absolutely!" said Lottie, without hesitation.

"Fine. Delighted to have you on board."

"I think I will be able to bring you another ten men at least," Lottie said.

"Marvellous. I assume you can stay on at your current hide-out? I hear the people of Le Chambon reclaimed the Town Hall yesterday but we still need to be vigilant."

"Yes but I'm not sure how I'll I square things with Fayol," said Lottie.

"Don't worry about him," said Diane. "We'll let him think he's still in charge but in reality, very quickly, events will overtake him. From today, you only take orders from me. Is that clear?"

"Yes," she said.

"I hear your husband's missing?"

Lottie felt the familiar ache in her chest and she nodded.

"Do you know where he is?" Diane's voice softened.

"No. At best, one of the camps in Germany, by now."

"It must be absolute hell for you!"

Lottie nodded and looked away.

"I'll try and find out. I have contacts but I can't promise anything. It's very likely they were taken to Le Puy and then on to Fort Montluc Prison, near Lyon."

"Thank you."

"In the meantime, Dede will bring you messages with your orders. Go back and wait." She got to her feet and held out her hand, signifying the end of the interview and as she shook it, Lottie caught the unmistakable aroma of expensive perfume.

CHAPTER 78

31St July 1944

St Julien Vocance, Haute-Loire, France

On this day, the American forces enter Brittany as part of 'Operation Cobra'.

The moon was Waxing Gibbous, at eighty percent of its full light. At midnight, Lottie and a team of twenty Maquis waited at St Julien Vocance, for the sound of the aircraft to arrive. She wasn't expecting a German reception committee but it would be wrong to be complacent and so they followed protocol and hid among the trees until the last minute. The area had been chosen deliberately for a large drop, since the Maquis' store of guns and ammunition had been badly depleted in the battle at Mont Mouchet. There had been no word about Michel or Marek but a source of Diane's had sent word that the prisoners taken from the villages at the gateway to the mountain had, as she suggested, been taken to Montluc Prison. There was no guarantee that either of them were there but it seemed likely. Lottie just hoped they'd survived the journey and she still had recurrent nightmares of Michel being tortured and the dreams were so disturbing that she sat up half the night, trying to keep awake. She longed every minute of every day for the war to end and it couldn't be long now that the Allies had broken out of Normandy and the Soviets were in control of several Polish cities. Despite her loyalty to the men, she'd grown to hate the mountains. Days once again began to merge and since there was no news about Michel and Marek, the wait was killing her spirit. She looked at her watch and, as usual, the plane was late. The sky above was clear and the Milky Way looked like a deep cloud of tiny lightbulb filaments. To kill time, she searched for the constellations of Orion, Ursa Minor and Cassiopeia and tried to make out Pegasus. It was something she and Michel used to do and the activity brought her closer to him. A noise from the woods behind alerted her and Lottie looked across at Charles and signalled to see if he'd heard it too, but he shook his head. She listened again but there was nothing out of the ordinary and as lookouts were all in place at various points along the kilometre strip, everything should, in theory, be fine.

*

At twenty-two minutes to one, the sound of a plane could be heard in the distance and Lottie gave the okay signal. She could tell the noise of a Wellington from several miles away. Surely the drop was due to be done by Halifax. The men emerged like woodland creatures and scurried with their torches to their positions. Still confused, Lottie gave the command to signal so the Pilot had confirmation that it was fine to make the drop. The huge iron bird, which was indeed a Wellington, flew high the first time before decreasing height and turning low, to make the approach and drop the canisters.

*

Without warning, out of nowhere, a machine gun started firing at the aircraft. The noise was deafening. Torches were quickly extinguished and the Maquis took cover. As the plane tried to gain height, it was clear to Lottie that something was terribly wrong. It banked sharply and turned once again and made a barely controlled approach as it swayed from left to right before hitting the ground and taxied, veering from side to side on the ground like a drunk, until it reached the end of the huge field and came to an abrupt stop. She couldn't understand why it had landed, as there was no smoke and the engines sounded fine. Shouting to the men to cover them, she dragged Charles in the direction of the plane, keeping low. The machine gun was now firing arbitrarily, desperately seeking out the Maquisards among the trees like farm boys shooting rats. Lungs bursting, Lottie made it to the now static aircraft and could see the crew moving around inside but no pilot was visible in the canopy. Still, it made no sense. Screaming at the crew in English, they appeared in silhouette in the rear escape hatch aiming revolvers at Lottie and Charles.

"We're Resistance. What happened?" Lottie yelled.

"The pilot's been hit."

"Where?"

"In the head. He's bleeding badly."

Lottie looked frantically back down the field. The strip of land was just over one kilometre. A Wellington required at least three thousand, seven hundred and fifty feet for take-off and it had managed to land.

"Can anyone else in there fly the plane?"

"No."

Behind them, the noise of gunfire was increasing as the Maquis battled to hold the enemy back.

"Is the plane damaged?"

"No, it doesn't appear to be." The voice was Irish.

"Are you the wireless operator?"

"No, the rear gunner."

"Let me in."

There was a silence as he contemplated her request.

"I said, fucking let me in! If you want to get home, we don't have time for a debate!"

Lottie turned to Charles. "I can fly this. Can you keep us covered?"

He looked at her as if she was mad. "You can fly *this?*" He looked at the length of the plane and back at her as if she'd lost her mind.

"Charles, I'm handing over command to you. There's no way I'm willing to pass the plane or its contents to over to the Germans. I have no choice."

"But you can fly *this?*" he repeated, unconvinced.

"Yes, let's just say it was a previous job."

Two figures were now visible in the doorway and they moved aside to allow Lottie into the aircraft.

Unceremoniously, she leaned out and handed Charles her gun. "Good luck, Charles," she called before the hatch was promptly closed and Charles, dazed, disappeared into the undergrowth.

Lottie looked at the startled men. "Pilot Officer Beauchamp, formerly Women's Auxiliary Air Force," was all she said by way of introduction as she slipped past them in the direction of the main cabin with only a cursory glance at the pilot who was lying on the floor, groaning and covered in blood. "Now, let's get this plane airborne and quickly." Looking around her, she saw where the bullet had entered the glass canopy. The pilot had been terribly unlucky but all she could do for him was to try to get him home, before the poor bastard died. Taking a deep breath, she dug deep and retrieved the information from memory that she needed to pull this off. "Get back to your positions and prepare for take-off," she said to the men, checking the fuel gauge. The undelivered canisters meant additional weight but there was no way she was leaving them for the Germans. Without further hesitation, she re-started the engines.

Lottie turned the aircraft and taxied back down the field on full throttle, propellers spinning and engines screaming, against a backdrop of gunfire. Suddenly, sitting up there in the pilot's seat she experienced a sense of wild exhilaration as they rapidly approached the end of the strip of field. Beyond that, there was nothing but a steep drop of about thirteen hundred feet from the top of the plateau, into darkness. There was no room for error. She had one shot at this. Leaning forward with engines flat out she watched as the precipice got nearer. As the nose was almost level with the edge, she pulled gently back on the column and felt the plane respond and begin to leave the ground. Below, there was the sound of rocks falling like an earthquake. The engines gave out a high-pitched squeal as she pushed them to their limits. It had been close but she'd pulled it off. Sitting back in her seat, she turned the yoke to the right and the plane banked away from the side of the mountains as it remained in the air and gained height. To her left she could see the dark shadows of Yssingeaux and to her right St-Sigolène as she pointed the aircraft north. The airspeed indicator read one hundred and seventy-two miles per hour as the plane continued to climb until, at four thousand feet she levelled out. Far beneath now, the silhouettes of the mountains gradually gave way to the flatter terrain around Vichy and Moulins before finally, by the light of a fiery dawn, they reached Orleans, Paris, Amiens and then Lille. Quickly, Lottie fell in with the rhythm of the plane, enjoying the sensation as it rose and fell on the air pockets. Every now and then she banked a little left or right, because she could and she loved the feel of it. If it had been a Spitfire and she'd been alone, she'd have spun and swooped and looped and dived but this was a grand-dame of the skies and was an altogether more docile animal. Far below, Lottie saw the English Channel and the pinky-white of the cliffs of Dover reflected in the early morning sun and she knew she was finally back to where she began her journey.

*

The aircraft touched down and pulled to a stop on the parched runway at RAF Oakington, Airfield and the crew broke out in a spontaneous round of applause, which made Lottie blush. From the hangar, two Jeeps tore across to the plane and by the time the crew opened the hatch, four or five military personnel had arrived with guns drawn.

"It's okay," said the navigator, with a smile. "The pilot's definitely one of ours!"

Lottie stepped forward in her Maquis uniform and jumped to the ground.

The Commanding Officer looked her up and down, frowning. "Who the hell are you?"

"My name, is Lottie Beauchamp." It was impossible to explain everything in a few sentences and she certainly wasn't going to be spoken to in that manner.

"I'm happy to tell you how and why I've flown your plane back to you but first, you have a dying pilot inside who needs attention, secondly, I'm in urgent need of a toilet, followed by a large glass of your best cognac!" She pushed past the thin-lipped CO with the puffed-out chest and, with a wink at the grinning crew, she walked in the direction of what she presumed to be the mess. Bemused and with no idea how to handle this attractive, unkempt woman, with the cut-glass English accent, the Commanding Officer had no alternative but to follow.

CHAPTER 79

20th August 1944, Fort Montluc, Lyon, France

On this day, the Lyon Sicherheitspolizei, under the direction Werner Knab and Klaus Barbie, took approximately 120 prisoners from Montluc Prison to Fort de Côte-Lorette. The prisoners are shot in small groups, inside the house.

According to a French Nazi collaborator, the piles of bodies reached six feet in height. The perpetrators stood on these piles to silence the victims. After the shooting, the executioners burned the house down using gasoline and phosphorus, then blew up what remained. Many of the victims were members of the French Resistance.

EPILOGUE

15th March, 2018 – Kent, South-East England

Lord Beauchamp and his daughter turned in to the long gravel drive of the nursing home and pulled into a visitor's parking bay. Looking around at the immaculate, white Georgian building and manicured gardens he nodded his approval. At the front door they were met by the manager, Mrs Gregory.

"Lord Beauchamp do come in," she said, holding out her hand. "I'm so sorry for your loss."

"Hugh, please. This is my daughter Charlotte." He smiled a little awkwardly, leaning on his walking stick for support after his recent hip replacement.

"Pleased to meet you Charlotte. I'm Patricia – Pat Gregory. I manage Alfriston Park."

Charlotte, taking her father's arm to offer support, nodded. "Hello. Pleased to meet you. What a lovely building. I'm sure my great aunt would have been very comfortable here."

"I hope so. Do come into the office. Can I get you some tea or coffee or something a little stronger?"

She had a kind face, thought Charlotte, feeling an irrational sense of relief that the manager of the home did not seem like a Nurse Ratchett. One only read about horror stories about these places but so far, she was pleasantly surprised. It had the appearance of a five-star hotel and smelled good too, not of urine and over-cooked cabbage as she'd braced herself for but of sandalwood. Above them in the hallway, a chandelier glittered and threw patterns onto the navy carpet and on a table in the centre was a large vase of brightly coloured, spring flowers. In a far-off room, she could hear the sound of a piano.

"Coffee, please," Hugh said, manoeuvring to a comfortable chair, wincing a little as he sat.

"Yes, coffee would be lovely," said Charlotte, sitting down. "Are you okay, Pa?"

"Yes thank you, darling." He waved his hand dismissively.

"The undertaker came yesterday. You have the address, so if you want to see her, just give them a call."

Hugh nodded. "Thank you. Did she go… I mean, was it peaceful?"

"Very but a little unexpected, to be honest. She joked a few weeks ago she'd 'knock up a few more years before retiring to the pavilion' and she 'hadn't needed a telegram from HRH, last year to remind her of how old she was, thank you very much!'" Pat smiled.

Charlotte grinned. "She liked cricket?"

"Very much so."

"How long was she here?"

"Just over eight years."

"What was she like?" Charlotte glanced at her father, wondering if she was taking over and asking too many questions but he seemed fine and was listening with interest.

"Fun. Bright as a button and very popular with the staff and residents. She was still doing the crossword until about six months ago. Her eyesight started to fail unfortunately but at nearly one hundred and one, that is to be expected."

Pat Gregory, thought Charlotte, was very tactful. In her position, she would have been curious to know why they'd never visited, before. She was, however, staring at her like one scrutinising a painting. Charlotte began to feel a little self-conscious and she felt herself colouring.

"I'm so sorry!" said Pat, averting her gaze. "It's just that you do look very much like her."

"Really?"

"Yes, uncannily."

"Well, I suppose genes go down the line," said Hugh. "Charlotte has the same colouring as her grandfather, Archie."

"I think there's a photo of her, of when she was much younger, in her belongings." Pat Gregory turned to a cupboard that contained a safe and pulled out a small cardboard box. "Apart from lots of books and some clothes, she didn't leave a lot, I'm afraid." Putting the box on the desk, she held out her hand, inviting them to take it. Instead, they both just looked at it.

"Would you like to see her room?" said Pat Gregory, head slightly on one side, eyes softened.

"Yes, please," said Charlotte, immediately. "Pa, if you'd rather not, I'm sure you can wait here for us?"

"Of course." Pat Gregory nodded.

"If you don't mind, I think I will," he said. "Unfortunately I'm not as mobile as I used to be."

"I'll order you some more coffee." Pat was standing at the open door, waiting for Charlotte to pass through.

"There's a lift or stairs."

"Stairs," said Charlotte. "Did she have visitors?"

Pat Gregory shook her head. "No. Not that I can recall."

"I wish I'd known her. It must be awful not to have anyone with her. We had no idea until your letter that she was still alive. It sounds dreadful but we didn't really know anything about her. She worked abroad for most of her life. Was she ever married, do you know?"

"Not that I'm aware of, although there was a crumpled black and white photo somewhere of a man. Very handsome. My dear, she was the most self-contained person I've ever met. She loved her books and when she could no longer read, she watched Attenborough or documentaries. Sometimes we'd take her to the local pub where she'd enjoy a glass of Cognac and some repartee with the locals but all in all, she kept herself to herself although we do know, first hand, she had a razor-sharp wit and didn't suffer fools." Pat Gregory stopped outside door number four, took out a key and opened it. Inside the room was sparsely furnished and the bed freshly made as though the occupant had just popped out. To the side of the high-backed chair there was a silver-topped walking cane, adjacent to a bookshelf that was crammed with tomes about archaeology and surprisingly, crimes of the Second World War. Charlotte stood for a moment, mesmerised by the space that was filled with the essence of a stranger who yet felt familiar. Her heart ached for a moment, with the loss of this woman whom she'd never known.

"I so wish I'd met her," she said, quietly, mainly to herself.

Pat Gregory nodded and smiled sympathetically. Charlotte wondered how many people she'd heard that from. People arriving lamely trotting this out when it was all too little, too late.

"What would you like us to do with all the books?" she said. "We've put her clothes in suitcases in the wardrobe."

"I've really no idea," said Charlotte, at a loss.

"Well, if you'd like us to donate them to charity, I'd be happy to arrange. We can keep one or two in the library here. As I said, there wasn't a lot but what she had, was good quality." Pat Gregory moved towards the wardrobe and opened it. Charlotte was glad her great aunt's clothes weren't still hanging up but her crimson slippers sat expectantly, neatly paired, at the bottom.

"Yes," she said, staring at them. "I'm sure my father will agree. It's a shame to send it all to landfill. You said there was a photo of Aunt Lottie?"

"In the box along with one other. She had hair just like yours. Long and thick. We weren't allowed to cut it short but she had it brushed every day and put into a French plait. Hers was white by the time she died, of course, but she still had eyes as clear and as blue as a fresh spring sky. The same colour as yours, actually. I know I'm going on about it but looking at you, it's like a young version of her has just walked in!" Pat Gregory gave a little laugh and shook her head.

Charlotte looked at her watch. It was time to leave this place. She didn't believe in ghosts but this was the closest she'd come to feeling the presence of someone who had passed. Taking a deep breath she made a silent promise that her great aunt would not be forgotten.

*

In the car, on the way home, Hugh Beauchamp sat with Lottie's box of belongings on his lap while Charlotte wove her way expertly in and out of the traffic, heading north-west.

"You must know *something* about her, Pa?" she said, suddenly.

"Who? Lottie?" Hugh was dropping off to sleep, having taken some more pain relief.

"Yes."

"I wish I did but as I told you in the car on the way, I know very little about her, really." He sighed. "She just didn't feature in my life. She spent the latter part of hers in Africa and Egypt, I believe. My father, Archie, didn't really speak about her to me, much. They kept in touch by letter I think but they must have all been burnt when he decided to downsize and I found him in the back garden, leaning on his Zimmer frame, stoking a large bonfire. I've a feeling she went to Cambridge before war broke out and then went back and finished her studies when it ended. She did something secret for Government during the war, I believe." He wrinkled his nose, deep in thought.

"What do you mean 'Secret'? Are we talking Bletchley Park or something?" Charlotte's interest was whetted.

"God knows. Abroad, I think. People didn't talk about the war, then and most of it would have been bound by the Official Secrets Act." He scratched his head. "Nobody really talked about anything, not like today where everyone's on Facebook telling each other what they had for breakfast. It wasn't like that in those days. All people had were letters."

Charlotte laughed. "Go on, this is fascinating."

He thought for a moment, "There was something... I seem to recall, about a chap being arrested and taken to a prison or concentration camp and she spent years trying to track down and prove what had happened to him. I think that was Aunt Lottie but I really can't be sure."

"So she didn't find him?"

"Oh, I doubt it. Would have been impossible, I think. Poor chap was probably long gone. Anyhow, your grandfather, Archie, sold The Lindens when my grandfather died because the place reminded him of things he wanted to forget."

"Like what, Pa?" She took her eyes off the road momentarily and looked at him.

"Oh, the war... his older brother Hugh was a fighter pilot and got shot down. I'm sure I told you."

"I don't recall. Did he die?"

"No. He was badly injured by all accounts and dreadfully damaged, mentally. He went back to The Lindens and shot himself in the barn. I don't think Father ever really got over it. He always said the title and the house should have been Hugh's. Instead of which, he got it. It bypassed Lottie, her being a girl and despite her being older than Archie. That's how I ended up being called Hugh and with the title. He must have thought something of his sister, though, because he asked that the first girl born into the family would be called Charlotte."

"What complete nonsense this hereditary Peerage is." She took her hand off the wheel and gave his arm a gentle squeeze.

"Indeed!" He thought for a moment. "Now, I *do* recall something about Hugh and Lottie having a Tiger Moth."

"No, *really?*"

"Yes. It was kept in the barn. I think it must have got sold at some point or maybe it went with the farm."

"Lottie was a pilot? How exciting! I'm really intrigued about what she did in the war."

"I don't recall any more than I've told you. She must have been barely twenty when war broke out. You know, Charlotte, the traffic looks quite clear. Hopefully we will be home within half an hour." Hugh looked around him.

"Are you tired?"

"A bit, it's the blasted painkillers. Will you come in for supper?"

"Well your operation was only two weeks ago. You'll be back on the tennis court in no time. Yes, I'll come in and say hello to Mother but I have to be at work by five."

"Yes, do. Hopefully she'll be back from bridge and she'll never forgive me if she misses you and we need to look in this box." He tapped it lightly.

"Yes, I wonder what's in it."

"Probably a priceless, ancient relic!" He chuckled.

*

As it turned out, the box contained very little except for some letters from Charlotte to her brother, Archie, a small, wooden ring, its patina darkened with age, an eternity ring with a stone missing, a wooden carving of a Spitfire and the black and white photo Pat Gregory mentioned, of a tall, dark man with what looked like mountains in the distance. She turned it over and it had the name 'Michel' and the date 'July 9th 1943 Le Chambon-sur-Ligne'.

"I do feel I need to know more about Great Aunt Lottie," said Charlotte, finishing her tea.

"How will you do that, Lot?" said her mother.

"The Internet, for starters." Charlotte glanced at her watch. "Oh, heavens, I have to go!" She got to her feet and pulled on her jacket, over her white shirt.

"Well, take the box," said Hugh, pushing it across the table to her. "Something in there might be of help."

"Thanks, Pa, I'll pop in on my way back on Sunday." She kissed them both put the box carefully in the boot.

*

By seven p.m., Charlotte was ready for work. Sebastian Kowalszyk looked across at her.

"Ready?"

She nodded, pressed a switch and began to speak. "Good evening, ladies and gentlemen. My name is Charlotte Beauchamp and as your Captain, I'd like to welcome you on this flight to Singapore. My co-pilot, is First Officer Sebastian Kowalszyk. We will be cruising at an altitude of thirty-eight thousand feet at an average speed of around nine hundred and thirty-three kilometres per hour. As we have a favourable tail wind tonight, we should arrive a little ahead of schedule at Singapore, Changi Airport, but we'll keep you updated. Whilst we're not expecting turbulence this evening, I would ask that when seated, you keep your seatbelts fastened. Our cabin manager is Lucy Chan. Lucy and her team will be pleased to assist you for the duration of this flight and I would ask that you listen carefully to the safety briefing. As this is a night flight, the cabin lights will be dimmed for your comfort except for on take-off and landing. From all the team, I wish you a pleasant, relaxed flight. Cabin Crew, doors to automatic."

The End

If you enjoyed *Lottie Beauchamp's War*, please consider adding a review on Amazon. Thank you.

Paula

ACKNOWLEDGEMENTS

With grateful thanks to Elda Abramson for her enthusiasm and editorial suggestions and to Penny Humphrey, Claire Hill and Jean Watson for being my faithful readers and providers of feedback.

Printed in Great Britain
by Amazon

27501323R00188